Acclaim for Roland Merullo and

In Revere, In Those Days

Roland Merullo

In Revere, In Those Days

Roland Merullo is a graduate of Phillips Exeter Academy and Brown University. He has written for *Newsweek*, *Forbes FYI*, *The New York Times*, *The Boston Globe*, *The Philadelphia Inquirer*, and other publications. He is the author of three previous, highly praised novels, the most recent of which, *Revere Beach Boulevard*, was a finalist for the L. L. Winship/PEN New England Award. He lives with his wife and two children in Massachusetts.

In Revere,
In Those Days

In Revere, In Those Days

A NOVEL

Roland Merullo

VINTAGE CONTEMPORARIES
VINTAGE BOOKS
A DIVISION OF RANDOM HOUSE, INC.
NEW YORK

FIRST VINTAGE CONTEMPORARIES EDITION, OCTOBER 2003

The Library of Congress has cataloged the Shaye Areheart/Harmony edition
as follows:
Merullo, Roland.
In Revere, in those days : a novel / by Roland Merullo.—1st ed.
ISBN 0-609-61032-5
1. Italian-American families—Fiction. 2. Revere (Mass.)—Fiction.
I. Title.
PS3563.E748 I5 2002
813'.54—dc21 2002003454

Vintage ISBN: 0-375-71405-7

Book design by Lynne Amft

www.vintagebooks.com

Printed in the United States of America
10 9 8 7 6 5 4 3 2

for my cousins

Acknowledgments

I WOULD LIKE TO thank, first of all, my wife, Amanda, for her steady love and her courage. My gratitude, also, to Eileen Merullo, Steven Merullo, and Kenneth Merullo for their lifelong support; to Craig Nova for the dignity with which he leads the writer's life and for many favors; to my friends Peter Grudin, Dean Crawford, John Recco, Blair Orfall, Arlo Kahn, Steven Cramer, Nadya Shokhen, and Volodya Tokarev for their encouragement and editorial advice; to Noelle Rouxel-Cubberly for her kind help with the details of Italian grammar; to Ed Desrochers for information about Exeter Academy; to Bob Jasse for his hometown enthusiasm; to the Massachusetts Cultural Council for a generous grant; to my aunts and uncles, living and dead, for their unfailing warmth, then and now; to my wonderful agent, Cynthia Cannell, for her loyalty and optimism; and to my superb editor, Shaye Areheart, and her fine crew, who supported this story from their first look.

Tell me:
Which is the way I take;
Out of what door do I go,
Where and to whom?

THEODORE ROETHKE
from "The Lost Son"

Book One

Book One

Prologue

MY NAME IS ANTHONY BENEDETTO, and I live what might be called a secret life. By this I don't mean that I'm some kind of sophisticated criminal—a safecracker, a cybercrook—masquerading as a good citizen. I'm not a former spy or undercover FBI agent who's been sent to live in hiding with a new identity. Just the opposite, in fact. Those would be exotic lives, and my life is plain and ordinary, a smooth stone among a billion stones on a beach. I have a good marriage, a lovely daughter, a home on six acres in the hills of central Vermont. I work as a painter—portraits mostly—and though I make a respectable living at it, I am neither wealthy nor, outside a small circle of critics and artists, well-known. I dress in jeans and running shoes, flannel shirts in winter and T-shirts in summer, and I drive a two-year-old Toyota Camry that has, on its bumper, only a small SAVE TIBET sticker far over on the passenger side below the rear lights. Even that, I sometimes think of scraping away.

If you passed me on the streets of this sleepy little town, you'd see an average-looking middle-aged man burdened by the usual cares and lifted by the small pleasures of the modern domestic whirl. What I mean when I say "secret life" is that I often feel the visible part of me is a plain wrapper that hides a gem. I feel that way about people in general: there is the wrapping, and then there is a sort of finer essence. She is tall, sexy, greedy; he is loud, brilliant, addicted to amphetamines. We are crude, generous, beautiful, vicious; we wear a patchwork disguise made from a hundred talents, habits, and needs, and underneath it lies this spark of something else, something larger than our labels and flaws. You can see that spark clearly in children before the coat of the personality grows too thick. You can sense it when you first fall in love, before the beloved's failings and troubles swell up into view; and then, later, if you've come to terms with the failings and troubles and have built a mature affection. It's not that I don't see the evil, pettiness, and pain in the world; believe me, I've seen it, I see it. It's just that I also seem to have an eye for the secret essence that lies beyond that, the gem in plain wrapping.

This is a story of the rescue of one soul. It's the story of an ordinary kid who had all the shell burned off him, all the armor. Something like that happens to most people in the course of a life, I think, though not usually at such a young age. It takes different forms: the death of a parent, spouse, or close friend; divorce, disappointment, disability. Afterward, you go through the world naked and raw, skinless, hopeless. Sometimes the pain only grows worse as the years pass, and you end your life in a cold pool of despair. Other times—if you are lucky, or blessed, or, as the Buddhists would say, if your karma is good—someone comes along and heals you, or helps you heal yourself.

I have lived now, healed and at peace, for half a life without ever feeling much inclination to tell this story. But two winters ago, after eighteen childless years of marriage, my wife, Regina, gave birth to a daughter. Our luck, our blessing, our good karma. And then, just about the time Rosalie reached the age where she was beginning to learn words, I was overtaken by an urge to write this down, to make it public. For her to read someday, I suppose. For myself. For the people who raised me.

One

THE STORY DOES NOT take place here in Vermont, but in a small city called Revere, Massachusetts, which lies against the coastline just north of Boston. Three miles by two miles, with a salt marsh along its northern edge and low hills rising like welts in an irregular pattern across its middle, Revere must seem to the outside eye like an uninspiring place. The houses stand very close to each other and close to the street—plain, wood-frame houses with chain-link fences or low brick walls surrounding front yards you can walk across in six steps. These days the city has a crowded, urban feeling to it: sirens in the air, lines of automobiles and trucks at the stoplights and intersections, thin streams of weeds in the tar gutters.

But forty years ago, Revere was a different place. There were amusements and food stands along its curve of sandy beach, making it a sort of slightly less famous Coney Island. And there were still some open lots pocking the narrow streets, blushes of wildness on the tame city skin. Not far from where I lived, a mile west of the beach, was a large tract of undeveloped land we called "the Farms," though nothing had been cultivated there since before the Korean War. For my friends and me, for city kids like us, the Farms was a landscape from a childhood fable: pastures, boulders, half-acre ponds, fallow fields where we turned over stones and planks and pieces of corrugated metal and reached down quick and sure as hunters to take hold of dozing snakes—brown, green, black. The snakes would slither and writhe along our bare wrists, and snap their toothless gums against the sides of our fingers, and end up imprisoned in mayonnaise jars with holes banged into the metal tops. We carried them home like bounty from a war with the wilderness, and sold them to younger boys for ten or fifteen cents apiece.

The automobile had not yet quite been elevated to the position of worship it now holds. The streets were freer and quieter. Hidden behind the shingled, painted houses were backyards in the European style, with vegetable gardens given preference over lawns, with fruit trees and grape arbors, and ceramic saints standing watch over a few square feet of flower bed.

Revere is a thoroughly modern place now, a corner of blue-collar America with chain stores and strip malls and yellow buses lined up in front of flat-roofed schools. A hundred new homes have been squeezed onto the Farms, streets cut there, sewer and electric lines brought in. But in some way I have never really understood, the city had a mysterious quality to it in those days, as if it lay outside time, beyond the range of vision of the contemporary American eye. *Provincial* is a word you might have used to describe it. But *provincial* means that a community believes itself to be living at the center of the universe, that it refuses to make an idol of the metropolis. Revere was provincial then, in that way. And, I suppose, proud of it.

Even in the days when Jupiter Street was quiet enough for nine uninterrupted innings of a local game called blockball, even then there was an underside to the life we believed we were living. The collection of bad characters known as the underworld, or the mafia, or the mob, had a number of nests in Revere. These people, in my experience, in the experience of almost everyone in the city, had little in common with the fantasy underworld you see these days on movie and television screens. For most of us, the face of the mafia was found in nothing more terrifying than a coterie of local bookmakers—neighbors, family friends, the guy beside you in the pew at nine o'clock Mass—men who made their living from the yearning of their neighbors toward some higher, softer life. In this way perhaps they were not so different from modern-day suburban portfolio managers.

The people in our neighborhood did not have executive jobs, did not commute into the city in suits and nice dresses, reading neatly folded copies of the *Wall Street Journal*, did not have parents and grandparents who had gone to college, and, with one or two exceptions, did not go to college themselves. They rode the subway into offices and warehouses in Boston, or drove their five-year-old Chevies to the factories in Lynn— where my father worked, in fact—and spent their lives in bland cubicles or hot, loud workrooms, performing the same few tasks again and again as their youth dribbled away. On Fridays they took a dollar from their pay envelope, walked down to the butcher shop on Park Avenue, and had a quiet conversation there with a man we called "Zingy." Zingy would take the money, record the lucky number—a wife's birthday, a father's license plate—then sell his loyal customer half a pound of mortadella and a package of Lucky Strikes. And the workingman would go home to his cluttered life in his drafty house and fall asleep clutching a tendril of a dream that he might "hit," that "the number" would come in for him and his family that one time, and then all the world's harsher edges would be rubbed smooth.

Of course, in Revere and elsewhere, one of the things that has changed in the last forty years is that the government has taken over Zingy's job. Now people walk down to a corner store and print out their lucky number on a blue-edged lottery form, and carry away the receipt (something that, after certain highly publicized arrests, Zingy stopped offering). But they go to sleep holding tight to the same dream. Only now, a portion of the profits goes to the state, to be spent by bureaucrats and politicians, whereas in earlier times the money went from the bookies upward—or, more accurately, downward—to a handful of violent, sly men in smoky private clubs, to be spent on jewelry for their girlfriends and vacations in Las Vegas.

The bookmakers were the mob's menial laborers, though, and didn't have exotic girlfriends or take exotic trips. Without exception, the ones I knew were affable, modest men who had stumbled into their profession by accident, or taken it up as a second job, the way someone else might put in a few hours delivering lost airport luggage or standing the night watch at an office building. But they were part of the fabric of Revere, too.

Occasionally, the uglier side of that fabric was turned to the light. In the 1960s there was a turf war going on in Greater Boston among different factions of the underworld—the Irish, the Jews, the various bands of Italians. This was closer to the movie version, to that brutal, hateful way of life modern moviegoers seem so attracted to—as if it isn't quite real and could never affect them. We would be listening to the news in our kitchen at breakfast and hear that a body had been found in a nearby city, or in Revere, a mile or two miles away—in the trunk of a car, on a street corner, behind a liquor store. Shot once in the back of the head, never any witnesses. Whenever these reports were broadcast, my mother would turn the radio off. I remember her bare freckled arm reaching up to the windowsill and twisting the nickel-sized black dial on the transistor radio, as though she might keep that aspect of Revere from my father and me, and maybe from herself as well. As if protecting us from life's unpleasant truths was as simple as slicing away the mealy sections of an overripe cantaloupe and bringing to the table only the juicy golden heart of it. "That's not Revere," she would say. As if she were insisting: That is not cantaloupe, that part we scrape into the metal bowl and carry out to the garbage pail.

I understand why she did that. Like most of the people in Revere, she and my father went about their lives in a straightforward, honest fashion, and didn't much appreciate the fact that the Boston newspapers and TV stations gave so much attention to the mafia, and so little to the ordinary heroism of the household, the factory, and the street. I've inherited some of my parents' attitudes. I don't much appreciate the fact that, to this day, the Italian-American way of life has been reduced to a television cliché: thugs with pinkie rings slurping spaghetti and talking tough. My story has nothing to do with that cliché. Almost nothing.

But the mob was a part of Revere in those days; it's pointless to deny that. The Martoglios shouting at each other at the top of Hancock Street when I delivered the *Revere Journal* on Wednesday afternoons was part of Revere. The dog track, the horse track, the hard guys and losers in the bars behind the beach, the crooked deals worked out near City Hall, the lusts, hatreds, feuds, petty boasts—it was all as much a part of that place as the neighbor who shoveled away the snow the city plow had left at the bottom of your driveway on the night of a storm, when you were off visiting your mother or sister or friend in the hospital; or the happy shouts of young families on the amusement rides; or my grandparents' neighbor Rafaelo Losco, who once, in the middle of a conversation with my mother, when I was five or six years old, broke from his cherry tree a yard-long branch heavy with ripe fruit, and handed it across the back fence to me.

Though I sometimes want to, I cannot paint a place, or a family, or a life—my place, my family, my life—in the pretty hues of cheap jewelry. I can't give only one-half of the truth here, because what I want to say to my daughter is not: Life is a sweet cantaloupe, honey; smile and be glad, eat. But: Life can be bitter and unfair and mean, and most people rise part of the way above that, and some people transcend it completely and have enough strength left over to reach out a hand to someone else, light to light, goodness to good, and I grew up among people like that—not in sentimental novels or on the movie screen, but in fact. They were imperfect people, who struggled to see the decency and hope in each other, and if I can be like them, even partly like them, I will, and so should you. A road across the territory between too extremes, a middle way—that's what I want to offer her. Between denial on the one hand and despair on the other, between sappiness and cynicism. A plain road, across good land.

Two

WE LIVED—MY MOTHER, father, and I—in a wood-shingled, gambrel-roofed house on Jupiter Street, in the western part of Revere, a seven-minute drive from the Atlantic Ocean. Domenic and Lia, my father's parents, owned the house; we rented the rooms on the second floor: kitchen, two small bedrooms, living room, bath. In winter the old iron radiators clanked and hissed, and my father tacked ribbons of speckled gray felt to the window frames. From the middle of June to Labor Day, we sweated in our beds.

On the morning after one of those June nights, we had just sat down to breakfast when the buzzer sounded at the door. I was eleven years old, there were three days left of school, and the morning air was touched, as it often was, with the salty breath of the ocean. I remember it blowing in through the screens, the soft, excited voice of summer, whispering something about an afternoon at the beach. And I remember the buzzer sounding, harsh and brittle, just as the food was being served. My mother let out an exasperated sigh at the ugliness of the noise. My father frowned, looked over at me, lifted his chin in the direction of the hallway. I trotted along the squeaking wood floor and pushed the plastic button at the top of the stairs. The handle clicked, the door swung inward, and one of my father's five brothers stood there with the sun shining through the porch screens on his bald head, one hand in the pocket of his fine silk pants, the other arm held slightly away from his body.

He looked up at me, blinked, pursed his lips, but did not make any move to step across the threshold. Something played beneath the muscles of his face, some half-suppressed comic pulse. "What are *you* doin?" he said, jingling the change in his pants pocket.

"Eating."

"What, eatin? What are you doin, *eatin?*"

"Pancakes."

He squeezed his eyebrows together, puckered the muscles at the corners of his lips. He still had not moved. His face was a mask of perfect seriousness, a battered and misshapen face, prototype for some Rushmore of the bankrupt and brokenhearted. He said, "Fluffy or flat?"

"My mother makes them nice, fluffy. She heats the syrup on the stove and melts the butter in it."

"What's the syrup?"

"Regular Jemima."

"And she heats it up, you shuah? That's what a gourmay cook in Paris would do. You positive?"

I nodded.

He jingled his change again, tugged twice at his big nose. "What else?"

"Three more days of school left."

"School? What, school? What three more days? You're not goin today. You're skippin. We need to ride around."

"I have to."

"Have to, my eyeball. You're skippin. How's your girl?"

"I don't have a girl."

"No?"

"No, Uncle."

"Then who was that gorgeous blonde I seen you walkin with down Broadway last night, then?"

"Aunt Ulla," I said.

At this, he almost smiled. He made a big fist and lifted it slowly into the yellow light. "You're goin around with my wife? I'll come afta ya."

"Tonio, who is it?" my mother called from the kitchen.

"Uncle Peter."

"Well, tell him to come up; your pancakes are getting cold."

"He likes them flat, you make them fluffy. He won't come."

"Listen to this kid, willya?" he said from the bottom of the steps.

"Aunt Ulla loves me, not you," I told him. "You're finished. We're running away to California without you."

He was starting up the steep wooden stairs now, shined shoes scuffing each tread, his head lowered, his nose like the rudder of a ship, holding him more or less on course. "California," he said when he was halfway up, the next to the last syllable pronounced "fawn." Cali-fawn-ya. "Where you gonna get the dough?"

"From you. She raided your bank account."

"What bank account?" he said, and the twist of a smile appeared on his mouth at last. "Who told you I have a bank account?"

He squeezed his hands into fists, huge scarred fists with which he had, at one time, fashioned his small moment of fame. He plodded up the last two steps and swung a roundhouse right, three-quarters speed. I reached up my left arm and half-blocked it, half-slipped the punch as he had taught me . . . only his other hand was driving an uppercut into my belly and would have caught me, hard, but just as it reached the front of my shirt, he popped the fingers open, flashed a silver dollar, slipped it into my pocket. In the next instant he had picked me up in one arm and was carrying me along the hallway as if I were a two-year-old. He hoisted me over the back of the chair and set me down there, gently, then touched my father on the side of the neck with the backs of three fingers, kissed my mother, took the empty seat at one end of the table.

"Gus," he said, swinging his eyes to my father and pulling twice more on his nose. "Gus, I had this unbleevable dream."

Three

AT ONE TIME IT had seemed that this uncle, Peter Domenic Benedetto, would break the mold he had been born into, the hard pattern of life in his city by the beach. For a few years it had appeared that even the cables of loyalty to a neighborhood and affection for a family—those twin steel bonds of the working class—could not hold him. Born fourth in a family of nine children, he seemed an ordinary enough boy at first. But shortly after he started school, some hidden gene bloomed in him, some inheritance from a deep ancestral past of field-workers and stone workers: he grew and grew. In the third grade he was a head taller than the tallest of his classmates; he had the arms and shoulders of a miniature man. By the sixth grade, he stood five feet eight inches tall. By the ninth grade, he was two inches over six feet, 180 pounds; he'd been introduced to boxing, and was already something of a local legend, sprinting up the steep hill of South Cambridge Street with a brick in each hand, knocking out school-yard bullies, happily and naturally taking on the role of protector of his family's good name.

He was not especially nice-looking—the big nose, the slightly protruding brow—not especially adept at schoolwork. But he had the gift of being remarkably at ease with people, all types of people, in all kinds of situations, and he had his phenomenal strength and an exquisite singing voice. His voice was at the high end of the tenor range, delicate, complicated, almost girlish in certain notes. In his middle age, the years when I saw him almost every day, that voice became a source of great shame to him; his rugged face was also a source of shame, as was the fact that he had worked his way up through the Golden Gloves finals, far up into the heavyweight ranks, only to be beaten senseless in his twenty-eighth professional fight, the fight that would have made him a national star instead of a local one. It was typical of him, probably typical of all of us, to be ashamed of what might elsewhere be considered a source of pride. We lived—men and women both—by our own skewed set of commandments: unblemished toughness, unquestioned self-sacrifice, generosity carried to the point of the absurd. Anything short of perfection was, for us, a species of failure. All our strength came from that, and all our wreckage.

For my uncle, that defeat in the ring marked the farthest stretching point of the cables of the city of Revere. After that brief foray into the outside world (he had been beaten at Madison Square Garden with his father, brothers, and one sister in attendance; he'd been knocked down twice in the first round by a black contender from New Jersey named Edgar Wellison; his nose had been broken, his lips rearranged. My father told me he had somehow stayed on his feet until the final minute of the tenth round, then fallen over sideways like a wooden soldier and spent the next six days in the hospital), Uncle Peter retreated to familiar territory and settled without a great deal of visible regret into the life he was living when he visited us on that June morning. The doctors advised him never to box again, and he never really resisted them. Though he joked about his fighting days with some grace and humility, he never brought up the subject first, never showed off old newspaper clippings, would even sometimes step outside for a few puffs from a cigarette when the subject came up. He sang in church and nowhere else, and then, after his only child reached the age of First Communion, stopped going to church. On his sprint up the slippery, dirty, bloodstained heavyweight hill, he had seen things and met people his siblings could only imagine—he'd been to exotic places like Nevada and Arizona, shaken hands with senators and show-business personalities, been treated to drinks and meals at fancy Manhattan clubs—and in one of those places he'd had the great misfortune of meeting Ulla Berensen, the sexy blond daughter of Norwegian immigrants. He courted her with lavish gifts he could not afford and elaborate promises he would never be able to keep, married her, brought her back to the clapboard house on Venice Avenue his boxing earnings had paid for, fathered a daughter named Rosalie, who became my close childhood companion, and for the next forty years he made money with his back, working odd days here and there as a laborer for friends who owned small construction companies.

One of the first things you noticed when you were introduced to Uncle Peter was that he could not be still for more than a few seconds at a time—it was no doubt a part of what had made him such a good boxer. He drove around the city on mysterious errands of his own making, took day trips to Rockingham Park to bet on the thoroughbreds when he should have been working, mowing the lawn, or taking Rosalie to the beach; he shifted and swung and danced (he was, my mother told me, a marvelous dancer) around any room he inhabited. Even on that morning, he sat at our kitchen table for only a minute or two, and then was up and pacing, setting his coffee cup on the counter and tracing a tight arc out to the edge of the hallway, swinging back, retrieving the cup, lifting it to his misshapen lips and setting it down again without drinking, going up behind my father and massaging the muscles on the tops of his shoulders for two seconds, winking at me, raising his eyebrows at my mother, swinging around, peering out the curtained kitchen windows at the Sawyers' house, studying the faded shellac of the hallway and a crack in the porcelain sink, sitting back down and stealing a sip from the cup, running a palm over his bald head as if to check for some miraculous second growth of thick black hair.

Even as a child I sensed that he had acquaintances from the darker worlds. What, exactly, those friendships meant to him—personally, financially—I don't think any of us ever really knew. Maybe they were his way of staying connected to what he saw as a larger life, something more impressive than the loan payments and trimmed lawns of the ordinary dimension. Maybe he owed some kind of illicit debt and spent his life doing favors for those people, working to pay it off. I don't know. Sometimes when we visited him at his house on a Saturday evening, or on Sunday after Mass, there would be a car parked out front at the curb, on the NO PARKING side, and a Joey or Mickey or, most often, a person he called "Johnny Blink," in the living room, oozing over the armchair like a toad in syrup. Even as a boy I understood that these relationships, this peculiar lifestyle of his, caused some trouble between Uncle Peter and Aunt Ulla. More and more as time went on, she would be upstairs when we visited, incommunicado, a terrible breach of family etiquette. A headache, Uncle Peter would say with his broken smile. One of her headaches. Or she had gone to church to say a novena, supposedly, or was visiting relatives up in Maine.

A man of infectious, indefatigable optimism, my uncle nevertheless seemed slightly tentative when you saw him with his wife, slightly diminished, as if she refused to buy a ticket for his grand performance and he knew it. At other times, too, he carried with him the scent of tragedy. It was as if he were a symbol of what might happen if we dared to reach past the boundaries of our place and our own people, a reminder of the kind of punishments that could be meted out by the non-Revere nations, by the moneyed tribes of the western suburbs and beyond.

But on that fine June morning he was lit up like a sparkler on the Fourth of July. He'd had a dream, an unbleevable dream, and had carried it down like a box of expensive silks from the bedroom on Venice Avenue. "Gus," he said, getting to his feet again and starting to pace. "Anna. I saw the numbah last night in my sleep. One, two, six. That's the numbah today, I know it like I know my own shoe size. How much can you put on it?"

Four

COINCIDENCE, FATE, KARMA, LUCK, the mood swings of a merciful God—it fascinates me now to listen to the ways we explain life to ourselves and each other. This is how the Lord has made the world, some people say, and, reading from a list of simple rules, they pack the entire mystery of the universe into one cheek, and spit it out at you through a syrupy smile. Or they insist, like petulant children, that nothing has any meaning, that everything from the angle at which sunlight strikes the surface of the earth to the chemical makeup of the blood running through a placenta is only the random careening of spiritless molecules.

These theories, I believe, come mostly from fear. My theories come mostly from fear. The fear of facing a life that remains unboxed and uncategorized: storms of bad fortune and shining rainbows of good luck that have no apparent connection to one's behavior. We send up prayers—that we should survive the hour, that our basketball team should win, that our sister's X rays should be negative, that this eighty-year run of evaporating joys should mean something. Or we stamp our feet, wave our arms, and insist it means nothing, leads nowhere, cannot possibly lead anywhere.

As if we know.

I went to school that day. Uncle Peter drove me, in fact—though it was only a few hundred yards from the door of our house to the steps of Barrows School. He left me off at the playground with a handshake, a kiss, and this piece of advice: "Always remembah who you are, Einstein, who your family is." And he promised to bring Rosalie there at 2:15, when the school day ended, and drive us up Route 1 to see a friend of his, a man with a built-in swimming pool, his own horses, and six flavors of ice cream in a walk-in freezer. All through my lessons I thought about it, the pool, the ice cream, the chance to meet one more of his legion of legendary friends, another Johnny Blink, Joey Patchegaloupe, or Bean-bag Pipistrillo. When the bell sounded and we spilled out the doors and down the cement steps, I waited on the sidewalk a little while, calling good-byes to my schoolmates as they drifted off along Mountain Avenue, fingering the silver dollar in my pocket, watching for his Cadillac. After half an hour passed and he didn't show, I made my way back down the short, not very steep hill of Jupiter Street toward my grandparents' house, carrying my disappointment in both arms like the remains of a beloved pet.

My father was, of course, at work. Instead of going up the steps, through the screen porch, and ringing the buzzer at our front door, I turned down the side walk and into the yard. My mother was leaning out my bedroom window, taking in a line of wash, the pulley screeching above the hot afternoon like a bothered gull. "Is that your report card?" she said when she saw me. "Is it good?"

I took it out of its envelope and held it open to her.

"Anthony, you know I can't read it from up here. Is it good, honey?"

"Two Fs, two Ds," I said. "The rest isn't bad."

"Anthony."

"It's good, Ma."

"Grandpa's waiting for you under the grapevine. Come up for a snack when you're finished. But change out of your good pants first if you're going to work in the garden, alright?"

My grandfather, Domenic Anthony Benedetto, was a slight, erect man, bald on top but not in the extravagant manner of Uncle Peter's baldness, always very soft-spoken and carefully dressed, a man who gave off an air of being completely at peace in his body with its thin shoulders and thin arms and thin, fine hands. What hair he still had was white and as fine as cornsilk, set off by a pair of eyeglasses, the top frame of which was the color of coffee beans. His eyes were a lighter shade of those same beans, his lips often slightly compressed over large, somewhat yellowed teeth. On warm afternoons he was in the habit of sitting under the grape-vine on a metal lawn chair and smoking; though, if the mood struck him, he might take the subway into Boston and visit friends at the tailor shop where he'd once worked. And if there was lightning in the summer sky, he would move the chair out onto the middle of the lawn and sit there, admiring it, daring the fates, while his wife and daughters called to him, frustrated and terrified, from the house, and the storm's first drops spanked the concrete walk.

We had, between us, a complicated language of silence. We had rituals—picking Japanese beetles from the grapevine leaves and drown-ing them in jars of kerosene, watching the Saturday night fights on his television, sneaking sips of wine in the cellar room where he kept his red-stained barrels, studying the fine points of Italian grammar (though, by that time, the language came almost as naturally to me as English), dis-cussing the small tasks he would assign me around the yard and pay me extravagantly for completing. We had our card games, little arguments, inside jokes, and, on days when I was feeling low, we had our clandestine trips to Sully's store for a sickly sweet chocolate pastry called sugar wheels.

He saw me and nodded. I walked over and stood beside the chair so he could put his arm around my shoulders. When I slipped the report card from its manila envelope again, he balanced his cigar on the edge of the concrete bench that ran the length of the shaded area, and took it from me. For more than a minute he stared down at it without speaking, his eyes moving slowly over last term's grades, the explanations of each subject, the teacher's comments, and my mother's signatures on the back, as if he had never seen an American report card before. The smoke from his cigar curled around us, and I could smell that, and smell his after-shave. The intermittent screeching of the clothesline pulley stopped.

"Is there anything better than A?"

"A-Triple-Plus," I said. "But nobody ever gets one."

He looked at me, tapped me once on the nose with a finger. He leaned sideways against me and drew a brown leather wallet from his pants pocket. It flapped open, showing a picture of his wife, my grandmother—sepia tones and old-world somberness—when she had been a girl of twenty or so.

"How many As there, count them, Mr. Joke-a-make. In Italian."

"Uno, due, tre, quattro, cinque, sei, sette, otto."

"Bène. Otto." He drew a five and three ones from the wallet, crisp as if they had just come from the mint (it was said that he liked only new money, and would go to the bank on Broadway every week and trade his wrinkled, soiled bills for ones like these), and handed them to me.

He nodded when I thanked him, a nod with great dignity and fellow feeling in it, as if we had once been the same body and were now, by some unfortunate accident, separated, and whatever he did for me was merely what one would be expected to do for a detached part of oneself. He picked up his cigar, all the while staring out over the ceramic statue of the Virgin and the flower garden my grandmother kept there, out past the rosebushes and the smaller vines that produced what we called "water grapes," toward the privet hedge that marked the boundary of his property. For a little while we stared out there together, as if making a scientific study of the molecules in the warm waves of air over Jupiter Street, or as if waiting a suitably long moment for the subject of my great academic success to have its play. Then he said, *"Ci mangiano vivi."* They're eating us alive.

"New ones?"

Another nod. "I waited for you to come before I went after them."

"Let me go after them."

He lifted his arm and released me, and I walked out from beneath the shadow of the arbor and into the sunlit garden. There were tomato plants of course, rows of them with their sharp smell; and peppers, squash, beans, basil, arugula and escarole, eggplant, carrots, beets, radishes, onions, garlic.

I made my way carefully between two rows. The tops of the tomato plants were at a level with the top of my head and had been tied to wooden stakes with white scraps of old shirtsleeves. On two plants near the end of the row, some of the leaves and limbs had been eaten down to their lime-colored skeletons. I traced the damage up from the ground, studying the square black turds, the ravaged leaves, two green tomatoes from which rough circles had been chewed. At last, I pinched the tip of a leaf and, turning it over, discovered one of the culprits there. It was fat from feasting on our crops, with tiny ivory feet, and it had a red horn, like the thorn on a rosebush, curling out from its forehead. Each of its green sections was dotted with a small black mark, windows on a jet fuselage. I cut off the leaf with my thumbnail and carried it over to my grandfather. He tore a page from that afternoon's *Record American*, set the leaf and caterpillar gently upon it, touched the corner of the page with his lighter, and we watched as the flames rose and the monster writhed, flipped onto its back, and soon melted. Grandpa Dom put out the fire with his foot, stamping and stamping and making something of a show, then wiping the sole of his shoe on the edge of the concrete. I went upstairs, satisfied, eight dollars and twenty-five cents richer for the afternoon—nine twenty-five richer for the day—and had a glass of milk with my mother, who was pleased by the As.

"Uncle Peter never came back for me," I said, to distract her from the subject of my school pants. She was baking something. I remember her turning away from the counter to look at me, her forearms dusted with flour. I remember being surprised at the wrinkle of disapproval in her voice when she spoke. She was not a bitter person, not by any means, but I remember the bitterness in her voice that day, hot and short-lived as the flash of a struck match. She said, "If your uncle's promises were dollar bills, we could buy two new houses with them."

"One for me and Rosie and our kids and the other one for you and Papa."

"You can't marry your own cousin, Tonio, you know that."

"Why not?"

"It's not legal, it's not right."

"We could have a separate house, and then you and Papa could live in peace."

"We already live in peace. What's that on the knees of your school pants?"

"No six kinds of ice cream, Ma. He never came back."

"He'll make up for it, you'll see. That's the way he is. He finds a way to make up for everything."

"When?"

"Tonio, let me see those pants."

"When, Ma?"

"Some other time, you'll see. You're like a son to him. What happened to your best school pants? Tonio!"

"*Ci mangiano vivi*, Mama."

Five

WITH HIS PENCHANT FOR impossible schemes and spectacular failures, with all the afternoons and evenings he'd walked out alone into the ten-acre parking lots of Rockingham, Hialeah, or Suffolk Downs, wringing a racing program in his hands and littering the tar with losing tickets; with all the twenties, fifties, and hundreds he'd tossed into the pot for someone else to win, maybe it was just the law of averages that caused the numbers to fall as Uncle Peter dreamed they would on that day: one, two, six.

Years later another possibility occurred to me: that my uncle had somehow found out in advance what the number would be. It goes against everything I know about how the number was determined on any given day—by the winning horses in three races at a certain track. But it is easier for me, given all the trouble that one flash of good fortune brought us, to picture Zingy or Johnny Blink whispering in Uncle Peter's ear in a loud bar near the beach, than to believe that God presented the information to him in a dream.

My father had bet ten dollars, Uncle Peter had bet twenty; another uncle, Leo, had been convinced to put down five. It was 1964; the payoffs in those days were on the order of 750 to 1, so, among them, on that afternoon, the three brothers took in the equivalent of several years' pay. When the news traveled around the family, a spontaneous festival formed itself at the house on Jupiter Street. Of that day I remember most of all the image of my cousins in the yard—thirty of them—a band of Benedettos aged four to twenty-two, the younger ones gathering into packs and roaming the two-tiered backyard, and the side yard, and the grassy alleyway next to the Sawyers' house. It was pleasure we were hunting, the fierce uninhibited joy of the child who has grown up in an environment where the flame of childhood has not been trampled out by addiction or poverty or the parents' demons.

We meandered and chattered, we shrieked and sang, sprinting, sweating, falling, arguing, crying out for each other. There was a kind of benign wildness in the air around us, as if the illegal windfall had pulled the last restraints off the chariot of our collective youth. At one point, on the upper tier of the back lawn, a square enclosed by the rear wall of the house, the grapevine, and two neighbors' fences, Rosalie went through one of the routines of the Revere High School cheerleading squad, which she'd memorized on two afternoons of peering through the fence at Paul Revere Stadium. She was twelve years old, too young to be a cheerleader. She would, in fact, in later years, harbor nothing but a bruised, smirking disdain for what she called "those nuns in foo-foo skirts." But on that afternoon, as the cousins ran and wrestled, she broke spontaneously into her routine, bouncing and kicking and barking out chants. "Gimme an 'R'! . . . Gimme an 'E'! . . ." The rest of us stopped and watched, panting, pulling strands of grass out of our hair, wiping our foreheads and faces with the sleeves of our shirts.

She was wearing a yellow dress with maroon and white stripes crossing at right angles to each other. "My tablecloth dress," she called it, affectionately. It flounced up around her hips when she pumped her knees, so that you could see her underpants and the tops of her pale thighs.

At the end of the routine, she flopped down on her back in the grass, the exhausted starlet, and then, while we were still applauding, she jumped up again, screaming. I thought a ground hornet had bitten her, or that she'd seen a snake. But it turned out she'd gotten the back of the dress in something one of the neighborhood dogs had left there. "A gift," we'd been taught to call it. As in "Rin Tin Tin from up the street left a gift in the backyard again, Ma."

But Rosie was going on thirteen, as we used to say, and too grown up for euphemisms. "I got shit on my dress, Tonio!" she cried out over the southern half of Jupiter Street at top volume. "My tablecloth dress! Dog shit, Tonio! Do something!"

In the foundation at the back of the house, there was a three-quarter-size door that led to my grandfather's wine cellar. Surrounded by a protective circle of girl cousins, Rosalie stood in the doorway, just out of view, and took off her dress. The young girl cousins carefully handed it out to the young boy cousins, who handed it over to me. Only a few square inches of the material were soiled, but the smell seemed to fill the backyard. Augustine, an older cousin who'd been named after my father, came by and held the dress while I sprayed it and sprayed it from the nozzle of the hose, and Rosalie called out instructions from her place by the wine barrels. "Be sure you get all of it, Tonio! Every last little bit! My mother will kill me if it smells up the car."

When Augustine and I had cleaned off as much of the gift as we could, we rubbed fistfuls of grass over the wet spot—so that the brown stain was replaced by a green one—then sprayed it thoroughly one more time. And in a little while we were all running again, making up games that blossomed and died, blossomed and evolved and died. With the wet dress sticking to her legs, Rosie ran beside me everywhere I went, pinching me, poking me, whispering secrets. The afternoon light softened, and soon evening fell over us, a sweet purple gauze. The voices of my cousins echoed against the houses like a happy symphony, and there seemed to be an endless supply of energy, of time, of good fortune. Anything was possible then: marrying a cousin, becoming rich, any good thing was possible.

From time to time, alone or in groups of two or three, we would pause for a breath and climb the wooden back stairs into the kitchen, take a sandwich or a piece of pastry from the table, run the gauntlet of aunts and uncles. One or two of them would stop us, put a hand against our neck or on our head or shoulder and ask about school, or friends, or our little lives, as if passing along an inheritance of warmth and good-will, one heartbeat at a time. Crucifixes flashing against bare throats, glasses of wine in one hand, the smell of brewing coffee, the fan wagging back and forth on top of the refrigerator sending out streamers of torn sheet in front of it, the television murmuring in the narrow room that had been fashioned from a hallway when the house had been renovated to make the apartment upstairs; jars of vinegar peppers, thin oily slices of salami on a plate, the soft white bread with sesame seeds baked into the crust, the bowl of fruit, the noisy tide of conversation, one or two of the aunts smoking, one of the uncles sitting with his knees spread, peeling the skin from a tangerine and offering sections all around.

My father and mother were there, sitting beside each other, the beam of sudden wealth—or, at least, sudden freedom from debt—shining in their eyes and mouths. My mother had taken hold of my father's hand, fingers intertwined, and was resting it in her lap, a sign that all was well in the world.

Around this nucleus of unwavering affection my cousins and I sprinted and whirled, until the neighborhood went completely dark and the radio music had been turned down inside, and men were standing on the back porch sucking light into cigar ashes, and I was being summoned, with increasing seriousness, up into the heat of the apartment for bed.

"Let me take him around the block once, Anna," my father said. He was holding one hand on the sweaty back of my neck, maintaining a pressure there just firm enough to keep me from running away again. We were standing on the side lawn, looking up at the window. My mother was leaning out of it on her elbows, as if she'd just finished taking in another line of socks and shirts. The hallway light was casting her head in relief, the shadows of the night covered her wrists and hands.

"Gus, it's almost ten. He has to be up at six-thirty for school."

"Just one loop around," my father said. "We need to have a special talk."

My father moved his hand to my shoulder, and we made one trip around the block that way. Smoke from his cigar floated across my face, a smell so pleasant to me that I would sometimes shut my eyes for a step or two and breathe it in deeply through my nose. It was a very warm night. Streetlights were reflected in the windshields of parked cars, and you could hear a laugh or a shout or television voices drifting out through the screens.

We climbed the hill of Jupiter Street, went across the short stretch of Mountain Avenue opposite Barrows School, then turned left and came down Saturn Street to the corner, made another left on Park Avenue, where there was more traffic, then walked up the sidewalk to the front of our house. There was the quiet tinkling laughter of domestic revelry floating out through the windows, a line of family cars still parked at the curb. "Let's sit here a minute," my father said, gesturing at the rough concrete stairs, "me and you." And we sat there, side by side and not looking at each other, like two men.

"I have to tell you something important, Tonio, alright?"

"Okay, Pa. That we're rich now?"

"We're not rich, but your mother's pregnant. Do you know what that means?"

"Having a baby."

"That's right."

"When?"

"Seven more months."

"How do you know, Pa?"

"We just know."

"Where's the baby now?"

"God has it."

"Where does He keep it?"

"In heaven."

"How does He let you know it's coming? A dream?"

"The doctor tells us. God tells the doctor and the doctor tells us and we go pick it up at the hospital on the right day, just like we did with you."

"Why does the woman's belly get big, then?"

He paused, glanced at me, then away. I turned and looked at his handsome square face in the streetlight, black-framed glasses balanced on the bridge of his nose, a dimpled chin, a high broad forehead, and a forest of dark hair his brother Peter would have killed for. He was smaller than Uncle Peter but almost as strong. And almost as bad with money. But more so than my grandfather or Uncle Aldo, the bank manager, my father went through his days wearing a mask of seriousness and purposefulness. Part of it came from the responsibilities of his job—he was a foreman in a plant that built jet engines. Part of it, no doubt, from what he had seen in Europe in 1943 and '44. Most of it, though, it seems to me now, was due to his inability to find a way to perfectly fit together his natural softheartedness and the code for manhood in that place and time. Sometimes the mask would crack. You'd get a glint of his dry humor, or follow the trail of his quiet sobs and find him burying the family dog in the upper part of the backyard on a cool October night. More often he'd simply pretend to be stricter or rougher than he was, though the act fooled no one, least of all my mother and me. "Tonio," he'd say, when I was being particularly disobedient. "Look at this, see this?" He'd turn his hand palm-up and point to the ridge of muscle between his wrist and thumb. "This is made to go against your bum, and it's gonna go there in another two seconds if you don't cut it out." Or he'd pull out the flap of his belt as if preparing to take it off. But there were no whippings in that house, no spankings. He was not an athlete like some of his brothers, not adept in business like some, not as socially at ease as Uncle Peter. At age nineteen he had been witness to the extreme end of the spectrum of human cruelty, and I think he struggled every day after that not to let it sour him, not to spoil my innocence with the legacy of war. That innocence would, in any case, be spoiled soon enough, though my father would not live to see it.

Laughter and voices floated out of the windows behind us.

He said, "It's in her belly now. It grows there a little every day. We can't see it yet."

"Why is it in her belly?"

"Because the seed for the baby gets planted there."

"Who plants it there, God?"

"Right. God and me."

"How, Papa?"

"What, how? We put it inside there."

"How do you put it in?"

"It's small in the beginning."

"In her mouth? Like food?"

"No, another way."

"How?"

"A trick."

"How, Pa? What kind of trick?"

He held the stub of the cigar between his middle finger and his thumb and launched it toward the street. It fell short, and I could see it blinking and smoking on the edge of the sidewalk.

"The way the world is set up," he said at last, "the way God sets it up, see, you learn a little bit at a time. Like you in school. Every grade you learn something a little bit different. It goes into your brain in a different place, a different little room, okay? First you learn to color, then you read, then you add, now you do long division, right? In my job you don't start building the whole engine for the airplane on the first day. You learn to read the plans first, you learn the different tools, calipers, trimmers, how you use them, okay?"

"Okay, Pa, but—"

"You're not at the age yet to learn everything about babies, or how to shave, or how to drive a car. Pretty soon you will. Hair is gonna grow on your face like on my face, see, on your body. You'll get big. Then we'll have a talk, okay?"

"Okay."

"We're going on a little trip, your mother and me, to celebrate our anniversary, get a little rest before your baby sister or brother comes, alright? We don't want you to feel bad that you're not coming with us. Your mother needs to get away now before this happens, understand?, because having a baby is hard work. She has to carry it around, she has to bring it to the hospital and deliver it. It doesn't mean anything against you that we're going."

"Where will I stay?"

"With Grandma and Grandpa. Rosie's coming over. The two of you are staying here, and Uncle Peter and Auntie Ulla and me and your mother are flying to New York. Three days we'll be gone; can you handle that okay?"

"Sure, Pa."

"Alright then, go to bed."

"Pa?"

We got up and went in through the narrow screened porch and toward the door where Uncle Peter had stood and pressed the buzzer that same morning. My father knocked twice on the wood, hard, and only then turned to me. "What?"

"When you get as old as Grandma and Grandpa, what things don't you know yet?"

An exasperated smile started to scratch at the muscles of his mouth, but immediately died there. He pressed his lips together. He raised one finger in the air and lowered it. "There's such a thing as being too smart," he said. "For a kid especially, there's—"

"I know, but what things?"

He knocked on the door again. "Probably you don't know the last little secrets," he said, "the things God keeps for Himself." He was look- ing straight at me now, the mask gone, the veneer of toughness stripped away. If I had known to look for them, I would have seen the bloody footprints of war there on his face, the dark questions at the center of my father's life.

"Like what?" I said.

"Like what? Like why He makes people get sick. Why He makes them die. Things like that." The buzzer sounded and the lock popped. "Now go on up now. Give me a kiss and go up and right to bed."

But even in bed, listening to the voices in my grandparents' apart- ment, the sound of spoons in coffee cups, a bubble of laughter in the yard—even there I could not let go of the conversation. I pictured an enormous book, thick as the library dictionary, the finger of God turning a page every year or so, letting you in on another small piece of the mys- tery. Hair on your face, cigar smoke and bundles of money, the secrets of pregnancy and death—I wanted to steal the book and hide in my room at night with a flashlight, poring over it. I wanted to know everything everyone else knew, without waiting.

"YOU CAN'T FEEL IT YET," my mother was telling me. She was sitting on the edge of the mattress. I could see her forehead and eyes in the faint light from Park Avenue, and the small space between her two front teeth. She had pulled the sheet up over my chest, then changed her mind and pulled it down again. "Later, you can put your hand here and feel her moving."

"It's a girl?"

"I think so," she said. "Won't it be nice to have a little sister in the house?"

I heard people on the wooden back stairs, and then on the walk beneath my window. "Wait till I get you home," Aunt Ulla was saying, in a voice that felt like a piece of sandpaper running along your skin. "Just wait."

"Sure," I told my mother. "Sure it will."

Six

THE BIG TRIP WAS PLANNED for that weekend, the last weekend in June. Uncle Peter had bought the tickets from a friend of his, a woman who knew somebody at the airlines—special price. He told me he'd made reservations at the finest, classiest, most expensive hotel in New York. He'd gone out and picked up a new suit, a new sport coat, a new pair of shoes because, as he said, "You can't go to New York City looking like a nobody."

But at the last minute Aunt Ulla must have fallen ill with one of her headaches because, as things turned out, my mother and father ended up flying off by themselves. Uncle Peter, Rosalie, and I drove them to Logan Airport on a hot, sunny Friday. We stood in the terminal building and watched through the glass as my parents appeared on the tarmac in a loose file of other travelers, as my mother turned to look for us and waved, as they climbed the portable stairway, turned again, both of them, swung their hands twice in our direction, as if they were just going to New York, to a hotel, as if they'd be home again in two days and then the world would be the way it had always been.

"Those are the kinds of engines your pa makes, see?" I remember Uncle Peter telling me. "At the GE, see? Look at them."

We climbed up to the open-air observation deck on the roof of the terminal—people did not bomb airplanes in those days, or fly them into buildings—and watched the jet back slowly out of its berth and roll off to the edge of the runway, only a few inches, it seemed, from the sea. We stood and stared as it gathered speed there, lifted up in a neat silver line, climbed, banked, folded its wheels in, and blinked off toward the exotic territory called New York.

Seven

OVER THE PAST TWENTY-FIVE YEARS, I have tried probably fifty times to paint my father's mother. There are old wrinkled snapshots of her all over my studio—as a young bride with shining black hair twisted into a bun on top of her head; as a mother surrounded by her brood; alone in her garden of gladioli and roses; with her husband in the mottled grapevine shade; with the statue of Mary in the background; with a child in her arms; indoors, outdoors, late in life, as I knew her: gray-haired, a silver-capped front tooth that blinked in the sunlight, the nose and ears gone too large, the flesh beneath her chin drooping, her eyes turned up slightly at the corners.

In her young, pretty days, in her old and not-so-pretty days, some persistent, unvarnished force shone through her, a steadiness, a deep, deep patience with the pain and frustrations of living. Looking at the photographs, you can see it there. But it does not translate into oils. Or, at least, I have never been able to accomplish the translation.

My grandmother was the sun around which the Benedetto family orbited. This, I know, runs against the cliché. In Italian families it is supposed to be the father who is imbued with some larger-than-human dimension. And in Revere, in fact, it was usually the father's word that held most of the weight in an argument, in a household code of laws—something carried over from the besieged mountain villages in the southern Italian countryside. In those places, invasion was a seasonal event, and it was the men, the warriors, who kept or failed to keep the family alive. Centuries later and thousands of miles to the west, it was the father whose arrival home at the end of the working day was a cause for celebration—

as if he had been away in battle and there had been some doubt about his safe return. It was the father who pronounced grace over steaming plates of food, who stepped out onto the porch and smoked on summer evenings while the women tended to their offspring and rinsed plates. If the Benedetto family had been a fifteenth-century Neapolitan royal clan—nine children and their nine spouses and their thirty-one sons and daughters—then my grandfather would have been installed on the throne, not beside his wife but a step above her, two steps above their Augustines and Peters and Marias and Aldos and the people they had married. My grandfather bore this exalted status well and quietly, neither making a great show of it nor shirking the harsher duties. But, king or no king, ask any of the surviving children where the spiritual power in the family resided.

My grandmother came to America when she was thirteen, was married by the time she was seventeen, gave birth to her first child at eighteen. Her adulthood was an unbroken dream of hard labor: carrying and bearing children; drawing forth meals, day after day, year upon year, from the cupboards, skillets, and gardens the way a conductor draws forth music from an assembly of musicians; scrubbing, dusting, pushing the carpet cleaner along the hallways while her younger children napped.

When I knew her best she was in her sixties and seventies, and until she became ill with Alzheimer's a few years before the end of her life, she would still put three meals together, weed her flower gardens, bake pies, and keep the house clean without benefit of paid help.

Her main pleasure consisted of surreptitious shopping trips to Boston—on the bus and in subway cars—where she would comb the department stores along Washington Street in all months of the year, buying Christmas gifts. After her children had all left the house and there was more time, she fell into the habit of watching the soap opera *As the World Turns* every afternoon, weeping over it sometimes as her mind failed. Every other spare moment seemed to be filled with prayer. I would come through the back door after school and find her at the table with her beads, eyes fastened on the wall as if a vision of an easier existence were painted there, and it was just a question of having the patience to wait until the colors came to life.

Even here I know I am not capturing her as she really was. Words stick on the surface. She worked a subtler dimension, the realm of the absence of ego. Even today, old neighbors I meet on visits back to Revere say, "She was a saint, your grandmother." And I want to say to them, Yes, right, but what is a saint? A stiff relic in the window of the church? How do you make a portrait of a saint; how do you talk about her without sounding false? What does it actually mean to be a saint in this world of lies and religious fanaticism? Who even believes in the possibility anymore?

I ask those questions of myself, in the studio, piling failures one upon the next. And always I go back to what seems to me a safe starting point: a saint is someone who, doing nothing dramatic, saying nothing profound, knows instinctively how to begin to rescue a child when, on route back to Boston from New York, descending through a soupy, surly fog, the jet that the child's parents are riding in catches its landing gear on the top of the concrete wall that marks the airport's eastern boundary, wobbles for one instant between an ordinary, taken-for-granted morning and the threshold of terror and mystery, then jerks sharply downward so that the nose strikes the tarmac, the enormous momentum lifts the tail up and over, and the jet, missing one wing, skids upside down and backward along the runway and explodes.

Eight

I REMEMBER SITTING BETWEEN my uncle and cousin in the terminal and watching the fog brush against the plate glass like the shoulder of a sleeping animal. It was an early-morning fog, a common occurrence in summer along the New England coastline, something that would soon burn away, leaving a clear, hot day. If the flight had arrived an hour later, there would have been no problem, no crash. We would have ridden home to Revere in my uncle's car and lived out very different fates. If the flight had arrived an hour later, if the pilot had not tried to land, if the angle of descent had been one degree different from what it was . . .

I remember I was dressed in school clothes for the event of my parents' homecoming, and that, at my grandmother's suggestion, I had picked a few flowers from the yard for my mother, and that Rosalie was sitting to my right, swinging her legs back and forth beneath the chair in a way that irritated her father. Years later, Rosie would tell me she'd had a premonition on that day, that she turned to me a few minutes before we heard the news—before there was any news to hear—and said, "What's wrong, Tonio? Something's wrong." But I do not remember her doing that.

I remember an announcement coming over the address system, and Uncle Peter lifting his head out of some reverie of greyhounds and colts, walking over to the ticket desk and then suddenly, absurdly, sprinting toward the emergency door and throwing his shoulder against it. At first, Rosalie and I thought he was only making one of his manic, comedic displays for the amusement of the other people waiting to be summoned to the gate. And then two policemen ran up and wrestled him to the ground. Uncle Peter threw a punch into the air—one inch to the side of one of the faces—a punch that would have killed a man, and the policemen redoubled their efforts, leaning all their combined weight on his arms and torso, and shouting for assistance. I threw the flowers onto a chair. Rosie and I went running to save him.

I remember stumbling around the yard at 20 Jupiter Street in the broiling heat of that afternoon, walking dazed down the narrow grass alley that separated my grandparents' house from the blue picket fence of the next yard over. I remember the smell of my aunts' perfume and lipstick as they took hold of me, under the grapevine, on the back steps, at the edges of the kitchen, pressed me against their chests and wrapped me in Roman Catholic platitudes about God's goodness and mercy. And I remember, when the afternoon had worn itself down to a blunt nib of spoiled, burnt hope, standing on the sidewalk in a loose collection of cousins and watching Uncle Leo's blue Studebaker make the corner from Park Avenue, come up the street, and stop at the curb. I looked at Uncle Peter. He was in the passenger seat, leaning forward, looking at me, his face a quivering chiaroscuro on which was painted misery enough for a hundred lifetimes.

I was swept into the small den, the TV was turned off, the other cousins banished to the yard. The aunts and my grandmother crowded around the door. My grandfather and uncles sat on the sofa and soft chairs, the room so small their knees were touching in an uneven circle. Uncle Peter's eyes were sending streams of tears down his face, and he stared at me as if I, too, might vanish in the next second, as if God were intent on taking the people he loved out of the world, one by one, like a merciless opponent plucking chessmen from a board. Uncle Leo was looking at the window, though the Venetian blinds were drawn. I remember all this as if it were painted on the insides of my eyes. Uncle Aldo and Uncle Francis maneuvered me so that I was standing between their knees, my back to the sofa, and facing my grandfather, who was sitting straight-spined in the soft chair closest to the door. I could hear Aunt Marie—who'd named her oldest son after my father—wailing in the kitchen, calling my father's name again and again.

"Antonio," Dom said when we were all still. He reached out, took my hands in his hands, and drew me across the carpet toward him so that I was standing close to him and my eyes were even with his eyes. "The plane, she crashed, you know it."

I couldn't swallow or speak. I could not move. I stared through the upper lenses of his bifocals.

"Eighty-nine people, they died."

I thought for a moment he was going to ask me to give him the words for "eighty-nine" in Italian. *Ottanta nove*, I was ready to say. I would have pronounced any number for him, any phrase. I would have taken out and handed over any of the empty little treasures of my school year—the test scores, the columns of As, the compliments of my teachers—in exchange for some relief from the weight of that moment.

"Three people, they lived so far; what they can find."

"Your mother lived," Uncle Leo blurted out, because he could not endure the pace at which his father was dripping information into the room.

"You mama, she's alive still, in the hospital now."

"Papa?" I spoke this as a question into a silence that was broken only by the wails and sobs in the kitchen. "Jesus, oh Jesus, oh Jesus God," Aunt Marie was crying out.

"You Papa . . . ," Dom said, and now he squeezed my hands harder and pulled me an inch closer.

"Your father pushed your mother and the other two people out the window," Uncle Leo piped up again from the corner of the couch. But his words, arcing over toward me like the thinnest lifeline of hope, carried no comfort. I could not turn away from my grandfather's face. "The plane was on fire," Uncle Leo went on. "People were burning up, screaming. Your father was a hero, like in the war. He saved them."

The sentences floated through the air like scraps of old thread. My grandfather's face was what mattered to me, *his* words, *his* assessment of the situation. He did not move, his grip did not relax; someone was murmuring to my aunt in the kitchen, comforting her.

"God called you father today," Dom said at last, and I watched a burst of feeling—electric and terrible—race along the lines of his face. "God called him up."

I looked to my left at the heavy black telephone on its skinny dark table. I smiled a wretched smile, a spasm of horror in the muscles of my mouth. More people were crying in the kitchen now, in the doorway, on the sofa behind and to either side of me. If there had been any chance of breaking away, I would have sprinted out through the kitchen and down the back steps, but I was trapped in that little circle of misery. I looked at Uncle Peter, who had leaned his face down onto his hands and lowered the backs of his hands to his knees and was weeping in high-pitched hiccups. I felt the skin of my face go loose, and a flood of tears, and mucous in my mouth, and my grandfather's arms taking hold of me.

Nine

THAT NIGHT I SLEPT on the sofa bed in my grandparents' parlor, a rarely used room of drawn curtains and plastic-covered armchairs. Rosalie slept with me. After a few restless hours, I awoke, in darkness, to the warm cotton smell of her pajamas, and the tangle of black hair down her back. I thought I had heard her crying. I thought the sound of it was what had made me wake up. But when I quietly said her name—"Rosie?"—she did not stir. I put the flat of my hand against her pajamas, against her back, and tried not to breathe so I could be sure she was breathing. "Rosie," I whispered. She slept on.

I sat up and rubbed my eyes and rubbed my face and saw that a frail light bloomed in the arched kitchen doorway. I shuffled across the carpet toward it. In the kitchen, my grandmother sat alone at the table, the night-light from her bedroom plugged into the outlet. Moths were driving themselves against the screens of the windows, buzzing and bumping and scratching at the metal threads. In her hands she held a small prayer book with a worn-out black leather cover, the pages edged red. Her eyeglasses rested halfway down her nose—a more modest version of Uncle Peter's nose—and she mouthed the words as she read.

When she realized I was there, she put her hand on the sleeve of my pajamas. A thin breeze, almost cool, floated in through the screens and across the skin of my neck. I shivered, stared at her, sleepily, miserably, half-listening to the moths. She pushed me gently down into a chair and went to the refrigerator, and in a moment the short sharp stink of stove gas reached me, then the sweet smell of bacon being cooked in its own fat. Soon she put a plate of eggs on the table, a glass of milk. She worked at the counter another minute, returned with another plate: two slices of toast, giving off small steamy breaths. She sat again, her hands and fleshy forearms on the plastic tablecloth, and for a few seconds we were as still as statues in the huge, half-lit silence, darkness breathing in through the screen, the emptiness of the dark rooms above us like an open mouth about to speak. She touched the toast slices with one finger and put a hand on my arm, not crying while everyone else cried, not trying to say anything to comfort me. Grandpa Dom slept, Rosalie slept. The aunts, uncles, and cousins had returned to their houses to sleep. She took up the prayer book and held it in her hand without opening it, without taking her eyes from my face. She looked at me out of a perfect stillness, as if willing me to understand something that could not be spoken. And for a few flickering seconds I thought I did understand it. Even to the deepest grief and pain there is a thin lining of disbelief, as if death and suffering are mostly, but not completely, real. It seemed to me on that night that she had taken my thoughts as if they were fingers, and was running them along the fabric of that lining, letting me feel the weave of it. But this lasted only a breath or two, before the tears came. I put my face in my hands, the way I had seen my uncles do, and wept without any self-consciousness, the top of my head so close to the plate that the next morning there was dried egg yolk in my hair, and she saw it and took me to the sink to wash it out.

Ten

THE NEXT DAY WAS very hot again, the sky unbearably bright, as if it were reflecting another world on fire. The fan hummed on top of my grandparents' refrigerator, and the house and yard were overlaid with a sad, superheated lethargy. My grandmother stood at the stove, sweating over her bubbling pots, resting a hand on my shoulder when I came within reach of her, pulling me close against her leg, pressing her fingers into the side of my face. Cousins sat in the shade of the grapevine or wandered the yard in pairs, staring out over the fences, picking up stones from the dirt of the vacant lot next door and tossing them back down again, glancing up and then guiltily away when planes crossed overhead on their approach to Logan. Neighbors brought over plates of lasagna and fruit baskets in plastic wrap. They sat in the kitchen for an hour or two hours, and with each new arrival I was summoned from my places of mourning—the sofa bed, the grassy alleyway—and presented to the guests so that I could accept their embraces, their kisses, their "Tonio, my God, Tonio. I'm so sorry for you, honey."

But I did not want sympathy and *pizza dolce;* what I wanted was to see my mother.

Rosalie acted as if I were a starving blind boy she had volunteered to chaperon. She brought me sandwiches, tall glasses of iced coffee with two inches of sugar in the bottom, cakes, cookies, bowls of pudding, pieces of fruit. But I would not eat. When, after lunch, the stream of visitors increased, and I realized none of them had come to take me into Boston to the hospital, that none of my begging and pleading was having any effect whatsoever on the aunts and uncles, I crawled beneath the large evergreen bush to the right of the front steps and sat there, nephew on strike, scratching nonsensical patterns in the cool dirt, refusing to appear when summoned, refusing to speak. After a while, Rosalie came and sat with me. We stayed there for a long time, not looking at each other, not talking. From our hiding place we could hear cars pulling up and doors slamming, and, once, the voice of a woman: "Such a handsome man."

One of us must have broken the silence. I don't remember who, or what we talked about at first—the memory of that day is broken up into pieces, hot, vivid, incomplete. At some point Rosalie took out her "Mary card" and held it in both hands in front of her against her bare raised knees. The Mary card was a piece of thick paper, not quite cardboard, probably an inch and a half by three inches, with a painting of a very young Virgin holding her infant son and looking up to heaven. Most of us had a talisman like that: a square of rough cloth called a scapular, which we wore around our necks; rosary beads; slivers of the True Cross; Saint Joseph medals on our desks, Saint Rocco statues on our end tables, Saint Christopher pendants dangling from the rearview mirrors of our cars. We prayed to Saint Anthony when we lost something, Saint Jude to help us with impossible cases, Saint Lucy when a cousin was hit in the eye playing stickball. We had our throats blessed by Saint Blaise in winter, we said novenas, went without meat on Fridays, nodded our heads when we spoke Jesus' name aloud or when we drove or walked past a Catholic church. The ordinary days were speckled with reminders that this life was a temporary life, not what it seemed; that there was a whole team of spirits above us, invisible in the ether, eager to help. You prayed to Jesus on the Little League field; you wrote down your sins every evening so you could make an accurate confession on Saturday afternoon. You said "God bless you" when someone sneezed, and "God rest her [or his] soul" whenever the name of a dead woman (or man) was spoken aloud. The Catholic child's mind was flooded with images: a tortured savior; a perfect mother; the agonizing cries of sinners burning in hell, without advocates, without hope.

So it seemed perfectly natural to me that Rosalie always carried the

Mary card around with her in her pocket. And absolutely unsurprising that she would take it out then. On that stifling day we were all calling on God—to heal my mother, to lift my father's soul, to give us some explanation for what had happened.

Rosalie stared at the card for a few minutes—I assumed she was praying—then tore it in half. She held one piece in each hand. I let out a choked-off shout, a protest, and reached out roughly to try to put the two pieces back together. Rosalie squeezed her hands around them, turned her back, and tore up each piece again, then tossed them in the dust and spruce needles.

"Rosie! It's a sin!"

"What God did to Uncle Gus, that's a sin."

"You can't say that!"

"He's not there. He couldn't be there and do something like this. Even the devil wouldn't do something like this to Uncle Gus. What if your mother dies, too? What if my father dies next?" She slapped at the dust so that the pieces of paper scattered. I reached across and grabbed at them, held one little scrap in my fingers. She pulled my arm back, put her body in the way. We wrestled and grabbed at each other's hands, angrier and angrier, grunting, saying, "Stop!" "Cut it out!" until she started crying, and then I started crying, and we sat with our backs against the foundation of the house like a set of sweaty, dirty-cheeked twins.

IN THE MIDDLE OF THE AFTERNOON, a car carrying three pairs of uncles and aunts left for Boston. I remember breaking away from Rosalie—who was staying close to me still, as if I were a balloon or a kite and the smallest breeze would carry me out over the ocean—and running down the sidewalk after it, calling out, "Take me! Take *me!*" until the car made the corner onto Park Avenue and pulled away.

Though I had spent almost no time in the house, where most of the rest of the family huddled and mourned, I knew Uncle Peter wasn't there. I knew it because when he was in the house or in the yard or out front leaning against the fender of a car with his arms crossed, he would almost always make a point of "checking in," as he called it. This meant that if I was outside playing with the cousins, he'd break away, every half hour or so, from whatever conversation he was engaged in, and stand at the screen door or step out onto the back porch until he saw me. He'd always done this, years before my father died, and, in a different way, he does it still. If he stopped by the house on one of his unannounced visits and I was asleep, he would slip into the bedroom and stand over me for a minute, usually reaching down and resting his fingers on my chest to make sure I was still breathing. This had been going on for so many years that I was no longer surprised to wake up and see him there, outlined in the diluted hall light with his huge arm held toward me and two of his fingers resting lightly on my chest. During the school year, especially, it upset my mother—the waking up, not the checking in. On more than one occasion, after Uncle Peter left, there was a small argument about it.

But he was my godfather, and in southern Italian culture that relationship carries with it a particularly heavy responsibility, as if you have been charged with taking care of a precious possession that belongs to someone else, a neighbor's diamond ring placed in your pocket, for life. You watch over it even more closely than you would if it were your own.

But it was more than that. It went deeper, even, than the fact that Uncle Peter was unhappily married, and poured out, on Rosalie and me and on one or two of the other cousins, the affection Aunt Ulla would not accept from him. It went deeper than the love he felt for my father—his favorite among the siblings. It had something to do with heroism; I am just now coming to see that. *Always remember who you are, Einstein, who your family is.* It had something to do with this idea he'd had, as a boxer, that by becoming heavyweight champion of the world, he would somehow lift all of us up and out of the reach of humiliation. No one could look down on him then, or on us. For being Italians. For being from Revere. The world would see us as we saw each other—as dazzling souls. It explains the Cadillac, and the expensive clothes, and the dream—impossible to fulfill—of winning enough money at gambling to buy us all the life we deserved.

Though there was no real reason to, he had this idea that I would conquer the wider world he had seen—and failed in, and fled. He loved his daughter more than he loved his own life, but he did not expect her to do this for the Benedetto family. He expected me to do it.

So he bought me baseball gloves and took me with him to Fenway Park. He drove me to school, taught me to fight, instructed me in the laws of style, of pride, of narcissism, perhaps. He treated me as if I would be a king someday and would lead my people. I liked it—what young boy wouldn't like it? I looked into his face hoping to see reflected there the proof that I was not ordinary . . . which may explain why I have spent the last twenty-five years trying to be as ordinary as I can possibly be.

And on the day after I learned my father had been killed and my mother badly hurt—how could God do such a thing to a special boy?—I looked for that image of myself reflected in Uncle Peter's face. I waited for him to come and lift me up.

But he had dropped off Rosalie and Aunt Ulla early in the morning and stayed only long enough to have a cup of coffee with his parents. He'd barely acknowledged me and left without saying good-bye, and for the rest of the day I looked for his car and listened for his voice. The previous twenty-four hours had been a series of mortar rounds with reverberating silences between: the commotion at the airport; the gathering of men in the TV room; the endless night in which I'd dozed and awakened every half hour and felt the truth of what had happened, the fact of it, appear out of the dark forgetfulness of sleep and slam against me, again and again. Shell-shocked as any soldier in any muddy trench, I expected what was left of the world to be blown apart, too. All guarantees had been revoked. What was to stop my mother from dying? Grandpa? Grandma? Rosie? Why shouldn't Uncle Peter fail to check in, even though he had been checking in every day I could remember for years and years?

Finally, late in the afternoon, half an hour after the carful of aunts and uncles drove away, I heard a car door close, and saw his face and shoulders above the trimmed hedge. I heard him say to Rosalie, "Where is he?" and watched his eyes flit over the lawn. When he saw me, he tilted his head toward the street once, quickly. I ran out of the yard and stopped next to him. "Get in," he said, "get in front, next to me."

I sat between him and Rosie. He was wearing a short-sleeved white dress shirt. I remember the light coating of hair over the sinews on his huge forearms, his thick wrists, the sight of both his hands on the wheel for once, the knuckles, the wedding band, the watch—everything reminding me of my father. The car squealed away from the house as if it were being driven by a teenager. Rosie took hold of my hand. We went up Jupiter Street and turned right onto Mountain Avenue and right again at the corner of Broadway, and near the end of Broadway we pulled to the curb in front of Russo's bakery. Uncle Peter reached two fingers into the pocket of his shirt and drew out a folded hundred-dollar bill. I had never seen one before. He pushed it into my hand and said, "We're goin in, and we're gonna buy every macaroon cookie and every éclair and every *biscòtti* they have, alright? Quick, they're closin up."

"And take them to my mother?"

He did not look at me. We got out of the car, closed the doors, and stood in the cool sidewalk shadows.

"And take them to my mother, Uncle?" I said again. My voice twisted upward and broke over the last two syllables. I had the bill in my right hand; Rosalie was holding my left arm near the elbow. I did not know that Uncle Peter was lost, adrift, that he was only falling back on old tricks—the money, the show—because he had no sense at all now of where the channel was, and where were the shoals. He had stayed away from the house all day because he could not face what had happened, could not face me. When he heard the word *mother* a second time, he looked at me blankly, then turned away. Someone who must not yet have heard about my father drove by and yelled out, "Hey, Peter B!" but he did not move even his eyes.

"Uncle?"

"We can't see her," he said flatly.

"Why not?"

"Why not, Papa?"

He looked at Rosalie and pursed his lips. He looked away.

"They let Uncle Aldo and Aunt Maria, they let—"

"You're too young. The doctors don't let you in that young."

"I want to *see* her!" I shouted over Broadway. "I want to *see her!*"

"We can't now, pal. . . ."

I crushed the bill in my hand, threw it against the front of his shirt, and sprinted down the sidewalk in what I guessed was the direction of Boston. I made it across Fenno and almost as far as the corner of Page Street—two blocks—before he caught me. He squatted down next to me and held me against his chest until I stopped fighting. "I can't, Tonio," he said into my ear. "I can't, pal, I can't. The other uncles and aunts, they had a meetin last night. . . . They don't want you to see her now. She's burned, your mother, okay? Now I told you. Burned up bad. She's in the hospital bed and can't get up. She can't see you, can't talk to you. I wanted to take you but now I can't, see? They'd crucify me. Let's wait two days, alright? Two days, then I'll take you, I give you my word, no matter who says anythin about it, okay?"

I leaned my head to one side, half-trying to escape, and saw Rosalie standing on the sidewalk fifty yards behind us, bending over with her hands on her knees, as if she'd been running all the way from Jupiter Street. "Papa?" she called.

Still holding me with one arm, her father turned and looked at her over his shoulder. "Papa?" she said again, weakly. She wobbled, she reached up and pressed one hand against her belly. We hurried toward her, and when we were still a few feet away, I saw that there were two thin trickles of dark blood on her right leg. I thought she had fallen and cut herself. "My insides hurt, Papa," she said, still bending over, and I could see then that the blood was coming down her thigh, past her knee, staining the top edge of one white sock.

"Jesus, Madonna," I heard Uncle Peter say. "Madonna, when things happen, they happen." He was fighting with the buttons of his shirt, taking it off. The word *tourniquet* came into my mind. I may have said it aloud, standing there, two feet from Rosalie. I may have burped it out in a spasm of panic.

My uncle had his shirt off and was bare-chested on the sidewalk, with the late-afternoon traffic rolling past and two women in black dresses watching from the door of an apartment house. He had balled up his dress shirt and was cleaning the blood from his daughter's leg. She had one hand on his bare shoulder. I could see the dark rich red soaking into the white fabric of the shirt. "Papa, Papa," she was whimpering. Uncle Peter folded the shirt over itself, enclosing the stains in white, then gently reached it up under her dress, between her legs, and said, "Put your hand there and hold it like that, honey; it's okay, nobody's watchin us. You're okay." He put one arm behind her knees and one behind her back and lifted her, and Rosie's eyes swung up and caught my eyes.

"Nobody's watchin, honey, nobody's watchin," Uncle Peter said as he carried her. She stared at me as we went the first few steps, then buried her face in her father's chest. "Nobody's lookin, honey. You're growin up now, that's all. Mama told you about it, didn't she? You're al-right. We'll take you home now for a little while. Tonio's here, we're all okay. We're okay."

I opened the car door. Uncle Peter put one knee on the edge of the seat and, reaching in, set Rosie down in the middle. "It's leather, it washes, don't worry, honey." There was a little blood on his hands and arms. "Reach in my back pocket and grab me the handkerchief, Tonio," he said. He cleaned off the blood, tossed the handkerchief onto the floor of the backseat, and we sat on either side of Rosie and rode up the hill to the house on Venice Avenue.

Uncle Peter told me to go out into the yard and play, to wait for him there, but for some reason I didn't do that. I remember standing in the kitchen with a glass of cream soda in my right hand. Rosalie was in the bathroom, cleaning herself, according to her father's instructions, with a warm washcloth. Uncle Peter was standing sideways in the parlor doorway with the telephone receiver trapped between his bare shoulder and his jaw, and he was taking the cap off a bottle of cold beer with a metal opener. He could not see me. He fumbled with the opener a little— he was distracted by Rosie, the phone—the muscles near his shoulders jumped as his arms moved, as if small animals were trapped there, below the skin.

"Ulla," he said into the phone. The bottle cap came off at last and skittered across the linoleum. "Home . . . our house. Rosie's got her, you know. She's bleedin . . . between the legs. . . . I know it, unbleevable, right? . . . I'll come get you, two minutes. . . . Whaddayou mean? This is somethin for you to do, Ul. . . . Look, I'm comin down there and I'm bringin you back here. . . . That's right. . . . I know that. . . . My brother just *died*, and my sister-in-law is probably gonna die, too. . . . I was out . . . out, nowhere. Driving around cryin. . . . Who abandoned you? What *abandoned*? What are you talkin about? Those are my brothers and sisters. . . ."

When he hung up the phone, Uncle Peter went out the door that led off the hallway between the kitchen and parlor. The door opened onto a tiny porch, just a landing, really, for the steps that led down into the backyard. I could see him through the kitchen window above the sink. He was standing near the railing, the tips of the fingers of his left hand resting on top of it, his right hand holding the bottle of beer at his hip. He took one drink from it and stood very still for twenty or thirty seconds, then he lifted the bottle up to his shoulder and threw it with a casual motion, one quick flex of the muscles of his shoulder and arm. The bottle flew end over end, circular trails of beer leaking out. It splashed into the round, blue, above-ground pool, bubbled there a minute, and slowly sank.

I SLEPT A DEEP, deep sleep that night, alone on the sofa bed in my grandparents' parlor. Rosie slept in her own house, in her own bed.

In the morning I sat at the kitchen table with my grandmother, eating toast and drinking coffee with extra milk in it, replaying everything I had seen and heard the day before. I was being cheated, I knew that—by God, by the aunts and uncles. Cheated or punished. My father was dead and my mother was going to die. Rosalie was bleeding from inside. Uncle Peter and Aunt Ulla were arguing. My grandfather had become a nervous man, overnight.

Instead of sitting with my grandmother and me as he normally would have done, still and calm, a sort of living statue before which we could lay the wreaths of our worries and plans, Grandpa Dom paced like a sterner, smaller Uncle Peter, lips pressed into a line, hands clasped and working behind his back. He stepped into the den and then out again into the kitchen. He went the length of the kitchen and disappeared into the small foyer near the back door. I could hear him speaking under his breath there, something I had never known him to do. Another few seconds and he reappeared, still muttering, checking the clock, checking his watch, disappearing again.

"Domenico," my grandmother said, as if she were warning him. "Rose Marie *verrà tra quindici minuti.*"

He emerged, a nervous ghost in the doorway, nodded at her curtly, nervously, and went on with his peculiar routine—the back door, the den, the back door again. On his loops through the den, he began now to address the telephone, in quiet but urgent Italian, commanding it to ring. When it at last obeyed, he was in the middle of the kitchen, heading the other way, and he turned and hurried back. I stopped eating and listened to him in there, speaking in his soft, aqueous voice. He hung up and hurried into the bedroom, then joined us again wearing a suit jacket over his white shirt and carrying his straw fedora. He touched my grandmother once on the elbow as if for luck, a touch with fifty years of companionship and the grief of one dead son in it, and signaled for me to follow.

I trailed him into the white heat of the morning and caught up with him just as he was leaving the yard. We turned left at the bottom of the street, sunlight sparkling on the car windows and on Park Avenue's drooping electric wires. We passed the awning shop, then Zingy's, then Sully's, a one-room corner store where my mother had sent me a hundred times for bread and milk. At Venus Street, a quarter mile short of Broadway, Grandpa Dom turned abruptly left, as if seeking shade. We went a hundred feet up the sidewalk and found a green Pontiac parked there with its motor running. My grandfather opened the passenger door, flipped the front seat forward, and motioned me in. Behind the wheel sat Vittorio Imbesalacqua, hair clipped short beneath a carpenter's cap, and beads of sweat on the back of his tanned, strong neck. Vittorio was almost thirty years younger than my grandfather. They treated each other more like brothers than friends, held together by a bond that seemed mysterious to me until I found out—years later, from Vito's daughter, Joanie—that my grandfather had sponsored her father's arrival in America, promised the authorities that the man would work hard, would do no harm here.

Every spring, Vittorio—"Victor Bones," as Grandpa called him—spent a whole workday pruning the vines on our grape arbor, in payment for which he would accept nothing more than a single shot glass of brandy in the late afternoon. He would bring his wife, Lucy, and his children, Joanie and Peter, to our Sunday gatherings, and sit with my grandfather on the concrete bench beneath the grapevine, sometimes holding a cigar between the fingers of one rough hand and taking the occasional puff. Famous for his physical strength and sublime abilities at bocce, he was the gentlest of men, quiet as a monk. He acted as if he were bearing some secret pain through the world and would never speak of it. And he had always seemed to hold some particular affection for me, always talked about my working for him when I was old enough, building houses. His son was just my age, a wild, funny, charismatic boy, who made fun of his own father's accent because some of his schoolmates taunted him about it.

My grandfather slipped into the front seat of the Pontiac and spoke to Vito conspiratorially, in Italian, mostly too soft and fast for me to understand. But I caught one word. Dom reached over the back of the seat and took hold of my hand, and we slipped off through the streets of Revere like fugitives in flight from a repressive regime. The word I thought I had heard was *"ospedale."*

We went along Mountain Avenue to Washington Avenue, and dodged through the back streets of Chelsea toward the ramp that led onto the Mystic River Bridge. My grandfather pushed open the small triangular side window so that the breeze blew into his face and tossed his fedora into my lap. I held the fedora there, watched him across the back of the seat, but I did not look at him or say a word, as if eye contact or speech or anything as noticeable as a drawn breath would cause him to order us back to Jupiter Street.

We climbed the long rise of the bridge, and saw Boston spread out there in the heat—the harbor, the Customs Tower, the hills of Charlestown scarved in smog, steaming, sweating. Grandpa handed Vittorio a dime for the toll, and Vittorio made a big show of refusing him, taking one hand off the wheel to bat at my grandfather's arm and bubbling in Italian that Dom was going to make him drive over the edge of the bridge and down into the water if he didn't stop; that it was bad enough, the driving, the sadness, what had happened to this boy, to his father, his mother, the other cars trying to push him over the edge, without the embarrassment, the humiliation, of someone else paying the toll for him when he was driving in his own car. He'd put the dime in his pocket, he said, he'd had it there all along, but then he'd set it out on the dashboard while he was waiting and it had somehow slipped off. . . .

At last, a coin—someone's—was handed over to the attendant, and we drove on, descending now, gliding this way and that along busy ramps and through short tunnels, through the close, clamorous city air.

By the time we turned onto Storrow Drive, Grandpa Dom had his hat on his head again; people were blowing their horns at the Pontiac and crowding up close on three sides. And Vittorio was leaning forward over the wheel, rolling along the speedway at thirty miles an hour while Boston drivers swarmed and cursed him, and his friend Domenic Benedetto snapped directions at him in a version of Italian laced with expressions known only to a few thousand souls born in the dry hill country east of Naples.

Finally we pulled up to the door of the hospital. Vittorio let out a breath he seemed to have been holding since Venus Street. He sank back into the seat, took out the swatch of old cloth he used as a handkerchief on his job, and toweled off his forehead, ears, and neck.

My grandfather squeezed his shoulder. "Don't wait for us, Victor Bones," he said in English. "You have the job going."

"But how can't I wait, Domenico?"

"Don't wait. You're in the middle of making someone's house."

"But how couldn't I?"

"Don't."

"But what now, you gonna walk home?"

"*Se ashpett, ci sara' un ingorgo. La* traffic jam!"

"*Ma perché? Sono soltanto le dieci!*"

"*Non ashpett!*"

They argued like this for a few minutes, as they had argued about the toll. It was a fixed aspect of their friendship, these little bursts of disagreement that were about nothing, and went nowhere, and almost always ended up with my grandfather, in deference to his age, perhaps, getting his way. With one hand on Victor Bones's shoulder, Grandpa made a signal to me, a finger hooking the air. I leaned forward and kissed Vittorio on his sticky cheekbone and thanked him, in Italian, three times.

And he said, "For what, *grazie*? You mother, she's like my own blood."

Once we were out on the sidewalk, Dom reached back in and dropped a dime on the seat for the return toll, then slammed the door on Victor Bones's objections and waved him back into traffic.

THE HOSPITAL WAS ALMOST cool inside and fearfully white—nurses' shoes, corridor walls, mattresses on wheeled metal carts. A miserable chemical smell pressed against my face, and after the heat of the highway, the sweat on my bare arms stiffened quickly into a gritty film.

My grandfather took me by one hand, and we went along the polished hallway. Doors stood open on scenes of beds and curtains, patients with sheets thrown off bare legs, casts, bandages, bottles, electric fans pushing air across faces that seemed sad and resigned to me. I saw no other children. In every room we passed I looked for my mother, but Grandpa Dom led me straight on, walking quickly, as if trying to outrun a posse of aunts and policemen.

We waited for the elevator in the company of a nurse who was pushing a woman in a wheelchair. The woman had damp white hair plastered down around her ears, and a slack mouth, and her shoulders—knobs of bone pressing up through the hospital gown—were curled in toward each other. As we waited, she let out a loud fart. I looked straight forward at our blurred reflections in the elevator doors, then rode up behind her, running the tip of my finger over the rubber wheel while she muttered and belched.

The fifth floor was another maze of corridors, waiting areas, bedrooms with the doors propped wide. At the third or fourth doorway, Dom steered me into a room with drooping plastic tubes and machines surrounding four beds. He led me to the farthest bed on the left side, and we stood there looking down at an old person with only one foot showing at the bottom of the sheet. Tubes were running into the person's nose and mouth, and under the sheets. A steady series of faint beeps emanated from a machine at his head. The head was shaved and partially bandaged, and there was a plastic mask over the mouth and nose and a stripe of swollen stitches along one cheekbone. The skin surrounding both eyes was a palette of purple, black, and dull yellow, and the arm we could see was wrapped completely in a cast. The patient was unnaturally still. I stared, wondering if it was a friend of Dom's who happened to be in the same hospital as my mother, or if he had brought me here first while the nurses were washing my mother and brushing her hair.

Grandpa Dom squeezed the top of my arm and said, "It's you mama, Tonio. She'sa sleepin now."

I was sure he was mistaken. I suspected a trick. My mother had eyebrows, a full pretty face, dark hair, life in her arms and fingers, two legs. She would never lie there silently like that with me in the room, no matter how sick she was.

I thought I heard my grandfather say, "She has a *coma*," as if he were mingling Italian and English again as he sometimes did. And at that moment I noticed the patient's chest pushing softly up beneath the sheet and realized it was a woman lying there.

As if from an enormous distance, I heard footsteps slapping the floor, a nurse calling angrily, her voice swallowed by an announcement on the corridor loudspeaker. My legs were shaking. My grandfather reached out and rested his fingers on the woman's forehead, on a clear patch of skin between two raw scratches. I noticed a familiar splash of freckles between her cheekbone and ear. I studied the closed, bruised eyes, what I could see of the nose and mouth beneath the plastic mask. Dom put a hand on the back of my neck and said, "Touch you mama, Tonio."

I tried to move my arm but could not. I closed my eyes and opened them. I stood there trembling. He took hold of my wrist and placed my hand above the sheet, near her shoulder. And for two or three seconds there was a slight change in the rhythm of the beeping machine, a quickening beneath the absolutely motionless surface. I looked up at my grandfather to see if he heard it. He nodded, yes. "Say in her ear you love her," he told me.

He stepped back and I slid along the rail in front of him so that my face was even with hers. He put his hands on my shoulders. I heard footsteps, close by now, and then the nurse was there at the end of the bed.

"We cannot have this, sir," she said.

"This woman in the *coma*," Dom said to her. "She's mama to this boy."

"Come away immediately. We cannot allow this."

I leaned down toward my mother's ear.

"Come away, please."

"Mama, it's me," I said. "It's Tonio. Mama. It's me."

The nurse pushed her arm in between Grandpa Dom and the railing of the bed and took hold of my shoulder. "Come now," she said. "She can't hear you."

"Yes, she can."

"No, believe me. She cannot."

I let her tug me away from the bed, listening all the while to the rhythm of the beeping machine. I looked back once, hoping to see my mother's eyes, or one of her hands reaching up.

Then I sat on a gray upholstered couch in the waiting room, with beams of harsh sunlight falling in through the window, and watched the nurse chastising my grandfather in the corridor, her hand wagging in front of his face as if he were the eleven-year-old. A stretcher was rolled past, there were more echoing announcements on the address system, two doctors came hurrying along with stethoscopes in their pockets. I tried to hold my eyes on Grandpa Dom, but they kept filling with tears. He stood facing her, straight-backed, the straw fedora in one hand at his side. He said nothing, offered no resistance, no defense. At last, she released him and he walked back and sat close beside me without speaking. He gave me his handkerchief, and we sat there like that, for ten or twenty or thirty minutes, until visiting hours began, at noon, and I heard the shoes of my uncles and aunts tapping in the hallway and then heard their voices. But by the time they saw me and started in on Dom's second round of chastisement, my mother had already passed on.

Book Two

One

MY PARENTS WERE WAKED at Alessio's funeral home, and buried after a service at Saint Anthony's Church, and life very gradually regained some semblance of balance for me. By this I mean that I stopped bursting into tears three or four times during the course of the day, stopped wanting to throw stones through school windows, and moved from my grandparents' sofa bed to the small spare room off the parlor, a room that had been used for storage but was now converted—the walls painted a pale blue, my bed and bureau brought down from upstairs and squeezed through the door, pictures of my mother and father set up on the night table in new dark frames. By some semblance of balance I mean that, gradually, over a period of weeks, the house emptied of visitors and fruit baskets, and "I'm sorry, Anthony, I'm so sorry" was no longer the first thing people said when I bumped into them on Park Avenue.

It has occurred to me from time to time since those days, as it has occurred to many people, I'm sure, that we live a kind of elaborate charade. In order to function in the waking world, we have to pretend to ourselves that death is some kind of rare affliction reserved for ninety-year-olds in hospital beds, or impoverished people in impoverished countries, or men, women, and children on other airplanes, in other cars, walking into other doctors' offices. The absolute certainty and complete unpredictability of it is too humbling and terrifying, too depressing to keep always before us. There is a Hindu saying: "Don't take the next breath for granted," which seems like good and wise advice to me now, but who, what earthbound saint, what goddess can follow it?

So we make plans, pursue an education, save money for some

probable future. We have to delude ourselves like this—who would ever have children otherwise, who would step out of the house?—it is right and good to do it. It is also partly false. And what happens to anyone who sees death at an early age is that he has that pleasant disguise ripped away from the face of creation. This is the awful predicament of eighteen-year-olds who have been sent to war: afterward—for a year, for a lifetime—everything but death seems like a lie to them. Every spark of beauty or kindness is shadowed.

Some people manage it, though, this perfect balancing of the constant awareness of death and the obligatory optimism of living. A few rare souls manage it. I believe now that what I saw in my grandmother, the night she cooked me eggs at two o'clock in the morning, was something like that: her understanding of the second-by-second fragility of our elaborately decorated worlds. I believe she knew that truth in her cells and bones, in a way most of us do not know it, or know only superficially, intellectually; and that my parents' deaths, while they were like a hammer blow to her heart, did not really shock her the way they shocked the rest of us. She had somehow learned to live by that Hindu saying, but there was no proper way of passing her wisdom on to anyone else. What could she possibly say on the subject to an eleven-year-old boy who had just lost both his parents? We mustn't take life for granted, Tonio? This is God's will, Tonio? This is the truth of our situation in the world: that we rope the wild beast of life with our thoughts, and corral it inside a fence of our fantasies and expectations, our sense of what is fair and not fair, but the corral, the fence, the hope of security and fairness and of keeping the stallion still—these are nothing but comforting illusions, apparently true for seconds or minutes or years at a time, but, in the end, not really true at all?

She was a peasant woman from a dirt-road village in the Italian countryside, intelligent but uneducated, not in possession of fancy phrases like that. So she cooked me eggs and bacon, and poured me a glass of cold milk to take the thirst and sourness out of that night. That was how she passed down her profound understanding of things: not just in plates of grilled veal cutlets, bowls of escarole soup, and glistening strips of vinegar peppers on slices of soft white bread, but in touches of her hand, in the steadiness of her eyes; in the sense you had that she would never judge you—even secretly—never criticize you too harshly within her own mind. She was a sort of gentle Zen master in disguise, a woman who spoke a language no one else around her could understand.

In the days and weeks after my parents died, I could feel her watching me, as if for signs of illness. Several times, through the soft quilt of sleep, I heard her come into the little room and stand beside the bed, checking in, like Uncle Peter. And in the warm seaside evenings just before darkness fell, in that sweet hour after supper, she would sometimes call me to stand with her in the flower garden she'd planted around her statue of the Virgin. "Antonio," she would say, though it sounded more like "Ahndonyo," and she would always be touching me when she said it. "Ahndonyo, you mama and papa, they're standin now just on the other side of a curtain, with the mother of God. The curtain, she seems to us thick, but she isn't, darlin. They're waitin for us there. They're watchin us." For a minute or two it would comfort me, this language of hers, this vivid faith in a world I could not see. And then I'd go back into the house and feel the weight of the four empty rooms upstairs, the enormous echoing vacuum where my parents' affection had once been.

My grandfather had a different method of dealing with what had happened to us. For days and days, for weeks after the funeral, he went around submerged in a stoic sorrow, sneaking sad glances at my father's picture on the parlor coffee table when he thought no one was looking. All during that time, he said nothing to me about death, my parents, God, or the nature of life. It seemed, at first, that he would never talk to me about what had happened, never again use the words *mother* or *father*, that he expected me simply to stop thinking about them.

Then, one afternoon, almost a month after the funeral, he came out into the yard, dressed maybe one-half of one notch less formally than he usually dressed, and he said, in English, "Tonio, now you and me, we're going down the beach."

I could only stand still and look at him, and, after a moment, say, "What, Grandpa?"

"We're going down the beach now."

"What beach?"

"The beach in Revere."

"Who?"

"Me and you."

"Swimming?"

"Not swimming, we're just going down there. To see the water. To walk around."

I stared up at him a moment more. He had his hat on, he seemed to mean it, but I had never known my grandfather to go to the beach. His affection for nature was confined to his vegetable garden and fruit trees. And even those he enjoyed at some distance, hiring Vito to come and prune the grapevine, and another friend, Nico Pentasco, to turn over the earth in spring, and spread the manure. He set out the plants himself, watered them, then washed his hands and put on his tailored trousers and white shirt and sat in the shade of the grapevine, reading *Il Mattino*. He listened to opera on Friday nights, while the other men on Jupiter Street were packing up the family station wagon with camping gear. He did not own a pair of blue jeans or short pants or a bathing suit. As far as his relationship to the ocean was concerned, we might as well have lived in Ohio.

I followed him out of the yard.

We walked down the street, crossed Park Avenue, and waited for the round-shouldered MTA bus to appear on top of the hill. When it arrived, we took our seats and rode to Revere Beach, a three-mile stretch of cold water, rounded stones, powdery gray sand, and amusement rides.

Once there, once we had stepped down out of the bus and into the shimmering air, Grandpa Dom seemed to stiffen. I could feel it in him the way I could feel all his changes in mood. It was as if the grit on the sidewalks, the kids in diapers splashing in the shallows, the tattooed carny taking tickets in front of the Dodgems, the seaweed and salty hot wind and the parade of high-school girls in bathing suits represented, for him, a circus of American disorder, unruly and rough as tackle football. Stiff and ill at ease, he led me down the long row of amusement rides, encouraging me to indulge wherever I wanted—the rickety roller coaster on its white-painted stilts, the echoing, rumbling Virginia Reel; the cheap games of chance—darts and blue balloons; BB guns and stuffed giraffes— the entirely artificial and wonderful little death-denying world that stood in a crescent of peeling wood and barking carnies just opposite the fine curl of shore. He never came on the rides with me, never threw a single dart. There was no mention of going in the water.

After an hour or so of this he bought a pizza, and two Coca-Colas in thick green bottles, and we carried them across Revere Beach Boulevard to the shade of the pavilion. We sat on a bench there and ate and drank, with legions of pigeons eyeing us from the hurricane wall, and seagulls flying in to stand and gawk, too proud to beg.

When we were finished, my grandfather wiped his lips very carefully with the paper napkin, back and forth and back and forth, folded the napkin, tucked it into the pizza box, closed the box against the breeze and the inquisitive gulls, set the empty bottles on the concrete near his shoe, and stared out to sea. After a time, and without any preliminaries, he began to speak to me, in Italian.

"I was born in a village they call Squillani," he said quietly, not look-ing at me, but out over the hurricane wall, toward the Nahant peninsula, and beyond. *Sono nato nèlla piccola paese quale si chiama Squillani.* "Between the cities Avellino and Benevento. In that place, there are hills wherever you look, green in spring like spinach—dark and green like that—and the rest of the year, brown like a potato after you dig it up and the dirt is dry and still holding to it.

"In Squillani we had one road covered with stones that went in cir-cles up our hill from the big road that led to Benevento. People lived on that road in stone houses with red tile roofs. People walked where they wanted to go, or they rode horses or in carts. There was one church, San Rocco. We went there every Sunday and feast day, and every morning during Lent. An old man rang the bells in the morning and again at night. On the feast days my mother would make bread and almond cakes, and you could smell them from five or six houses away, and it would make you want to go toward that smell.

"Sometimes, on Saturdays when the weather was not too cold, my father would take my brother, Salvatore, and they would go hunt rabbits in the mountains past Benevento. The only bears left in Europe lived in those mountains. Even now it is that way. He would borrow a rifle from his friend Enzo Moccia. They would leave before it was light on Saturday morning, and return very late. Do you understand me?" he asked. *Mi capisci?*

"*Sì.*"

"*Tutti le parole?*"

"*Sì, tutti.*"

"*Bène.* When I grew old enough, a little older than you are now, I used to ask my father to let me go with them. After a year of asking, he agreed. It made me happy to think that I was old enough to go with him and Salvatore and not delay them. Salvatore and I slept in one bed, close together. Bapo would wake us by hitting us once in the middle of the forehead with his second finger. Hard. It was dark in the rooms of our house, dark and cold outside the windows. Salvatore would take out the cheese in the dark and take my mother's big knife and cut three pieces of cheese and four pieces of bread—two for our father—and tie them up in a clean cloth. My job would be to carry three empty wine bottles to the well and fill them with water and push the purple corks into them and wait there. The birds would be singing in all the trees while I waited. The sky beyond Tufara, which was the next village to the east, would start to show a light the color of a drop of wine in water. Not long after I saw that color, I would see my father and brother coming down the path carrying the rifle and the food. They would take one bottle from me each, and we would go down toward the big road without talking. The birds would be whistling then, calling one to the other, and the dogs near the bottom of the hill, the ones who didn't know us, they would be barking.

"We would go to the bottom of the hill and wait there on the road to Benevento. The sun would just be showing his face now, throwing down light on the tile roofs of the houses and the tops of the hills. But everything—all the stones and leaves and the tops of our shoes—would still be wet with the *rugiada*. Do you know this word . . . in the morning, when the grass is wet—"

"*Sì.*"

"How do you know it?"

"I heard Grandma say it."

"How many times?"

"Once."

"What is she, in the English?"

"Dew."

"How does she spell herself? *Com'e si scrive?*"

"D-E-W."

He grunted, nodded, peered down at my forehead for a moment, plucked at the crease of his pants. "After a while, my father would make one of his cigarettes and smoke it, and after another little while we would hear the cart coming from the direction of Roccabascerana. We would hear the wheels, the hard feet of the old horses. The cart would stop and we would climb up in the back with the man's metal pots and rope, and the boxes of soap that he and his wife made with their own hands. My father would sit in front with the cheese and bread so we wouldn't eat it. My brother and I would sit in the back with our legs hanging over and our stomachs crying for something more to put in them. Sometimes Salvatore would have hidden two or three cooked chestnuts in his vest pocket. He would take them out and peel off the shell with his teeth, and break them one by one in half, and we would chew on them in the bouncing cart. Slow, we would chew them, to make them stay longer in our mouths, and when they were all finished there was a feeling in your stomach worse than when you started.

"It did not take long for the day to get hot. Soon we would begin to sweat, and we would watch the dust lifting up behind us. Sometimes, when it was very hot and we knew we still had a long way to go, we would all sing 'O Signore' or 'Lenta Va La Luna' and drink a little of the water to make the time pass.

"At the market in Benevento, the man—I don't remember his name anymore—he would let us off, and we would walk from there up into the mountains to the places where you could hunt. Sometimes there were berries on the bushes there. Sometimes my father bought some sour cherries or two pears at the market and let us eat them.

"When we got high up to the places where you could hunt, Salvatore would go into the woods on one side of the path and I would go in on the other. We would throw stones there and make noise and stay far out to the sides. The rabbits would be afraid of us and would run out into the path, and Salvatore and I would hear my father shooting the gun. After a time the shooting would stop, and he would whistle, twice, very loud, the signal that we could come back out, and then we would go onto the path and take the rabbits and carry them back to him by their ears, with their blood dripping near our shoes.

"Once, I heard a loud noise in there, and saw a bear, just the front leg and part of the shoulder. The bear was brown, Tonio, and he looked as big as two kitchen tables one on top of the other. I ran back to my father. Salvatore ran back. We waited with the gun, shaking, but we did not see him again. Once, Salvatore chased out a fox. My father shot it below its ear and sold the fur for a lot of money, and with some of that money he bought us a hunter's knife to share, with a white ivory handle."

"What's that, Grandpa, *avòrio?*"

"What the elephants have on their horns. White, hard. *Avòrio . . . capisci?*"

"*Sì.*"

"Salvatore had that knife in his belt when he died in the First War. . . . Sometimes, in the autumn, we would go farther up, to where there was a field of tall grass. We would chase out birds there for my father to shoot. Afterward we would eat the bread and cheese and drink the water, looking out over the tops of the hills toward Napoli. My father would clean whatever he had shot and put it in a cloth sack that he kept folded over his belt and that was stained with blood and marked with black letters you couldn't read anymore. He would take a handful of the thick grass and wipe his fingers clean, and the blade of the knife clean, and tell us stories about the city of Napoli, the statues and churches and palaces there, the thieves, the market, the boats that left there every day, carrying people to other countries, to America. We would sleep a few minutes sometimes, the three of us against each other to stay warm. And then Salvatore and I would carry the sack down the hill, taking turns. We would wait near the edge of the market—sometimes a long time— until the man with the cart was finished with his business, and if we had money and if it was the right time of year, Salvatore and I would buy four or five peaches and eat half of one, each of us, and bring the rest home for our mother and sisters. Sometimes I would fall asleep sitting on the cart with my legs hanging over. Just like that.

"When we came back to Squillani, it would be dark. Our father would give the man one or two birds or one rabbit for letting us sit in his cart. We would walk back up the road to our house, and I would almost be too tired to put one of my feet in front of the other. My father would carry the cloth sack, and Salvatore would carry the empty water bottles, and I would carry nothing and fall farther and farther behind them, looking down at my feet. At home I would wash my hands and face and my feet at the well, then go right to sleep without even eating anything and wake up so hungry, it was like the nest of bees in your belly.

"But every time my father asked me to go I went, and in a few months I was strong enough to walk and not fall behind.

"Then, one time, after I had been going with them for two years, we were coming back in the cart from Benevento, and the birds started to sing and whistle and fly inside the trees like they were crazy birds, and the air near us felt like there was a sound in it but nobody could hear that sound. And then the man's horses started to kick and jump and try to break loose from the cart—the same two old horses that always walked along, one foot and then the next foot, like they were falling asleep. The man could barely keep them from running off the road. The chickens near people's houses there, and the dogs and the goats and the birds—all of them were making a terrible noise like the end of the world—*tutti facevano un rumore terribile, come se fosse la fine del mondo.* I looked at Salvatore and saw him bounce up in the air, off the cart. I looked over

my shoulder at my father, and he was looking back at me and his face
was a terrible face, all with the fear of death on it. It is a terrible thing to
see a father's face that way."

He interrupted his story for a moment then, as if realizing what he
had just said, and what visions it might raise in my mind's eye. I became
aware again of people on the sand, and cars going past behind us in the
sun, and the shimmering quiet bay. And I did in fact think of my father
in the last seconds of his life, with the flames around him, my mother
with the child in her belly, burning up, and people screaming and dying
around them, and the jet going along the runway at an impossible speed,
backward, upside down, the sound of tearing metal above everything
else, the horror of it, something very close to my image of what hell must
be. I had read about the crash, sneaking the newspaper into a corner of
the front porch at night and kneeling on the floor there in the light from
the street, and in the previous weeks I had imagined those moments in
great detail, hundreds of times. Night and day they would press themselves into my mind: the fire, the pain and blood, the sound of screaming. I saw my mother with her bandaged face and missing leg. I
remembered the smell of the hospital room, the beeping machines, the
wails and cries that had come from the room when the aunts and uncles
went in there, with the doctors and nurses working to pull my mother
back from the other life into this one. Those thoughts hung always just
outside the goings-on of the moment, like clouds of ash and smoke
swirling against the lid of a closed eye. The smallest movement, a word,
a photograph—any one of a thousand things could lift the eyelid.

But when Dom fell back into the hypnotic, quiet rhythm of the story,
those images floated back again and hung at a little distance. He was
talking steadily and quietly, staring out over the ocean, one arm behind
me on the back of the bench but not touching me. His legs were crossed
at the knee and his hat was sitting on a piece of newspaper on the green
wooden slats on the far side of him. His voice changed slightly, as if the
place it was coming from were a barrel slowly filling with water. And
slowly I began to feel the enormous sadness that was in him, and to
understand that it was always there, buried below the quiet, ordered exte-

rior. That he needed to have perfect new bills in his wallet, that he needed to have a crease in his pants, a laundered and pressed handkerchief— these things moved and shifted and formed a new picture of him. I began to feel a different kind of connection to him, and to sense that there might be some hope for me at the end of his story, some explanation for his own grief and mine, something he had been turning over in his thoughts all those quiet afternoons, some particle of proof, as impossible as it seemed to me then, that God had ordered the world a certain way, and might have been present to help my parents in their last agony, and might be able to help me now.

"I was on the ground then," my grandfather said in the watery voice, "at the edge of the road next to a pear tree. I had fallen with my shoulder against the trunk of the tree. It hurt so much I could not move my arm. Even now, Tonio, when there is going to be rain or snow, it still hurts. The pears weren't ripe but they were falling from the tree all around us. They hit against my legs, my chest, my face. I was crying for my father to help, but he couldn't hear me because there was a noise all around, a tremendous noise, biggest noise you can imagine.

"Everything was moving. Nothing was the way it was supposed to be. The trees, they were leaning sideways, the road was breaking open, the pears were falling before they were ripe. Nothing would stop moving even for one second, and then everything stopped all at once and the air was filled with dust as thick as smoke. In their yards near the sides of the road, men were yelling everywhere like crazy people. The cart's two back wheels were broken in pieces. I heard animals making their noises all together, and I heard my father yelling, 'Domenico! Salvatore! Domenico! Salvatore!'

"Salvatore had a lump on his forehead as big as an apricot, and my arm couldn't move and hurt me very much, and my father had cut his elbow and there was blood all through the arm of his shirt. But we could walk. We left the man there with his cart, and as fast as we could we went the rest of the way along the big road that led to the smaller road that led up to our village, Squillani.

"There was dust in the air everywhere, Tonio. There were people hurt everywhere, people helping each other, screaming, crying, praying to the saints, to Mary, to Jesus to help them. There were little children who could not stop crying, and dogs that could not stop barking. As we got close to the bottom of our road, we saw two or three stone houses, cracked open as if the walls were only as strong as the shell of the egg. While we watched it, one of the houses fell down completely, like something made of paper. Somebody's bed was there, right in the open air in a pile of cement and rocks. My father kept saying we should walk faster, walk faster.

"In Squillani, not far from the top of the hill, there were more broken houses. The higher we climbed on the road, the more broken they were. It was like walking in a dream of hell. Dirt and ash and leaves floating everywhere, the screaming, the smell of smoke. It was still daytime but the day was dark, like God had hit his elbow on the switch that turned off the sun. People lit torches and made big fires. In the light from the fires you could see their faces and their broken houses, pieces of broken roof sticking out through windows, trees that had fallen down on gardens, trees lying across the street, houses with broken backs. Carts upside down on a pile of stones. Every few minutes the ground shook again, less than before. We stopped, and stood holding on to each other with our legs wide apart. 'Don't be afraid,' my father kept saying to us. 'Don't be afraid.' But his face was all covered with dirt and sweat, and his shirt was all dark blood, and it was very hard to look at him and hard to have to stop and stand there, not knowing what we would find when we got to our house, not knowing if the world was going to open up and swallow us or let us live.

"But before we even got up to our house, which was beyond the top of the hill, on the back side, the east side, some of the boys who were a little younger than me came running down in the dark. They were calling the name of the sister I loved more than I loved my own father and mother, more than Salvatore, more than God, Tonio. 'Eleonora is buried! Eleonora is buried in the earthquake!' they said to us. Sometimes even now when I sleep, I hear them saying it. Even now. We ran the rest of the way up the road in the dark. When we reached our house, it was standing strong with only the windows and one or two parts of the walls broken. Our mother was out in the street in front, waiting for us, crying two dirty streams down her cheeks. The house next door—Alfredo Pierni's house, Dr. Pierni's grandfather—was broken in three pieces. One piece was leaning over sideways, and one piece was perfect as it always was. And the other piece was only a pile of glass and wood, concrete, big stones, everything in a place it wasn't supposed to be. The quilt from a bed was there in the dirt, an apron there, the handle of a broom. I can close my eyes and see those things now, the way they were. My sister was under that . . . under those stones. My brothers and the men who lived near us were working by the light from the fires, lifting the stones up—they had only two metal bars and some pieces of wood—and pushing them over into the street.

"Salvatore and my father and I went to work there, too. We were all tired and hurt—my arm would not move—but we worked. People had lit torches all around the half of Alfredo Pierni's house that was crumbled— there was no electric then, Tonio—and the women and girls had brought some food there—bread, water, peppers, a little cold horse meat and wine. Sometimes the boys would stop working and get something to eat or bring some water to their fathers, and people were crying everywhere, and some people—men and women both—would start to scream or to pray out loud every time the hill shook again under our feet.

"Sometimes, in the early part of the night, we thought we heard Eleonora calling out a name from under the rocks."

"What name?"

Instead of answering, he paused again, touched his hat so that it moved an eighth of an inch closer to the center of the piece of newspaper, so that the world was that much more in balance. He looked up, swallowed, and went on. "We would stop and listen. Then everyone would start to move the big stones away from the place we thought we had heard the voice.

"There were ten or eleven men and maybe twenty boys, but we were all tired and in some places the walls had fallen down in pieces bigger than this bench we're sitting on, you and me. They had to be broken up with a hammer before you could move them. You would cut yourself on a nail or a piece of tile or glass, and you would have to stop working and move away from the standing part of the house whenever the shaking started again.

"We could hear the bells of churches in the valley ringing all the time, and the women were praying to our saint, Stefano. It was midnight, then it was after midnight, and I was like a boy walking in sleep. We got near the bottom of one part of the pile. Someone yelled out that they saw an arm sticking up from between the rocks. I remember hearing someone say that"—Grandpa Dom repeated the phrase: *"un braccio che sporgeva"*—"and I was so tired, I heard it as if from under the water. I started to climb over the stones toward that place where they had seen the arm. My mother was crying very much now, and calling out Eleonora's name. The women were around her. It felt like a dark dream feels. Then someone lifted me up out of the dream, Bartolomeo Agello, the strongman, the giant, who moved the biggest pieces of stone and who had a moustache that hung down on both sides below his face. He lifted me up under one arm, and Salvatore, my brother, up under the other arm. He carried us away, like you carry two puppies, so that we wouldn't see Eleonora being taken out from under the stones, and we didn't see her ever again after that, only the box they put her in to bury her, the way you saw your father and your mother in the church."

He fell abruptly silent, the last few syllables—*"nèlla chièsa"*—drifting away on the sea breeze. I waited for him to finish the story, to add a neat moral, a last drop of advice. But he only folded his hands in his lap and would not look at me. We sat there that way for a long time, staring out at the water. Every now and then he would move the fingers on his left hand forward so that they touched the back of my shoulder, and then take them away again. From time to time I would peek up at him, but he would not meet my eyes. A sadness hung in the air around us. It was somehow embarrassing. A mother holding a young baby stopped to ask him the time, and my grandfather shook his watch out from under the cuff of his shirt, and told her the hour, in his stilted, accented English, and we were back in America again. Seagulls floated in the air in front of us, climbing and climbing and letting the clams in their beaks drop onto the hard sand and break.

My grandfather picked up his hat and stood. I threw the pizza box and the two Coke bottles into one of the tall green trash barrels, and we walked to the bus stop on Ocean Avenue. We waited there, people walking past us toward the beach, people eating, smoking, laughing, as if there were an unlimited amount of time for those things. I worked the story this way and that in my mind. I gnawed at the shell of it, trying to reach a soft center. I had seen my grandfather every day of my life—in the yard, in the house, walking down the shaded sidewalk from his card game at the New Deal Club, in shirt and sport coat, his shoes shined, his nails trimmed, the white tufts of hair very neatly combed back. I believed I had a complete and perfect sense of his life. It was an ordered life, strict, scheduled, a man's life, it seemed to me then. There was a great deal of love in it but not much laughter or tears, no exorbitant sprays of feeling, no fear. In some meandering and wordless fashion then, groping in a dark inner sea, I connected it to my father's life, to the lives of my uncles, an assembly of turtles moving by instinct along grooves worn in the earth 20 million years ago, heavy with armor, all the soft innards protected, the head and eyes pulling back at the first sign of something alien, the first unfamiliar sound. Only in the dark green depths did they swim and play, and even then it was always with an awareness of the soft underbelly, predators knifing up through the wet darkness. Only within the family and within the walls of the home could they ever be really at ease, and even then they needed to keep this shell over everything, this manliness.

The houses of the city slipped past beyond the bus window, paint over shingle over plywood, over life, and I struggled to set things in order in myself, to find my place in that parade of souls. My father's father sat beside me, silent now after his long burst of speech, the city rolling past, invisible airs stirring and settling between us. He had pushed aside the armor for a moment so that I might have one glimpse of the tender way a man was made. The feeling of it swept across the vision of my mother's face and body, my father's casket, the same images that had haunted me, hour by hour, for weeks. An awareness of the magnitude and honesty of his gift came over me, a sense of being loved beyond question, beyond what I might do or fail to do, beyond what I deserved. I turned away so that he wouldn't see, and I blinked and blinked and rubbed my sleeve across my eyes.

By the time we stepped off the bus at the corner of Jupiter Street, my face was mostly dry. The sun had swung around and down beyond the end of Park Avenue, and the smallest breeze was slipping in along the grid of the planetary streets, and my grandmother and Uncle Peter were standing at the top of the back steps, watching us come up the sidewalk toward home.

Two

EVEN THE DEATH OF both parents doesn't occupy the whole spirit and mind of a child. Even the intricate constellation of a large, warm family can't fill in all the open space in a universe. I had my own life to live, I could not avoid it. And so, carrying my huge cargo of grief, I worked in the garden when my grandfather needed help, accompanied Uncle Peter whenever he let me, played with my cousins on Sunday afternoons, swam at Revere Beach, read baseball books in my small room before bed, walked down to the Little League field for my games. I had three close friends—Peter Imbesalacqua (who would, years later, after decades as a compulsive gambler, testify against a mafia capo and be put into the Witness Protection Program), Leo Markin (who would enlist in the marines, serve honorably in Vietnam, then leave Revere forever and make his home on a tiny Pacific island), and Alfonse Romano (who would also serve in Vietnam, but return home and make a career as a policeman, eventually becoming the youngest chief in Revere's history)— and after the first period of my bereavement had passed, our games and explorations more or less resumed their normal summer pattern.

I don't see Leo or Peter at all now, and see Alfonse only a few times a year, but in those days the four of us were inseparable, a band of benign troublemakers. We all had our stories. Leo's mother had died when he was a small boy. Alfonse's father had disappeared and was never spoken about. And Peter—Vito's son—seemed to have been born too close to the border between ordinary mischief and something worse.

Some days we would meet at my house and walk east down Park Avenue, one of us bouncing the pink rubber ball off housefronts, one of us rattling the broomstick along people's chain-link fences or knocking it hard against the light poles and NO PARKING signs. We'd pass the afternoon at the stickball courts calling out a fantastical play-by-play: Maris, Mantle, Monboquette, line shots into the screen in left. Some days we'd wander across Proctor Avenue to the Farms, and move through the fields and abandoned orchards there with snakes squirming in our mayonnaise jars, and our shoes and socks black with mud. Some days we roamed the yards on either side of Jupiter Street, as if the neighbors' fences had been placed there only so we could refine our climbing skills. We set off M-80s behind Thayer's garage, climbed onto Allen McCarthy's roof, peered into his parents' bedroom, and saw his mother in her underwear, touching perfume onto her breasts. We sprinted down Zwicker's driveway holding bunches of stolen grapes against the front of our shirts. Once, we broke into the booth at the top of the bleachers at Paul Revere Stadium and stood there, calling high-school football games in deep voices, making ourselves into heroic tight ends and fearless linebackers. On that day, in the middle of our imaginary play-by-play, we saw a boy climbing the rows of the grandstand toward us. We made quick friends with him. The boy was new in town, slightly older, blond, tanned. He had a southern accent, and he impressed us by holding his cigarette lighter so that the flame licked lightly against the dry boards of the announcer's booth. Two nights later he picked a lock, sneaked into the basement of Lincoln School, soaked some old books and papers in gasoline, and burned the eighty-year-old building to the ground.

From time to time, the balloon of good feeling among the four of us would swell up too large, blocking our sense of our individual selves. We would argue over some small thing, pair off, wrestle in the dirt of someone's front yard, and walk away scratched and triumphant, or scratched and beaten, sewing up the friendship again in an hour, or a day, or a week. We traded baseball cards and Pepsi bottle caps, fished for flounder off the Point of Pines Bridge, and, sweaty, dirty, happy, drank glasses of lemonade in each other's kitchen on hot August afternoons.

All that had happened before, all of it had been happening for as long as I could remember. What was different in that summer was that I began to be drawn into an exploration of my own solitude. Some mornings, after eating breakfast with my grandmother and grandfather in their sunny kitchen, I would step outside, turn right instead of left when I reached the sidewalk, away from my friends, and roam the city alone, as if the puzzle of living and dying could be worked out on Revere's rough tar streets. Or I would climb the Park Avenue hill to the cemetery, kneel and cry for a while at my parents' graves, pick bits of leaf off the seeded plots, finger the new-cut letters on the gray granite, then walk back and forth along the avenues of headstones, reading dates and names, as if putting my mother and father in such a long list of the dead might make things a little easier to bear. I had allowance money—a jar full of bills and coins in a corner of my little bedroom—and almost unlimited freedom. On some days I would dip into the jar, take the bus to the beach, and dive again and again into the cold water, then cross the Boulevard and buy a stuffed quahog or two slices of pizza, and carry my meal to the far end of the sand and eat it slowly, staring out to sea. Other days I'd climb the steep hill of Venice Avenue, intending to see if Rosalie or Uncle Peter was home; but I'd pass by their house and keep walking, down to Arnold Street, around the ramshackle factory that made wrapping paper, down to Olive Street, where my mother's best friend, Lois Londoner, lived. Usually I'd walk on past her house without stopping, venture from there across the creek into Chelsea—a poorer, more tattered Revere—and walk as far as a corner deli where an old, one-legged Jewish man sold lox and cream cheese on a bagel, my secret passion, for sixty cents.

I was too young to be so far afield alone, but a secret and mysterious solitude was singing its first notes in me. Vaguely, blindly, in some dim, curtained sector of my thinking self, I was beginning to suspect that the face of the world was a mask, and I haunted the corners of Revere like a ghost, seeking its edges.

On one of those walks, I found myself in Point of Pines, a part of the city that hangs off the northern end of the beach, and where, even now, the houses are generally among the most expensive in Revere. Angelo Pestudo, the famous underworld boss, had a home there; everyone knew it. Uncle Peter had told me stories about him; I'd seen his name in the papers. I had not gone looking for that house especially, but when I came upon a stucco mansion set back from the street, with a circular driveway, dark cars, a high wall, a swimming pool in the back from which I could hear the happy shouts of girls, I knew who presided over it. As I was passing the brick gate, I glanced in and saw a pretty girl there. She was thin, brown-headed, delicate-featured, about my own age, stepping barefoot down the hot tar driveway with a beach towel wrapped around her waist and her wet hair plastered back from her forehead. A heavyset man stood close to the house, watching her. I was walking very slowly, ambling, roaming, and after another step or two I realized she was coming to retrieve a beach ball that had skipped down the sloping drive and come to rest against one of the abutments of the gate, three feet from me. To save her a few burning steps I went back and rolled it up the drive. She stopped it with her foot—like a soccer player—looked at me as one might look at a servant, then picked it up and turned away without so much as a nod of thanks.

Three

THE SCHOOL YEAR STARTED—sixth grade—and I set to reaping another harvest of As and compliments. It was a kind of addiction for me: I
would have done anything to cling to my place at the top of the class and
keep the warm stream of adult approval turned in my direction. My
grandfather went into the hospital that October with what the doctors
called "a very minor heart attack," which turned out to be the first in a
string of very minor heart attacks that would eventually kill him. And
probably he saw in me, upon his return, what I can see now in myself
from a distance of thirty-five years: that there was something unnatural
in my scholastic perfectionism, that an eleven-year-old boy needs some
sweet water to drink other than the flattery of his elders; that there is a
body there, supporting that flaming brain, and it ought to be given its
share of the joy of use. When Grandpa came home from the hospital, one
of the first things he said to me was "I met somebody in there, Antonio,
who gave me the idea for you. After Christmas, I show you what it is."

The idea for me. He said it as if there were one idea for each person
in the whole of his or her life, one plan, decision, or secret word that
could be fitted like a key into that person's private padlock. The lock
would pop, a thick steel door would swing open, revealing a landscape,
and a road across that landscape, and you would only have to follow that
road for your bereavement to transform itself into a life that was fulfilling and logical and free of pain.

The idea for me. For two or three weeks I was obsessed by the
thought that there *was* an idea for me, that Dom had carried it home
from the hospital like a dose of exotic medicine, known, in Brazil or

Ghana, to cure the confusions of orphans. And then, when he didn't mention it a second time, the idea of the idea for me sank gradually into the background, where it remained until the year passed on.

It was an odd and sorrowful Christmas season—gifts for me from every aunt and uncle and half the cousins. Books, two baseball gloves, school shirts, four pairs of thick socks, and the feeling that I could dampen the mood of any room just by stepping into it. There was a snowstorm on Christmas Eve, and I remember sneaking out my grand-parents' front door, away from a kitchen full of relatives, and walking the solar-system streets block after block, Jupiter to Mercury to Pluto and back. I watched the flakes swirl and shift in the streetlights. I listened to snow shovels scraping on front walks, and the whine of the wind between houses. I remember stopping at the corner of Mars Street and Mountain Avenue to study the spectacle of the approaching city plow, a circus of whirling gold lights and clinking tire chains, and a curved blade throwing up a surf of snow. The rumble and roar of it matched the mood of my hidden self—a dark, futile anger in the middle of a joyous night. I remember I was wearing the woolen gloves and hat my mother had knit-ted for me the Christmas before, shuffling along in my galoshes with the metal clips up the front, kicking up snow as if it were calf-deep dust, walking and walking, up one hill and down the next, and wallowing in an odd, vengeful satisfaction that the storm had broken the ordinary easy rhythm of the holiday. I made the corner from Park Avenue onto Jupiter Street, chilled and sweaty at the same time, and walked the last hundred yards across the vacant lot to my grandparents' house. A glad yellow light poured from both kitchen windows. A car door slammed out front, and the sound echoed up the snowy street like a child calling out. I stamped my feet, pulled open the back door, and the bulge of happy talk was punctured with my first step through.

There was a film of self-pity over everything I said in those days, every-thing I did. I am ashamed to remember it. Uncle Peter sensed it, and made one or two gentle suggestions. "Get yourself a girl," he said. "Have a regular thing you can look forward to every day—a candy bar, a TV show." For a person so constitutionally incapable of bringing any amount of order to his own life—his uneasy marriage, his troubled finances, his addiction to betting, his inability to understand where he should settle on the spectrum that ran from his high, sweet singing voice to his association with the Johnny Blinks of this world—for all that foolishness, he was in possession of a certain intuitive wisdom that rose into view at difficult moments, a little sandbar of sanity that showed itself only at the lowest tides. In his own way—short on logic, long on heart—he must have sensed the sour note in the chorus, not only of my life, but of the greater family's. His response was typical: in his parents' kitchen, on that snowy Christmas Eve, he waited for a quiet moment, and said, without, I'm sure, having cleared it first with Aunt Ulla, "We're havin a party up our house. New Year's. Everybody has to come."

Four

IT WAS A DIFFICULT TIME for Uncle Peter. Even before the death of my parents, he had begun a slow financial decline that would find him, in the last decade of his life, accepting handouts from nephews and flashing his worn-out charm on the aides in the poorest of Revere's nursing homes. He had already gambled away all of his huge winnings on 1-2-6, so I don't know how he managed to pay for that New Year's party. Maybe a wealthy relative of Aunt Ulla's died in Norway and left them money. Or maybe he'd had what he called one of his "miracle days" at Suffolk Downs, or had accidentally fallen into a regular working schedule in order to be able to buy Ulla and Rosalie the gifts they wanted for Christmas, and found he had a little bit left over. Maybe the other couples paid for the food and entertainment in exchange for Peter and Ulla having the "time," as we called such things, at their house. I don't know.

Everyone came. Every relative as far removed as second cousin, the cousins of my grandparents from Brooklyn, my mother's sister Janice from New Jersey (who never wrote and never called, and lived the life of a recluse there, taking in stray dogs), neighbors from Jupiter Street, family friends, the boyfriends and girlfriends of my older cousins, Uncle Leo's golfing buddies and our eccentric dentist Dr. Rose (who, with his fingers in your mouth, would go into endless detail about the latest trip he and his wife had made—to the Greek islands, to Tahiti, to the coast of Spain), Johnny Blink, Freddie Roof, Archie the Lip, Ulla's mother and father—so out of place with their hay-colored hair and tight-lipped politeness. Everyone.

Uncle Peter had arranged for a trio of musicians to play, friends of his of course. They set themselves up in the finished basement—Rosalie's playroom when she had been a little girl. This proved to be a mistake, because the younger cousins naturally took over that room, and in the early part of the night the musicians were forced to spend as much time protecting their drumskins, clarinet keys, and accordion bellows from flying toys and meandering two-year-olds as they did piping out their "Silent Night's" and "O Sole Mio's."

Upstairs there was a makeshift bar—tended by Peter himself for the first half hour or so and then abandoned to the whims of his guests— and folding metal tables that Jeanne Mulligan (the Irish caterer who cooked Italian) had covered with enough food to feed six football teams. Cold cuts, antipastos, rolls and breads and crackers and cheeses, dishes of meatballs and lasagna, plates of tripe and stuffed peppers, plates of squid and eels and flounder, eggplant parmigiana, a bowl of shrimp and a quart of cocktail sauce, half a dozen pies, cookies, candy, a coffee urn going in the kitchen, sodas for the kids from a second cousin who owned the soda company and who brought along his wife and three beautiful daughters.

Dom and Lia and the aunts and uncles poured themselves drinks and fixed themselves plates of food and took up more or less permanent positions on the parlor sofa and soft chairs and the folding chairs Peter had borrowed from Saint Anthony's Holy Name. But, for us, for the cousins, being still on that night would have been a kind of sin against the commandments of our bodies. Roughly according to age, we formed ourselves into groups. The middle group, to which I belonged, roamed the upstairs rooms, bouncing across beds, closing and opening doors, talking and singing and shouting, improvising games of tag on the staircase. Or we circled down into the cellar when the music stopped, and tickled the younger cousins, talked to them, brought them, as we had been brought, into the warm fold of our blood-affection. We were the Benedettos, after all, and by the simple force of our love for one another we were going to fashion something worthwhile out of the mud and stone of our fate.

We had always taken an unadulterated joy in belonging to one another, but at no time in my memory did it show itself more than on that night. Even now there are such "times" among those of us who are still alive. Mostly now we gather after funerals, but there are happy events, too—a reunion, an eightieth birthday, a fiftieth wedding anniversary. My eye has been sharpened now, with age; I am more critical. I can see the insecurities and small feuds: who has made more money than whom and is a bit too proud of it, softened, spoiled. Who failed to invite whom to a child's wedding. Whose daughter or son missed a funeral or a wake, forgot an important anniversary, ended up in trouble, borrowed money he or she did not repay. Looking at faces is my profession, and in some of the faces at these gatherings I see the shame of a half-failed life, the ache of an annoying mate, the shadow of anger and debt, and a certain provincial close-mindedness.

But even in spite of our flaws and failings, there remains some happy unity to that group, an instinctive loyalty that dilutes individual troubles. In some way I cannot analyze, we have learned—we have been taught—to ignore each other's mottled surfaces and focus on what lies deeper. We want the best for each other. We say, "I love you," before we hang up the phone. We look into watery old eyes and see reflected there a past that is impossible to reproduce in this fast and broken-up modern age, an age in which the younger members of the family have struck out on their own to make their fortunes, and ended up living like kings and queens on small, lonely, perfectly landscaped suburban islands.

Sure, the lens is coated with nostalgia. Surely some of the family's rougher edges have been sanded down by my selective remembering. But there was a rare love there, palpable, obvious, all-inclusive. The death of my parents only added fuel to that love. It burned brightly in Uncle Peter's house that night.

After the party's opening stanzas, the smallest children were put to bed upstairs, watched over in shifts by the older girls. And then the bar, some of the food, and most of the action made its way down into the basement room.

There, gradually, as the last two hours of the year ticked away, a circus atmosphere sprouted from the soil of our stale grief. Uncle Leo—usher at the nine o'clock Mass, electrical engineer, teetotaler, a man who did not eat sweets and did not swear and would not kiss his wife on the lips in public—began stealing ice cubes from the bar and going around the room slipping them down the backs of the women's dresses. Aunt Gina retaliated by putting a cube down Uncle Peter's shirt, and he squirmed and danced and writhed and eventually, magically, shook it out of one pantleg with an expression of such comical surprise on his face that Uncle Aldo had to run for the bathroom. There was something wrong with the door handle there, and Aldo accidentally locked himself in. We heard him pounding and yelling at the top of the steps, and the more noise he made, the more vehemently Peter signaled for us to ignore him. My stomach ached, I could barely breathe from laughing. Rosalie was next to me with her arms wrapped around herself and tears sliding out of the sides of her eyes. I turned to look at my grandmother just as Uncle Spudsy sneaked up behind her and dropped a cube down the back of her dress, and she twitched and made faces and jumped around in her seat in a way that lifted her younger self to the surface. Grandpa Dom reached out, a bit drunkenly, and kissed her on the mouth. For a few minutes, while the band took a break, someone set a record on the phonograph, and a woman's voice sang in Italian:

> You better mar-ry a fire-man
> He'll come and go, go and come

And I understood the words, but not what the adults found so hilarious in them. I laughed anyway. Cousin Timmy laughed until he wet his pants. Even Aunt Ulla and her parents laughed.

The cellar hysteria drew people down from the parlor and the upstairs rooms. Soon all but the smallest children were awake again and sitting sleepy-eyed on the floor against their mothers' shins, or in their fathers' laps, and Uncle Peter was stepping through the crowd like a maître d', filling glasses, coaxing a song out of the accordion player—a man named Benny Bostingaluccio, whose face was the color of a McIntosh apple and lined with veins, and whose nickname was Benny the Map. Father Bucci had his arm around the back of Aunt Laura's chair and was leaning his bright pink face down toward her, an expression of childish joy in his eyes and a coffee mug half-filled with whiskey in his lap. Rosalie slipped outside with Cousin Catherine and returned to sit close to me with tobacco on her breath.

Finally, at 11:30, Uncle Peter went to the front of the room and stood there with his hands on his hips, looking at us the way, at the end of a difficult week, a master carpenter might look at a broken-down garage he has not quite finished rebuilding.

"Sing! Sing!" people shouted. But he would not oblige them.

"Sing, you bum!" Uncle Aldo called out.

"Go back in the bathroom, Aldo, willya?"

"Sing," Aldo said. "You want to make us happy, sing for us once like old times."

But Uncle Peter pursed his lips at the foolishness of the idea, stubbornly shook his head. "No singin," he insisted. "No singin until we have somethin tremendous to sing about in this family." And then, after a theatrical pause during which he pulled his thumb and second finger down over his nose three or four times, checked his fly twice, rubbed his bald head, pressed the back of a wrist to his eyelids, he said, "But if Tonio lets me, I'll tell one story."

A cheer filled the room. Heads turned to me, I smiled, nodded.

"I have to tell one story, don't I, Tone?"

"Or you could sing," I said, and a roar of laughter rose up. Someone squeezed the back of my neck. Someone else reached over and patted me on the arm. Even Aunt Janice winked.

"Madonn, now the godson's gotta give me the needle. What about the rat story? Huh? Alright?"

Rosalie and I nodded together. Uncle Peter gathered himself, standing with his shoes almost touching at the heels and spread out at a ninety-degree angle, his dark trousers holding a sharp crease, his fingers playing up and down along his ribs as if there were piano keys there and he was practicing the scales. He was wearing a light gray sport coat with wide lapels, small circles of sweat beneath both arms. Toying with us now, he set to tugging at the sleeves of his shirt so that the expensive cuff-links showed, flicking a bit of invisible lint from one arm, taking out his handkerchief and wiping it back and forth across his forehead. He looked up, checking his audience, working it, then shook out his arms and began:

"This is last summer," he said, though he pronounced the word "summah," as we all did, and said "yahd" for yard, and "fiyah" for fire, and exaggerated his already troubled grammar to add another drop of comic effect. "Hot up my yahd like a fiyah, like Africa." He winked at me, yanked on his belt. "Hot like you wooden bleeve up my house, and I'm out front clippin the hedge. I have my shirt off"—he moved his hands up and in toward his chest to help us imagine him without his shirt—"and I'm pourin out sweat like a hoss."

Now he spread his hands, made them into loose fists as if holding the handles of the hedge clippers, and brought them together and apart like Benny the Map with his accordion.

"And I'm thinkin, Hottest day of the whole summah, and Ulla has me out here doin the hedge. The sweat's pourin down into my good pants, and just when I'm about to give up and go inside, Mrs. Accetullo comes ovah from across the street. She looks at me like I belong in Danvahs State Hospital. 'Watcha you haht, Pietro,' she says, and she shakes a fingah at me like this heah.

"Watcha you haht," he repeated, one finger sarcastically wagging so that the muscles of his arm and shoulder shifted and rolled beneath his sport coat. "After that I'm ready to quit forevah . . . pay some high-school kid to do the hedge clippin around heah. Watcha you haht. But I hear the screen door, and I know by the sound of the feet that it's Ulla, so I staht goin a mile a minute, chippin, choppin, a-beep, a-bah. Sweatin. Ulla comes up behind me with a glass of ice coffee, but I keep workin another minute like the hedge is the most important thing in the world when it's ninety-nine degrees out and the game is on channel five, right? Then finely I stop.

" 'Take it easy, honey,' she tells me.

"I say, 'I'm takin it easy. You should see me when I'm really goin.' "
And she gives me one of those Norwegian looks, you know, those looks
they learn because it's too cold to really talk up there." He skipped his
eyes from chair to chair until he found Ulla's parents, sitting at the back
of the room with their drinks held in both hands between their legs. He
shrugged at them half-apologetically. "The Norwegians are beautiful
people, right? Of course they are, the best . . . the second best." He
winked at his in-laws and went on. "Where's Tonio?" I says to her.

" 'In the pool with Rosalie,' she says.

" 'Who else is in theah with em?' I says, because the boys in this
neighborhood, they're like little bulls, like *animale*. But before she can
answer me, I look across the street at Mrs. Accetullo's house, and I see
this heah unbleevable thing come out from undah her cah." He glanced
at his father, who was sitting not far from Rosalie and me, and for just a
moment he seemed like a six-foot-three-inch boy, as if the entire performance were merely an elaborate reaching out for some sign of approval,
some signal of forgiveness for the person he'd become, a former boxing
champion who spent his days now carting wheelbarrows full of wood
scraps around construction sites, and being paid in cash. "Pa," he said,
almost losing his momentum. "I swear to God it was a *ratto* the size of a
wattamelon." He held his hands two feet apart. "Ulla *skeevas* rats like
Adam and Eve *skeevad* the snake. She screams in my eah; I thought the
siren down the fiyah station went off, Pa. I thought I went deaf. I have
the clippahs in my one hand and my ice coffee in the otha, I'm sweatin
like a hoss, I'm half deaf, and this *ratto* the size of a German sheppid
is comin straight across the street right at us. " 'Peetha!' my wife is
screamin in my eah. 'Peetha! Do something!'

"She runs up the stairs and grabs her dress between her legs like this
heah. Really, I'm not kiddin ya. What? Like this heah, I'm tellin ya.
Look, up high between her legs. . . . Meanwhile, the monstah is comin
down undah the hedge about this fah from my feet"—he twisted his hips
and belly back and forth as he said this, going up on his toes like a linebacker attempting a ballet move, and some of the smaller cousins stand-

ing on the stairs started imitating him—"and waddlin into my property like he pays the taxes.

"Now, natchrally, the neighbors heah Ulla screamin, and they're out on their porches wonderin whether we're havin a big fight or what. 'What's he up to now?' they're askin each other. 'What's he doin to that poor nice woman he married?' 'What kind of a mess is he makin out of things over theah?' So I'm on the spot, Ma, like always, right? Right, Tone? Rosie, am I right? On the spot like always. So whadda I hafta do? I put down the clippahs and the ice coffee, I take the rake I was usin to rake up the hedge with, and like a nut I staht chasin the monstah down the side of the house. There's a little alley theah, ya know?" He pointed up and toward the side of his house. "Grass. Leads from the front to the back, and I'm chasin the rat, and I staht raisin my rake up ovah my head and bangin it down right behind him, but not hittin him because I worry if I only wound him—it's an old rake—he might turn around and go for my throat . . . or worse. And if I kill him, I'm gonna hafta spend the rest of the day diggin a grave in the backyahd in the ninety-nine degrees while the game is on, okay? So I'm playin' now for time, see? The rat's just goin into the backyahd now, and Ulla went straight true the house and is on the little back porch, screamin, 'Peetha! Peetha! Rosalie and Tonio are inside the pool, Peetha!'

"Gus and Anna's kid is in the pool, natchrally. The godson. Doesn't come up my house all summah"—another wink in my direction—"he has to be theah on the day the rat comes. And I know the rat is goin in right afta them, too. They love the watta to begin with, rats. Wheah else is he gonna go on a day like this? And so now Tonio's fatha is gonna come home from the GE ovahtime and find a note sayin his kid just got bit by a rat up Uncle Petah's and him and Rosie are up the Mass General now. That's it for me, that's the end of my reputation, right? My good name." He pulled at his nose. "But just at that minute, I see Ruggierio Longo, who lives behind us. The old man, a paisan of Mama's, right, Ma? He was heah a little while ago, but he went home to bed. It's ninety-nine degrees out, and he's ninety-tree, but he thinks he's in the Old Country still, and he's out in the sun pullin weeds from around his peppahs like the *padrone* is comin in ten minutes to make an inspection, can you imagine? Ruggierio hears Ulla screamin. He comes ovah to the back fence, and I'm tryin to defect the rat away from the kids, so I yell out, 'Ruggerio!'

" 'Pietro!' " he yells back. This guy is a prince, Papa, I'm tellin you. If we were ever in trouble, he would climb ovah the fence and dive in the pool to save the kids if he had to, ninety-tree yeahs old.

" 'Ruggerio!' I'm yellin. *'Ratto! Ratto!'*

"By now the rat is scared to death—Ulla scared him with that Norwegian screamin she does—and he's gone by the pool and is headed for the fence at about twenty miles an awa. 'Ruggerio!' I'm yellin, right? And I'm still behind the bastid—excuse me, Father—just missin him with the rake, a-boom, a-boom. Am I right, Tone? Am I makin this up? Tell em."

By this time, Uncle Peter had worked himself up into a fit of tics and nervous twitches and was sweating as profusely as if it was, in fact, ninety-nine degrees in the room, lifting an imaginary rake above his head and banging it down in front of him, his face pinched tight in concentration, his bald head speckled with droplets, his eyebrows up, lips tight, eyes wild.

" 'Ruggerio!' " he yelled so loudly that one of the babies started to cry. He didn't notice.

" 'Pietro, doan-a-worry, Peitro! I'ma smashing the *bastardo.'*

"Ruggerio has a spade up over his head. He's ready. I'm followin the rat with the rake, just missin now, hopin the monstah will find the hole in the fence where Ruggerio's dog comes true and pisses on Ulla's flowers. The rat comes to the fence. I give one more tremendous smash with the rake just on the edge of his tail. He squeezes true the fence, just barely squeezes true, and BOOM! Ruggerio kills him with the shovel, once, on the head, bang, the rat's layin theah dead as a rock."

Uncle Peter stared down at his feet. A droplet of sweat hung for a second at the end of his nose, then fell onto the top of his left shoe. "I stand there a minute, puffin and huffin," he continued, "waitin to see that he's really dead and not just playin. Finely I go ovah to the fence, and Ruggerio has a smile on his face from one end to the otha. 'Atsa way, Ruggerio,' I tell him. 'Beautiful. I was tryin to get him since the front yahd. You're ninety-tree, you take one smash with the shovel, and BOOM!'

" 'Whatta we gonna do with him, Pietro?' the old man asks me, lookin up, but by now I'm already turnin away. Ulla's there, the kids. I did my duty, right? Wasn't my property he died on. 'Ul,' I say, 'go get Mr. Longo a nice glass of ice coffee, willya? Least we can do.' "

He finished his story with a shrug, a sad clown's face, a peek at his father. For a moment in his battered lips you saw a line of doubt, as if perhaps this wasn't the kind of story he ought to have been telling about himself, wasn't really the kind of thing he ought to have done. His audience had settled down, we were chuckling, smiling, wiping tears, the younger children still imitating his rat walk, the awakened baby whimpering. Aunts and uncles sighed, shook their heads at him, erupted in little aftershocks of giggling and snorting.

Peter retreated to the bar to fish another beer from the leaky metal barrel there. It was ten minutes to midnight. People were checking their watches and looking around the room, searching for something to fill that small remaining piece of the year, when Rosalie stood up and rat-walked to the place her father had just abandoned. Among the cousins, she'd always had a reputation as an actress and a mimic, but, until that moment, she had never taken the wider stage. Now she stood in front of the family and struck a pose, feet splayed, small belly pushed forward, shoulders thrown back, and hands waving. "It's Peter!" one of the aunts yelled out. Rosalie paced back and forth through gusts of laughter, tossing her shining black hair, swinging an arm in front of her, punching an imaginary shoulder, sticking an imaginary cigar into one corner of her mouth, and twisting her eyebrows down toward it as if there were something absurdly sour and offensive in the taste.

"And so he squeezes true," she said. "He squeezes true, and BOOM!"

The air in the basement room pulsed and throbbed with laughter, as if we had all been pressed together inside the body of a guitar, and

Rosalie had taken it from her father's hands and strummed one happy chord. My grandmother was holding her chest in both crossed arms and rocking back and forth in her chair. My cousin Angelina was standing beside and slightly behind her, clinging to my grandmother's shoulder and swaying forward and back like a girl on a carousel horse. Sabatino, one of my grandfather's cousins from New York, was ho-ho-hoing like Santa Claus. And Johnny Blink stood against the wall, next to Uncle Peter, smiling the dull, dazed smile of a person who did not understand the language being spoken, but realized dimly, vaguely, secondhand, that something humorous might have been said.

Rosalie let it run its course. She glanced at her father, checked her mother's expression, winked at me. Her eyelids drooped slightly as they often did, giving her face a sleepy, sultry look. Her lips turned up just at the corners, and she seemed to me at that moment much older than she was and indescribably beautiful. "Alright," she said when the laughter had almost subsided, "who's this?" Her face changed suddenly, became serious. She met my eyes. I felt a tickle run across the skin of my arms and up the back of my neck, and then she looked away, stood up very straight, elbows slightly back, one finger adjusting an invisible pair of eyeglasses on her nose. She swung her head sharply to one side. "Anna," she said, with a perfect imitation of an inflection I had not heard in six months and would never hear again, "how long till we eat, huh? Where's Tonio? What happened to Roslee? Is she here for supper or what?"

"Gus, relax, will you?" she answered, in my mother's voice now, with my mother's gentle sarcasm and raised eyebrow. "Go change your underwear or something."

There was a second's pause, as if no one in the room could believe she had done what she had done, and then the remaining chirps and warbles of laughter converted themselves, by some mad alchemy, into a flood of weeping. I felt it penetrate my chest and rise up through my throat. I stared at my cousin, who stared back at me. There were tears running down into my mouth. I swung my head around the room at the perplexed faces of the younger children, at my aunts and uncles with their cheeks shaking and their hands across their foreheads as if to shade their eyes from a burning summer sun.

Upstairs, in the abandoned parlor, the grandfather clock Aunt Ulla had inherited struck a few notes for the new American year, a somber, reliable song that promised some small improvement in the nature of things. I seemed to be the only one who heard it.

Five

ON NEW YEAR'S DAY, not long after breakfast—which was late that morning, and simple after the feast of the night before—Grandpa Dom called me into the narrow den and told me to sit in the soft chair, he had something he wanted to say. I lived then in constant fear of a certain kind of conversation I'd often imagined: my grandparents telling me, in voices that were sad but firm, that it wasn't right for a boy my age to be living with old people, that I was being shipped out to Uncle Peter's house so I could spend more time with Rosalie, or to Uncle Leo and Aunt Eveline's house so there would be a dog and three boy cousins for me to play with, or that I was being sent away to Maine or New Hampshire to attend some school for orphans that the priest at Saint Anthony's had told them about.

Sitting there in the TV room with my imagination going full tilt, I felt as alone as a stranger on the streets of a cold stone city. But then my grandmother came into the room carrying a wrapped present the size of two shoe boxes side by side. Dom slipped into the kitchen and reappeared, standing near the door, holding something behind his back.

"We wanted to give you this now instead of Christmas," he said, "so the new year would bring the good luck for you instead of the bad." He nodded to his wife. She handed the box across. Sitting where my grandfather had been sitting when he gave me the news about my parents, I peeled off the paper, lifted the cardboard cover, and saw a pair of skates there, hockey skates, and another pair of warm socks—my fifth—to go with them. I looked up. As Dom brought his hands out from behind his back, the object he'd been holding slipped from his grasp and clattered down against the radiator. He cursed quietly and picked it up—them up—two shellacked hockey sticks with VICTORIAVILLE written in red letters down the shaft.

"The idea for you, Tonio," he said, holding them out with a certain tentativeness, a certain vulnerability that made me think of Uncle Peter. "There was the hockey player in the hospital when I was there. A professional. In the room across from me. We used to talk. When I told him about you, he said this would be the idea for you. What do you think?"

THAT AFTERNOON, DRESSED FOR the arctic, my grandfather and I carried the new skates and sticks to the bus stop at the bottom of the street. It was a holiday, the buses running infrequently, and I remember we waited there a long time, stamping our feet and swinging our arms to stay warm. We rode to the beach and boarded one of the blue subway cars waiting to leave Wonderland Station, me with the box balanced on my thighs, and Grandpa Dom sitting very straight in his wool overcoat, scarf, earmuffs, and gray felt fedora, holding between his knees two unscratched hockey sticks with black electrical tape wrapped in even bands along their blades.

Rocking side to side against each other, we rumbled across the trestle at Beachmont Station—last stop in Revere—and rolled and clattered past the white wooden church steeple on the corner there. The train went through the frozen reeds of the salt marsh, past the stables of Suffolk Downs, past the lonely yellow screen of the drive-in movie, and the triple-decker porches of East Boston. We slipped behind the airport, where big silent jets glinted winter sunlight, taking off and landing, one after another, with such grace and ease that I could not look at them. When I opened my eyes again, we were in the tunnel beneath Boston Harbor, the train squealing to a stop at stations with names that seemed exotic to me, that seemed to stand as labels for pieces of another world: Deer Island, Wood Island, Devonshire.

Near the end of the line we left the train and climbed into the city. Gusts of cold wind coursed around the skeletal beginnings of what would someday be called Government Center, blowing sheets of newspaper across the memories of the old Scollay Square, its burlesque halls and gangs of sailors careening through the streets in search of a little warmth.

"There were houses here at one time," Grandpa Dom said to me, pulling the scarf away from his mouth with one finger. "The West End this used to be, when I first came to this country. They knocked it down."

"Who?" I said. "Why?" But such a cold wind came up that we lowered our faces and plodded on.

Carrying our awkward cargoes, we walked down the quiet sidewalk of Tremont Street, through Boston Common, across Charles Street to a wrought-iron gate that admitted us to a park with frozen flower stalks and bare gray trees. There was a pond in one corner of this park, and skaters there. Girls were spinning circles in the frigid air, boys racing back and forth slapping a puck and shouting.

Dom sat me on a green slat bench and removed the cover from the box. Kneeling on the lid so as not to soil his trouser leg with the dirty trampled snow, he helped me lace my feet into the cold skates. They were stiff as wooden boots. I stood, wobbled; he rubbed his gloved hands over my cheeks, then straightened his scarf and said, "We try it."

We tried it. With girls in leotards making graceful pirouettes in the white-scratched center of the pond, and teenage boys flying here and there at the far end, and a few adult couples gliding along, arm in arm, my grandfather and I made one circumnavigation, tortuously slow, me with my ankles splayed, knees buckling, arms whipping like windmill blades; and my grandfather holding the parka hood at the back of my neck with one hand and shuffling along near shore in his rubbered shoes, feeding me a steady stream of encouragement: "Atsa way, Antonio. Atsa my boy. Oops. Alright, okay. Up we go, Marciano. Up, Graziano. Atsa way. Now we goin, you and me. Now we skatin."

One loop and I was exhausted. My ankles ached. My cheeks were pinched by the icy air, and my breath was leaving me in great white clouds. The lobes of Grandpa Dom's ears showed beneath his earmuffs, white as teeth. A quick pulse skipped along the veins of his forehead. When we regained the bench and he had caught his breath, he said, "Ock is the idea . . . for you, Tonio . . . eh? Don't you think?"

Six

AFTER THAT DAY, to the amusement of his friends and family, my grandfather—a tailor from a part of Italy where snow was as rare as a full belly—made himself into a student of the game of ice hockey. He watched the NHL on television, pored over the *Record American* sports pages, took me twenty or thirty times to Boston Arena on St. Botolph Street, where the Revere High School team played its games, and three or four times to Boston Garden to see the Bruins play. He enlisted Vittorio Imbesalaqua to build us a wood-framed net for the backyard, and then a plywood goalie that guarded all but the corners of it, and he would send me out there on weekdays after school with the five pucks he'd bought, and make me stay outside until I'd put fifty shots into the strings from twenty feet away. On vacation days and Saturdays, we met the 12:15 bus at the corner, rode to the beach, caught the subway into the city. We learned to transfer to the Green Line in order to avoid the cold walk through the wastelands of Scollay Square. At the Public Gardens we made one loop, then, as the weeks passed, two and three and four loops around the hockey players and the figure skaters—Grandpa Dom in shoes, me in my new skates.

When we had rested a bit, we staked our claim to one corner of the pond, and my grandfather stood near the bank in his rubbers and ear-muffs, leaning on his stick for balance, and slapped the puck more or less in my direction. I missed three-quarters of his wild passes, and had to slip and scrape and stumble to the far bank to retrieve them, dodging better skaters or watching them dodge me; learning to absorb their anger if I interrupted a play, bumping into young women cutting figure eights;

falling hard in a tangle of legs, apologizing, getting up, skating back to my place with the puck flipping and fidgeting against my stick.

Slowly, week by week, we learned. It wasn't long before Dom could send the puck with some regularity in my general direction, and I could cross the pond alone without falling. Later, I learned to cross my ankles one over the other when I made a corner, and stop with both blades perpendicular and my weight leaned back, throwing a shower of ice up onto the cuffs of his pants.

After each of these lessons, he would take me to a bakery on the edge of what had once been Boston's West End. We would set our sticks and my skates in the corner, as though they were the tools of a hardworking tradesman and his apprentice, and sit by the window sipping hot chocolate. On one of those days—it was early in March, the ice had been slushy and soft and we knew hockey season would soon be over—he spent an especially long time cleaning his eyeglasses with his handkerchief, massaging the lenses, testing the hinges. And then he said, without quite looking at me, "The same fella told me about the hockey, he said there are schools where you can go. Fancy. For kids who are smart like you. Scholarships they have. . . . Prizes for people who aren't rich."

I watched him put the glasses back in place. "What do you think, Tonio? What do you think about it?" I watched him fold his handkerchief and fold it again and smooth it with his thin fingers before putting it back into his pocket. I watched him brush some crumbs from the table into his palm, and drop them in the saucer. Something was different. His eyes wavered when he looked at me, he seemed ill at ease, not quite sure of my affection for him. "It wouldn't be now, but later. For the high school. You would have to live away."

"Away where?"

"At the school. New Hampshire. Maine. You would have to go away like I went away when I was a little older than you, even though it makes you afraid. Sometimes you have to do that to find the life for you." I watched him. "What do you think? They have hockey teams there. They have people who go to the fancy colleges afterward, who turn into doctors."

The life for me. I had just discovered the idea for me, and now he was talking *life*. I finished my macaroon cookie and looked out the window at the street.

"You can stay with me and Grandma, Tonio," he said. "Until we die. That's not why I'm saying it."

Seven

I THINK OF THAT MOMENT in the West End Bakery as the point where my spirit and my cousin Rosalie's spirit began to run along different roads. That conversation planted something in me, gave me permission to do what I did not yet even know I wanted to do: go out into the wider world the way my uncle Peter had, and see how long I could stay on my feet there. Frightened and confused, I nevertheless began, on that day, to look for my true place in the world.

The beginning of our separation had little to do with the fact that, being a boy in the 1960s, I could play ice hockey, and, being a girl in the 1960s, Rosalie could not. What began to draw us apart was connected more with what my grandfather had said about conquering fear. It was a subject he knew something about. In 1908, age fourteen, he'd left Italy alone and sailed, in the hold of a ship filled with strangers, across an ocean, then hand-built a new life for himself in a country that was filled with opportunities . . . for which millions of immigrant men and women had to claw and battle. He knew the price you paid for having the courage to leave—that feeling of being cut off, forever, from the warm soil in which the people closest to you had their roots; the feeling of speaking an alien tongue in an alien land; the feeling that your success in the new world, however impressive, would always be edged with a memory of the life still endured by the people you'd left behind, your every hard-bought comfort lined with guilt.

It was that way with Rosalie and me. I know enough now not to make judgments about it. It was not better to leave Revere or Squillani; it was not better to stay. What's better is, somehow, in the middle of the roar and whimper of a thousand local voices, to hear clearly the music that plays inside you, and to dance to that and nothing else.

If it were possible to ask Rosie's opinion on the subject now, I suppose the response would be a shrug, one of her classic tough-girl smiles, a comment like: "Oh, Tonio, don't you know? Every life is the same, just like every dinner is the same, don't you understand that yet? A little different flavor maybe. A little fancier or more expensive, quicker or more drawn-out. Same basic shitty result in the end."

It's not true, though. Even the same basic shitty result—even death—varies, depending on what kind of life it closes the door on: authentic or stunted; plain, sensible, and enriched with love, or elaborately decorated and empty. No one who knew her would say that Rosalie's life was a fulfilling and healthy one, or that her death at age forty-one was anything but the last in a series of small and not so small tragedies. Though her father had never lived his dream, he had at least tried to live it, and had made his uneasy peace with the demon of failure. Rosie could not do that. She was penned in by some primal hopelessness so terrifying that the door could not be opened on it. She was a master at hiding all this—the fear, the vulnerability. Until the night she died, she was chained to her place by the fear of some ultimate humiliation at the hands of the outside world; as if, within the limits of the city of Revere, anything could be borne, but beyond them, nothing.

Eight

SHE WAS A BEAUTIFUL GIRL, exotically beautiful. Later in life, people would often ask if she had Gypsy or American-Indian blood. She had the thick black hair Uncle Peter must have had in his youth, and her mother's pale eyes, a color not so very far from the color of the gas flame on our grandmother's stove. She was fourteen months older than I and, until my second year of high school, slightly taller. She had a great natural talent for drawing and painting, an aversion to dogs and a special affection for birds, a habit of interlacing her fingers and putting her hands on top of her head, so that her forearms pointed out from her skull like the brim of an oversized hat.

She was always a bit uncomfortable with her own girlishness and prettiness, always saucy and cool, as if she had been thirteen since the day she turned three. She would hide behind that coolness, with her friends and schoolmates especially, and then, just when you saw it for the disguise it was, she'd rip it away and speak some bare truth at you, shock you, try to embarrass you even—especially if she herself was embarrassed.

I remember once, walking with her around the block of Jupiter and Saturn streets on a Sunday afternoon eight months or so before my parents died. I know it was October, because she would stop from time to time and pull a few bright red or orange leaves from the edge of someone's lawn and put them into her fist like a florist making up a bouquet, and I remember her saying, in the middle of a conversation about school, "I kissed Caesar Baskine last night. I let him put his tongue in my mouth. Have you ever done that with a girl?"

She was eleven at the time. Caesar Baskine was a seventh-grade boy from the housing projects, notorious even then for his playground sadisms and collection of pornographic playing cards. Of all the boys in Revere, all the boys in eastern Massachusetts, all the boys along the Atlantic shoreline from Prince Edward Island to Patagonia, Caesar Baskine was the last boy her father would have wanted to be allowed to place his tongue in Rosalie's mouth.

As the years passed it was always that way. "I had a whole cupful of whiskey last night, Tonio, and I went to bed so drunk the room spun like a Ferris wheel. Have you ever done that?" "I smoked pot with some of my friends down the beach last week. Have you tried it yet?" "I snorted cocaine." "I had sex." "I went a hundred and ten miles an hour in Joey Mitchell's car on the Lynnway." Later: "I lost twenty-seven hundred dollars at Atlantic City in two hours. Seize the day, right?" And still later: "I moved back in with Caesar. He said it won't happen anymore, he promised."

It seems to me now that, more than any of the other cousins, Rosalie and I inherited our grandparents' courage. That was a key element that linked us. The difference was that my courage was emotional, or psychological, and Rosalie's was physical. In time, my adventures would take me to the distant bright bays of the wealthy, to their schools, their homes, to harbors lit with their careless optimism and noblesse oblige. And hers carried her always closer and closer to the forbidden, uncharted channel of some night world inhabited by demons.

My wife—a woman who knows something about the subtleties of self-hatred, whose brother returned from Vietnam a walking manifestation of it—was friends with Rosalie for the last twenty years of her life, cared about her almost as much as I did, tried almost as hard to help. Her comment on the day of Rosalie's funeral still rings in my ears. "The idea that she was supposed to hate herself was planted in that woman very deep, Anthony, very early on. You tried to get to the roots and dig them out. I tried. But whenever she got close to digging them out herself, some devil whispered in her ear that she'd be adrift then, that she'd float out into deep water and end up lonely and abandoned and broken."

Nine

BUT THE CABLES OF AFFECTION that bound Rosalie Benedetto and me were spun from fibers of blood and history and a million small Revere moments. We knelt next to each other at the altar rail at the children's Mass at Saint Anthony's, tickling, pinching, and whispering while the priest worked his way toward us with the chalice. We stood on the pedals and pumped our bicycles up the long slope of Mountain Avenue, then coasted back down, no hands. We sat cross-legged in our grandparents' parlor with bowls of ice cream in our laps while she rattled off a string of numbers: "Sixteen, four, thirty-one, eleven, five, five, twenty," and I said, "Ninety-two," the moment she was finished, and she called me Einstein the way her father sometimes did, and told me to be careful or one night I'd wake up with smoke coming out of my ears. We'd sit in her room and I'd watch patiently while she made copies of dollar bills, with a fountain pen on good paper, very carefully transcribing the elaborate edging, the numerals, the shaded leaves on the right and left sides, working hour upon hour to get it exactly right. A teenage counterfeiter. An artist of the doomed and confused.

Every Sunday, Dom and Lia would invite one family to 20 Jupiter Street for lunch—Aldo and Marie and their children one week, Francis and Julia and their children the next, and so on—and then, after lunch, the table would be cleared, reset with cold cuts and bread, desserts, fruit, coffee, and the other aunts, uncles, and cousins would arrive. In the space of thirty minutes, our ordinary backyard would convert itself into a kind of Circus Maximus. There were thirty-one grandchildren. A few were too young to venture away from their parents. A few were too old to want to spend Sunday afternoon at the circus. The rest of us occupied the bottom of Jupiter Street—and, in colder weather, the rooms of the first floor of our grandparents' house—like a band of undersized heathens.

It seems to me now that we spent most of those afternoons running. We would chase each other down the grassy alley next to the Sawyers' house, or through the stony, weed-covered vacant lot next door, or around the grape arbor and up onto the elevated patch of lawn, along the borders of which my grandmother grew flowers, and in the center of which a gnarly crab-apple tree tossed its worm-eaten fruit. We'd sprint, sing, taunt, and wrestle, squeeze behind the neighbors' garages and sheds, hide in their shrubbery, throw baseballs, kick footballs, fly kites, jump rope. We'd stand still for a minute or two and eat a handful of my grandparents' grapes, squeezing the pulp and seed into our mouths and tossing the bitter skins over the fence into the yard next door. Or send a few bocce balls down the dusty court in desultory imitation of our parents. Or, as the afternoon cooled and we grew more sedate, we'd sit on the lawn or the front steps and listen to the older cousins—Michael, Patti, Julia, Nunzio—tell stories from the battlefields and tender parlors of high school.

When we were young, especially—seven, eight, nine—Rosalie and I loved those afternoons, loved the stature and grace of our older cousins—sports heroes, war heroes, famously popular girls at Revere High. But almost every Sunday we'd end up slipping away from the communal fever for half an hour, tugged free by some need to share a quiet intimacy we believed we had invented. We'd spend this time in simple ways—walking down to the corner of Park Avenue to watch the buses and cars go past; walking up to the school, sitting in the shade of its balcony, and looking out over the planetary streets sunken in their Sabbath rest. Or we'd sneak down the cellar stairs and forage around in the dusty room where Grandpa Dom kept his barrels of homemade wine, and where we hid the treasures of the season—pieces of quartz, polished chestnuts, scraps of wood and ceramic tile and metal with which, in the vinegary shadows, we engineered elaborate imaginary worlds.

We showed each other our private parts once, as we crouched in the small space between the Cappuccios' garage and their back fence.

Once, we kissed like grown-up lovers—on the bed in my room, no tongues involved, just a passionate embrace and a drawn-out pressing of lips to lips.

Even before my parents died, we shared a fascination for the inexplicable: why God made some boys and girls retarded, or crippled; why Mrs. Castellano was mean and Mrs. Abbruzzo kind; why there existed such creatures as mosquitoes, caterpillars, and sharks, things no one wanted. Why her mother loved her some days, and seemed not to love her at all on others.

Aunt Ulla was a sort of shadow-mother to Rosalie, a woman of irreconcilable contradiction, a figure who haunted the margins of the family life from the moment she said, "I do." She taught her daughter to put makeup on her face, and mocked the color of her hair. She threw together careless meals, and spent hours cleaning the kitchen and Rosalie's room. In certain moods, she would wrap her arms around her daughter and squeeze her against her chest, fondle her cheeks, put an arm around her on the divan. And then, on the same day, sometimes in the same hour, she'd slap her in a fit of anger or poke her in the ribs to make her move, or push her roughly against the refrigerator when Uncle Peter wasn't home and she thought I wasn't watching. She hissed threats that would wrinkle the skin of your arms, and she laughed a laugh that could make you feel happy to be connected to her. She pushed Rosie mercilessly to do well in school but seemed incapable herself of understanding even grade-school homework. For years, Rosalie circled her, a hungry dog circling a piece of meat roasting in the flames. From time to time the flames would seem to lessen, and she would dart in for a lick or a nibble, a bit of nourishment . . . and be burned again, and retreat to a wider circle, and gradually, after an hour or a week, move close again, make another hopeful, pitiful assault on her mother's heart.

And then, not long after my parents died, she seemed to just give up. She stopped circling, kept her mother at arm's length, paid her back with interest for the hungry years, never returning a kiss or a kind word, barely making eye contact; turning her smile, and her beauty, and the saucy, smirking joy of her presence in her father's direction, and in mine.

As we grew older, as Aunt Ulla retreated more into her moods, headaches, and bottles of pills, Uncle Peter became a kind of friend for us, a 220-pound equal. On certain summer afternoons, he would be "taking a beach day," as he called it, and would appear in front of the house in his Cadillac—without ever calling first—send Rosalie to find me while he talked and drank coffee with his parents, and then ferry us off to one exotic destination or another: the docks in East Boston (where he had a childhood friend in the scrap-metal business . . . "crap metal," he called it when the friend wasn't around), the pond at Breakheart Reservation (he loved to swim and would go out into the deep water and dive and resurface a dozen times like a seal), Revere Beach, Nahant Beach, ramshackle and elegant houses in different North Shore neighborhoods, where he would vanish into the back room for mysterious consultations with Johnny Blink or Freddie Frisco. Rosie and I would be left to make odd conversational gambits with Mrs. Blink, if there happened to be one, or Freddie Frisco's elderly uncle, leaning over sideways in his wheelchair with the television on too loud. Or, once, with our host's girlfriend, who lay in queenly fashion on the sofa with her skirt hiked up to the middle of her thighs, her slender legs flexing and gleaming in a pair of silk stockings, and a small pet monkey pulling at the buttons of her blouse with hairy fingers, like some miniature version of the fellow with whom my uncle was taking counsel in the back room.

I read somewhere that boredom is the beginning of the spiritual path. Perhaps that is true. Maybe we need to get tired of this world's enticements in order to be drawn toward those of the next. But, for Rosalie's father, boredom was an enemy to be hunted down and killed. Boredom, for Uncle Peter, consisted of two unpeopled minutes strung together. He did not like to be alone, and believed no one else liked it, either. Conversation and companionship were breath and pulse for him, and he was happiest holding court at the kitchen table on Sunday afternoons, or wandering out into the yard, catching hold of a passing niece or nephew by the shirtsleeve and saying, "What's goin on? What are you doin? Who was that boyfriend I seen kissin you down Hill Park?" He'd pay unannounced visits to the homes of his brothers and sisters—before work, in the middle of the afternoon, sometimes at ten or eleven o'clock at night—just to sit over coffee or a glass of wine and talk for a little while. An almost fearless man in the physical sense, he seemed to live in constant fear (a fear my parents' deaths reinforced) that this breath and pulse of companionship might suddenly expire, that the family might evaporate before his eyes. It was as if he were an acrobat with plates balanced and rings spinning and bowling pins somersaulting in the air all over the city, and his first duty in life was to drive around making sure nothing ever touched the ground.

I understand now that this manic gregariousness would be an exhausting quality in a mate. But it was a wonderful quality in an uncle. When my parents were alive, and, especially in the long barren stretch after they died, nothing was sweeter than to see Uncle Peter's Cadillac draw up in front of the house, to hear him say, "Let's go," to climb into the front seat beside Rosalie and head off with the radio playing and a roll of bills flashing and to end up following his naked, muscular back into the water of Breakheart's Upper Lake, or the swinging tails of his sport coat up the driveway of a house in Somerville or Medford or Nahant, behind the door of which any sort of creature might be waiting. For Rosalie, especially when she felt motherless, and for me, especially after I became an orphan, nothing was sweeter than that.

Ten

ON THE DAY ROSALIE TURNED FOURTEEN—a little more than two years after my parents died—Uncle Peter took some time off from his latest temporary position—as a bricklayer for a friend named Isaac "King" Bundt, who was building a strip club on Squire Road—and drove us to Suffolk Downs. He parked, not in the enormous lot where the ordinary clients left their ordinary cars, but around back, a few yards from the security entrance. Two wheels up on the sidewalk, a foot or two south of a fire hydrant, illegal in six different ways. He stood up out of the car, shrugged the sport coat onto his big shoulders, smoothed the lapels, shifted his belt buckle left and right with one hand, slammed his door. I happened to glance at Rosalie while this was going on. She was watching him, trying to get it exactly right—the shrug, the lapels, the imaginary belt buckle. She even slammed the door with the same exaggerated carelessness as her father. He didn't notice.

We followed him along the sidewalk to a chain-link gate with a strand or two of rusting barbed wire on top. The sentry there was winding and unwinding a whistle on a string around his middle finger. "Little John B. in the sixth," he said to my uncle, by way of a greeting.

Peter patted him on the belly; the man reached out two fat fingers and tapped the top of Rosalie's head and my head as we passed. Beyond him, we found ourselves in a rich cosmos of horse smells and sagging wooden stables leaking hay. Thin small men with brightly colored silk shirts and leathery faces sat on corral fences with their elbows on their knees, talking, smoking, staring at Rosalie in her tight jeans as if she were bringing them a delicious hot lunch and they had not yet eaten breakfast. Or they paced back and forth in the dirt like animals who were themselves about to be saddled and ridden.

Every one of them seemed to be on intimate terms with Uncle Peter— which was not exactly a surprise, given the state of things in the other places he took us. Trainers, jockeys ("the great, unappreciated American at-letes," he liked to call them), maintenance men, security guards, hangers-on—they nodded to him in a serious way, the way of comrades about to go into combat; or they grinned, snapped a salute, mouthed a crude punch line in Spanish. He laughed, hugged, threw a mock jab, slapped rear ends, squeezed forearms, winked, flashed the thumbs-up, exercised his talent for making everyone around him feel they were extraordinary, that a homely face or lowly profession was merely a mask, a costume, a mistake that hid the most royal and noble of souls.

He led us along one of the dirt side streets and into a stable—dark, sweet-smelling, vaguely ominous. He stood with his hands on a half-door and told us, "Don't move for a minute. Let your eyes get used to the not-so-much light."

When my eyes got used to the not-so-much light, I saw that he was smiling at a thoroughbred on the other side of the half-door the way wealthy collectors smile at paintings they have just purchased. The horse was like nothing I had ever seen—no other horse, no circus animal or zoo animal, nothing. It stood in the shadows, eyeing us, ducking its dark head and snorting, as if pleading with us to let it run. The muscles of its black flanks twitched. It stamped its delicate feet in the hay. Rosalie let out a squeal of delight, wrapped both arms around me and squeezed so hard that, for a moment, I thought Uncle Peter had given her the horse as a birthday gift.

"Somethin, huh?" he said. "I'm gonna buy you kids one like this when you graduate high school. We'll build a little stable for him in the lot next to Grandpa and Grandma's house. We'll get ridin lessons, alright? Whattaya say?"

What could one say?

He led us out of the stable and down another dirt avenue, past one turn of the oval track, to another sentry at another, smaller, chain-link gate. "Little John B. in the sixth," Peter said to him. And then: "My brother Gus's kid, Tonio. And Rosalie, my sweetheart, my girl. Today's her birthday."

This fellow, owner of an enormous bulbous nose and an abundant belly, pushed one arm elbow-deep into his pants pockets, wrestled out a roll of bills, and peeled off a ten. He folded it twice and placed it daintily in my cousin's hand. "There you go, Rose," he said. "Buy yourself something nice from Angelo Cece."

Two more pats on the head. We stepped past Mr. Cece, through the gate, and moved toward the grandstand. As we walked, Uncle Peter leaned down and said out of the side of his mouth, exactly as if we were adults, "Angie Pooch. Went to be a priest out of high school, then quit because he couldn't stand a life without women. Has the most gorgeous wife you ever seen, and she's happy as a clam every time you see her. You believe that? Ugly *chidrool* like him?"

He sauntered along, separating a crowd of bettors in front of the grandstand as if he were Moses. The places along the rail were all taken—it was only ten minutes until the next race—but he walked up and stood so close behind someone, practically sweating down the back of his collar, that the man eventually sidled over enough to create one more space. Peter motioned Rosalie into the space, motioned me in, waving and making a face when I hesitated. "Their first time heah," he announced. "My girl's birthday." Our neighbors to either side moved and shifted an inch, two inches, and soon there was room at the rail for all three of us. Cigar smoke floated around our faces. Horses pranced a few feet away. Drawn-out announcements—not unlike the announcements you hear before a boxing match—floated and echoed above our heads: "Aaaand wearing the r-red silks and carry-ing one hun-dred nineteen pounds, Maxine's Chief." Women with binoculars and cheap jewelry, men studying racing programs beneath the visors of their golf hats, the red and yellow silks, the smells, the tote board in the center of the infield with its code of numbers—Suffolk Downs looked to me on that day like a sweaty, smoky paradise, an Oz. Rosalie was acting like a nun on her first visit to the Vatican.

"Why do the jockeys have whips, Papa?" she asked excitedly.

"Those ain't whips, honey."

"They look just like little whips, Papa. Look, he's hitting his horse with it."

"Those there are fly swattahs, honey. They use them to keep the flies off the hoss when he's runnin."

"How can the flies stay on them when they're running that fast?" I asked.

Uncle Peter gave me a peculiar look—critical, perplexed, as if there was something obvious fluttering in the air over Rosalie's head and I was too stupid to see it. "Flies stick on you when you run, Tonio?" he said. "Sure. Alright, then. What makes you bettah than a hoss?"

"My uncle was a champeen boxer," I said, because it came to my mind to say it, and he looked down at me, pinching his eyebrows together, and for one-tenth of one second I thought he might cry.

"Almost champeen," he said, recovering. "Almost champeen you can take to the loan office at the bank on a sunny day, and the lady there will give you a calendah to take home."

As the minutes ticked down to the start of the race, the activity around us, casual and pointless when we arrived, took on an urgency you could feel in your fingertips. The thoroughbreds were being turned toward the starting gate. Some of the people around us hurried off in the direction of the grandstand, from which a thrilled murmur spilled into the air. There was a quickening everywhere, a jump in pulse that could be read in the muscles around Uncle Peter's eyes.

"Now I'm gonna teach you two guys how you win money on the ponies," he said. "So listen." He took a cigar from the inside pocket of his sport coat and lit it with a fancy inlaid lighter. "See this?" He held the lighter up toward me, as if it were evidence in an ongoing case against him. "Gold and motha-of-pearl. Your aunt gave me this when we got engaged." He stuck the cigar into one corner of his mouth, plopped the lighter back into his pocket, yanked from another pocket a dog-eared program, unrolled it to a page on which the horses in the sixth race were listed, squatted down so we could see, and began making circles and

In Revere, In Those Days 115

check marks with a golfing pencil, covering the page with the hiero-
glyphics of the gambling life. Six-furlong speed, track condition, odds
the last six times she went off, speed out of the gate, weight, jockey,
trainer. See?

Rosalie, who hadn't passed in a math assignment since two Christ-
mases ago, was following his pencil and nodding her head with the confidence of an MIT sophomore. Something seemed to have been lit in her,
some fuse in the curl of the DNA. I can see the moment as clearly as if it
were etched onto this page—Rosalie's birthday, the murmuring crowd,
the sun making tiny regular ribbons of shadow on the just-raked track as
the horses pranced and whinnied. And Uncle Peter turning his jaw out
away from us so the smoke from his cigar would drift in the other direction, pointing with the nub of the pencil, looking at her, at me, to see if
we understood.

We understood well enough—me with my facility for grasping and
storing up semi-useless bits of information, and Rosalie in a different
way, with her organs and bones, her whole self. There was a mysterious
symmetry of blood operating in that moment between her and Uncle
Peter, a confluence of need, a fitting together of small discontents and
urges. From birth, it seemed, her father had been infected with a horse-
player's faith in spectacular possibility, a preference for grandiose failure
over mundane survival. That view of life, that deadly faith, was a se-
quined jacket he had been trying on her since she'd been old enough to
use a spoon. Trying it on and eyeing it. Taking it off. Folding it up neatly,
setting it on a shelf in a closet that Aunt Ulla never used. Trying it on
again, six months, a year later. Biding his time until he had an ally in the
house. On that afternoon, for the first time, he set the jacket over Rosalie's
shoulders and saw that it fit her perfectly. In the first moments of her fifteenth year on earth, by a dusty oval not far from America's first public
beach, my cousin had been introduced to the idea for her.

All my uncle's calculations and notations were purely for our benefit,
a first lesson in the grammar of the track. He had been given what was
known as "a tip" on that race. He told us we each had two dollars to bet
with. He would place the bets for us, since we were below the legal age,

but it was up to us to pick a horse. "I'm goin with Little John B., though, myself, just so you guys know. I think he looks like the hoss that wants it the most, don't you?"

We hurried up to the windows and placed our bets a few seconds before the bell sounded. We watched the race with the tickets in our sweaty hands, in a crowd of screaming adults, and, a few minutes after it ended, we stood beside our happy friend at the betting window as he counted out new bills into our palms. Little John B. in the sixth, it turned out, had been good information.

Eleven

LATER THAT SAME SUMMER—it was a breezy weekday afternoon with
storm clouds bunching and swirling above the hills—I left the yard after
lunch and set out on one of my solitary walks. The best part of those
walks was that I never knew where they would lead me. I never allowed
myself to have any destination in mind. I might make a sudden stop opposite Bibsy the shoemaker's, cross Park Avenue there, climb the steep
hill of South Furness Street, then wander down Vane to Broadway for a
five-cent ice-cream cone at Cardell's. Or I might continue straight up
Park Avenue and pray at my parents' graves, then leave by the back gate
and walk the streets of Malden, the next city west, until I came to my
cousins' flower shop, where they would feed me a Moxie and ginger snaps
and drive me home. Or sometimes, seeing a bus come over the hill, I'd
sprint to the nearest orange-banded lightpole and climb aboard, jump
off again at the top of Shirley Avenue, and stroll down past the delis and
shoe stores, the butcher shops with Hebrew letters in the windows, ending up at Revere Beach Boulevard and the amusement rides.

Occasionally that summer I would bump into Rosalie there, on the
Boulevard, and we'd spend a little time together, replaying our latest adventure at the horse track or the "crap-metal" yards, before she drifted
back to her older friends and I went on alone. Those meetings with her
were fleeting and coincidental—almost always near the beach. Leaving
Jupiter Street with her Malden Street friends, she would seem to me to be
swinging out and out, into the cool darkness at the edge of the universe,
and then I'd see her on the Boulevard sidewalk, and she'd see me, and
we'd move close again for a few minutes, and it would be like watching a

comet looping back into view—racing, burning, passing just close enough so you could feel the tug of its gravity, then shooting away again into the dark. I'd go on about my solitary adventure with a twist of disappointment in my belly, a new layer of loneliness set neatly on top of the old.

On this stormy August day, I had turned right at the bottom of Jupiter Street and was heading nowhere in particular when I was overtaken by a desire to see her. Because of the weather, I suppose, I had the sure sense that she was at home, instead of at the beach. So I crossed at Achenbach School, angled down Dale Street to the corner of Venice Avenue, and began the long climb. A few hard raindrops slapped the street, the clouds whirled in purple shreds. I hurried on.

When I was still a block away from her porch, the rain started to fall steadily, smacking against my shirtfront and face. I broke into a run, skipped through the gate, up the front steps, knocked once on the door, and pushed through. There was a grumbling of thunder outside. I went through the parlor, kitchen, and TV room, looking for her, taking an orange from the counter and spinning it in the fingers of one hand as if it were a baseball. I opened the cellar door and called her name down into the darkness. I climbed the stairs to the second floor. There was another clap of thunder, a hard ticking of rain against the windows. "Rosie?" I tapped once on the door of her bedroom, pushed it open, and saw Aunt Ulla half-lying, half-leaning against the headboard with Rosalie's pillow supporting the small of her back. She was wearing a cream-colored summer dress with a pattern of small blue and yellow flowers on it—I remember it perfectly—and the dress was pulled up around her hips and a man was kneeling between her legs with his back to me.

I thought, at first, for that first instant, that it was Uncle Peter, helping her on with her stockings, or massaging her feet as he sometimes did. I thought she might be having one of her headaches. And then the expression on her face reached me, there was a small convulsion of the muscles around her mouth, and she said the syllables of my name in a way that made me want to have another name. The man was built like a sumo wrestler. He was not Uncle Peter. He swiveled on his knee and looked at me over his shoulder, dropped his eyes to the orange in my right hand as if it might be a pistol, and then drove them like dark-handled knives back up and into my face. I had seen him somewhere. In one of the houses we'd visited with Uncle Peter, or at a family party, or sitting behind the wheel of a car in the driveway while Peter leaned down to say a last word. He had an unforgettable face, handsome in a terrifying way: bright green eyes, short hair the color of the spots on a banana, and a wide forehead, on the left side of which, just above his eyebrow, a lump the size of a marble pressed up from beneath the skin. His lips pulled back slightly, as if he might snarl. I stood very still. Aunt Ulla was pushing at the bottom of her dress and trying to sit up, and rain beat against the window beyond the bed. The man knifed his eyes into me for another moment, then stood—lightly, quickly, the way a much thinner man would move—and brushed roughly past me and out the door without speaking. "Smithy!" my aunt called after him. I heard Smithy's feet on the steps, quick feet, and then the front door slamming closed, and then thunder.

"Tonio," she said. She was sitting on the edge of the bed by this time; she seemed to be trying to catch her breath.

Two words squeaked out of me. "Rosie home?"

She shook her head, chewed on the inside of her cheek, pulled down the front of her dress. "She's out with her father. They went out."

I stood there as if everything but my eyes had been paralyzed. She tugged the dress down another inch. The walls, the carpet—every surface of every object in the room—Rosalie's bureau, her Beatles poster, the fabric on the pillows of her bed—seemed to be humming just beyond the range of the human ear.

"They left twenty minutes ago. They went to get you first. They were going up Route One for ice cream and then to a farm in Topsfield where they have horses. They were supposed . . . I thought they went to get you."

"Are you alright, Auntie Ulla?"

She stood up without answering, and seemed only then to compose herself into the aunt I knew, cool and distant, taller and blonder and bigger-chested than the other aunts, the only one among them who wouldn't offer you something to eat the moment you'd taken two steps into her house. "Come downstairs now," she said. "I'll make you an ice cream." I shuffled my feet, surprises multiplying in the charged air. We went downstairs. I sat at the kitchen table while she moved between the cupboards and refrigerator, keeping her back to me. In a minute there was a bowl on the table, next to the orange I'd appropriated—four Oreo cookies with mint–chocolate chip ice cream spooned carelessly on top, a glass of milk. A sharp crack of thunder rattled the panes of the glass in the back door and echoed down into the valley where I lived. The rain followed with such force, it seemed it would press through the walls and leave us lying flat, side by side, in muddy puddles. I did not like mint–chocolate chip ice cream.

She sat opposite me and lit a cigarette, tapping it against a glass ashtray and blowing smoke straight up in the air. For a little while I toyed with the ice cream anyway, reaching past it with my spoon and breaking off pieces of the black wafers. I could feel her eyes on me. At last, when I had pretended to eat for what seemed a long time, I looked up.

"That man was a doctor," she said. "Auntie Ulla is sick."

"You are?"

She sucked hard on the cigarette, nodded with a throat full of smoke.

"Are you very sick?"

"Yes."

I looked down. The ice cream was melting around the edges of the bowl. There were flashes of lightning in the yard, and the tremendous rain, and I wondered if Rosalie and my uncle had been caught in it, up at the horse farm in Topsfield.

"I never told anybody but you," she said. "And you can't tell anybody either. Ever. If you told somebody, it would make Uncle Peetha so sad he'd have a heart attack, he might die."

"Alright."

"You have to promise me."

"I promise."

"You have to remember that Uncle Peetha will die if you tell anyone, if you ever tell anyone—Rosie or Grandpa and Grandma, your friends, anybody, okay?"

"Alright."

She looked at me for a long time, then stood and stared out the window with her back to me until the cigarette was smoked all the way down and the rain had eased somewhat. I could hear the grandfather clock ticking above the sound of it.

"Thanks for the ice cream," I said. "I'm not that hungry now."

"You can't even tell Rosie that you came up to see her today," she said over her shoulder. "Can you remember not to do that? Otherwise, she'll know about the doctor."

"I'll remember."

"I have to go someplace now, to the drugstore to get my medicine. If I had the car I'd drive you home, but it's not raining that hard now. When you get back, tell Nana and Grandpa you just went out for a walk someplace, to the park, and you got wet, alright? I'd let you have my umbrella, but then they'd know you were here, and they'd find out about me, and they'd get sick, too."

"Alright."

For some reason I had held on to the orange during all of this. As I was going down the hall and toward the front door, Aunt Ulla stopped me and took it away.

I was already developing the habit, in those days, of pretending to know less than I knew, pretending not to understand something an adult had said when I sensed they did not want me to have heard it. Twice, I had even raised my hand in class and answered a question wrong— though I knew the correct answer—because it was beginning to seem to me that there was something slightly shameful about my harvests of As, that the teachers might embarrass you if you seemed too eager to learn, that people wouldn't like you as much. So, as I was going toward the door I tried, without saying anything, to make my face and somehow my arms and shoulders into a mask and a posture of stupidity. It made me feel very young. I nodded at Aunt Ulla in what I hoped was an innocent, stupid way, and then I turned around and ran down the steps into the rain with my arms up, making a little false yell as if I were seven or eight and Rosalie were there and we were playing one of our games. I kept this up until I was through the gate and down the sidewalk far enough so that she could no longer see me, and then I dropped my arms and walked home in the last breezy splashes of the storm.

Twelve

I HAVE STOPPED TRYING to explain to my friends—artists, professors, intellectuals, people who, for the most part, don't have warm feelings about organized religion—what a central place Saint Anthony's Church occupied in my childhood years, and occupies still, in my memory.

My parents' bodies were blessed in that church before being brought to the cemetery for burial; my uncles, aunts, and cousins were married there. Along with the names of a few hundred other early benefactors, my grandparents' names are cut into blocks of pale marble near one end of the altar rail—you can still see them if you go there. My father used to tap me on the chest with the offering basket when he ushered at the nine o'clock Mass; my mother used to press her eyes closed at the elevation of the host and bring the tips of her fingers to the spot between her eyebrows. In that church I saw my uncle Louis, a tough guy in his youth and an ironworker into his sixties, bubbling over with tears at the sight of his brother's coffin being wheeled down the aisle. That brown stone building, for me, is a museum that holds the solids, vapors, and liquids that make up human existence: the joy of birth and the sudden mysterious disappearance that is death, the wailing of babies, the shrieks and laughter of young children, the love of God and the terrors of hell as described to us by pale nuns in spectacles, the confusion of a Catholic boy's sexual awakening. The smell of incense, the glass-clean soprano notes falling over us from the choir loft; old Vincenzo Festa, with his half-inch-thick eyeglasses and terrible speech impediment, grabbing hold of my arm as I walked down the aisle after Mass, and trying to make it clear to me, for the hundredth time, how close he and my father had been all their lives, like brothers, like twin souls knit together. Given the trembling flute-note of love in his voice, given a bundle of memories like that, how could I possibly walk into Saint Anthony's and be thinking about Vatican politics?

For a certain part of my boyhood, roughly the years between ten and fourteen, I would go to Saint Anthony's every other Saturday afternoon with my grandmother, for confession. Sometimes Aunt Marie or Cousin Laura would join us, but most often we went alone. It was a ritual for us, what we had instead of hockey practice. Uncle Peter would leave us off in the parking lot, and we'd walk side by side up the shallow stone steps between the statues of Christopher Columbus and Anthony of Padua. There were heavy dark doors, as if we were stepping into the Middle Ages, and beyond them the dim, smoky quiet of the vestibule. You dipped your fingers into a white marble basin of holy water and touched them to your forehead and chest; you heard the heel of someone's boot knock loudly against a pew and the sound echoing up to the sixty-foot-high ceiling; you saw a priest without his vestments striding briskly across the altar on some errand, trailed by an altar boy in floppy black cuffs; you stood for a moment letting your eyes adjust, watching the dust motes drift across beams of sunlight that angled down through the stained-glass windows.

My grandmother and I would walk up the side aisle, past the confessionals and the stations of the cross, and light two candles at the altar rail, then go back, kneel in a pew, and wait our turn.

The priests—Fathers Castaletta, Bucci, and Bellini—had rotating duty in the confession box. Father Bucci was a friend of Uncle Peter's and generally considered the most lenient of the three. Father Castaletta was hard-line, strict; on certain days, positively mean. I used to hope we would draw Father Bellini, who was almost deaf. There was something strangely soothing about kneeling in a pew, contemplating your sins and God's wrath with such somberness and regret, nervously waiting your turn, then hearing Father Bellini's voice booming out into the nave: "YOU WHAT? HOW MANY TIMES? BUT HOW COULD YOU DO THAT, KNOWING OUR LORD LET HIS SON BE CRUCIFIED FOR YOUR SINS?

The tactic never varied. Father Bellini would berate the poor sinner, go on and on about how awful his or her transgression was, how incredible, how absolutely unbelievable . . . and then, once he or she was suitably humbled, "Father B.," as we called him, would change from the Old Testament God into the New, and in a slightly kinder but not much quieter voice say: "ALRIGHT, THEN. NEVER MIND. IT'S NOT THE END OF THE WORLD. YOU THINK IT'S THE END OF THE WORLD FOR SOME-BODY LIKE JESUS? YOU THINK HE HASN'T HEARD WORSE THAN THAT, A THOUSAND TIMES WORSE? OF COURSE HE HAS. SURE HE HAS, HERE'S WHAT YOU HAVE TO DO, THEN: FOR YOUR PENANCE SAY ONE OUR FATHER AND BE SORRY YOU DID IT, OKAY?"

On one of those Saturdays, I saw a woman—she must have been visiting from another parish—come out with tears streaming down her face. More often, though, people would step from behind the heavy curtain, glance up for a moment at a friend or relative waiting in the pews, and shrug their shoulders as if to say, "Well, what can you do? I drew Father B. this week; he let me have it."

On the Saturday after I'd stumbled upon Aunt Ulla and her friend Smithy, Fathers Bellini and Castaletta must have been visiting the sick or playing golf. After my grandmother had taken her turn, she held the curtain back for me, and I went in and knelt and waited. The panel slid open before me, revealing Father Bucci's profile, and I started in, by rote: "Bless me, Father, for I have sinned. These are my sins. It has been—"

"Tonio," he interrupted, "how's Little League?"

"Good, Father."

"How's your team?"

"We're seven and three, Father, so far."

"Seven and three. Alright, not bad. What position you playing?"

"The bench, Father. The bench and shortstop."

"What bench? Your uncle says you're a star, as good as your cousin Nunzio. What's he up to, anyway?"

"Nunzio? He has a summer job with the MDC, cleaning up—"

"No, your uncle."

"Uncle Peter?"

"The one who never comes to church. Where the hell has he been lately, out golfing every day instead of coming to visit his friends?"

"Last week he took Rosalie up to Topsfield to see horses."

"And he didn't bring you along?"

"He just missed me, Father."

"Missed you. How could he miss you—"

"I went out for a walk."

"I'll give him *miss you*. I'll take him out in the back parking lot, and I'll knock him out with one punch. You tell him I said so."

"You sure, Father?"

"No. Tell him Father Bellini said so. Tell him he yelled it out all over the church."

"That would be a lie, wouldn't it, Father? I wanted to ask you—"

"There are lies and there are lies. That would be what you call a little lie that doesn't hurt anybody. Half a venial. Then there's the three-quarters of a venial, that maybe hurt somebody a little bit. Then there's the big lies, full venials. The big ones you confess, the other ones you say an Act of Contrition and ask Mary to ask Jesus can he look the other way. *Capito?*"

"*Capito*, Father. But how do you tell the difference?"

"Easy. The difference comes down to one thing: did you do it out of love or did you do it to get something for yourself?"

"What if somebody else asks you to lie?"

"About what?"

"About something you saw."

"Then it's the same way. That something you saw, will it hurt somebody if you tell them? Will the lie make you get something just for yourself?"

"Yes to the first part, Father, and no to the second."

"Then it's not a sin. What else? Any other gigantic sins this week? You kill anybody? Steal any cars, anything like that?"

"No, Father."

"How old are you now, twenty-one?"

"Going on thirteen."

"Any girlfriends yet?"

"Three of them, Father. I like to go out with three at the same time if I can, so it doesn't get boring."

There was a pause. I saw his face move closer to the screen. I could smell his aftershave. "You're a joker," he said at last. "Your father was like that, too, you know. You could never tell with him when he was joking, his face wouldn't change. And your mother was a very special woman. She saved your father's life after he came back from the war, did you know that?"

"No, Father."

"He would never have put the pieces back together again without her, do you understand?"

"What pieces, Father?"

"The pieces of who he was. His soul's pieces. Your mother and Vito Imbesalacqua saved him. Ask your grandpa someday what Vito did for your papa when he came home."

"I will, Father," I promised.

"I pray for them every single day. You'll see them in heaven, okay? That's the way God does it. He takes them away from you for a little while. Seems like forever, but it isn't. You believe me?"

"Yes, Father."

"What about your cousin Rosie? Any boyfriends?"

"Caesar Baskine."

"Now you're joking again."

"I'm serious, Father."

"You're kidding."

"Last week he took off his bathing suit down the beach in front of everybody to prove he already has hair near his penis."

"He did that?"

"Yes, Father. Next to the bathhouse. Rosie told me, and it's not something she would make up. Two old women saw his naked bum and started to yell for the police, and then Caesar and his friends ran away."

"And Rosie is going around with him?"

"I think so."

"Does your uncle know?"

"Not yet, Father."

"Alright. I'll go up the house then and have a talk."

I glanced at the crucifix on the wall to my left, at the dark curtain, at Father Bucci's silhouette. "Call first," I told him.

◆

AFTERWARD, I SAID MY TWO Hail Marys at the altar in penance for the multitude of my sins, and my grandmother and I stepped out into the day, feeling as though we'd been washed clean, inside and out. For a child, perhaps for adults as well, there was no feeling quite as deeply calming as the feeling of believing yourself to be forgiven and loved by God. I sometimes wonder now if the whole spiritual search doesn't consist of that and nothing else: a movement toward that feeling, toward an unshakable belief in your own goodness, in some pure and persistent essence that hasn't been ruined, no matter how ragged and selfish a life you've led.

I remember the way the sunlight struck my face when I stepped out of the church on those afternoons, the way the tight line of houses on the other side of Revere Street seemed to have been polished and set clean against the salty air. The flagstones on Saint Anthony's patio, the wrought-iron railings there, even the chrome and glass of the automobiles in the lot—every object in the world vibrated with a quiet, gentle approval, as if the atoms of creation were comrades-in-arms welcoming you back from war. The feeling lasted sometimes as long as several hours, and for that time you saw the world as mystics and saints must see it: the eye with which you viewed creation was a purified eye, free of self-doubt and self-loathing.

As we usually did, that day my grandmother and I walked three blocks to the corner of Revere Street and American Legion Highway, where there was a coffee shop owned by Uncle Aldo's godfather, a man who went by the name of Jerry the Zazz. Among a number of other delicacies, Jerry the Zazz served English muffins that were pressed flat to the grill in snapping puddles of butter, and milkshakes in tin shakers with dew on them. There was an odd collection of new and slightly used items for sale on the shelf that ran along the wall below his plate-glass windows: small television sets, cameras, a vacuum cleaner; once, a puppy in a cage. When I asked my uncle about these things, he told me they had "fallen off a truck," which did not quite make sense. It was true that Jerry the Zazz's place sat on the corner of a busy highway, and that trucks passed it day and night. But, looking at the unmarked TV sets, the puppy, the leather gloves in boxes, the golf clubs in bags, it seemed impossible to me that they could have fallen from one of the passing trucks and not been damaged. And it was difficult to picture Jerry the Zazz out in the street, between orders, rescuing lost objects from the edge of the curb.

My grandmother and I took our regular table and sat looking out on the highway.

I have a peculiarly good memory for visual details, for certain moments. It's not exactly a photographic memory. I can't read a page of text and repeat it verbatim without looking. But I can summon pieces of my past and "see" them as clearly as if they have been thrown onto a screen in some interior theater. There are times when this is more curse than gift—I sometimes wish, for example, that the humiliations and botched love affairs of my early adulthood would blur a bit in my inner eye—but it helps with the kind of painting I do, and it's not the kind of thing a person can change in any case.

I remember that my grandmother was wearing a dark brown dress on that day, with a maroon thread sewn in curlicues on the collar, and that her church hat was made of velvet or velour, black as a burnt match, with tiny mother-of-pearl beads and a fishnet veil. She took the hat off and set it to the right of her coffee cup, and Jerry the Zazz himself brought us our food.

He was a very small man (some scholars say that Pygmy blood mixed in with the southern Italian gene pool at some point in history) with a nose that seemed to have been formed from a slightly different shade of clay and pressed too hard into the middle of his face. His beard must have been especially heavy, because every time I saw him—mornings and afternoons, weekdays and weekends—his cheeks and chin were covered with a thin carpet of stubble that made me think of the wicks of candles. His eyebrows were black, too, though his hair was perfectly white and thick, and parted on one side in a neat pink line.

He was polite enough to me, usually asking how old I was, or what was the name of my teacher—as if this information had a life span of two weeks and he needed to renew it every other Saturday. But the way he spoke to my grandmother went beyond politeness. He set her coffee and slices of toast on the table, then invariably reset them, moving the handle of the cup half an inch so that it would be easier for her to take hold of, or rotating the plate two degrees so that the toast faced her at a certain angle. He would then take a step backward, into the aisle between our table and the counter at which his other customers sat on red bar stools. And he would take up the end of his apron in both hands and wipe his fingers clean, leaning slightly toward her as he did this. He let go of the apron eventually, but kept the small forward tilt of his upper body, sometimes pressing his hands against the outsides of his trouser legs like a man frozen in the first instant of a deep bow.

"Lianna," he would address my grandmother, in what I recognized even then to be extremely formal and elaborate Italian. *"Come il mondo ti tratterebbe sul questo pomeriggio meravigliosissimo?"* How would the world be treating you on this most marvelous of afternoons?

"Abbastanza bène," my grandmother would answer, leaving her hands in her lap so that he would not feel that his conversation was keeping her from her food. Quite well.

"And what," Jerry the Zazz would go on, "would be the condition of the health of your wonderful husband, Domenico?"

"Quite well," my grandmother would say.

"And this life of ours in America, this rich life of ours, is it generous with all your children and their husbands and wives, with all your grandchildren? Are they well?"

"Very well."

Hearing this, Jerry the Zazz would nod and bring his dark eyebrows together like caterpillars consulting each other as to the advisability of risking one small further advancement in the line of questioning. He would glance at me, seem to remember my presence. And then, having made his decision, he would straighten up an inch, step back another quarter of a step, and sweep his short arm through the air as if he were smoothing the shoulders of the oxygen molecules there with the veined back of his hand. "Excuse me, I'm interrupting you," he would say. *Scusa, ti disturbo.* "I'm delaying your afternoon. Please eat. Please call if I may help you."

Then he would walk very stiffly and self-consciously around the counter and go to work rinsing dishes and tending his grill, but I would always have the sense that three-quarters of his attention remained on our table, on my grandmother. She would sip from the coffee cup with the smallest of smiles at the corners of her mouth, then set it back on the saucer, break off a piece of the buttered toast and nibble delicately, not quite looking at me.

On that day I poured the milkshake into my glass, glanced at the back of Jerry the Zazz's head, took a sip, looked over the bar again at his white hair, then leaned toward my grandmother and said, "He loves you."

"Chi?" she said indignantly. Who?

"Jerry the Zazz," I whispered. "He's in love with you."

"Ma che dici?" she whispered hoarsely. But what are you saying?

A quick red flush had risen to her cheeks, and I had a feeling similar to the feeling I'd had one day when I came home early from school and accidentally saw her naked. There had been some kind of a teachers' meeting; we'd been let out an hour early. I had hurried home to change into my play clothes and had come in the back door without making much noise. I went through the kitchen, not paying attention, stumbled across the threshold of her bedroom, intending to say a quick hello, and knocked right into her where she stood at her bureau, fresh from her bath, spraying herself with Jean Naté, and wearing not a stitch. She saw the expression on my face and went into such a roll of trilling laughter that it rang in my ears long after I'd run out of the house.

It was like that now. For one or two seconds I felt as if I had caught her in something. There was the quick blush, a flicker of embarrassment, the secret smile, then she laughed quietly, turning her face out toward the window so Jerry the Zazz wouldn't hear.

"It's true, isn't it?"

She looked back at me, shrugged, glanced over the bar. I kept watching until she was forced to speak. "I was with his wife very good friends when we were girls in the North End," she admitted, so quietly that I had to strain to hear her. "His wife, she died very young, when she was bringing him their first child. All these years now he lives like a *celibe*. Grandpa says he's waiting for the day when he can propose to me to get married, but it isn't true."

"It looks true."

She smiled again, the small, secret, inward-turning smile you see on some paintings of the Buddha.

We sat there a long time that day. Probably the conversation with Father Bucci had lifted an enormous weight from my conscience, allowed me to move the scene with Aunt Ulla and Smithy off to the edges of my memory, because I felt especially happy and calm. It is not so easy to be a Catholic kid, to have God bleeding there in front of you every week, tortured for your sake. You can end up feeling like a walking, talking mortal sin, a scratched-up dirty doll, constantly watched. For a little while that day, I felt freed from that. My two Hail Marys had made me holy in God's eyes. I remember asking my grandmother what she asked for when she prayed.

"Nothing, Tonio," she said. She had finished the toast and was brushing the crumbs together on the plate, pressing her fingertip down on them and bringing the finger to her mouth.

"What do you say to God?"

"Nothing. I don't talk, darlin. I listen."

"He talks to you?"

"Not like we talk, you and me."

"How then?"

"He talks by what He makes in the world."

"What does He say?"

She lifted up her eyebrows once. She looked at me the way her son Peter sometimes did, as if the ordinary fences that stood between the adult mind and the child's had been uprooted and carted away in the space of two breaths. It seemed to me that she was assessing my readiness to hear certain information, and that she was on the verge of deciding I needed to wait.

"Tell me, Grandma."

She looked down at the table, and her attention settled on one of Jerry the Zazz's rumpled cloth napkins. The napkin was as yellow as an egg yolk, with thin green vines sewn along its edges—I can close my eyes and see it now as if it were here on the desk in front of me. I have paintings and drawings of it everywhere on my studio walls, in file cabinets and dusty folders, pencil sketches, pastels, oils on canvas in various sizes. "What's the story with the napkin, Anthony?" my dealer, Jeremy Stearns, asked once, and I did not even try to answer him. Grandma took hold of the napkin in her fingers and shifted into Italian: *"Devi guardare molto attentamente,"* she said. *"E' una lingua che vedi, che non ha nessun parola."*

You have to look carefully. It's a language that you see, that doesn't have words.

I looked and looked and had no idea what she was talking about. It was only a napkin. Most days it still is.

Jerry the Zazz came back to check on things, and asked about the napkin. "It was dirty, Lianna?"

"No, no. It was fine. Everything is fine."

"She was telling me about God," I explained, and the Zazz turned to me as if I'd spoken the name of someone he'd known many years ago.

"Ah," he said, "God." He patted me on the shoulder twice and walked away.

When we were finished with our food, I went behind the bar and used the telephone. A few minutes after that, Uncle Peter appeared, beeping the horn out front and smiling at us through the windshield of his car. Aunt Ulla was in the seat beside him, waving at me, burning her eyes into me. My grandmother squeezed into the front seat next to her. I climbed in back. We rode up Revere Street and along Broadway and, stoplight by stoplight, I could sense the holiness, the goodness, leaking out of me. By the time we turned onto Park Avenue, the world was ordinary again—telephone poles, curbstones, and the smoky summer smell of the streets.

I must have asked about Rosie, because I remember Uncle Peter turning to his wife and saying, "Why doesn't she go to confession anymore?" And Aunt Ulla saying, "Why don't you?" under her breath, without looking at him.

When he pulled up in front of my grandparents' house, Uncle Peter reached across the back of the seat and took hold of my left forearm with one of his big hands. "Stay a minute," he said. "Man to man." And I could feel a kind of electric current pass into me from the back of Aunt Ulla's blond head. When she and my grandmother had gone down the walk toward the back steps, Uncle Peter turned around to face me. There were little streams and twitches of trouble running in the muscles around his eyes. "Whatta you so nervous about?" he asked me.

"Nothing. What are you?"

He frowned, squeezing away any possibility of making a joke. "What do we do about her?" he said, and he looked terrifying to me at that moment, a man who could kill another man without much hesitation or regret.

"Who, Uncle?"

"Whatta you mean, *who?*" He peered at me from beneath a tangle of scars, until I squirmed and looked away and heard: "Rosie, who else? What do we do about her and this heah mongrel she's goin around with?"

Thirteen

WE DID NOTHING. I started junior high that year, a ten-minute walk from home. Rosalie rode a bus to the old Garfield School, not far from the beach. That building has been torn down now, replaced by a beautiful modern structure with lots of glass and light, but in those days Garfield School was a dilapidated brick box, a local disgrace, a sort of minimum-security prison for ninth-graders. There, in that seaside cauldron of guerrilla cliques, fistfights, and antiquated classrooms, Rosalie began to melt away from her father and grandparents, and from me. I would see her on Broadway, walking past the fire station in a knot of ninth-grade girls, most of them smoking, all of them having perfected the hard smirk and sloped shoulders that served to protect them from the various humiliations that haunted the corridors of Garfield School. If she saw me, she would wave and call out my name, detach herself from the loose formation of friends just long enough to rub her cheek against mine, make a kissing noise, and peel off a few affectionate sentences, like bills from a roll in her jacket pocket.

"How ya doin, cuz?" she would say, tilting one shoulder down and flicking the butt of the cigarette with her thumbnail, or blowing smoke straight up into the air in an unconscious parody of her mother, never quite meeting my eyes, never quite still.

"Good."

"McKinley's nice, isn't it?"

"Sure, great."

"Goin out with anybody?"

"Not yet."

"Why not?"

I shrugged, looked away.

"You know what Grandma says: when you meet the somebody for you, you'll be happy forever."

"I know. You goin out with anybody?"

"Caesar, but not really."

"Are you alright? Your eyes look different."

"It's the cold air. I'm with my friends now, gotta go, okay? But I'll call you. You can come out with Caesar and me some night, alright? We'll get a pizza at the Brown Jug or something, hitch a ride to New York for a cup of coffee, okay? Bye, alright? Be good."

I'd watch her hurry away, flicking the cigarette once at the side of her leg, catching up with her friends in front of Rosa's Subs and squeezing into the middle of them the way her father squeezed into his place at the rail at Suffolk Downs.

That fall Rosie was arrested for the first time—for possessing a small amount of marijuana. It was a harmless transgression of a foolish law, a matter of being in the wrong place, with the wrong friends, wrong cop walking the beat. But it was 1967, in Revere, and marijuana seemed to many people then—some of our relatives, even—like the advance guard of a monstrous new evil that was stalking their way of life. She was released into her parents' custody. No one in the family talked about it.

Fourteen

IN A STRANGE WAY, that afternoon with my grandmother—at church and in Jerry the Zazz's—was the high point of that period of my life, the summit of my self-esteem and happiness. It would be years before I'd feel holy again, or good, or blessed.

At some point after the short, hard moment in Uncle Peter's car, something broke in me, and in my feelings for Revere. I'm not sure I have lived long enough, or will ever live long enough, to see that break through a clean lens. But I believe now that this change in me had something to do with the important place Caesar Baskine had begun to occupy in Rosie's life. I was not jealous of him. I think that if he had been a different kind of boy, I might even have been mature enough then to be happy for my cousin, to want to do things with them once in a while, to wish them well. But it was as if the pettiness and roughness in him was a virus, and it made his relationship with Rosalie into a mutation of the normal pattern of teenage love. The virus twisted her; it infected Uncle Peter, and it infected me.

What happened first was that the streets, housefronts, and landmarks of the city—things that had always seemed to me to be painted in the colors of a perfectly good-natured welcome—turned inhospitable overnight. It was as if the sun had risen one morning a different color. It began to seem to me that Caesar Baskine was a truer representative of Revere manhood than I was, than Uncle Peter was, than Grandpa Dom was, and so I began to be estranged from my own place. And since that place had been so much a part of the person I thought I was, I began to be estranged from my own self, as well.

If it hadn't been for the consistent affection of the Benedetto family, it is possible I would have snapped in two completely in those years, and ended up like some of the sad-but-pretending-to-be-happy middle-aged men I saw in the crowd at high-school football games. My uncle Francis had gotten me a job in the little wooden stall where coffee and hot dogs were sold at halftime, and amidst the great convivial tide of fans there, I would always see a few solitary souls, washed back and forth at the edges of things like broken pieces of shell in the surf. You could see the discomfort in their skittering eyes when they ordered, in the uncertain way they reached out for the paper cup—"This one mine?" They could not quite summon the unself-consciousness necessary to just do things the way people did them in Revere. They could not quite buy the local act, be part of the local scene, fit into a gang the way Rosalie did with her friends on Broadway and down the beach. And they had never found the courage to go away for a year or two, or forever, and make up an act for themselves. They functioned well enough, but there was not much joy in their functioning, not much style. Jostled by the crowd, they stepped away from the booth with their steaming cup in both gloved hands, then remembered, turned back, fished a nickel out of their coat pocket and reached out over someone's shoulder to toss it at the tip jar, and the nickel always missed, always rolled down into the dirt, and you would hear them saying, "Sorry," as they drifted back toward their place in the grandstand.

I might have ended up that way if it had not been for my aunts, uncles, and cousins. They were a strong sheath of muscle and tendon surrounding a fracture in a bone, and they held the bone steady, and held it, and held it, until, eventually, years down the road, the fibers cemented themselves together again and the bone was fit to bear weight.

I'M NOT SURE I HAVE the courage and the clear-sightedness to tell this part of the story, and I'm not sure I understand the sequence of events precisely enough to describe them well, but I know the beginning.

The beginning was McKinley School, the place Rosalie called "nice." It was not nice, not for me, at least. It was a hulking, three-story structure with a slate roof and bloodred brick walls. There were wide-gauge screens over the windows on the first floor, and a small tar playground with two bent, netless basketball hoops and piles of litter against the fence. During my time there, eighth-grade boys initiated seventh-grade boys into the pleasure of attending by means of a ritual called "poling." Small gangs of self-appointed polers would mill about the playground before the morning bell and chase down any seventh-grader foolish enough to wander onto the premises a few minutes early. The seventh-grader would be lifted up by the mob, held parallel to the ground—all this accompanied by howling and grunting and screaming, and observed with special interest by the seventh- and eighth-grade girls. The polee's legs would be spread, and he would be driven like a ramrod into the metal pole that supported the backboard, testicles first.

I saw Stephen Brown poled. I heard the noise he made—a stifled scream—saw the metal pole shiver, watched him writhing on the dirty tar, his legs shifting back and forth, one arm held between his knees and his head arched back so that the veins in his neck stood out. There was a great deal of status in having been poled, and when he recovered in a few days, Brown became a kind of honorary eighth-grader. The honor seemed a dubious one to me.

There were good teachers at McKinley School in those years, teachers who cared, who encouraged, who made a valiant stand at the gates of the fortress of spelling and reading and math. But there was a teacher who turned his eyes away from a wrestling match at the back of the homeroom and, later, slipped a few dollars into the hand of the winner because the loser was a notorious troublemaker in class; teachers who pushed students against the blackboard, hard, who lied to us, pitted us one against the other with classroom balloting for "most conceited girl," "best-built boy," and the like; teachers who were caught up in the kind of cult of roughness that ruled the playground and, to some extent in those years, the city itself.

The king of this cult was a boy named Johannes Orto, widely acknowledged to be the toughest kid in McKinley School. Orto was not particularly mean, but he was as tall and heavy as an average-size grown man, tremendously quick with his hands, fearless, and as stupid as the trunk of a tree. I remember the math teacher, Mr. Craxis, becoming frustrated with his antics once and shouting at him across the heads of the other students: "Orto, what was our deal? You just sit there in this class, right? You sit there in the back row, and you make no trouble, and I give you your C for the year. Did you forget that already?"

The teachers were besieged; they cut deals, they ceded the playground to Orto and his crew the way governments cede distant provinces to bands of guerrillas. Or they tippled and mumbled behind their desks and failed to notice that my friend Peter Imbesalacqua had pinned a condom to the window screen of Room 7B in such a way that the afternoon sun cast a perfect shadow-phallus on the yellow shade. Class after class, we snickered over that, three-quarters of us having not the faintest idea what a condom was actually used for, or where in Greek mythology we should place the god Trojan-Enz. Weeks went by before someone in authority noticed and had the condom taken down.

Probably McKinley would have seemed less like a correctional facility and more like a school to me if I had continued to grow at a normal pace. My cousin Ernie's son—my godchild—is a student there now, and I've driven him to school two or three times, and visited his classroom. It all seems so ordinary, nothing like the noisy, terrifying McKinley of memory. The boys and girls stand as high as my waist or chest or shoulders, and carry their books down the oiled, squeaking corridors like somber little soldiers in a jumbled peacetime march. They skip out the front door, they chase each other back and forth across the miniature lawn. The older ones drift off together in knots of three and four to sneak a cigarette or talk about a scandalous romance. They look harmless and very young, the way my friends and I must have looked to our elders. What seemed to me then like the outer edge of hell must have seemed, from the teachers' point of view, like a sweaty day at the beach. We were, after all, merely acting out the insecurities and psychological dramas of our parents: the girls were required to be streetwise, at once flirtatious and cool, and the boys were required to be tough. Those were the commodities in which our mothers and fathers traded in the adult world. That was what they had instead of money.

But I had stopped growing. Average size in fifth grade, slightly below average in sixth, I stepped into the classroom on the first day at McKinley School and discovered that my classmates, boys and girls alike, had risen up around me over the summer like skyscrapers around a four-story office building built in the 1920s. In seventh grade, I stood four feet ten inches short. One afternoon before the start of English class, Janet Siskovitch somehow got hold of my penny loafer and held it up over her head, and I reached and jumped and could not come close to snatching it back from her. Arnold Wiggio, also my size but a bit stockier, was thrown out the window in music class while Mr. Johnson plunked blindly at the keys of his upright piano and half heartedly urged us to sing "My Country 'Tis of Thee." Wiggio was unhurt—the window was only ten feet off the tar of the playground—but with the shoving and rabbit-punching, the fistfights and threats, the poling, the little game in which a house key was scraped against the back of a hand until the skin broke and bled, the swaggering Orto and his cigarette-smoking lieutenants, McKinley was a jungle biosphere: what counted was force and cunning. Lacking those, you might resort to camouflage: try as best you could to blend into the cracked paint of the walls or the metal and concrete of the stairwells; or you might work out a system of joke-cracking and wise remarks and, betraying your cousins and friends, ride like a trembling bird on the shoulders of the rhinoceros, pecking away fleas and beetles now and then, making yourself useful, staying safe.

My arms were like twigs next to the arms of most of the other boys. I prayed for hair to grow above my top lip. At night, I used to stand in my little room in my grandparents' house, take hold of myself around the ribs and pull upward, as if puberty might be summoned with a few good yanks of the bones. I developed all sorts of clandestine strategies for showering and changing at the YMCA, anything to hide my smallness and hairlessness. In spite of what I'd told Father Bucci, I had been an all-star shortstop in Little League, but I did not even bother to try out for Babe Ruth League, the next level up. The diamond was too large there, the pitches too fast, the other players twenty or thirty or fifty pounds heavier and sometimes a foot taller. Instead, I played stickball at the tennis courts with old neighborhood friends—some of whom were close to my size—buried myself deeper in the shame of good scholarship, and spent hundreds and hundreds of hours cultivating the idea for me: shooting pucks at the plywood goalie Vittorio Imbesalacqua had made, and passing every winter afternoon at the MDC rink, or at the pond in the Public Gardens with my grandfather.

A small, slight man himself, a tailor in a time and place where most of his acquaintances were stonemasons and construction workers, a quiet, dignified, opera-loving man in a race of boisterous Americans and gregarious Neapolitans, Grandpa Dom seemed to have an acute understanding of the perils of being a small man who didn't like to hurt other men. I found out much later that it had been his idea for Uncle Peter to bring me out into the backyard three or four times and give me boxing lessons. I took to those lessons the way I took to my schoolwork—diligently, patiently, obediently. Blocking punches, throwing punches, dodging punches—I could do those things well enough. The problem was, I did not want to do them. I did not see any reason to smash my fist into someone else's face, and that philosophy was a great liability for a boy at McKinley School. Anyone could challenge me, push me, slap me around, and the most I could manage was to take hold of their wrists and wait until the fight was broken up, and then lace up my hockey skates on the weekend and bang into bigger boys to prove to myself that I wasn't a coward.

I made the Bantam Team, then grew an inch and a half in eighth grade, and another inch and a half in ninth, and earned a spot on the Revere High School Junior Varsity, though I was still the smallest member of the team and did not see much playing time. Once, in a game against Winthrop, with my grandfather and Uncle Peter in attendance, I took the place of an injured left winger and skated half the length of the rink with the puck before a defenseman put his shoulder into my chest and nearly knocked me out. That was the extent of my local heroism on the ice. Still, it used to give me a strange sort of pleasure to be knocked down like that, checked, tripped, smashed into the boards. I would get up, set my helmet on straight, and chase after the player who'd checked me, protected by the pads and the rules, more or less fearless.

But there were no pads on the street, and no rules, and no point to the things that went on there, as far as I could see. Except that, in the seventh, eighth, and ninth grades, the girls—even my favorite cousin—seemed attracted to boys who liked to fight. Even the teachers seemed to admire them above everyone else. And if the cousins and uncles weren't telling stories about Uncle Peter's days in the ring, they were reading from a mythology of masculine violence: Frankie Lucca had broken someone's nose for insulting his sister; Uncle Aldo had beaten someone to a pulp for stealing his wallet at the Revere Theater; John-John Sawyer, who lived next door, liked to punch his hands against the shingles of his parents' garage to toughen the skin.

These stories—partly true, partly embellished—were passed along by men and women both, to boys and girls both, proudly, innocently, like parables, like prayers. The war in Vietnam was tearing the neatly pressed fabric of the country to shreds in those years—1967, 1968, 1969—and young men went to war because of stories like that, because the battle-field was the ultimate test of their toughness, and toughness was the ulti-mate test of their goodness. That is the trick the nation plays on its poor and working-class sons and daughters.

But in those years, I would have given anything—anything—to be tough in that way. Sitting beside me under the grapevine on the night Martin Luther King, Jr., was killed, smoking a cigar and staring out at the tomato plants, Uncle Peter said, as if temporarily converted to non-violence, "Tough doesn't matter, Tonio. I broke Burly Goodman's jaw down the beach when I was your age. One punch. He was a linebacker on the football team and three years older than me, and he said something about Italians I didn't like. You think that did me any good in the long run? You think I'm proud a that now?"

"You sound proud."

He frowned, looked away. "Lissen," he said when he turned back, "I wasn't smart in school, I wasn't nice-lookin, even when I was a kid, alright? I had one thing goin for me, I was strong, I was tough."

"The most important thing," I said. "The best thing to have going for you."

"Bullshit," he told me. It was the first time he'd used a word like that in my presence. "Look at me now. I'm a slave for other people. I sweat, I break my back, and whaddo I have?"

"You have a Cadillac, you have a nice house. You have the prettiest wife of anybody. The most friends."

He seemed not to hear. He let out a breath of sweet smoke, reached down and wiped something off his shoe. "I showed you how to box, didn't I?"

"It doesn't work when I fight in the street. I'm afraid. I hate it."

"Everybody's afraid. Lissen, forget fightin, I'm tryin to tell you. Forget it. You gut a great life layin out ahead of you. You're gonna be somebody special, a doctor, a senator, and you're worried about bein tough in ninth grade?"

But that advice was like a whisper of encouragement in a chorus of howls and jeers. The future was a speck of *might be* against an enormous, ninth-grade *IS*. Rosie had drifted away from me and toward the meanest, roughest kid in the city—didn't that show what was important, and what wasn't? I was a dwarf with skinny biceps who went to church every week and got all As without trying, a scrap of a boy washing back and forth at the edge of manhood, leaning forward tentatively from the back of the crowd and saying, "That one mine?"

"What do you think?" my grandfather asked me when I came home after a particularly miserable day. "What do you think about going away to one of those schools we talked about? Not now, Tonio, but maybe next year or the year after? What do you think?"

Book Three

One

IT WAS A BLUE, brilliant, seaside September morning. The tops of the
two old maple trees in front of Mr. and Mrs. Sawyer's house shifted and
tossed in a light breeze. Uncle Peter pulled up to the curb in his brown-
and-gold Cadillac—the last new car he would ever own—and lifted my
suitcases from the sidewalk into the trunk with an artificially happy expression on his face, as if he had just lost a high-stakes poker game and
was pretending the money didn't matter. Aunt Ulla had left him a few
weeks before. Left him, left her teenaged daughter, Rosalie, left a note,
flown to Norway with a wealthy new American boyfriend on the vacation she had always dreamed of, a vacation that marked the end of her
association with the Benedetto clan, and the end of her time in Revere,
Massachusetts.

Many years later she would step into my life again, once, briefly, a
gray-blond, bejeweled, seventy-five-year-old drifting along the edges of a
small crowd at an art opening in Chicago. The show was called "Faces of
Revere," and on the walls of the gallery were portraits of some of the uncles and aunts, of Dom and Lia, Father Bucci, Rafaelo Losco and his
wife, Teresina. I was standing with Jeremy Stearns, my dealer, and a
young woman who collected portraits and whose name I do not remember. I looked up and saw Aunt Ulla hovering in front of the four-foot-by-
four-foot face of her former husband. I recognized her immediately. My
first instinct was to slip into the men's room.

But the collector and Jeremy moved half a step to the side and sank
deeper into business talk, and I set my plastic glass down and made myself walk across the room and say hello.

"Hello, Anthony," she said, in a voice coarsened at the edges with money and age. In her pearls, pantsuit, and carefully applied makeup, she seemed as polished and hard as the gallery's marble floors, but she also seemed at peace with herself in a certain way, as if she had at last found the place she'd been destined for. It surprised me—the poise, the air of casual distance, of confidence. It surprised and angered me. I had not realized until then how ambitious she was, how badly she had wanted to find herself in a station higher than a wood-frame house on a crowded street in Revere. Until that moment, I had not realized those things about myself. She clasped my hand in both her hands and looked up at me. "Very, very wonderful work."

I nodded, gestured toward the canvas, and said, "Someone you might remember."

"Oh yes, of course." She half-turned toward the painting, and then, since I was watching to see what effect it might have on her, she caught herself and faced me full again. "How *is* Peter these days? Are you in touch?"

Rosalie had been dead three months—Ulla had sent an arrangement of flowers to the funeral home; my uncle, struck down by his grief, was a patient in a rehabilitation clinic on Revere Beach, where I visited him on Sunday afternoons and pushed him along the Boulevard in a wheelchair. "He's fine," I said. "We have lunch in Boston every Friday."

She knew I was lying. For a moment the veil parted, the same veil she'd always worn around me, and I could see that my lie had made friendly contact with the liar in her, as if we had at last found the frequency on which we could speak without static. Or as if the fact of Rosalie's death and Uncle Peter's misery somehow justified the decision she had made all those years ago. Her eyes flickered to either side, and she said, in a quiet, pleasant-seeming voice that was not quite a whisper: "You hate me, don't you? You've never been able to forgive me."

"You didn't come to Rosalie's funeral."

She flexed the muscles near the right corner of her mouth. She looked away, but only for the time it took to blink. "I wanted to," she said. "I tried to. I got packed and dressed and took a taxi to the airport. . . . But I just couldn't face all of you. I cashed in my ticket and went straight home and didn't get out of bed for three days."

I stared at her. The usual marks of age on her pretty face. The false sociability. The poise, manufactured gregariousness, and fear of ordinariness you sometimes find in the upper classes. I said, "You're everything I hope my daughter won't grow up to be."

One spark of hurt then. She opened her mouth and closed it. And at that moment I remembered, very precisely, the look on Rosalie's face on the day I told her I was going off to the eleventh grade at Phillips Exeter Academy: a tough-girl smirk built on a foundation of cauterized wounds, as if her mother's leaving and my leaving were only two more events confirming the true architecture of the human soul. I shifted my weight, ready to walk away, but Ulla rested a hand on my arm, a proprietary hand, all the past in it.

"Rosie forgave me before she died."

Do you really think so? I almost said, but we had reached a territory I was not able to navigate, the territory of my old, impotent rage. I turned my back and left her there, standing beside the painting of Uncle Peter.

But that was many years after the day I left Revere. With the obvious exception of my mother and father, we were all alive, together, and more or less healthy then, and, until Uncle Peter's arrival, the morning wore a somewhat forced air of celebration. Rosalie had promised to ride with me to Exeter, New Hampshire, and see that I was safely settled in, but when he pulled up in front of the house, Uncle Peter was alone. "You're number two in her life now," he joked by way of an apology.

"Which makes you number three," I told him.

He cuffed me on the shoulder. There was uneasy laughter from the small delegation that had assembled, Uncle Aldo and Aunt Laura, Grandma and Grandpa, my little cousin Nicky, who wanted very badly to be a hockey player someday, like me. I hugged and kissed them, stalling, hoping to see Rosie drive up in Caesar Baskine's GTO. But she'd had enough abandonments for one season. Uncle Peter slammed the trunk. I took one breath and looked around at the houses and telephone wires, the rusting TV antennas, the lines of cars at the curbs, the garden and the grapevine, and the windows on the second floor of my grandparents' house. Then I made a small, awkward wave, climbed into the passenger seat next to my uncle, and rode away.

WE MADE A PASS through the cemetery—"for luck," Uncle Peter said. He slowed down but did not stop at the graves, then cut across the northwest corner of Revere and up onto Route 1. For the first few miles he sat staring straight forward, eyebrows pinched together, left wrist draped over the top of the wheel, his bald head nearly touching the roof of the car. I noticed he was still wearing his wedding ring, though he had announced to the family that he and Ulla were separated (we were Catholics; the word *divorce* was not used), that the marriage was over. If he ever met the rich bastard who had stolen her away from him, he said, he'd kill him with his own hands, drag the body out into the middle of Broadway, and then walk down to the police station and turn himself in.

When we passed Danvers State Hospital, he shifted his weight, glanced at me across the seat, and said, "What's this all about anyway? This goin away to a rich kids' school. Grandpa talk you into this?"

"They gave me a scholarship."

"I know they gave you a scholarship. You're gonna be a great hockey player someday; you're the smartest kid ever to come out of the city of Revere. Who wouldn't give you a scholarship? What I'm askin is why did you take it? Revere High wasn't good enough for you?"

I did not know why I had taken it. Because Rosalie had sailed away from us with a thick-necked future felon; because I was terrified by the slow failing of my grandfather's health and the slow accumulation of the weight of age on my grandmother; because, though I had grown five inches over the summer, I was still not at peace with the rough idolatries of the neighborhood I had once loved. I had my hockey games—after years of hard practice, I had made the varsity squad at Revere High and seen some playing time; I had my friends; I had, still, the comfort of family gatherings. But in some way I could not fathom, my parents' deaths had begun to hurt me more instead of less, as if, as my body changed, the sadness had spawned offspring in my cells—an ancestry of absence, a genealogy of grief. I did not want to be a kid anymore, fussed over and vulnerable. I wanted to make a life for myself, without waiting, a life beyond the borders and barriers of Revere.

"I don't know why, Uncle," I told him. "I don't know."

"Beautiful," he said, in a harsh, sarcastic tone he had never used with me. It was like one of his playful punches thrown too hard. And I threw back, as he himself had taught me to.

"You're pissed off because Aunt Ulla left," I blurted out in my nervousness, my fear of *him* abandoning *me*.

"Mr. Psychologist now."

"And because Rosalie's out of the house most of the time. You're pissed off at me because of them."

He turned his face to me, and it seemed ugly at that moment, all twisted lips and scarred eyebrows, all shadow. "Since when do you talk to me like that?"

"It's true, though."

"Don't throw the truth like a punch."

"You started it."

"You're the one who's leavin."

"I'm not leaving, I'm going to school. I'll never leave, I'll never leave you. You've been a father to me for five years. I'll never leave you as long as I live."

He kept his eyes forward, blinked, swallowed. "You're in a small club then," he said, trying for a joke and just missing.

A few miles of highway slipped past the windows—billboards, neon signs, cheap storefronts facing broken-up tar lots—a spiritless and gaudy landscape, all money and the legacy of dreams of money.

"And you'll find somebody better than her," I said. "You'll see. Lots of women will want to be with you."

"Sure," he said. "Hundreds. Thousands."

I kept watching him. He flexed his fingers on the wheel. "They'll be after your money," I said. He turned his jaw toward me, a little broken light playing at the edges of his lips. "They'll go out with you just to be able to sit in a car like this."

"There you go. My pal Tony Mer sold me this car, said the same thing. 'Flocks of them, Petah,' he said. 'You won't know what to do with the women you'll attract with a vehicle like this heah.' "

"Not as long as you keep wearing that ring, though."

He looked down at his hand, and I could see that the anger had already washed out of him. I remembered my father's quick temper and quick apologies, and my own—a Benedetto inheritance, for better and worse. "Forgot about it, can you imagine?" Uncle Peter pushed a button with his left little finger, and the window hummed down. "Hold the wheel, Tone." I reached across and steadied it while he tried to pull the ring from his finger, yanking it up against the knuckle, grunting and struggling, making a show, finally giving up. He could have gotten it off easily if he'd really tried, I knew that. I said nothing.

He took the wheel from me again, and we sped north, away from the subject of my betrayal, and Aunt Ulla's. Shortly after we crossed the New Hampshire line, there was an exit marked EXETER, RAYMOND, EPPING, which led us down a ramp to a tiny tollbooth. It looked like an outhouse there beside the road. "Five cents, please," the collector said when we stopped. Uncle Peter pulled a roll of bills from his left pants pocket, peeled off a five, put it into the collector's hand, and pressed his foot to the gas.

"Right there," he said, when we were on a two-lane highway headed west, "is how you know you're in New Hampshire. They have yellow lines on the road instead of white, and they make you stop for a nickel."

I laughed a little two-note laugh, my half of the peace treaty. We drove on.

I had been to Exeter Academy once before, with my grandfather and Uncle Aldo, for an interview and an admissions tour, but Uncle Peter had never seen the place. I can't honestly say I watched his expression as we went along the road and into the town—I was too busy studying the new surroundings myself—but I could sense his mood: a city dweller's disdain for the woods, at first, and then for the single street of quaint shops, for people who would live in such a place, so far removed from the rush and tight quarters that, as the saying goes, meant the world to him.

The school itself is set just south of Main Street, separated from the commercial district by a few blocks of clapboard-sided eighteenth- and nineteenth-century homes. It is a fabulous place, three hundred acres of sprawling lawns and perfectly maintained brick dormitories, a little oasis of privilege among the strip malls and pine forests of southeastern New Hampshire. But when the campus opened out in front of us in the afternoon light, Uncle Peter did not say so much as a single word, did not grunt or exclaim, did not even turn his eyes. We reached the main quadrangle; he turned left into a parking lot and stopped to ask a passing student, "Where's Amen Hall?"

The name had been a running joke in the family since I'd gotten my dormitory assignment. "Amen," Rosalie said, on one of the two times I'd seen her. "It's what you say at the end of something, isn't it, not the beginning?"

The student leaned down toward us, his eyes skittering over the Cadillac's flashy fenders, my uncle's improbable face, me. " 'A-men' is how it's pronounced," he informed us. "Rhymes with *Cay*man, as in Cayman Islands, you see. It's that one. You go straight down there and park wherever you wish. *A*-men Hall."

"You see?" Uncle Peter said mockingly when we had started off. "That's what you're up against. *A*-men. Rhymes with *Cay*man. You see?"

But the moment we stepped out of the car, he seemed to shrug off all traces of whatever sense of inferiority or bitterness we might have carried with us from the sweatier kingdoms. It helped me. He stood up out of the car and did his thing with the belt buckle, shook his arms a couple of times, lifted his gaze to the specter of *A*-men Hall—neat brick, four stories, freshly painted white trim around the windows—and he was immediately at home again, in the world of people, absolutely fearless and sure. We carried my bags to the third floor, Room 21, and set them on one of the beds in the innermost of two rooms. He paced, poked his nose into both closets, opened and closed the drawers of the plain brown desks and bureaus, scuffed his shoe on the canvas-colored linoleum, squeezed the doorjambs, went over and stood for a minute at the window, as if the building were his castle and he was searching the grounds for a derelict gardener.

While we were hanging up my shirts and sport coats, there was the sound of shuffling feet in the outer room, and a slim, handsome black boy about my own size put his face in through the doorway and beamed a warm smile at us. "Joey Barnard," he said, taking Uncle Peter's hand and pumping it up and down. "You must be Mr. Benedetto."

"Peter," my uncle said, in a state of shock.

"And you must be Anthony. We're roommates."

"Tonio," I said.

"Joey Barnard. West Sacramento, California. I'm all moved in. I'll give you a hand if you want."

It took us ten minutes to carry up the second load from the car, and about half that time for me to decide how I felt about Joey Barnard. He had the same natural ease as my uncle—in fact, they were chatting like old pals when I came back from the bathroom. You could see the tracks of some kind of heartache in the skin around his eyes, though he had a graceful way of covering it with a smile and tilted head, his hands opening out and up as he spoke.

Uncle Peter shook Joey's hand again, squeezed his shoulder, said, "Alright then, I'm leavin you two guys to your studies and so on, your girl-chasin. Walk me down to the car, Tonio. Joe, we'll see you weekend after this one. You're comin out to lunch with me and Tonio's grandparents, it's all set."

We stood beside the car in the New Hampshire light, older boys sauntering past with an air of comfort and ease that seemed the stuff of dreams to me. "Alright," Uncle Peter said, "he seems like a nice kid. They're good people, some of em. Your grandpa used to have a colored friend when he worked in Boston. Shocked the whole neighborhood when he invited the guy home. Mr. Earl. Never forget it as long as I live. Grandma's mother was livin with us then. She hid in the parlor and peeked out at him like he was from Mahs. Mr. Earl." He took the roll of bills from his pants and peeled off two fifties. "Had one of my miracle days at Suffolk. Heah." There was no point in trying to refuse. I folded the bills into my palm and pushed them into my pocket. His eyes swung up to mine, old scars, gray-green irises, a little water. "Lissen," he said, putting his hands on my shoulders and squeezing me, "don't ever let nobody make you feel less than they are, that's all. Okay?"

I could not answer.

"Alright. Nothin wrong with cryin. Your pa and your mother would have been proud as hell that you're in a place like this. Do good, alright?" He was crying himself now. We were a warm flotsam of Mediterranean emotion on the cool North Atlantic tide of passing students, parents, teachers in tweed.

He hugged me very hard, climbed into his car, and drove away without glancing back. I stood there and watched him go, watched the great cloud of guilt that followed him, a guilt that would never be washed away, the sense that he had somehow rubbed his weird awful luck off on my mother and father, and would have to spend the rest of his life now making it up to me. I stood there with tears on my face and watched until the gold fenders disappeared.

Upstairs, Joey Barnard was sitting sideways at his desk, studying the orientation schedule. He looked up and said, "What a great guy your dad is."

Two

FOR A BOY LIKE ME, a boy who loved sports as much as he loved school, Exeter was a three-hundred-acre paradise: baseball diamonds, basketball courts, two indoor hockey rinks that had been built the year before, just across the road from Amen Hall. The classes were never larger than thirteen students, all of us sitting around a hardwood table on the same level as the teacher. No poling, no fights, no problem being seen carrying home a stack of books. It was, in a sense, a community of orphans, which meant that the salt of seeing parents and children together was not constantly being dribbled into the raw bloody wound left by the death of my mother and father.

Instead of the regular Monday-through-Friday schedule, we had classes on Monday, Tuesday, Thursday, and Friday, and half days on Wednesday and Saturday. Mandatory sports at least four days a week—six days for varsity or junior-varsity teams—and, on the four full days, there were even two class slots after sports and before dinner. Jackets and ties had to be worn in class and at the dining hall. Lights out at 10:30 for juniors like Joey and me, with the occasional extension to 11:00. Anyone caught out of the dormitory after the check-in hour could be placed on probation. Any student found using drugs or drinking alcohol—one time— would be expelled immediately. Girls from the town or from other boarding schools were allowed only in the Common Room on the first floor, and only during certain weekend hours.

At my grandparents' house, I had been accustomed to an almost un- limited freedom—walking wherever I wanted, staying up as late as I wanted (often they went to bed before me)—but I did not chafe very much under the thick blanket of Exeter rules. And, though there were some extraordinarily wealthy boys among my classmates, the distance between their lives and mine didn't seem so large.

In those years, boasting about a family's means went against the prevailing social winds. It was the late sixties, a brief moment in which American materialism was called into question, prior to the all-out worship of things and money that would mark the next thirty years. Scholarship boys like Joey Barnard and me were required to wait on faculty tables at dinner one out of every three terms—a practice that has since been abandoned—but even that did not trouble me. In fact, aside from a boy named Higgenbotham, and some faculty members—who seemed, in their tweed, tortoiseshell, and proper, reserved manner, like another species of adults than the one I'd grown up with—the issue of class and wealth was not much of an issue for me in my two years at Exeter. I was an innocent in such matters then. I knew that some of my classmates had fathers and even grandfathers who'd graduated from "the Academy," as it was called; that some of them went to the Riviera over summer break, that some of them had famous last names from the worlds of industry or government service. But I had no drawer in which to file that information. I had been outside of Massachusetts twice, both times to visit my mother's sister Janice in New Jersey: how was I to react to the idea of the Riviera? And my last name was famous, too, in the place I'd come from.

The other part of it was that I just did not feel like playing the working-class ethnic kid at Exeter, because I discovered almost immediately that I had at least as much in common with my new friends as I did with the Leos, Peters, and Alfonses I'd left behind. Now, in middle age, the pendulum has swung back. I find myself drawn to old friends from Revere and tugged away from some of the people I know in the wider world—people who grew up with summer homes purchased by their grandparents, who went to places like Exeter without any of their family members being upset about it, or surprised. How strange it has all turned. How much more of my own prejudice I have to confront now, when I encounter a person like Higgenbotham.

Jeffrey Lewis Higgenbotham IV was his full name, but I did not know that until I saw it on the program at graduation. He was a junior, like me, and lived on the third floor of Amen Hall, too, in a double with someone named Madhur Jarasapwanatha, a tremendously wealthy, unnaturally quiet boy from what was then called Ceylon. As if everyone else at the school had shrugged them from their own shoulders onto Higgenbotham's (no one called him Jeffrey or Jeff), he carried around with him every imaginable symbol of class and wealth. Grandfathers on both sides of his family were Exeter graduates—his parents, he told me the second time we spoke, had gotten engaged at Palm Beach. ("What a coincidence," I said. "Mine got engaged at Revere Beach.") He lived an hour northwest of New York City in a rural enclave of polo fields, golf clubs, and Tudor mansions. His maternal grandfather had patented the rounded piece of metal on which garden hoses are hung in loops, and made a fortune from it; his father and one of his uncles played polo; one or two of his aunts sat on the boards of charitable foundations. At Exeter, he had a closet packed with beautifully tailored sport coats, three tennis rackets in presses; he wore a gold watch; he taught me to play bridge in the basement smoking room (I taught him the Italian card game *briscola*); he went around with his chin in the air, his wise proclamations falling upon the heads of the rest of us like coins tossed out the castle window. He was a breathing, living, walking-around cliché . . . and the first time I saw him he was pissing out the window of his third-floor dorm room into the New Hampshire night.

Joey and I had become fast friends with Madhur at orientation, and on the second day of classes we wandered down to his room after dinner to sit and talk. He had a two-room double, just as we did, though in the northwest corner of the building. As I followed Joey through the door, I became aware of a tall, narrow-shouldered boy standing with his back to us at a dark window. "Course, course," he said, looking at us over his shoulder, but keeping his pissing apparatus discreetly out of view. This "course," I would soon learn, was Exeter jargon for "of course," and was supposed to be inserted into speech wherever possible. If asked whether or not you were prepared for a history test, for example, the right answer was either "Course I am," with a slight emphasis on the last word, or

"Course not, course, course," delivered with the tailing-off inflection one finds in eastern Maine.

"Course, course," Higgenbotham said. "It's Barnaby and Benetto. Benetto, step over here. My mum saw your name on the dorm list and warned me about you. Not to go home with you on weekends and so forth, never to form too close an attachment to the criminal worlds. So that's the first thing I'd like to do."

He shook himself with great flair, yanked the zipper up, slammed the window down, slapped his hands together as a substitute for washing them, and crossed the room with a couple of manly strides. "Benetto," he said, as if we were two colonial explorers meeting in a sub-Saharan out-back, "Higgenbotham." And then: "Barnaby, very pleased."

How, I wondered, could a fifteen-year-old boy act like this without getting his ass kicked every time he opened his mouth?

"You were peeing out the window?" Joey asked him.

"A privilege of the four-year boy," he said.

"You're a senior?"

He shook his oversized head and turned his eyes toward me for a second appraisal, as if, by coming into the room with someone who asked questions like this, I had confirmed his mother's worst suspicions. "Upper Middler, same as you and Benetto here, same as Maddy. However, I *will* be a four-year boy when I'm a senior, and we're all supposed to be crazy by then, so the authorities are bound to make allowances. Come, sit down."

We arranged ourselves on his bed and desk, while he struck a pose in the one soft chair. "Benedetto," I corrected him, at the first opportunity, and he gave me a puzzled look, squinted, paused, then said, "Higgenbotham, as I mentioned."

Higgenbotham, it turned out, was a hockey player, too. When he learned I would be trying out for the squad, he began to give me profiles of the coaching staff, the varsity stars, my likely competition for the team from last year's JV. This was done with complete disregard for the fields of interest of the other two boys, but for a while at least, for the first few weeks, we were all a bit hypnotized by Higgenbotham, by the apparent seamlessness of his act, and were content to listen to him the way he seemed to expect to be listened to. "Mr. Rislin, you see, was a star at Princeton. All-America, in fact. Don't let the quiet voice fool you. He'll work you to skin and bone in practice if you earn a spot, and he likes fellows that can hit." And so on.

What saved Higgenbotham, to the extent that he was saved, was that once we'd gotten past that first blinding display of what we took for sophistication, it was easy enough to see that he was just a boy underneath, like the rest of us: a thin wrapping of adolescent arrogance over the normal pubescent anxieties. That fall, I saw him once in the presence of his polo-playing father. They were walking laps around Amen Quadrangle on a particularly fine October afternoon, the father smoking a pipe and talking, and Higgenbotham going along with him shoulder to shoulder. His father had an odd gait, elbows pulled stiffly back as if he were in uniform and at attention, the legs swinging in his trousers like puppet's legs, loose, thin, weightless. It was Higgenbotham's gait; it had looked very original on him until you saw the father. I was struggling valiantly to make small talk with the daughter of one of my teachers when they passed. Higgenbotham acknowledged me with a tiny nod, but made no introductions. When they were just beyond us, I heard him say, "But Father, don't you think they'd prefer . . ."—and the voice was a little boy's voice, a third-grader's warbling plea.

He had a bit of a speech impediment, too, a very slight lisp, and the habit of being careless with people's last names. The thin shoulders, the splay-footed gait, the struggles with Latin and calculus—try as he might, he was one of us. It would turn out that he was a fairly good hockey player—not good enough to play at Yale, where he ended up enrolling after graduation, but good enough to play second defense on the varsity team, junior year. And it would turn out that this was his only athletic ability, a rare occurrence in my experience of people who play hockey. He could not throw or catch a Frisbee on the lawn when we played on Sunday afternoons. He swam across the new Olympic-sized pool like a harpooned whale, splashing and gasping and throwing his mouth open in an expression of agony. Wrestling with smaller boys on the carpet of the Common Room, he always lost, and usually he tripped at least once running the bases in club baseball games, tripped, scraped his forearms, banged his nose, banged his bat off the catcher's mask as he took his flailing swings.

But he stumbled and splashed good-naturedly, the confidence of his bloodline buoying him, just as the confidence of mine sometimes buoyed me. We kidded him without mercy, called him "Figgentop," tripped him in the corridor, made so many jokes about his penurious nature that, finally, on a Saturday night near the end of senior year, he felt obliged to buy milk shakes for everyone in the Grill. But it was impossible to taunt him in any mean sense. At McKinley, he would never have been poled; it would have seemed somehow sacrilegious.

On that first night I was enchanted by him, just as Madhur Jarasap-wanatha and Joey Barnard seemed to be. There was a kind of purely American glamour to him, confident, bumptious, unself-conscious. He represented everything I had worried about encountering at Exeter—the genteel snobbishness, the nonchalant bigotry—and to find it wrapped up in a harmless, foolish package like Higgenbotham immediately stripped it of most of its power. Joey and I retired to our room in time for the proctor's check of lights, and lay in our beds with a shaft of moonlight slicing in between the shade and windowsill and across the few feet of darkness between us. "Ever know anybody like that in West Sacramento?" I asked him.

And he let out a low, sweet chuckle and said, "Man. Oh, man, no!"

Three

JOEY BARNARD HAD A SISTER named Regina (who would, ten years into the future, become my wife) and a brother named Francis Assisi Montgomery Barnard, who was serving in the navy in Vietnam and who would come home wounded but alive and eventually check into a drug-rehabilitation center outside Portland, Oregon. Both his parents were living. They rented one-half of a brick duplex, a house with a lopsided front porch and dusty backyard. Joey was Catholic; an athlete, too, a miler; and had grown up loving books in a not particularly bookish family, hating to fight in a neighborhood where street fights were part of the coming-of-age ritual of every boy. So we had the most important things in common.

I learned all this from our conversations in those first weeks, from the snapshots he showed me, the three framed pictures of his family he kept on his bureau. He was a skinny, happy, outgoing kid, but behind the bright eyes there was some slow-shifting trouble. Every now and then as the fall term progressed and the academic pressure increased, I would come back to Amen 21 and find Joey lying on his bed, rigid as a corpse, staring up at the ceiling when he should have been studying. "Having a mood," he called it. He'd greet me with a flat "Hi, Anth," lie there for another half an hour, completely silent and still, then go into the bathroom across the hall, wash his face six or eight times with cold water, and come back into the room and play The Impressions into his headphones, or sit at his desk writing a letter to his sister.

Little by little as the term went on, as he began to feel he could trust me, he would bring out small pieces of his Sacramento life and set them up in the room like exhibits in a museum of domestic agonies. The lights would be out. We'd be lying in our beds, ten feet from each other, and Joey would roll onto his side and talk to me in a voice without intonation. His father was a quiet man, he said, a driver for a bread-and-cupcake company, a person who just could not seem to save any money. He'd been an infantryman in World War II but had seen only a few days of combat. His mother "had some problems, too." She'd go three or four months as a perfectly sober wife and a good mother, and then walk out of the house one day as if she were going to buy groceries, and return with two bottles of sweet, cheap wine. She'd drink steadily through dinner, glass by glass, the rest of the family trying to pretend everything was fine. After dinner she'd sit at the table and work her way into the second bottle, usually getting about halfway to finishing it. She'd stand up then—it would be just before bedtime—and begin walking through the rooms of the house like a spirit, ranting about her life: that the kitchen was dark, that the front steps sagged, that grass wouldn't grow in the backyard, nothing would grow there, that they'd be stuck in that dark, sterile place for the rest of their lives, that her husband hadn't been able to save fifty cents in twenty-four years of marriage, that her children were doomed. On and on it would go in this flat, brutal tone, until one by one the rest of the family slipped off to bed. Joey would lie awake in the darkness, listening to her voice as, deprived of an audience, it slowly lost volume. Once she stopped talking, his mother would begin to pace back and forth across the kitchen. He'd listen to her footsteps on the linoleum, hear her compulsively rearranging the chairs, washing the rest of the second bottle down the sink, walking, coughing, muttering. Eventually she would turn on the radio, and when he heard the faint strains of jazz, he knew it was over for another few months. Next morning, he'd see an aspirin bottle on the windowsill over the sink, and his mother would hug him and his sister and send them off to school with peanut-butter sandwiches and chocolate Kisses in their lunch boxes.

"She builds it all up," he'd tell me. "She lets it all build up inside of her, Anth. Sweet all the time, sweet and sweet and sweet and the sweetest thing you can imagine. Other people let it out in little bursts. She builds it up."

The worst thing was, he said, that he could feel it in himself, that same sudden onslaught of sourness, that same urge to see nothing at all good in his life. "It gets passed down in the blood, Anth," he told me. "It beats you up, then it goes and beats up on your son or daughter, and their sons and daughters. I'm going to solve it, though. I'm going to MIT and become a research scientist, and I'm gonna find the gene for whatever this is called and figure a way to bleed it right out of people."

We had a physics class in common, a teacher named Mr. Strink, who stuttered and sprayed and walked around the lab compulsively knocking a pencil against the watchband on the inside of his wrist. We'd sit at the same table in the dining hall—breakfast, lunch, and dinner—complaining about the terrible food, finding hairs in it, pieces of newspaper, bits of buckshot, convinced the kitchen staff was out to poison us. For our fall sport we chose cross-country running—to get in shape for hockey, in my case; to stay in shape for winter track, in his—and would run together through the flat, sedate streets of the town, day after day, as the leaves turned orange and red and lay like quilts over the unfenced lawns, as the weather turned cool and rainy, then raw, then cold and sharp, as we made the transition from new boys to veterans.

If the workout consisted of sprints, I'd see Joey only from behind. But if it was a three- or four- or five-mile run, he'd jog along beside me for the first ten minutes or so. We'd make a little conversation between breaths. Then, at a certain point, he'd pat me on the shoulder, say, "See you in the showers," and pull effortlessly ahead, lifting his knees, swinging his skinny arms, gliding through the string of runners in front of me as if he were on skates and the rest of us were slogging through snowbanks in boots. College scouts from the best track schools in America knew his name, but he kept them at bay, and kept the varsity cross-country coach at bay as well. He did not want the pressure of a varsity sport just yet, he said. Indoor track would be fine in the winter season; he wanted a little breathing room first, some time to get used to this fancy East Coast life.

Physics, math, history, English, Russian, piano lessons, mandatory chapel, dormitory meetings, student council, chess club, rifle club, mixers, cross-country practice, hours and hours of homework—Exeter's way of dealing with the flaming hormones and nascent homesickness of a thousand boys was to keep them constantly busy. And, in my case, at least, the strategy worked. I was happy there.

Beyond the occasional mild disagreement with Joey or temporary trouble in a class, the only sour note for me in this new life was the absence of my favorite cousin. Rosalie never wrote, was never home when I called from the pay phone in the basement corridor, never came up to visit. Just after noon every other Saturday, Uncle Peter's Cadillac would appear in front of Amen Hall, and I'd always peer out the window hoping to catch a glimpse of her. My uncle would step out, tugging the lapels of his sport coat together and fastening one button; Nana Lia and Grandpa Dom—if he was feeling well that week—would climb out and look around as if surprised all over again by the lawns and groomed shrubbery, the well-mannered young men in neat clothing, the quietness and order and air of wealth. After some hugging and kissing, they'd take me, or more often Joey and me, to a restaurant we liked at the northern edge of town, and we'd eat half-pound hamburgers and hot-fudge sundaes and talk about home.

It got so I'd know when Uncle Peter was about to bring up the subject of Rosalie's absence. The meal would be finished, we'd be strolling down Main Street in the cool air, past the glass storefronts, he and I would pull ahead a few steps, and he'd say something like: "I don't know, Tonio. I don't know what's wrong. He's a piece a garbage, this kid she's runnin around with, you should see him. Big mamaluke. Doesn't look you in the eyes when he shakes hands, always snifflin and snortin, drives around with his music blastin, his shoulders down like this heah. She falls all over him. 'Come up and see your cousin,' I say to her on Friday nights. 'He misses you like you can't bleeve.' And she says she will, she'll be ready to go at ten-thirty on Saturday, she promises. And then ten-thirty on Saturday comes, and she's out, or sleepin, or in such a mood I don't want her to come with me anyway. I tell her be in by eleven, she comes in at one. I tell her study in school, she gets all Ds. I tell her, whatever else you do, never smoke, she smokes. She's in the house three, four minutes, then she's on the phone, out the door again, in the mamaluke's car, gone. I yell, we have talks. What I am suppose to do, spank her like her mother used to? What am I suppose to do?"

These conversations lay like stones in my pockets. I'd carry them around with me for days afterward. I'd write Rosalie upbeat letters filled with anecdotes about the boys I was getting to know, the food I was eating, the things I was learning, funny stories from the dorm, from class. I'd tell her to come up and bring me a sub sandwich from Rosa's, that I was shrinking away on the dining-hall food. All through September and October, I called Uncle Peter's house after dinner two or three nights a week, hoping to catch her, giving up, finally, after a night when I realized she was there, a few feet from the phone with a finger to her lips, shaking her head at her father.

One sour note.

❯

SO I BEGAN TO make myself not care so much about Rosalie. I practiced not caring about her, not thinking about her. It didn't help much. I believe we are joined to certain people in this life and that we have to live out our joint fates fully, squeeze every last drop of blood and tears and laughter out of the relationship, live and suffer with them until whatever cable it is that holds us gradually wears away and snaps. Rosalie has been dead for years now, and the cable has not broken; I still can't really make myself not care.

But my rich new life went on. I became accustomed to its rules and rigor, to the feeling of waking up in a strange bed in a brick building filled with people I barely knew. There were fresh layers to my sexual education: Mr. Pleverer loitering in the locker room after sports and staring into the showers; the piano teacher running a hand over my back once, in a lingering way, as I played my lessons for him in our weekly class; someone—Higgenbotham, we guessed—taping *Playboy* centerfolds up inside the door of the john. We stared out our windows at the teachers' daughters crossing the quadrangle toward their parents' apartments, as if we were staring at goddesses disguised in braids and backpacks.

I wrestled with Russian grammar and the laws of physics. On Thursdays I came to expect, in my post-office box, an envelope with my grandfather's handwriting on the front. Inside, there would always be a new five-dollar bill and one folded page of stationery with his wavering script: *"Caro Tonio, Qui tutto a posto, ma ci manchi molto."*

The campus was bounded to the east by playing fields, a river, and woods. Once or twice during the week and always on Sunday afternoons, I'd take walks there, stopping to sit on a stone or a fallen tree and reread Grandpa Dom's latest letter, to say a prayer for my father and mother, to try to find a way to push two worlds together inside me. Then I'd get up to wander the paths along the shore of the river, swinging out into unfamiliar territory, farther and farther away from the warm orbits I had known.

Four

THE WEEK OF THANKSGIVING marked the beginning of the winter sports season, and tryouts were held then for varsity and junior-varsity teams. Joey and I skittered nervously through our classes on the Monday of that week, our thoughts fleeing the somber avenues of eighteenth-century English literature for the terror and thrill of the track, in Joey's case, and the ice rink, in mine.

That Monday afternoon I walked with him in a light snow from the main quadrangle, across the campus, past Amen Hall, and up the long concrete ramp of the new sports complex. Even by New Hampshire standards it was a cold November day. An inch of fluffy snow had already accumulated; the soles of our shoes squeaked as we went. We were too nervous to say much. Others were making the same trip—a parade of boys, in hats or hooded jackets, walking alone or in small groups—with the same hopes. But for Joey and me I think there was an extra charge to that hour. Comfortable as we had grown at the Academy, there was still a way in which we had something to prove to ourselves. There was, still, a subtle demon living in us, something we'd carried there from coarser places, rougher places, places where people came of age feeling the little nagging spank of inadequacy. For Joey, naturally, the demon was an older, crueler one. It would have been easy for him to hear, in the proper accents that surrounded him at every moment of every day there, the voice of the oppressor. It would have been easy for him to read the word *nigger*—a word I heard spoken aloud at Exeter only two times—on the walls of the Academy Building, where the portraits of the white-faced principals of the school—1781 to the present day—hung in a neat row, where all the triumph and disgrace of American history seemed to rever-berate from the old walls. It would have been easy enough for me to re-member that fifteen friends in the Amen Hall Common Room had chanted, "Beat the Wop," while we watched a boxing match between the Italian champion Nino Benvenuti and the U.S. Virgin Islander Emile Griffith, and use that moment to fuel a kind of continuous victim fan-tasy. But Joey and I weren't made that way. We weren't angry young men, we didn't aspire to be; we wanted to succeed at Exeter for our own sakes, not as mascots for a beleaguered race or ethnic group.

Even so, on that cold afternoon, I believe we were carrying some small banner before us as we made the walk across campus. For some-one like Higgenbotham, there was, no doubt, the pressure of his lineage, a whole genealogy to live up to. For us it was wider than that. Failure—in sports especially—would hold a bit of extra pain in it. Coming from West Sacramento, coming from Revere, it would be one thing to carry home a report card with a few Cs on it; something else entirely to be chased off the playing fields.

I remember being in the middle of the elaborate dressing ritual that hockey requires—jockstrap and protective cup, shin guards, shoulder pads, the white athletic tape, and long knit stockings—when Joey came by my locker and tapped me on the shoulder. He was already dressed—in sweatpants and running shoes and a sweatshirt with JAMES MARSHALL WILDCATS on the front—and he had a deadly serious expression on his face, as if we were going into battle. My hands were sweating. I wiped my palm on the lucky red T-shirt my grandfather had bought me, and we shook hands, sternly, like three-quarter-sized men.

In order to reach the rinks from the locker room, you walked down a tunnel so new you could taste the concrete in the air. You passed through a set of glass fire doors and into another tunnel with benches along the walls and black rubber matting on the floor. You put on your skates there, lacing them up slowly so as not to cut off circulation to your feet, pushed your hands down into the huge scarred gloves, grabbed your stick, and waddled up toward the ice.

The sport of hockey has become associated now with bare-knuckle brawls and raving fans. But that is professional hockey, that's the corruption of money. On the college and high-school level, it was then, and still is, a sport of tremendous grace. There is contact, of course—the game would not be the same without it, and it helps to be rough and fearless—but the true heart of ice hockey is speed and awareness of others, not force. When I stepped onto the ice that day and took my first long strides, I felt released from the plodding pace of the walking world, half-freed from the chains of gravity, set loose in space. Two or three flexes of the leg muscles and I entered another universe, a quicker, smoother, more exciting zone in which sticks clacked against the glassy surface and pucks boomed against the boards, and the coach's whistle shrieked and echoed like the sharp cry of a hawk hunting a frozen canyon.

Coach Rislin threw handfuls of pucks out onto the ice from a burlap sack, and set to studying us as if we were objects in a medical experiment. Over the course of the next two afternoons, he ran us through skating drills, passing drills, shooting drills, sent us flying toward the net, two forwards against one defenseman, had us sprint from goal line to blue line, stop and sprint back, sprint to the red line and back, the opposite blue line and back, the opposite goal line and back, until we were huffing out clouds of vapor and pulling mouth guards from between our teeth to take in more air.

All the running I'd done that fall, all the afternoons spent shooting at Vito Imbesalacqua's plywood goalie, all the early-morning hours of Bantam, JV, and Varsity hockey at the MDC rink in Revere, the bruises and sprains, the little bursts of fear and elation, the awkward hours with Grandpa Dom holding the hood of my sweatshirt in the Public Gardens— all of that sailed around with me on the ice during those two days. It was as if I'd been studying a language for years, then traveled for the first time to the country where that language was spoken, and found I could make myself understood there without too much trouble. On the Wednesday before the holiday, we had only half a day of school. Just after the noon meal, Joey and I made the walk across campus again, climbed the ramp, went through the fire doors, and saw our names on the bulletin board under a heading that said, "The Following Students May Pick Up Varsity Gear from Ricky on the Monday After Thanksgiving Between 12:00 and 2:30."

It was a fine thing to be able to tell Uncle Peter on the way home.

He had something fine to tell me, too. "Good news, Tonio," he said, when we'd paid the five-cent toll and were heading south along the highway. "Rosie and I are moving in upstairs, over you and Grandma and Grandpa."

"What about your house?" I asked him, watching his face wrinkle and twitch and almost being able to read what he was hiding.

"Sold it," he said, squeezing the wheel so that the muscles of his forearm flexed. "I sold it last week. To the bank."

Five

I SAW ROSALIE THAT NIGHT. I'd been home less than an hour, just enough time to unpack my clothes and give my grandparents the latest news from school. She breezed through the back door, wrapped me in an exaggerated hug, and said, "Let's go, Tonio. Caesar wants to take you for a ride." Before I could really look at her, before I had a chance to ask what had been happening in her life, she had swept me out of the kitchen and into the front seat of Caesar Baskine's light-brown GTO.

In all eras and all places, there have been men whose only real talent is an instinct for physical intimidation, a love of inflicting pain. I have seen them in Russia, in Mexico, in drafty Canadian bars. I've watched them walking their tough-looking girlfriends down the sidewalks of down-at-the-heels Vermont factory towns. The anger in their bones links them across all geographic and political boundaries, all the centuries. They seem to be challenging the very air around them as they move, seem to take even the most passing, casual glance as a personal insult, holding their hands out away from their hips as if ready to draw from a holster. Apparently free of physical fear themselves (I wonder, though, if they aren't, in fact, ruled by it), they can sense it in others as surely as a thief senses an unlocked door.

This comes close to describing Caesar Baskine, though there were somewhat softer secondary characteristics that adorned his basic nature like flowers tattooed on a fist. I had known him slightly when I was growing up, had heard the stories about him—fighting stories mostly—seen him a few times standing on the corner with some of Revere's famously tough older boys. When I was still in junior high and spending a lot of time at the skating rink, he would occasionally make an appearance there and extort dimes and quarters from kids like me—younger, smaller souls—coming up close in front of you as you were carrying your skates to the door, putting a hand on your shoulder, giving a little push, and saying, with a fake-innocent expression and no offer of repayment, "Hey, how about loaning me some money for the bus?" With this approach he might make a dollar or two in the space of half an hour, but it wasn't really the money he was after. What he was after then, I'm sure, what he would chase for the rest of his life, was the sense of being large in the world—in the life of the city, in my cousin's life—as some kind of a balm for the fact that he seemed to himself, in his most private moments, so painfully small.

As soon as I pulled the door of his car closed, he reached across in front of Rosalie and smacked me, backhanded, on the breastbone, in what was at once a gesture of affection and a signal of physical superiority. You're one of us, the greeting announced. Here, get in line behind me. He had grown since the last time I'd seen him, not so much taller as wider—a square head on a square, thick neck, on rounded, muscular shoulders—and now he flaunted, in the unfortunate fashion of the day, a pair of reddish-brown sideburns that stood like bristled boots on his jawline. The front seat was lit by the street lamp. I could see a few days' worth of rusty beard on his chin, between the sideburn tips. And there was a lively, almost an overjoyed glint in his pale eyes, as if, after years of planning, he had finally recruited Rosalie's cousin over from the choirboy crowd to the forces of evil.

He wasn't evil, though, not really, at least not then. Mean perhaps, even sadistic, but the main force twisting him was a nastier version of what Uncle Peter suffered from: a barely concealed and desperate need to be thought well of. It was my only small advantage over him.

He pushed down on the accelerator and zipped his racing machine between the cars parked on both sides of Jupiter Street. At Mountain Avenue he did not so much stop as hover, pushing the nose of his GTO halfway into the traffic lane, making two cars coming down the hill left to right move out and around him, then screeching in behind the second of those cars and crawling up on the poor woman's bumper, gunning his engine with one foot on the clutch, swerving right and left, until, by the time we reached Mercury Street—five blocks—she was obliged to pull over and let him roar past.

Rosalie was pushed up close against him, leaving me unanchored on my half of the seat. I slipped my right hand down between the cushion and the door and held on, where they couldn't see. I pressed my feet into the floor mat whenever we tilted to a stop. We careened along Broadway to Revere Street and then down to the beach, running yellow lights as they went red, the half-muffled exhaust system bubbling and backfiring, the car rocking at stop signs as Caesar revved his 389-cubic-inch V-8.

It was 1969, but we cruised the Boulevard in classic fifties fashion. From time to time Caesar would see—or pretend to see—someone he knew, on the sidewalk or in a car going the opposite way, and he'd make a big show of flashing his headlights or sounding his *ah-oo-gah* horn. This would be followed by a glowing elaboration of his friend's credentials. "Johnny Mikelewski, best running back in the Greater Boston League," he'd say. Or: "Ernie Livinio's little brother. Beat the crap out of some Puerto Rican guy in Chelsea last week, sent him right to the friggin hospital."

"Great," Rosalie would say. "My hero." But her sarcasm had a lining of affection to it. Caesar would smirk and lift the back of his hand up near her face, as if he were barely holding himself back from striking her. Or as if he were giving my imagination something to work on in later years. Then he'd pinch her thigh, hard, and she'd squeal and wriggle and nuzzle up against his arm.

At the northernmost end of the Boulevard the amusements and food stands gave way to a row of comfortable brick houses with small lawns, and there was less light, fewer people. Caesar pulled the front of his car in tight against the hurricane wall and killed the engine. We got out.

It was a raw, blustery night, no moon. Caesar put one hand on top of the wall and swung his legs over; Rosie and I followed. We walked down the sand toward the water, where the lights from the Boulevard could not reach us, and I felt the neat quiet world of the Academy slip off my back like a linen shirt floating away on the wind. The staid classrooms, Joey Barnard, Coach Rislin tossing pucks onto the ice—those things might have belonged to a soft, fake life I had dreamed about one night.

We walked to the edge of the water and stared out over the splashing, whispering surf. Boston Light blinked there, a fickle star caught between the noisy blackness of the sea and the silent, white-spotted sky. Caesar reached inside his RHS football jacket and took out what looked like a hand-rolled cigarette. "Ever try it?" Rosalie said, turning to look at me for the first time.

"Try what?"

She tilted her face sideways and turned her lips down at me the way I'd seen her father do a hundred times. "Grass," she said impatiently. "Dope."

"No."

"You'll like it. It makes you calm."

I'm already calm, I wanted to say, but by then Caesar had lit the cigarette and, clamping his lips down on the trapped smoke, was tilting his head up and back in a stylized, thick-necked ecstasy. Rosalie mimicked him, I mimicked Rosalie. We passed the thing back and forth a couple of times, then Caesar tossed the tiny nub of it into the surf and said, "Hah!" very loudly.

The damp shoreline swirled and tilted. I turned away from them and walked south along the edge of the water, letting the cold waves lap against the soles of my sneakers, feeling the wind scraping my cheeks and bare hands. I had gone less than twenty yards when the row of streetlights curling off toward Winthrop took on a cast I can only describe now as angelic. Revere Beach had become a stage set for a mildly ecstatic vision, a vision empty of the ballast of pain I seemed to have been carrying around with me for centuries. The night was no longer cold. The past and the future fell away neatly, and I coasted through the narrow strip of present with such a sense of ease and joy that I forgave Rosalie immediately and completely for her association with Caesar Baskine. Why turn away from someone who offered this: six puffs that erased all the pain of the past?

I swung around and saw them there in the distance, kissing, her body pressed against his as if she wanted to be welded to the buttons of his shirt. Strangely then, I was overcome by an urge to pray. I went down on one knee in the damp sand, and looked up at the sky above Boston Light as if the Jesus of the nine o'clock Mass were floating there, waiting to offer a word. But there was no Jesus in the sky, and no words came to me. What came, instead, was a sense of my mother. There was no real image, certainly not an image of the last time I had seen her—burned, unconscious, wired up to the beeping machinery of the last hours of life—just a faceless, scentless, soundless memory of her essence, as if she were standing there behind or beside me, with her feet on the wet beach stones and wet strands of seaweed. Look at this, Ma, I seemed to be saying to her without actually speaking the words. Look at us now, torn there and here as if we had no blood connection at all. Tell us where we go now. Tell me who I go with.

Then I was walking back along the shore, closing in on the spectacle of Caesar groping my cousin in the cold wind. To divert them, I stuck my rear end out, jutted my chin up into the air, and said, as Higgenbotham liked to say it, "The Acahdemy. I am a student at the Acahdemy."

Caesar laughed, reached out to clap me on the back and nearly knocked me into the water. Rosalie took my elbow—I had been waiting for her to touch me—and led me up the soft slope, then seemed to change her mind. She drifted away, down the beach again. For a time, Caesar and I stood rooted in the sand, watching her. Then we floated over to the hurricane wall, leaned back against it, and immersed ourselves in a dull, quiet reverie. I was dimly aware of the surf, the cars swishing past at our backs, Rosalie's coat swinging toward us down the beach and then passing by in front of me close enough to touch.

"It's *freezing!*" she screamed, falling into Caesar's lap like a starlet. She turned her eyes to me, and in them was something so close to hatred that even through the drug it hit me like a slap. She held on to him, one of his knees to either side of her. He pulled a set of keys from his jacket pocket and dangled them in front of her face. "Run up and start the Gee-Toe, Rosie," he said.

"Right, boss. Yes, massah."

When she'd gone, Caesar and I walked a little ways down the beach, aimlessly, twenty feet apart, flinging stones in the general direction of the surf, kicking shells, then, finally, making a wide loop back toward the car. The first elation of the drug had already given way to something arid and sour. My head was aching, the steel needles of Rosalie's eyes were still lodged in me.

"So how is it, that school?"

"Pretty good."

"Pretty good? You left Revere High hockey for friggin *pretty good?*"

"They have three football fields. Five basketball courts. Two hockey rinks."

"Big shit."

"You'd like it," I said, though even through the remnants of the drug, the idea was utterly absurd to me, comical, farcical. I pictured Caesar Baskine in Mr. Goodyear's history class and could not keep a short, mean laugh from bubbling out of me.

He seemed to know I was laughing at him, seemed to have been expecting it. He shoved me once in the shoulder, not very hard, and said, "Your cousin can be a cunt, know that?"

The word fell against my ears like a club. I walked on a few steps. I wanted to hit him. I wanted to have him out on the ice with me so I could skate circles around him, put the blade of my stick between his skates and lift it up, hard, into his groin; trip him as he skated toward the goalpost, or send him crashing into the boards. "You're lucky she has anything to do with you," I said.

"Yeah?"

"You know it, too. You're the cunt."

"Screw you," he said, but with palpable affection.

"You're a big dumb piece of shit; you have a barbell for a friggin brain. Your face looks like a hamburg somebody forgot to cook." I had no idea what I was doing, talking to him like that. In another setting, he might have swung his fist into my teeth and left me lying there in a pool of my own blood, but I had accidentally struck the right note with him. I was speaking his language, spitting fearlessness into his face. He loved me for it.

"Screw you, Einstein," he said tenderly. "You friggin Jew."

We went on a few paces, close to the seawall by then. I could see Rosalie sitting in the front seat of the car, looking at herself in the rearview mirror, playing with a strand of hair. This way? That way? Which way will he like it better?

"You guys get to know each other on the beach?" she said.

"He's no queer," Caesar answered, as if I'd been tested, and managed a passing grade. "He's okay, the friggin Jew."

Rosie laughed.

Caesar's crude assessment of her rattled in my brain as we drove through the dark marshland near Oak Island and back toward my grandparents' house. Rosalie sat between us, one hand on top of his thigh. She lit another cigarette, blew a stream of smoke against the dashboard. No one spoke. We were all cool. Not a Jew or a queer among us.

By the time we made a last screeching turn onto Jupiter Street, the sourness of Rosalie's cigarette smoke had slithered down into my stomach. Caesar pulled the car to the curb.

"Thanks for the ride," I said. Rosalie laughed, glanced at me, looked away when I hugged her. Caesar crushed my hand. "You're okay," he said.

"Great car."

I waited there until the taillights disappeared onto Park Avenue. I went down the walk at the side of the house, stumbled down the small half step that led into the backyard, and stood there holding on to one of the grapevine posts. After a few minutes I stepped into the garden and vomited twice onto the frozen stalks of the tomato plants. There were lights on in the kitchen. I sat out under the grapevine, spitting, rubbing a sleeve across my mouth, letting the last of the sourness drift away. I thought about my mother, about the feeling I'd had on the beach, the sense of her. It seemed to me then that it held some key to the night, to Caesar and Rosalie and me, and to why I had stopped loving this place. But I could not quite get my fingers around it and turn it in its lock. I bent forward and looked back up over my shoulder, past the edge of the grapevine to the dark windows on the second floor, and struggled to remember her face and her body as they had actually been—the small space between her front teeth, the hair pulled up and back from her forehead, the freckles near her ear, the muscles of her calves. Now, though, all of that was mixed up with Caesar's words, with my cousin's hand on his leg, with a dozen images from Higgenbotham's magazines, and Amen-Hall-smoking-room comments about faculty daughters.

After a while the cold air reached me, and I climbed the back steps into the kitchen, closing the door a little too loudly. My grandfather came out from his bedroom. He took hold of my elbow briefly as he passed, telling me, quietly, to sit. Without its leaves, the table was an ordinary-sized piece of furniture, covered with a plastic cloth and supporting a centerpiece of plastic fruit in a raised white dish. Dom had his slippers on. He opened a cupboard and took out an unlabeled jug of red wine, uncorked it, poured two glasses. Whenever we had family gatherings at that table, the custom was that the adults were served full glasses of wine, and the cousins were served wine mixed with what we called "orangeade." For the youngest, it was pure orange soda; for those in grade school, orange soda mixed with a spoonful of wine, swirling like blood in a glass of neon orange. Only the older cousins were served more wine than soda, and looking down along the table, you could guess our ages by the color of the drink in front of us. You could read there who could drive and who was allowed to go out on dates, and who still had before them the great adventure of crossing over from the continent of childhood to some new land of kisses and speeding cars.

With the deliberateness of a priest at the altar, my grandfather set the two glasses of wine on the table in front of him, went to the refrigerator, poured into my glass no more than a capful of soda, and set it carefully before me. The mixture seemed too dark for me. I looked up at him, and he was sitting straight-spined, lips pressed tight, the satin lapels of his bathrobe lying unwrinkled on his thin, flat chest. He seemed to pray over the wine for a moment before the lenses of his eyeglasses swung slowly up to me.

"Bevi," he said quietly. Drink.

When I had swallowed a sip, he said, still in Italian, and almost as if he were talking to an adult, *"Allora, raccontami comè la tua vita là."* Alright, tell me about your life there.

We sat at the table until just before midnight, two hours past his usual bedtime, and I told him everything: what I was studying in each class, what the teachers were like; how Mr. Luckey, during a discussion of Conrad's *Victory,* had tried to cure a boy named Braithwaite from saying *Eye*-talians; how, the night before vacation, when the Academy bell struck twelve, we all opened our windows and screamed out over the dark quadrangle, howling, barking, making the sounds of chickens and donkeys until Mr. Williams came out, and the police drove up from town, and one by one we quieted down and slipped back into bed. I told him about Joey, his running and his moods; about the hockey tryouts and Higgenbotham's pinups covering the wall of his room, hidden—when his parents visited—by a discreetly tacked-up tapestry he claimed had been in his family since before the Civil War. The weather, the food, the sound of the Academy bell tolling out the hours over the cold campus, the way I would take the money he sent me and walk to the sub shop in town after dinner to fill my belly, the way we would sometimes stand in the stairwell near one of the faculty apartments and listen to Mr. Williams and his wife screaming at each other; the mixers with Brookles Country Day and the Pennyworth School, girls pressing their chests against the front of your sport coat when you danced to a slow song, the feel of their hair against your cheek, the smell of their skin.

"Have you kissed one yet?" he asked me simply, straightforwardly. *Ne hai gia baciata una?*

"Non ancora."

"Perché?"

"I don't know why. I'm shy with them still."

"Alright. You won't always be. You need that other half of you to make the life right. Every man needs the woman half in his life. Almost every man needs it." He nodded at his own words, swirled the last two drops of wine in his glass, then drank, set the glass down directly in front of him, moved his hands out to either side a few inches and then brought them in again, slowly, tenderly, fingers outstretched against the sides. "Like this you want to hold them when the time comes," he said. *"Cosí."*

❯

I CHANGED INTO MY PAJAMAS, brushed my teeth, walked back to my small monk's room with its bookshelves, statues of saints, and pictures of my parents, and I pulled the covers up over my chest. The wind whistled in the leaves of the Sawyers' maple trees and against the eaves of the house. The wine ran warmly in my hands. I brought them up together above my body, holding them a few inches apart as if there were a glass there, and then wider.

Six

AFTER THE TRADITIONAL FOOTBALL GAME against Winthrop (Caesar with his seven unassisted tackles and two penalties for unnecessary roughness; the cheerleaders cartwheeling in the cold so that their underpants showed, then bouncing up and shouting, "We're from Revere, and no one could be prouder, and if you don't believe us, we'll say it even louder! WE'RE FROM REVERE, AND NO ONE COULD BE PROUDER!"), after the turkey and lasagna and the rounds of dessert, coffee, and talk, Rosalie and I put on our coats and hats and walked the grid of streets, block by block, the way we liked to do on that holiday.

There were flakes of snow in the air, kicking sideways in a fickle wind, and the city was quiet and still, so that I felt my old love for it swirling and rising around me. The houses and the yards were miniature worlds—fenced in, closed in, private, mysterious, and yet, at the same time, connected to the life of the street, sharing a common, humble fate. Green shingles, gray clapboards, white window trim, TV antennas, statues of the Virgin, the pocked green cinder-block wall of the football stadium—all of it seemed to be singing to me: "We're from Revere, and no one could be prouder!"

I wondered if Rosalie could hear it. I wondered if she ever thought about the other part of the cheer: "And if you don't believe us, we'll say it even louder! WE'RE FROM REVERE!" Why assume that a listener wouldn't believe it? Or that saying it louder would convince him? Why were the Exeter cheers all "Rah . . . rah . . . hail to the grand old school" types of things, straight off the playing fields of Eton, dry and empty as a verse from an out-of-date hymnal in a dim colonial chapel? One shore was jumbled, raucous, and lit up with glaring insecurities and a desperate, infectious pride. The other was orderly as arithmetic, closed, staid, too certain of itself. I wondered then if Rosalie, if anyone in Revere, if anyone in the world other than Joey Barnard, had any good advice about how to keep a ship afloat in the rough waters between.

"What was that look you gave me?" I asked her at the top of Mercury Street.

"What look?"

"Last night, on the beach. You looked at me like you hated me."

"You were acting phony."

"How?"

"You were pretending you liked Caesar."

"He seems like a pretty good guy."

"Stop it, Tonio. I know you can't stand him. You're phony now since you went away to that school. You even talk different. You have niggers for friends."

The word burst against my ears, like *cunt*, like *guinea*, all the vicious syllables we reserve for the Other. I had heard it often enough in Revere, but never on Rosie's lips, and I went along a few steps with my eyes straight ahead and my hands clenched in my pockets. "Saying nigger to them is just like someone saying guinea or greaseball to us," I managed, when I had calmed down a bit.

"So what?"

"So, treat other people the way you want them to treat you."

"Yes, Father."

"His name's Joey. He's my best friend there. I'm going to bring him home some weekend. You say that word around him, and I'll take Caesar outside and kick his ass in front of everybody."

"Right. You look like a stringbean next to him. He'd beat you to a pulp with one finger."

"And that's the most important thing, right?"

"See what a phony you are now? You want it both ways. You want to beat up Caesar, and you want it not to be important that you *can* beat up Caesar, which you never could in a million years anyway. Who are you,

Tonio? What are you, a boy in a magic-show act, a little different costume every day depending on who you're with?" She leaned her head
back and laughed, in a way that seemed borrowed and almost cruel. Two
snowflakes fell on her face and immediately melted. Her eyes were
closed, her mouth open, and her black shining hair was caught in the
collar of her coat and bent upward in a curl. For that instant, she looked
like a grown woman in terrible pain. "Next thing you know you'll be
hanging around with queers," she said.

. "Why all the meanness all of a sudden?" I said. "What did I do?"

"Nothing."

"You never used to talk like this before."

"I'm just joking, it's a joke. Don't be a girl about it."

On Mars Street, a man in a T-shirt stood in his front yard, teasing a
German shepherd with scraps of turkey meat. Snowflakes landed on his
bare arms, but the pain of the cold did not seem to reach him; or possibly
it reached him and was indistinguishable from the pain of the rest of his
life, unremarkable. He was holding his right arm out, jerking the hand
upward a few inches whenever the dog leapt for his treat. "Work for it,"
he said. "Come on, Sinatra. Want it." His wife stood behind the storm
door in her housedress, a glint of wry admiration on her face. The man
ignored her, ignored us as we passed.

"You could go out with any boy in the whole high school," I said,
pressing all my weight down against the urge that was rising up in me,
an urge to hurt her back.

"That's right, I could. And I picked him."

"Why?"

"Why? Because he has a nice car, I like his face, I like the way he
kisses. And he doesn't pretend I'm pretty."

"You are pretty. You're beautiful, Rosie, like your mother was."

"Right, thanks."

"It's true."

"Thanks for the comparison."

She pulled a quarter step ahead of me.

"Where is she, do you know?" I asked.

"Do I care?"

"Does she even write or anything?"

"Do I want to talk about her, Tonio?"

There was a small brick hospital just opposite the top of Mars Street, on the other side of Mountain Avenue. The smell of cooked turkey was floating out through the kitchen vents, but there was something oily and sour about it, something deathlike. "I came up to your house once," I said. I had been squeezing the words away from my lips for half a block. "Your mother was in your room, she—"

"I don't want to hear it, Tonio. I don't want to think about her. I don't want to talk about her ever again, that's all. She should have died. I would have been happier if I came home that day and it was her dead body there on the kitchen table instead of the note."

"She left you a note?"

"I *don't . . . want . . . to . . . talk . . . about it*, Tonio."

"What did it say? You never told me."

"Tonio, *stop!*"

I stopped. We reached the top of Jupiter Street and headed down the short hill, wrapped in a silence that was as different from our old silences as the skin on an old woman's face is different from her granddaughter's. We passed DeRosa's yard, Achenbach's, Zwicker's, Sawyer's, Famigletti's. When we reached our grandparents' house, her house now, Rosalie touched me on the shoulder, not unkindly, and said, "Go the rest of the way alone, okay?"

"Rosie, come on."

"I didn't mean that about your friend. I don't ever use that word."

"Why did you say it then?"

"I don't know, I'm confused now. My head is confused."

"Rosie, talk to me. Come with me. We always go as far as Pluto Street on Thanksgiving. We've been doing that since you were eight and I was six and a half. I have to have somebody to talk to here, about things, I—"

She kissed me on the lips, sprinted up the steps, and disappeared through what had once been the front door of my parents' house.

❦

THERE WERE CARS PARKED along the curbstones on both sides, as always, and the houses were quiet on that holiday, though you could sense people inside, families around a table, men propped up in front of a television, watching football. I walked as far as Pluto Street and then kept going, angling down Dale Street past the Jehovah's Witness Temple, past the wrapping-paper factory with the sagging roof, along Fenno Street to Page to Olive. My mother's friend Lois Londoner lived there. She and my mother had both been trained as physical therapists, and had met in the years before I was born, when they worked at the Walter Reed Hospital in Washington, and then at the Soldiers' Home on the hill in Chelsea. I knew Lois had had a stroke a few years before, and as I walked, the idea came into my mind that she might be alone on the holiday and want some company. I did not feel like going back to my grandparents' house, in any case. For once, I did not want to be around the other Benedettos. I do not know why.

Lois answered the door in her housecoat, pressed her trembling cheek against mine. She invited me in and immediately began setting out plates of various desserts on the table. She said she'd cooked a Thanksgiving meal for old friends, but there was no evidence of it in the room, no smells of turkey and stuffing, no dirty plates in the sink. There were six or eight birdcages in the kitchen, and a few more in the corridor that led to her dining room. Parakeets, a toucan, two parrots. From time to time, as she shuffled around opening bags of cookies and splashing them onto plates, cutting ragged slices of boxed cake, I would hear a squawk or the batting of feathers against thin metal bars. The parrot was the only real noisemaker. *"Who's there? Who is it?"* he would screech, a deaf old man shouting into a telephone receiver.

"It's Anthony," Lois said, exactly as if she were talking to a friend, and it occurred to me that the only Thanksgiving dinner she had prepared was the one she'd fed to her birds. "Anna's son."

"Who's there? Who is it?"

"Anthony Benedetto."

"Who's there? Who is it? Who?"

Between his cackling questions, I could hear the clock ticking steadily in the parlor. Lois poured me milk from a glass quart bottle, and her hands shook so much that a little bit of it spilled on the tablecloth. In a moment she was next to me again with a yellow sponge, the impulses going from brain to hand in broken bursts, so that she jerked the sponge awkwardly over the spill and nearly bumped the full glass off the table.

We sat and made small talk for a while. I told her about Exeter, about that day's football game, about the aunts, uncles, and cousins she knew. She listened eagerly, pushing the various dishes a quarter of an inch left or right or closer to me, as if I might not have seen them. After a short while, the conversation ran out of gas and coasted to a stop against one wall.

"Who's there? Who is it?"

I was concentrating hard on the cookies and milk, scraping my brain for new things to say. I could feel her watching me.

"Your uncle comes to visit," she said at last, and I looked up.

"Which one?"

"Peter. He never stays very long. He'll show up at the front door, ringing the bell, and by the time I get there he'll be looking this way and that way, peeking in through the curtains, shuffling his feet. He always brings a fresh loaf of bread or some macaroons from the bakery on Broadway, but you have to practically pay him to come in and sit down. I don't think he's ever yet finished a cup of coffee I made him, then he's up and kissing me, saying he has to go, has to meet somebody, has to get his car fixed, has to get some little something done at the dentist."

"He's like that," I said, and I heard the words echoing across time. I saw my mother at the kitchen counter with her hands dusted in flour, saw her turn and look at me over her shoulder. *He's like that, Anthony.* In her voice there had been the same species of frustration I now felt with Rosalie. *She's like that.* She moves, dances, keeps herself always just beyond the reach of your arms, of your affection, as if she believes that, at its deepest levels, love is nothing but a sticky trap, a death sentence.

Because I couldn't stand the silence pressing in against us, I blurted out, "I had the feeling sometimes my mother didn't like him."

"*Who's that? Who's there?*"

"No, she liked him. Who couldn't like him?"

"Nobody," I said quickly.

"But she was worried about the influence he had on your father. She brought your father back to life, you know, right back from the dead. When she met him in the hospital, he was a broken man. He never talked to you about what he saw in the war, did he?"

"No."

"He was wounded very badly. Did he tell you that?"

"My mother did, once. Wounded in the knees, she said."

"Feet, knees, and his back. And he'd already spent four months at the Walter Reed and hadn't really gotten much better. He didn't want to get out of bed to do his therapy, didn't want to see any visitors. He used to wake up in the middle of the night on the ward and scream and scream and then sit there, bolt upright, shaking worse than I'm shaking now. She'd come in and calm him down. But in the daytime she'd talk tough to him, wouldn't take any funny business. 'Time for your exercises now, Augustine. This isn't summer camp,' she'd say. 'Your life's ahead of you, not behind you. Show me what you're made of now. Just get up and walk through the feelings and do what the doctor told you to do.'

"He was angry at first, and stubborn. And then, little by little, you could see him falling in love with her. Before they could be released, the patients used to have to go out into town to prove they could get by in the world—prove that they could walk, reach around and take the wallet out of their back pockets, get on and off a trolley car, that they were stable enough, mentally, you know. At first, she used to go out on these pretend dates with him and act like it was a duty, but you could see she was falling in love. Your father was such a handsome specimen of a man, for one thing. And once all that shadow came away from his face, once he started to walk again and get out in the sunlight again, he was like a regular movie star. We were all a little bit in love with him.

"When they got married, your mother made him promise to move out of Revere within three years, but he never could do that. He never could have left his brother, for one thing."

"Why?"

"Why? Because he felt sorry for Peter, I guess, because he worried that he wouldn't survive if they left him—"

"No, why did she want him to move out?"

"Because she thought there were better places for children to grow up. And she worried what might happen to your father if he stayed in the city, working at that factory. The noise, the commotion. She worried that if he kept spending so much time with Peter, you'd never have enough money to move out. She and your father used to take drives up to Newburyport on Sundays when you were a baby, and she always said that was where she wanted to live, out in the country. It was her idea, you know, for you to go away to a school like where you're going."

"No, it was my grandfather's."

"Your grandfather got it from your mother, believe me."

"No, he heard it from someone he was in the hospital with, a hockey player."

She looked at me for a long time, folded the fingers of her shaking hands together. "Your grandfather's a very smart man, Anthony, the way your uncle is. Smarter than he pretends to be."

"What do you mean?"

"I don't mean anything, but it was your mother who used to talk about you going away to school, about you being something nobody else around here has ever been."

"There are doctors here," I said. "Lawyers. There are some rich people in Revere."

"Rich wasn't what she had in mind. Doctor wasn't, either. She'd seen enough of doctors, believe me, not to want one in the family."

"What then?"

"Just different, inside yourself. A different kind of man. She used to come down here and have lunch with me sometimes when you were in school and I didn't have to go to work until three o'clock. Different was what she wanted for you. Some other place, some other way. She never said specifically."

IT WAS DARK BY THE TIME I left her house, Lois's kindness and loneliness and the courage with which she bore her fate all tugging at me for the first few blocks.

Instead of retracing my steps, I took the longer, flatter way home— Fenno Street to Broadway to Park Avenue—adjusting my past as I went. *Who's there? Who is it? . . . A different kind of man.* Later that night, in as casual a tone as I could manage, I asked my grandfather what was the name of the professional hockey player he'd been in the hospital with, but all he said was, "That's too long ago now, Tonio, for me to remember."

Seven

WE HAD A STRONG TEAM that season—my Upper Middle year, as they call the junior year at Exeter. Higgenbotham played second defense; I was the left wing on the third line; and we had a Lower Middler goalie named Giorgio Cabanhas, who would one day be named All-America at Cornell. Because four of his stars had graduated the previous June, Coach Rislin liked to refer to that season as a rebuilding year, but we won four of our first six games, and went into the Andover game at the end of the season with a record of ten wins and four losses.

The Phillips Academy at Andover and the Phillips Exeter Academy are sometimes confused with each other, though they are not connected in any real way. They were founded by cousins—Henry and John Phillips—in 1778 and 1781. They attract the same kinds of students, their campuses resemble each other to a certain extent, and they're less than an hour apart, one in northeastern Massachusetts and the other in southeastern New Hampshire. There is a two-hundred-year-old rivalry between them: at Exeter, in the area of sports, a win over Andover carries as much weight as the rest of the season's games combined.

Uncle Peter had been to most of our home games that year, sometimes bringing Uncle Leo and Aunt Eveline and one or two of the younger cousins along. He would sit at center ice, in the top row of the concrete benches, and feel no compunction at all about standing up at quiet moments and shouting, "Antonio Benedetto!" at top volume. It embarrassed me the first few times. I don't think Rosalie was right in saying I had turned into a different person since going to Exeter, a phony person. But I had been made aware that there was a more restrained way of doing things, and shouting out your nephew's name in public did not exactly fit in with that. When I scored my first goal—it was against Choate in the second period of a runaway victory—I skated back to the bench out of breath and happy, and, after a few seconds, felt someone thumping me from behind. It was my uncle. He'd run down through the crowd and was leaning far out over the wooden partition that separated players from fans, and he was hitting me on my shoulder pads, hard, with both hands. Coach Rislin half-turned toward him and twisted up one side of his mouth, but that subtle hint was like a child's whispering in the noisy circus of Uncle Peter's affection. When I turned around I was looking directly at the top of his bald head. His face was tilted up toward me, the eyes lifted against the edges of the lids, the big nose sticking forward and down. The strain of the awkward position had caused the blood to run into his face, and his old boxing scars stood out against his pink skin like tiny porcelain chips. It was an astounding face, really, the face of an old warrior, at once humble and magnificent, ugly and resplendent. At that moment, held out like that into the territory of the players and coaches, it was a glowing coal of triumph, as if my little victory had reignited all of Uncle Peter's youthful glory in the ring and we were linked now, standing together victorious above the hurt that, for the last 150 years, had been flung at every immigrant who ever set a tattered valise down on American soil.

All that winter I waited for him to bring my grandfather to one of the games. Grandpa Dom had seen me play at Revere High, but I wanted him to see me at Exeter, in the elegant uniform—maroon with white numerals—a better player now, and at home in the big new world into which he'd propelled me.

But that winter my grandfather's trim vitality began to abandon him. He'd been in and out of Massachusetts General Hospital four times with chest pains, and I lived with the constant fear that I would never see him again. Two nights before the Andover game, I called home. Uncle Peter answered, said Grandpa was resting, that he wanted to come to the game but the doctors wouldn't allow it.

"Is he okay?"

"Sure. He's just resting, Tonio."

"Really?"

"Natchrally really. What do you think, I'm makin it up?"

"He's not dead?"

"What, dead? What's the mattah with you? The pressure goin to your brain up theah? Lissen, let the nervousness make you stronger, alright? Let it be like gas in a car. There's gonna be scouts in the stands. It might make the difference between gettin into Hahvahd, you know, and havin to settle for somethin less."

The locker room on that Saturday was quiet as a wake. We dressed in silence, Coach Rislin pacing back and forth with his clipboard and maroon wool jacket with EXETER sewn on the back in large letters, the smell of concrete and liniment in the air, the sound of sticks clattering, locker doors slamming.

When you first step out onto new ice it is very slick and fast. There are no blade marks to slow down the puck, and passes come at you like black artillery rounds. We went through our regular pregame drills, passing, shooting, making plays, skating together in a large circle, then crowding around our goalkeeper and slapping him on the helmet, or knocking our sticks against his shin pads, for luck. When the horn sounded, the starting six stayed out on the ice, and the rest of us banged through the gate and took our places on the bench, clouds of breath in front of our faces, sticks upright between our knees, little twists of nervous energy skipping about in the belly. In a slow moment during one of the drills, I'd glanced up at the back of the grandstand, hoping to see my uncle there. Joey Barnard raised an arm in salute; I answered by raising my stick. But there was no family. So in the quiet, tense seconds before the puck was dropped, it was a surprise to hear the sound of my uncle's voice yelling out, "BEH-NEH-DEH-TOE!" One or two of my teammates looked at me and grinned over their mouth guards. The "oh-oh-oh" echoed around the concrete arena. The game began.

Andover had lost only twice that year. They were solid through all three lines, but had two exceptional players—a first-line center from Quebec named Andrew Boldeaux, and a defenseman named Jacob Mellmann.

Mellmann also played middle linebacker on the football team, and his style in both sports was similar: hit, hit, hit. He was, I suppose, a sort of more-polished, better-educated version of Caesar Baskine. That week in practice, Coach Rislin had made Higgenbotham take on the role of Mellmann. Higgenbotham had worn a blue practice jersey, and had made a sincere effort to intimidate us, throwing his thin shoulders into people, tripping, hooking, even tackling me once when he knew I had him beaten.

Higgenbotham was no Mellmann, we all knew it. For a defenseman especially, he was a bit on the timid side. But the exercise accomplished two things at once: it gave Higgenbotham more confidence that he could knock people over occasionally without costing us goals, and it broke down the exaggerated picture of Mellmann we'd built up in our minds.

Still, deflated reputation or no, he was an impressive sight: legs like tree trunks, a thick waist, and a pair of shoulders you don't often see on high-school hockey players. He was a deceptively quick skater, too. Whenever I wasn't on the ice, I studied him, but I couldn't find any weakness in his game. He never rushed the puck, preferring to hang back and latch on to our forwards as they came into his zone. He'd fall back, fall back, draw the forward in, then, abruptly, the distance between them would close and Mellmann would be stepping up with a shoulder and perfect balance, knocking Eddie Westin or Michael Courtman to the ice and sweeping the puck away with an air of cleaning up a small mess after having chased the riffraff out of his mother's backyard.

Boldeaux was a player of a different sort, an artist, a magician, light as a leaf on his feet. He spun, he twisted, he feinted and deked, the puck glued to the blade of his stick as he sprinted his glorious zigzags up through the middle of the ice. The scouting report on Boldeaux was that he relied more on his moves than his shot, which was mediocre, so the strategy was to keep him outside a certain radius and make him shoot from there at our acrobatic Cabanhas. We managed to do that for the first period, and it ended in a scoreless tie. The locker room was silent, as before, the syllables of Coach Rislin's terse sermon falling on us like beads of sleet.

In the early part of the second period, the center on my line, Andy de Vetterling, knocked the face-off between the legs of the Andover center. I had cut diagonally across behind him—a play we'd worked on in practice—and I caught the puck on my blade and went over the blue line with only Mellmann between me and the goal. I skated straight at him, faked left, slipped the puck neatly between his feet, and was most of the way around his right side when he took an extra skip-step, an improbable ballet move for someone that size, and drove his shoulder pad into my helmet. I went down face-first and slid into the boards, hard, getting a glove up in front of me at the last second. Stars, a whistle, the hot, sweet taste of blood. I lay there letting the world spin and the pain rise and rise and then begin to fall away. In a moment I could see the ceiling lights, then a circle of swirling faces. Bill Liston, the trainer, was kneeling next to me, wiping blood away from the top of my lip and pinching my nose gently between his thumb and second finger to see if it was broken. I sat up, was helped to my feet. "BEH-NEH-DEH-TOE!" I heard from the top of the arena, but it was like someone else's name being called through thick seaside air. Held by both arms, I wobbled back to the bench through a fog of dizziness and pain, and sat out the rest of the period, leaning my head forward into a bag of ice and spitting blood onto the rubber mat between my feet. I can't say much about that period, except that it ended, again, in a 0–0 tie. During the intermission, Mr. Liston worked on me some more, checking for a concussion, plying me with aspirin and water, applying bags of ice, massaging the back of my neck. By the time the horn sounded, I was clear-eyed again, and steady on my feet.

Boldeaux hit the post twice that day. Six minutes into the third period, he took the puck from his own blue line, shifted and spun through half our team, made a fool of Higgenbotham with a left-left move no one had ever seen before, went in alone on Cabanhas, faked right, flipped the puck to his forehand, and fired a wrist shot that banged loudly off the pipe and caromed straight out front. Cabanhas covered up until the whistle blew, then lay there an extra few seconds, composing himself. The contingent of Andover fans cheered and howled at the brilliance of it, the bad fortune, and for a little while after that we stumbled and slipped around the ice like beaten boys.

With three minutes left to play, my line skated on to take a face-off in our own zone. My head had cleared completely, leaving only some swelling and a small throbbing in the middle of my face. Someone had tossed an orange peel onto the ice, and as the referee cleared it up and checked to see that there were no scraps left anywhere, I heard my uncle shout, "Tonio, Tonio, Tonio! Grandpa's here!" I barely kept myself from looking up. The puck was dropped, we cleared it, and for another minute and a half chased it back and forth in center ice. We were near the end of our last shift and very tired, all of us; everyone on the ice was tired. Chaz Metier fought with an Andover player on the right wing, kicked the puck loose, chased after it in a burst of energy, captured it, looked up, fed it across ice to me. I was already moving toward the goal—one of the best things I'd been taught in the Revere hockey program was to always be in motion so that if the puck did come my way I'd have some momentum and might catch the defense flat-footed. Which is more or less what happened. I was moving when the puck reached me, tapping into some last reserve of energy. One stride and I was across the blue line, Mellmann right there. He'd been on the ice for probably 60 percent of the game and was exhausted, half a step slower than he might otherwise have been. I crossed my right skate over my left and took the puck diagonally away from him, toward the left corner. Just as he shifted his weight, I reached the puck forward and slid it behind the heel of his stick and across in front of the toe of his left skate. Metier was streaking for the net there. He took the pass, skated two strides, and lifted a perfect wrist shot over the goalie's stick-side arm and into the left upper corner of the net. The red light flashed, the arena exploded in cheers, horns, and stamping feet, and we wrestled Chazzy to the ice and pounded him black and blue.

With something like ten seconds to go, Boldeaux made another of his astonishing runs, swerving, shifting the puck all the way across from far left to far right without even glancing down. When Courtman tried to pin him against the boards, he spun completely around in midair, some-how keeping his feet, recovered the puck, and moved straight in. He beat the other defenseman, had an open shot from fifteen feet out, half-beat Cabanhas, too. But Giorgio managed to get a piece of his glove on the shot, lifting its trajectory enough so that it clinked off the crossbar and banged into the glass behind. Boldeaux chased it, madly, furiously, and the horn sounded, ending the game. As we poured off the bench and onto the ice, I held back for one small moment, looked up at the scoreboard to fix it in my memory, then turned and searched for my grandfather in the cheering crowd. I found him this time, two rows down from Uncle Peter's usual place, between my uncle and Joey Barnard. Uncle Peter was hugging and kissing them, bouncing up and down like a boy, but my grandfather was facing straight forward, staring at me, one of his gloved hands held out in a loose fist in front of him. For a second or two, I could see my father there, in my grandfather's posture and in his face.

IT'S NOT A VERY IMPORTANT THING, I know, a tiny triumph like that. Much as some athletes and fans like to think so, sports is not the same as life. There are lessons you can learn, sure, but the stakes are never as high. Still, it can sometimes happen that there is a crucial interior puzzle a person is working through, and it gets solved in an exterior event—one spark of grace in a high-school hockey game, a painting that turns out just right, a lucky conversation with a friend. Occasionally now, in certain moods, struggling in my studio, cleaning up after an unproductive day when all the nasty demons have been singing in my ears—that making faces on canvas is a waste of time in a world where people are hungry and poor, that I have no special contribution to make in any case, no special talent, that the pool from which I draw is only a muddy puddle at the far edge of the truly important things—at such moments, sometimes without trying to, I remember my grandfather's face and gesture on that afternoon at the Exeter rink, and it lifts me up a little bit.

Eight

I WONDER SOMETIMES WHAT would have become of my cousin Rosalie if she'd had a couple of triumphs like that in her high-school years. Not sports or academic success necessarily, but any little bright moment she might have held on to and looked back at from time to time. I wonder if those kinds of exterior successes aren't, at least partly, a substitute for something else; if we seek glory in politics or sports or business or the arts only in order to fill what is really an interior void. The empty place where a mother's love should have been, for instance. Once, only once, in her cocky, bulletproof, pretend-nothing-hurts voice, Rosie said to me, "I think Caesar's a substitute for something, Tonio. I think drugs are a substitute, and sex, and everything." But though I prodded and pushed her and made a nuisance of myself, that was as far as she'd go.

The rest of that year went smoothly for me. I took a driver's education class with a man named Roberto Whistlestop, who was almost deaf and ridiculously nervous, and yelled out, "Stop sign! Stop sign now!" when we were still in the middle of the block. I played club baseball four days a week, watched Joey run track when there were home meets on Wednesdays and Saturdays. I adjusted myself to the pace and stress of academic life at Exeter, studying three hours and more every night. On Sunday mornings I walked down to St. Michael's for Mass, and soon developed a wild infatuation for a girl there. I used to stare at her thin legs when she walked up to Communion, braids bouncing on her shoulders. I used to think of her at night as I lay in bed, the freckles across her nose, the turned-up top lip, the hem of the skirt knocking against the back of her legs when she walked. Once, late on a Sunday afternoon, she and a friend came to the tennis courts for a game, and Jarasapwanatha rushed into my room, saying, "Ahnthony, Ahnthony, the geerl from the choorch is pilaying." We borrowed two of Higgenbotham's racquets and raced down there, hit the ball into her court a few times, asked her name—Penny Toddeman—but it never came to anything beyond that. I was too shy to try to talk to her after church, miserably, agonizingly, shamefully shy. And, though I found two Toddemans in the Exeter white pages, and even carried the numbers down to the pay phone in the basement once with a pocketful of dimes, I never called.

Joey Barnard came home with me for Easter dinner, and it took the family about half an hour to forget he was black and stop being extra-nice to him. Because of his brother in Vietnam, he had conflicting feelings about all the antiwar protests—which endeared him to us, because my cousins Jamie and Augustine were in Vietnam, too, and we felt the same way: wanting their sacrifice and courage to count for something, on the one hand; and on the other hand just wanting them home. Joey said he had never tasted cooking as good as my grandmother's—which was the right thing to say—and ate so much of her lasagna that the family talked about it for years and years. After the meal we walked to the beach together in the April sunshine. Black faces were not seen on the streets of Revere in those days, and there were a few nasty looks, people staring out car windows, turning their heads at us as we passed. I could tell Joey noticed, but I didn't think it was something we could talk about. Though Rosalie kept her distance from us, she did come up to him as he was leaving and shake his hand in a friendly way. And she did let it be known later—to others, not directly to me—that he was "a nice kid." High praise from her, in those days.

She still refused to write to me at Exeter, or speak to me on the phone. When the school year ended and I came back to 20 Jupiter Street, I saw almost nothing of her. Uncle Peter had gotten me a summer job, mixing and carrying mortar for a bricklayer in North Revere, and Rosie spent all her nights and weekends out with friends, with Caesar. When I did see her—in my grandparents' kitchen, in front of the house, at the beach with her gang of girlfriends—she was always in a hurry and glassy-eyed, and she treated me as if I were an old pal with an infectious disease, probably a fatal disease, the symptoms of which were that you would be forced to stop rushing and rushing, and made to sit still and tell everything about yourself, honestly, to someone you loved. After a while, it hurt me so much that I stopped trying to talk to her, to get her to stand still. I breathed cement dust and read Kerouac and went to the beach on weekends with Leo Markin, Alfonse Romano, and Petey Imbesalacqua. I sat with my grandmother and grandfather in the yard, worked in the garden, went to church, played golf with Uncle Peter a few times on Sunday afternoons, or went with him to the horse track for an hour or two of talk and losing.

In short, my life became tame and ordinary, something it had not been since the death of my parents. It probably would have remained that way, too; I would have started to have faith in predictability and comfort if, late in the summer, Rosie hadn't tried to kill herself.

It happened on a rainy August Saturday, in the middle of the afternoon. She had been out someplace with Caesar, and when he left her off in front of my grandparents', she walked back up to where she had lived before her mother abandoned the family—the forest-green house with cream trim on Venice Avenue—went into a neighbor's garage, found a rope there, knotted the rope around a crossbeam and around her neck, and stepped off the empty fifty-five-gallon oil drum she had been standing on. The neighbor, Mr. Tokarev, heard the barrel topple. He ran into the garage and cut her down with his hacksaw. He called the ambulance, called Uncle Peter at the house on Jupiter Street, and said, according to what my uncle himself later told me, "Peter. Viktor Tokarev. Your daughter try to hang up her own body with the rope in my garage. I cut her down. The ambulance men, they take her in hospital now. I never tell nobody long as I live."

It is supposed to be the case that those who fail at suicide actually want to live, and are only sending out a last desperate cry for help. Perhaps that's true, but it seems too simplistic to me. Since that rainy afternoon, I have formed a sort of mild obsession with people who try to take their own lives. I study newspaper accounts, formulating an imaginary profile of the victim, wondering about the personality quirks of the parents, the atmosphere of the home, the love life, the genetic predilection. Maybe Rosie was calling out to be saved—somehow it does not seem like her—or maybe there is just some invisible boundary to fatal unhappiness, and a person doesn't realize she's crossed over until it is too late.

By the time she reached the Mass General, Rosalie was conscious, welts already looping around her throat as if, wrapped and ribboned, she were being presented to the emergency-room physicians as a gift. The Revere ambulance attendant—another friend—told Uncle Peter that the first words she said when he revived her were "I have to talk to Tonio," but that came to me thirdhand, and I'm not really sure I believe it.

She had turned eighteen a month before. By virtue of some old clause in the Commonwealth of Massachusetts statutes at that time, the state had the right to place her under psychiatric observation for thirty days because she had committed the crime of not wanting to live. We did not talk about her hospitalization—in the family or outside it—just as, over the previous year, we had not talked about Aunt Ulla's disappearance. In both cases, Uncle Peter told his brothers and sisters the news, in person, told his parents, told me, maybe one or two of the older cousins, and then it was as if we wrapped that piece of our history up in an old wool sweater and pushed it under the bed, against the baseboard there, and left it to the darkness and dust. The code of silence was that instinctive, and so was our desire to protect Rosalie from the swirling eddies of Revere gossip. I tell it now, here, I tell everything here, only because I have come to believe it was this penchant for silence, this concern for what people might think, that, years later, ended up trapping her in her web of addiction and abuse, and eventually killing her.

Still, a tickle of guilt sparks along the nerves. I can hear a voice saying, Why bring the rotten part of the cantaloupe to the table when you have guests, why tell? Because secrecy and shame corrode the soul is why. Because the truth gives it air and light. It has always been that way. It's one of the few life lessons our wonderful family never quite seemed to master.

Perhaps the reason was that we did not trust other people to be as generous in their judgments as we were in our own. We are, after all, the descendants of southern European village life, with its lethal gossip and unredeemable reputations. I'm sure that neither Grandpa Dom nor Nana Lia nor any of the aunts, uncles, or cousins thought less of Rosalie because of what had happened. I'm sure of that. Afterward, they didn't shun her, or make a special condescending fuss over her. I don't believe they thought less of Uncle Peter, either, though his faults as a father were obvious enough. If anything, it seemed to me, we loved Rosalie more because of her troubles. Her disguise had been ripped away. She was naked and humbled in front of us, no false little skirt of success, respectability, or manipulation to cover the ordinary human failings the rest of us hide by instinct.

Still, even though he must have known this and felt it, Uncle Peter bore, after Rosalie's first suicide attempt, the heavy weight of local disgrace on both shoulders. The eye of the world meant too much to him for things to be otherwise. I was old enough to feel it clearly by then, to see the change in his posture and hear the broken note in his voice. But I had not the smallest idea what to do about it.

The day after she was sent to the psychiatric ward of the hospital in Woburn, thirty minutes to the north, we drove up there together, Uncle Peter and I, heading away from the house on Jupiter Street with enough food for an army. When we'd gotten clear of Revere, he turned to me as if I were the resident expert on all mysteries now that I'd completed a year at Exeter, and asked, "Where did I go wrong, Tonio?"

"Nowhere," I said.

"The other cousins, the other families in the city, they don't have things like this."

"Sure they do," I said. "They just hide it better, that's all."

I was talking as he wanted me to talk, as if I knew something, when in fact I did not. I was seventeen, and caught in a kind of terrified awe over what Rosalie had done. The night before, I had been awake past midnight, picturing the coarse rope burning the skin of her neck, picturing Mr. Tokarev scratching through it with his hacksaw, catching her in his arms, carrying her across to his house and up the short set of stairs and making the call to the police station with his fingers on her pulse. I was sure her unhappiness had something to do with Caesar, and I hated him, despised him, dreamed up elaborate fantasies of murdering him. "Maybe it's because of Aunt Ulla," I said.

Uncle Peter always slouched to one side when he drove, left wrist guiding the wheel, left foot tapping to a radio tune, his free hand crushing the stub of a cigarette into the ashtray, adjusting the temperature or the volume, picking at the edge of the upholstery. He pursed his lips but did not speak.

"Or Caesar maybe."

"Caesar," he said bitterly. He yanked twice on his nose. "You know who Caesar's uncle is? Angie Pestudo. You know who Angie Pestudo is?"

"Sure. I saw him in his yard once. I threw his daughter's ball back to her."

"When?"

"A long time ago."

Another pause without any eye contact in it. "Caesar's got a nice career all marked out for himself a couple yeahs down the road. He'll go to work for Angie or Eddie Crevine, breakin legs. Perfect for him. Where does that leave your cousin?"

"With bad people."

"Right. With bad people the rest of her life. With a guy who makes his livin breakin legs. How long you think it will be until he starts hurtin her?"

He was a kind of prophet, my uncle.

We drove a little ways through the commercial trashiness of Route 1, oversized signs squeezed into roadside lots: FURNITURE, SEAFOOD, CAR UPHOLSTERY, DISCOUNT SHOES—as if we were speeding through a hell of voices shouting promises that would not be kept. A question floated into my mind, something I had been wanting to ask about for as long as I could remember. "Are you connected to him, Uncle?"

"Who?"

"Pestudo."

He swung his chin around and fixed me with a look for so long,

I thought we'd end up driving across the breakdown lane, across the sidewalk, and straight through the window of an auto-body shop. NO APPOINTMENT NECESSARY. "Ah you serious?" he said at last, turning his eyes forward again and tugging on the wheel once to bring us back between the white lines. "Who put that idea in your head?"

"Nobody. I just always wondered. You used to take us to those houses, Johnny Blink, Joey Patchegaloupe. I thought maybe they were mafia guys."

"Mafia guys? Johnny Blink? Johnny Blink couldn't spell mafia if his next meatball sangwich depended on it. Johnny Blink doesn't know what the R stands for on the shift of a cah. When we were kids, we used to tell him it meant Rev. He'd put his father's Packard in Reverse and push down on the gas a couple times. Almost broke your neck until he figured out we were jokin."

I laughed. But the story felt like a decoy to me. Like putting the puck over on your left side, drawing the defenseman's attention there, while with your body and skates you were moving right the whole time.

"Smart has nothing to do with being part of the mafia, though, does it?" I said.

He reached across with his right hand and tugged on the lobe of his left ear. "Only with not gettin involved."

"Are you involved?"

"You're not gonna let it go, are you, Tonio?"

"Not today, no."

Another one of his patented looks. We careened down an exit and skidded to a stop at the lights.

We were in the suburbs now, or some neosuburban no-man's-land between whatever Revere was—the metropolitan area, the outer ring of the inner city—and the leafy communities farther north; some terrain of slightly larger ambitions and slightly larger lawns and slightly better schools. A nowhere, it seemed to me, in spite of the tidy, soft feel of it. A nowhere between reality and the woods.

"I'll tell you somethin I never told you before," he said. Then we went two blocks without a word. "One day, when I was done with boxin, Angie Pestudo called me up and invited me down his house. It was near Christmas, the day before Christmas, I think. He had his cellar set up like a private club—a bah with a bahtendah, a TV. Guys sittin around in leather chairs, twistin their pinkie rings and scratchin their balls. Walkin in there was like walkin into another country, Tonio, and he was the king. 'Benedetto,' he says to me, 'you're a hell of a fighter.'

" 'I'm retired now, Angie,' I told him. 'My fightin days are done.' We were sittin at one end of the room, away from the TV. Everyone else called him Mr. Pestudo, but I called him Angie because when we were kids in junior high we used to pal around. He was a fat little wiggly then, no good at sports. I used to rough up people who teased him, and I used to spend a little time at his house once in a while because his mother made a nice eggplant pahm. 'My fightin days are over,' I says. He had a cigar in his hand, thick as two of your fingers, and he wobbled it back and forth the whole time but didn't light it. He liked to drink milk and Coke, can you bleeve that? Milk and Coke with ice. Some days he'd take a big risk . . . milk and Pepsi. 'Why don't you come work for me?' he says. 'What are you gonna do now that pays better?'

" 'I'm goin in with my father,' I told him. 'We're startin up a little landscape business.'

" 'What does your father know from landscaping?'

" 'Not much,' I said. I was makin it up as I went, Tonio. I was pissin my pants that day. Thirty-one years old. Broke. Just married. Baby on the way, my boxin career all over, Angie Pestudo backin me into a corner. 'He's got a little money put away,' I said. 'I have the strong back.'

"Angie rolled the end of the cigar around in his mouth and never moved his eyes off me. 'Why don't you put that strong back to work for me?'

" 'My dad wants me,' I said. 'This was always a dream of his, landscapin.'

"He was looking at me, Tonio, a look that could melt the bones in your leg. Grandpa had a dream about landscapin like you have a dream to go to Chelsea and sell ladies' underwear in Kresge's for the rest of your life, okay? But I had the story goin now, I couldn't back off.

" 'Two hundred a week,' he says. In those days, on two hundred beans a week you could have a built-in pool in the yahd and go to Florida a month in the wintertime. I shake my head.

" 'Three hundred,' he says. One of the ball-scratchers turns around now; Angie's starin at me. What am I gonna say?

"I say, 'Angie, listen. I have nothin but respect for you, and an offer like that, comin from you, a generosity like that, I'll appreciate it until the day I die, bleeve me. But I couldn't hurt some guy for owin money. I spent my whole life owin people money, you know me, you know how I am. Nobody would bleeve me if I went up to them and said, "Lissen, you owe Mr. Pestudo. Pay up now or else—'

"See, I worked that angle. That I was too softhearted."

"Are you?"

My uncle pretended to be checking the signs on the cross streets. He slowed down, he looked right, looked left, brought his eyebrows together, and when he started up his story again, it seemed to me that a key chapter had been left out, that something else had happened there in Angie Pestudo's basement, but he would never tell anyone about it as long as he lived.

"So eventually he let me off the hook and shook my hand and let me walk outta there, and he never bothered me about it again. And you know who ended up takin the job of collectin debts for Angie Pestudo, breakin legs? Ever hear of a guy named Fat Smithy?"

A line of chill ran along the skin on my arms. A tractor trailer passed us, and for a few seconds the noise kept me from speaking. "Does he have a lump on top of his eyebrow?" I asked when the truck had pulled ahead.

"*Did* he," my uncle said. "They found him in the trunk of a Buick in Mahblehead. Last week."

"They did?"

He nodded.

"Who killed him?"

"Eddie Crevine, most likely. Chelsea Eddie. One too many legs he broke, one too many things he knew about Eddie's deals. But that was him. Like a little Ping-Pong ball was buried there under the skin, a mahbel. Somebody who was in the room that day told him about Angie offerin me the job. He went up to Angie the next day and Angie gave him the position. Nice life, huh? Go around hurtin guys. One thing I never did, Tonio, I never borrowed money from those people. No matter how desperate I ever got, you understand?"

I nodded, but there were words bunching up in my mouth. What do you do in those houses then? I wanted to ask him. Who are those people to you, really? But it was somehow impossible to speak the words. Maybe I was afraid of the answer he might give, I don't know; afraid of spoiling my sense of who he really was. I'm almost sure now that he never had any official connection with the underworld—he would have lived a richer life. But it held a certain perverse attraction for him, as it holds for so many people: the false promise of being able to live above the law and all moral consequences; the sense of being tied to a group of people by a blood oath. Pete Benedetto had been famous at one point in his life, at a young age, so it was natural enough that he'd want to hold on to some of that, want to be something more than "just anybody." What were his options? He could be a construction worker, or he could be a construction worker who drove a Cadillac and was on a first-name basis with Angelo Pestudo, who was welcome at the home of Joey Patchegaloupe. It makes me sad to think about it now. I want to say to him, You could have had a plain, small life, Uncle; you could have been just an ordinary laborer, and we all would have felt the same way about you. But it's too late for that now.

I turned and looked out the side window. We were passing a line of plain capes with no fences around their yards, one-year-old Buicks and Oldsmobiles out front. We stopped at a red light not far from a driveway in which a thin man wearing short pants and sandals was washing a car as tenderly as if it had a soul.

"How do you know Fat Smithy anyway?" my uncle said.

I pushed the tip of my finger against the metal button and rolled the window down another inch.

"Tonio?"

"I saw him in your house once."

"My house? On Venice Ave.? At what, a pahty?"

I couldn't look at him. I watched the thin man in short pants and wondered if I would end up like him someday, massaging the roof of my Oldsmobile on a sunny afternoon, mowing my little lawn and painting my little house and pretending to myself that there wasn't something enormous and terrifying about the world, that children weren't trying to hang themselves, that men didn't break people's legs over a debt and then end up in the trunk of someone else's car with a bullet in their brain. Probably now, my life is not so different from that man's life, but it seemed to me at that moment like a suburban charade, a life that was too safe, too *nice* to be able to hold much truth in it. I studied that world for a few seconds, the light turned green, and then I heard myself saying, "He was kissing Aunt Ulla, I think, or touching her. They were in Rosalie's bedroom. I came in without knocking. I was eleven or twelve."

Block after block we went before my uncle said, "Where was I?"

"Out with Rosie. You'd gone by Jupiter Street to pick me up and take me to see a friend of yours who had horses. But I was out taking a walk that day. You missed me. I went up to your house looking for Rosie."

He swerved the car to the curb, banged the shift into Park, and cut the engine. He looked at me for a long time without speaking. I looked back. There was no love for me in his eyes at that moment. At last he said, "This is true what you just told me?"

I nodded.

"And you knew for five yeahs without sayin anything?"

I looked down at the ashtray. "I didn't know what it meant then," I said.

"You still don't know what it means."

"It means Aunt Ulla was cheating on you."

He was staring forward now, tapping the bottom of the wheel with the side of his second finger.

"It means she was a bad mother, a bad wife, that she's going to hell when she dies, and so is he."

He tapped and tapped, as if counting through his options. "Did Rosie know?" he said after a while.

"Not from me."

"Did you ever tell anybody?"

"Nobody."

"Why?"

"Not to hurt you," I said.

"Why'd you tell me now then?"

"Because he's dead now," I said. "Because you can't kill him."

I had turned my face away from him and was staring out through the passenger-side window without seeing anything. After a terrible stretch of silence I heard an odd noise and looked over to see him working the ring finger of his left hand back and forth between his teeth and cheek. He pulled once, and the ring slipped up easily past the wet knuckle. For a few seconds he studied it, nostalgically it seemed, or as if wondering how much he could sell it for. Then he started up the car again and drove, the ring clutched in his left fist, his arm hanging over the side. Somewhere in the next block he opened his hand and let the last of his connection to Aunt Ulla fall into the street.

Nine

WE PULLED UP IN FRONT of a three-story building that was set back from the road behind a sloping, parched lawn. It was a modern structure, oblong and cheerful, but the cheerfulness made it ugly: too many stripes of yellow and pastel blue—as if it had been built to hold teenagers who'd tried to kill themselves, but was trying to pretend otherwise. My uncle and I were each carrying a shopping bag full of food. We went past a sleeping receptionist in the lobby and stepped into an open elevator. When the doors closed, we stood side by side, facing them. I studied his blurred aluminum reflection, and it seemed to me that his head and neck were shimmering with anger. The feeling of it filled the moving metal box in which we stood as if the air around us were saturated with a poisonous gas that was just on the verge of combustion. By the time we reached the top floor, I realized that part of what created this feeling was his stillness. It might have been the only time I remember him not moving—no rearranging of the feet, no impatient working of the lips, no talking. He had a wife who'd cheated on him, a daughter with rope burns on her neck. One humiliation, one sadness after the next. The doors opened on a sweaty, chemical smell, but at least it seemed possible to breathe again.

There was another receptionist on this floor, a woman with wire-rimmed eyeglasses sitting at a cluttered desk. Behind the desk stood a pair of white metal doors with small windows in them. There was metal mesh in the glass, and though we had been told it was a minimum-security ward, that no one here had ever tried to harm anyone but herself, the place felt just like a prison to me. Even at some distance from the doors you could hear the chaos—women shouting, loud radio music, the occasional eruption of freakish laughter—and, still without looking at him, I knew what Uncle Peter was feeling. Above the symphony of confusion and misery, I heard the receptionist say curtly, "Leave the food here. One of you in at a time." A nurse walked past with squeaking shoes.

"This heah's her brother," Uncle Peter said, and I looked at him then, not because of the lie, but because the voice coming out of his mouth had the quality of a lit fuse to it—sparking and sputtering, the small reserve of patience burning down toward an explosion I could feel in my own chest. For all his size, bravado, and tough reputation, he was really an exceedingly gentle man. I had never heard him reprimand Rosalie in anything other than a quiet voice, as if he turned down the volume when he was angry at her instead of turning it up, or as if he believed children were made of the thinnest glass. You could make a little noise around them now and then. You could tell stories, smoke cigars, carry them down a hallway under one arm. But you always had to set them down gently; you always had to be aware of your advantage in size and strength; you always had to keep a sort of soft cushion of chatter and affection between them and life's hard edges.

I had always thought of Uncle Peter's boxing career as something noble, almost harmless—you wore padded gloves, after all; you had a referee there to stop the fight if things got too bad. But standing close beside him at that moment, I had, for the first time, a sense of the violence that has to lie in a boxer's heart, the willingness to beat another human being bloody—not in imagination, but in fact—aim your punches at the open cut above his eye, smash his lips into pulp, knock him down, knock him out, send him to the hospital on a stretcher. "This heah's her brother," he said in the sizzling voice, "and I'm her father. We drove an hour to see her, bring her some special food she likes." The sentences snaked out into the air around the woman's desk, sparking.

"One person at a time may meet with her in the visiting room," she repeated in her flat, soulless way. "The orderly will watch you through the windows of the ward. Leave the bags here."

I could feel the heat radiating from Uncle Peter's arms. It seemed impossible that the receptionist did not feel it, that she could maintain this careless manner while sitting so close. She was thin, harmless, officious, gray-headed, and she was moving the papers on her desk aimlessly, a signal for us to leave. *Don't*, I almost said to her out loud. Don't not look him in the eyes now. *Don't.* Uncle Peter stood with his thighs pressed against the edge of the desk, beads of sweat above his top lip. It seemed to me that in another second he was going to pick up the desk and the woman both, carry them over to the elevator, and throw them down the shaft.

"I'll wait," I said, trying to calm him. "You go in first, Uncle."

He did not move his eyes from the woman's face, and at last she looked up through the lenses and smirked. He made a small movement then, almost a twitch. The fingers of his right hand moved half an inch before he caught himself. I'm sure she missed it.

"Where's the visiting room?" I asked her.

She pointed her pen at a set of doors.

Touching Uncle Peter then—I put one hand between his shoulder blades—was like touching the lid of a pot in which the water has started to boil. His spine was electrified, the muscles surrounding it as hard as the side of a furnace. We walked toward the doors the woman had indicated, and I saw movement through the glass, the beautiful swirl and lift of my cousin's black hair. Uncle Peter went up to the doors and pushed, but they were locked from inside. I saw part of the orderly's face in the glass, and when he unlocked the door and swung it out toward Uncle Peter, I had a glimpse of Rosie sitting in a chair with her hands between her knees, pushing them down into a white hospital gown. I raised one hand in a shy greeting, but she did not look up, did not even move when her father stepped into the room. The door closed.

I paced back and forth in the reception area, listening to people yelling and laughing, like caged birds. I looked at the cheap framed watercolors on the walls, nature scenes—meadows with green hills in the background, rivers twisting through colorful autumn woods—and I wondered what I could possibly say to her. I felt as if I was walking along a polished linoleum path, with hell to one side and heaven to the other, only the heavenly scenes in the paintings had something dishonest about them, something so clean and nice and unblemished and fake that I almost would have preferred to be on the other side of the doors, with the screamers. Almost.

I must have waited out there four or five minutes before the doors slammed open and I saw Uncle Peter stride through them, straight at me. He had Rosalie by the upper part of her right arm and was half-dragging, half-lifting her across the little foyer. He took hold of me with his other hand, and we made it onto the elevator before the receptionist looked up from her phone call. The elevator doors closed on the sight of her astonished face, the phone still in midair, the orderly just coming into view. I held on to Rosalie's hand. "Come on," Uncle Peter was saying to the elevator through his teeth. It was the voice he used with horses at the track as they made the last turn. He was pleading with the god of luck. "Come on, come on now." He was holding out a set of keys to me. "Tonio, go to the bottom and get the car, you know where it is. Drive it around front and get in the passenger seat and open both doors."

A faint dull bell. Second floor. Uncle Peter and Rosalie were out and moving toward the stairwell, and I continued to the ground level and walked out into the lobby—a decoy—stepping very calmly through the front doors and moving toward the car with the feeling of walking in a dream, my chest as tight as a drumskin, and the keys in my sweaty hand. When I was in the car, I tried to remember everything Mr. Whistlestop had taught me. I concentrated very hard on each movement. Put the key in the ignition. Turn it. Pump the gas once. Foot on the brake. Shift into Reverse. I backed the car carefully out of its space, put the shift into Drive, and was making a slow, careful loop toward the entrance when I saw Uncle Peter and Rosalie burst out into daylight like doomed lovers running toward the edge of a cliff. I had almost come to a stop when I saw the orderly banging through behind them. I heard him shout. Uncle Peter stumbled over something on the sidewalk and went down on one knee. He pushed Rosie on toward the car. It was safely in Park now, I was sliding across the seat, lifting the chrome door handle, watching her, watching what was happening behind her. Uncle Peter had turned but had not quite straightened up when the orderly reached him, and he made a movement so quick and short it was like the pumping of a piston in a firing engine. I saw the orderly grab his own throat and fall on his back on the sidewalk like a character in a silent film, his feet kicking as he gasped for air. There was something awful and at the same time almost funny about it. And then Rosalie was in the car on one side of me, and her father behind the wheel, and there were other people coming out the doors, and I turned to look at them over the top of the seat as we drove away.

Rosalie stared forward in a dull, hypnotized way, as if she'd just awakened from a feverish sleep. I squeezed her hand. After a long moment, she squeezed back, then held on to me tight. We made it to the highway without hearing any police sirens. Uncle Peter traveled south only two exits—six or eight minutes—then left Route 1 and went the rest of the way on back roads, through Wakefield and Saugus, Cliftondale, North Revere, then down Mountain Avenue to Jupiter Street. Rosalie burst into tears when we stopped in front of our house. She shook and wept and sobbed with her head leaning sideways against my shoulder. Her father just sat there for a while, then he said, "We forgot the food," but nobody laughed. He came around, lifted her up in both arms, and carried her down the sidewalk into the yard with her legs hanging down on one side of him, and her hair hanging down on the other.

Ten

MY GRANDMOTHER TOOK ROSALIE into the back bedroom, and I could hear the quiet tones of her voice there, but not individual words. Grandpa Dom, Uncle Peter, and I stood at the front windows of the parlor, waiting for the police. We did not look at each other or say very much. It was probably ten minutes before they appeared, a blue-and-white Revere cruiser with two officers in the front seat. We walked outside, and my grandfather and I stood on the screened porch while Uncle Peter went down to face them.

On the porch there were two metal lawn chairs against the back wall, and a concrete floor, painted gray, that scratched against the soles of your shoes when you crossed it. Except to have access to the upstairs apartment, we hardly used it, preferring the privacy of the grape arbor in the backyard. From the porch you walked down six steps to a concrete walk. There was a flagpole to your right—my grandfather raised the American flag every morning with great solemnity—on a tiny lawn bordered by hedges high as my chest. Uncle Peter stopped there, at the end of the walk, at the edge of our property, his back to us and his hands held at his sides in a manner that suggested he would use them again if he absolutely had to, but would rather not. The two officers faced him at a distance of three feet, badges blinking in the sun.

"Mario," I heard my uncle say in a tight, small voice, "I took my daughter home."

Instead of answering, Mario looked up at the porch. Beneath the visor of his cap, his eyes went from my grandfather to me and then back again, assessing the second line of defense he'd have to go through if he managed to get past Uncle Peter. He ran his gaze over the front windows of the house as if he might see Rosalie there, glanced up at the second story, at the flag, at the hedges, swallowed, shifted his weight. "We got a call," he said when his eyes had moved back to my uncle's face.

"I took my daughter home. She's havin a tough time now. I decided home was the best place she could be now."

The younger policeman was staring at us as if we were felons. His partner, Mario, said, "What are we supposed to tell the hospital? You hit the guy."

"He's alright, isn't he?"

"Sure he's alright, but—"

"Tell them you know me since I'm eating cookies and milk in first grade and that I'm a good father."

"Nobody said you weren't, Pete. But they want you for assault; they think you're a kidnapper."

"She's my daughter," he said, as if that explained everything.

The officer's eyes floated around again, seeking out an avenue between two loyalties. Then my uncle put a hand on his shoulder. I think there aren't five people in the New World who would have put a hand on a policeman's shoulder at that precise moment. The younger cop looked at him as if he had fondled the queen of England, but Peter wasn't interested in the younger cop. The younger cop hadn't eaten cookies with him in first grade and did not register on the scale of things that mattered, was not someone he would have called "a Revere person." Probably, the younger cop had been born in the city and never had any intention of leaving, but just by virtue of the look on his face at that moment, he had ceased to be a Revere person for Uncle Peter, for my grandfather, and for me. Being a Revere person meant that, above and beyond everything else—the laws of the Commonwealth, the rules of the Church, the opinions of the richer, better-educated world—you had an instinctive empathy for other people's pain and embarrassment. It was the same thing as "having class." Having class was demonstrated by pulling another chair up to the table and setting an extra place when an unexpected visitor rang your doorbell at dinnertime—but this had to be done immediately and naturally, without even the smallest sign that it might be an inconvenience. It meant taking care of a neighbor's child on short notice because the neighbor was having a rough day, or sending a flower arrangement to a friend's mother's wake, even if you couldn't afford to, even if you and the friend hadn't been on the best of terms lately. It meant walking up to someone who had beaten you—in an election, in sports, in an old romantic involvement—and offering congratulations, or going into a bar and offering to buy a round, no matter what number of strangers were sitting there, no matter how low your bank account, or your mood. There was a little bit of showing off in all of this, of course. But there was also a genuine largeheartedness, a sort of socialism of the soul.

I watched my uncle's fingers squeeze the blue-shirted shoulder, twice, in an encouraging way. Mario, the gesture seemed to say, whatever you do now you're going to have to live with in this city for the rest of your life. Everybody is gonna know. You'll walk down Broadway—next week, next month, next summer—and people will think, There goes the guy who put Pete Benedetto in jail for bringing his own daughter home.

All of Jupiter Street seemed to go silent and completely still. Mario, my uncle, and the younger cop might have been painted on canvas.

Mario scraped one fingernail down the cleft of his chin, twice. "She's alright then?" he said. I saw my grandfather make a small, approving nod beside me.

"Recoverin," Uncle Peter told him. He had stepped onto the sidewalk and turned his friend so that they were facing partly away from the younger officer and looking down the street toward Park Avenue. They might have been scouting out their tee shot on the first hole at Cedar Glen. The tone of my uncle's voice changed, grew softer. His old self seemed to rise from the place where it had been buried when Aunt Ulla left him. You could see it in the way his arms and shoulders worked, the way he pressed his hands together as if in prayer and shook the fingertips forward and back, then swung them out and around, holding up only the index finger of each hand and making circles like a clown balancing two plates above his ears. He lifted one foot an inch off the ground and reset it in a slightly different position, tugged at the cuffs of his long-sleeved shirt, put a hand in his pocket and shook it so the change jingled, scuffed his other shoe, shrugged, wiped something from his bald dome, turned his big nose in toward Mario's, touched him lightly on the elbow, the forearm, looked up at a bus passing on Park Avenue. All the time he was talking. "Baskine," I heard. "Her mother . . . What can I do?" The matter was already decided, obviously. It was just a question of smoothing out the last little wrinkles in Mario's conscience, lending him a warm overcoat to help him through whatever wintry bureaucratic troubles he might encounter back at the station. After a few minutes, I suspected they were no longer even talking about Rosalie, but about some greyhound on which Uncle Peter had inside information, a car he'd heard someone was selling cheap, the sister of a mutual friend who'd suffered a miscarriage and was recuperating now, and should they visit or just send a card.

When they were finally finished, my uncle stepped over to the younger officer and shook his hand, squeezing the forearm at the same time and tilting his forehead down an inch so that the gesture had about it a feeling of both apology for an inconvenience and the consummation of a binding contract. Mario got back behind the wheel. The younger officer sent one last suspicious glance in our direction, slammed his door, and sat staring straight ahead. I watched the cruiser glide to the bottom of Jupiter Street, the little flash of brake lights there, the long policeman's pause, then it turned right—the opposite direction from the police station—and disappeared.

At first, Uncle Peter could not quite look at us. He squeezed his nose a couple of times. He stood on the sidewalk with his back to the porch and his hands on his hips, glancing left and right. Then, at last, he turned, mounted the stairs, opened the screen door, and said to his father, "Mario Andreottla, Pa. He used to come to the back door when we were kids and call me like this heah: 'Hi-oh, Pee-tee!' Remembah?"

Eleven

WHEN MY UNCLE AND GRANDFATHER went inside, I stayed out on the steps and looked across the street at the green-trimmed windows of Millie Santosuosso's house. My grandfather's flag stirred in a small breeze, causing the rope to tap against the pole. It was a thin rope, hardened by rain and sun, and when it hit the pole, the hollow metal echoed like a meditation bell in the small front yard. Only one week remained before I was supposed to be back at Exeter—Joey Barnard had called a few days earlier, excited about starting the new term—but it seemed impossible to go back there after what had happened with Rosalie. One of the peculiar aspects of being a Revere person, of having class, was that, since we shared so thoroughly in each other's suffering, there was a certain amount of guilt associated with success and happiness, with getting out and away. It is, I think, to this day, the quality that keeps people from ever moving out of that place or places like it. Our antennae were so finely tuned to the potential for misery in the world, the asphalt-and-salt martyrdom of neighbors and friends, that good fortune always felt like a mixed blessing. Sure, you wanted to hit the number—everybody wanted to—but what blaze of envy would your new wealth spark in the hearts of the other people on the street? What kind of tragedy would God visit upon you for thinking too much of yourself and flying off to some overpriced Manhattan hotel where you didn't belong? Sure, I wanted to be back with my friends in Amen Hall, skating on the magnificent rinks, sitting in my sport coat and jeans around a hardwood table, while groundskeepers mowed the lawns outside and Mr. Haydock talked to us about the French Revolution. But how was I supposed to leave my cousin with the rope burns on her neck, my uncle with his big debts and broken-up family? Or, leaving them, how could I ever really be at peace with myself up there, in my little New Hampshire paradise?

I remember Ray Recupero raising his hand once in catechism class and posing a question to the nun: "How can a person be happy in heaven, Sister, if he knows that somebody else—maybe his cousin or his neighbor or his friend, anybody in the world—is burning in the fire in hell?"

A Revere question, I think. The question of a good Catholic boy. But more than that as well. Now, from a distance of 150 miles and thirty-five years, it sounds in my ear like the great unasked question in the discussion of American poverty: how can anyone ever move out, move up, without dragging an enormous stone of guilt and sorrow behind them? What little bell tolls in the mind of the boy from Bedford Stuyvesant who graduates from Harvard and settles in the suburb, or the girl from a Virginia hollow or a plain Midwestern factory town who sits in a restaurant in Soho listening to her friends complain about the salad dressing? How much of that chorus of sweat and compassion accounted for Joey Barnard's dark moods? How much of it was part of what threatened to glue me there that day, right there, to the weed-edged sidewalks of Jupiter Street, for all time?

Twelve

IF THERE WERE REPERCUSSIONS from the kidnapping, they never reached me. No doubt one of the uncles, aunts, or family friends was asked to make a phone call to a childhood pal who had become a judge, district attorney, or chief of police. That was the way things were done then in Revere, in eastern Massachusetts. That is the way things have been done everywhere, since the beginning of time. There is the written law—precise, logical, merciless—and then there is the messy, merciful, half-corrupt human web of debt, affection, and influence that hangs around the law on all sides.

Rosalie recovered, the welts around her neck healed. The day before the start of the school year, we went to the beach together—far down toward Point of Pines where none of our friends were likely to see us—and waded around in the ocean for half an hour, feeling for an old innocence there on the sandy bottom.

It did not work very well. We had not been innocent in that way for the better part of a decade, since the day my parents' plane crashed; we had barely spoken for the better part of a year. But the whole afternoon had about it a feeling of reconciliation, even rebirth.

This may have been because Caesar hadn't called or come by since the rainy Saturday when Rosie tried to kill herself. I was buoyed by the hope that he was gone from her life now, for good, that proximity to death had somehow cleared her vision. Uncle Peter seemed to have been infected with the same optimistic delusion: in the days when Rosie was being nursed back to health by my grandmother, he regained some of his old cheerfulness. He scraped and painted the square-topped picket fence that protected the hedge out front, helped his father and me put the early tomato harvest into canning jars, to be used for gravy in the middle of winter; he even jogged around the block a few times in a T-shirt, shorts, and shoes. We both had an instinctive sense that if we could just get Caesar Baskine out of the picture, Rosalie would blossom into the woman she was meant to be—an adult version of the happy, feisty, confident soul she had been in early childhood. She'd marry a man we liked, have children we adored. We'd gather for Sunday meals and go to the beach together on Saturday afternoons, and, for another ten or twenty or thirty years, we'd put off the thing we feared most: the breaking up of the Benedetto family.

Rosalie and I splashed, shouted, dove under the cold water a few times, then ran back up the shore and toweled ourselves dry. We left our shoes and shorts there and carried our towels north along the sand, past the PRIVATE—RESIDENTS ONLY signs that were posted at the place where Revere Beach legally ended and Point of Pines Beach legally began. We walked around the point to the bridge over the Pines River. It was dead low tide. We squeezed between the pilings of the bridge and walked under the highway. From there we could look out over the river—a wide inlet, really, an estuary—and past the salt marsh to the sprawling gray General Electric plant where my father had worked until five days before he died. A waterlogged wooden beam had washed ashore. We laid our towels on it and sat.

"Looking forward to school?" she asked after a while.

"I'm thinking of not going."

"Not going!"

"It's phony up there. It's not real."

"And this is?" She swung her arm toward the strip of auto dealerships and donut shops that stood on either side of the highway. She shoved me so hard that I almost slipped off the beam. "You're a big hockey star, you're a genius. And you're gonna stay here, you dope? And what, spend the rest of your life down Bill Ash's eating slices of pepperoni pizza and talking about some great slap shot you did when you were fifteen?"

I shrugged and looked straight ahead at the factory buildings. "I'm not a star, Rosie, and I'm not a genius, either. Your father says I'm the smartest kid in Revere. I'm not, and you know what? I wouldn't care if I was. It doesn't matter to me anymore, being smart. I've had enough of it in my life."

"So now what? You're gonna try being stupid for a while, see if that's any better?" She shoved me again, not so hard. "Boy, do I hate this modest crap," she said. "It's ten times worse than bragging. You're going back up to that school and you're going to Harvard and become a doctor, or I swear to God I'll never speak to you again as long as you live."

"You hardly speak to me as it is. We haven't had a talk since before I left home. I call and you pretend you're not there. You hug me but you can't look me in the eyes."

"I don't want to talk, Tonio. You don't get it."

"But why? If something's wrong, we can change it, we can fix it."

"I don't want to fix it."

"It drives me crazy when I hear you say things like that, Rosie. It's a kind of giving up. You have all these people who love you, who want to help you, make your life happy, and you . . . It's like whenever somebody's nice to you, you spit in their face, you think they're a loser, you—"

Two police cars sped across the bridge into Lynn, sirens wailing. Rosalie covered her ears with her hands, then got up and walked to the water and began tossing stones and pieces of shell into the current. Her life seemed to me then like a twisted, knotted piece of wire. I had believed for a long time that I could pull on it here and there, unravel it, make it more or less straight. I had been in love with her since I was two, a completely illogical and innocent love. But something broke in me there on the beach: I began to give up. I stared at her, half in love still, half furious.

She had already made most of the transition from beautiful girl into the beautiful woman she would become. The beauty was courtesy of her mother's genes, perhaps. She'd inherited Uncle Peter's natural athleticism, too, and had the tight waist and strong legs of a gymnast without ever having done an hour of exercise in her teenage life. I was seventeen then, an age when the sight of a girl in a bathing suit—her shape, her skin, the way her hair fell against the tops of her bare shoulders—would imprint itself upon my mind long after the actual human being had disappeared from view. I'd be sitting in my room with a book in my lap, or washing my chest in the shower, or lying in the dark between the sheets, and the curve of the muscles of a girl's calves, or the flat place between the front of her hip bones, or just the memory of the movement of her legs would come absolutely alive again in my inner eye. It would be, then, as if I were standing still and running at the same time. Some new chemistry would sprint up through the middle of me, a reflex built into the species a hundred million years ago. Of what use were the strictures of the Church and the cautions of the nuns against that?

For a few seconds I allowed myself to look at my cousin that way, as a kind of revenge, maybe, a weird offshoot of my frustrated love. She had her back to me. She would bend over and feel around in the sand next to her feet, then straighten up and make an overhand toss, and I could see her breasts shifting against the fabric of her bathing suit when she reared back, then her spine and the backs of her legs. For a minute or two I was swept up in it. For a minute or two I pursued an absurd little vision of Rosie and me having some kind of future life together, saving each other. Not married, naturally, but allies of some sort, confidantes in the world beyond Revere, a grown-up brother-and-sister team.

"Let's get out of here, Tonio," she called, and for the time it took to draw and release one breath, I thought she meant something else.

I picked up our towels, we squeezed back between the damp pilings. She said, "You haven't asked me about Caesar."

Something in the way she said his name rang in my ear like a caution.

"I noticed he didn't come see you," I said carefully.

"Didn't come see me. Didn't call. Didn't nothing."

"I noticed that."

"Know why?"

"Why?"

"Because we had a big fight that day."

"I thought that might be it."

"Know what the fight was about?"

"What?"

"I was pregnant."

We startled a trio of seagulls as we turned the corner. They flew a little ways up the sand, singing a loud chorus of complaint. From where they had been perched, you could look all the way down the curl of Revere Beach, past the high white hills of the roller coaster.

"Shocked, right?"

"When are you having it?"

"I'm not. I went to a doctor, in Nahant. He took care of it."

"What do you mean?"

She was crying now, suddenly, one hiccup of grief in the salt air, tears on each cheek. I took hold of her hand and she wrenched it away, then, after three more steps, she grabbed my wrist in a vice grip. We walked on that way, as if I were hostage to her misery and she were marching me down the shore toward some encounter in which one of us would be imprisoned and executed, and the other set free.

"He took it out of me. . . . I was bleeding for a week, Tonio."

"Took it out of you? What do you mean, 'took it out of you'?"

"He pulled it out. He killed it."

"What do you mean?"

"Come on, Tonio. Grow up."

I swallowed. I said, "Alright, I just—" And then: "Does your father know?"

She shook her head so violently that a teardrop flew off her cheek and landed against the skin of my shoulder. A jogger passed us on the sand, headed north. He stared at Rosalie for a few panting breaths, ran his eyes up and down the front of her body, plodded on.

"I'm not going to be able to have babies now, ever. Caesar was so pissed off, he said he'd never speak to me again. He wanted it. He has a job lined up, and he wanted us to have a little house and a little baby. And I didn't want to. I don't know why. Don't ask me why. A girl I know,

Elaine, she told me about this doctor in Nahant. You can practically see his house from here if you turn your head that way. I had to decide right away because the longer you wait, the bigger a sin it is. I couldn't talk to anybody about it. I went out there all by myself, and there was a woman there, his nurse, and she let me into the house, and he took me into the cellar office and pinched it out of me with tweezers. It hurt like mad, Tonio. I bled and bled all over his table and his rug, and they kept me there and held towels against me, and she fed me eggs and bacon, and I threw them up all over myself. It cost three hundred dollars and now—"

"Where did you get three hundred dollars?"

"I got it. Don't ask me where I got it, and I did it, and now I'll never have kids. I can't go to church now; I can't even go *by* the church without feeling like a devil. I can't even look Aunt Laura in the face anymore."

"Aunt Laura gave you the money?"

"Don't ask me, I said." She let go of my wrist and struck out at the air with her left hand, once, twice, uttering a sound like someone who'd been kicked in the stomach.

We walked over to our sneakers and dungaree shorts, carried them up to the wall and sat there, brushing sticky grains of sand from between our toes with the corners of the towels. Cars passed behind us on the Boulevard, and I was ambushed by a memory of my father sitting on the gritty front steps with me on a hot happy night. *How does the baby get in there, Pa?*

Rosie sat back on the wall with her knees bent and her arms around her shinbones. We looked out to sea, squinting.

"Is that why you . . . tried to—"

"No. I knew you'd think that."

"Why then?"

I looked away from her, out at the Nahant Peninsula, at small sparks of sunlight reflecting from the windows of the shoreline houses there.

"I don't want to be with him," she said. "I don't care if I ever see him again."

"Don't then."

"I will, though. I know I will. It's like I knew it the first day I saw him. He knows it too."

"Bullshit, Rosie."

She laughed a two-note false laugh. "First time I ever heard you swear."

"That's bullshit superstition. You're too old for that now. You can do whatever you want with your life. You can go live in Boston, or California, France, Italy. Good-looking, smart boys will want to go out with you. You're absolutely beautiful; you're one of the nicest girls I've ever met—"

"Out of all those thousands?"

"You're smarter than you give yourself credit for and a million times too good for shithead Caesar Baskine. That's just bullshit, what you just said."

She shuffled her feet an inch back and forth on the wall and pulled the tops of her thighs in against her chest. I turned then and saw the thin twist of a smile at the corners of her mouth, another moment I've never been able to quite get down on canvas to my own satisfaction. Even if I had, I would never have exhibited it, not that smile, not on my cousin's face. Because it was the closest thing to evil I ever saw in someone in our family. It was clear to me then that my words, the logic and caring of them, were like lengths of kindling Rosie was collecting. She was going to take all the kind and uplifting things everyone in the family had ever said to her, any belief in anything hopeful or good, and pile them onto an enormous bonfire.

What my wife would say to me on the afternoon of Rosalie's funeral was true: at some point the idea of self-destruction had been planted in her, and we tried and tried and could not dig it out. Who planted it there does not matter. What matters is that Rosalie might have turned away from that idea, and instead she indulged it. She chose Caesar Baskine and kept choosing him, even after he had gone to court a dozen times, to jail twice. Even after he had repeatedly beaten her. In some perverse way, she liked to have people talk to her the way I was talking to her; it brought that small, bitter, superior smile to her mouth. It was, for her, just the kind of dumb faith in resurrection that her loudest inner voice mocked. The world could be a good place, we were saying to her, a peaceful, hopeful place. She knew better.

Something passed through me when I saw that smile. In the way young people know something, a wordless way, I understood that whatever unblemished love had existed between us was finished. There would be a connection, still; there is a connection even now—we named our daughter after her, in fact. You don't stop loving someone because she no longer loves herself; it's just that the love has no place to go, no port in which to unload its cargo. Your ship plies the coastline endlessly, looking for a calm bay, for welcome. It might occasionally be signaled closer to shore, but it is never allowed to dock.

We walked back to Wonderland Station and took the Park Avenue bus home without saying much beyond what we had already said. She kissed me at the door, I remember that, a kiss on the lips that had nothing but the past in it. And the next day, when Uncle Peter knocked on the door of my little bedroom, I was packed and ready to leave.

Thirteen

IN THE MONTHS OF SEPTEMBER and October, a rare kind of healing light falls across southern New Hampshire in the late afternoon. The uniqueness of that light has something to do with the proximity of the ocean and the mountains, and later, as the season deepens, with the colors of the dying leaves. People come from all over the world to see the autumn colors, but I think it is really the light that draws them to that particular part of New England: they come in hope of a cure.

Across the street from Amen Hall were tennis courts and the new athletic complex, and then, stretching as far as the river and a little ways beyond, an expanse of open playing fields: for baseball, soccer, football, and lacrosse. I did not have a late-afternoon class that term, and sometimes, between the end of sports and the start of the dinner hour, I would wander out on those fields, cross the concrete bridge over the river, and walk in the woods alone. There was a profound joy for me in those walks, and it soothed some of the trouble I'd brought back from Revere. The fields seemed like living creatures shifting and settling in the mysterious light, almost able to speak.

Because we had both wanted to do something different in the way of a sport that fall, Joey and I were rowing intramural crew. Practices lasted from two to four, and were held on a wide section of the river that was far from Amen Hall. After those workouts, my legs and arms would be weary and there would be only an hour or so between the time I got back from the boathouse and the time I had to head off to the dining hall, and there was always a paper, exam, or oral presentation to think about. But my solitary walk in the woods had begun to seem like the most important part of the day, and I usually found the energy for it.

On some of those afternoons, walking out of the woods and toward the campus in that light, with the smell of the river around me and the *plock . . . plock* of tennis balls on the clay courts in the distance, I would be filled with a feeling that seemed to me to have nothing to do with Revere or the Benedetto family or my friends at the Academy. I am tempted to say it was only that first sense of existential solitariness that sets the adult apart from the child. But it was deeper than that. I came across a poem not long ago, a very bad poem with a title I liked—"The Ordinary Self Greets the Soul"—and that might be a way of describing those moments: as if I were being introduced to a piece of my truest identity, something steady and gleaming, almost eternal, that stood beside or beneath the ordinary run of thoughts and feelings I was used to calling "Anthony Benedetto."

One afternoon, walking a few minutes later than usual along a path in the woods, I turned a corner and was startled to see a woman sitting there on a flat, waist-high boulder in the middle of a clearing. She was so still, I didn't see her until I was nearly right next to her. I let out a small grunt of surprise; she didn't move. Her eyes were closed. I thought at first she was sleeping, but who slept sitting up? When I recovered, I went over to her and asked if she was alright.

She opened her eyes. "Yes, fine," she answered, in a voice you would use with someone you knew well, a voice stripped of the tacked-on decorations that keep people at a distance—that signal approval, or disapproval, or a desire to be liked, or a desire to be left alone.

"I'm sorry I disturbed you."

"You didn't."

I nodded, apologized again, and went on along the path. It was one of those encounters that seems to happen too quickly; afterward, you run through all the things you might have said, might have done differently. I did not like the fact that I had been startled, that I had tried to cover over my embarrassment by asking a question that did not need to be asked. It made me feel young again, just when I was beginning to feel so mature. Crossing the river, I realized I had recognized the woman, and I remembered her name. Mrs. Coughlin. Her teenage son and her husband—who had worked in the admissions office and whom I'd spoken with briefly on my first visit—had been killed in a car accident on Route 101 near the end of the previous school year. The principal made the announcement in chapel, taking off his glasses and holding a handkerchief up to his nose and mouth. It was recommended, but not required, that students attend the wake, and Joey and I and Higgenbotham and Madhur Jarasapwanatha had walked down to the funeral home in our sport coats and ties to shake hands with her and the other family members and to tell them how sorry we were.

It was my night to wait on faculty tables, and I was late. I trotted back across the fields, wondering what quality it was in the way she had spoken to me, what had seemed so different there.

Fourteen

THOSE WALKS, that quick encounter with Mrs. Coughlin, marked the start of another life for me. It is a difficult thing to write about. Difficult to write about because the life that began there—fragile, unsure, wavering like a candle flame beside an open window—was an interior life, hidden from the camera lens of the commercial world. In America, though all of us experience it, that dimension of things has usually been suspect, the province of bohemians, loners, and ten-dollar palm readers at sidewalk booths. We are a country of scientists and entrepreneurs, of factual certainty and cold, hard cash. We put our energy into things that can be measured—as if accomplishments can change the raw fact of dying, or as if, like the pharaohs, we can pack our treasures into the coffin with us and carry them past the customs checkpoint of death.

I am that way, too, as American as anyone, and that fall I was caught in the same web of hope and anxiety as all my friends, the same kinds of thoughts: girls, schoolwork, college. But beneath all that, in a deep, hidden part of me, something else was beginning to stir. I do not know why, or what to call it.

I had been elected Student Council representative from Amen Hall, my grades were solid if unspectacular, I had grown to above-average height and started shaving every day. I was feeling more and more at ease in my classes, in the basement smoking room with my friends— some of them hockey players, most of them not. I felt healthy and strong.

Coach Rislin stopped me outside the post office one morning between classes and said, "Benedetto, you turned into a poplar tree over the summer. Poplar trees don't make good hockey players, understand? Between now and when the season starts, I want you to eat like a tiger, okay? Like a rhinoceros."

"Like an elephant," I suggested.

"Right. Like an elephant. I want some meat on those bones."

I did not need the encouragement. Most days, between breakfast and lunch, I went down to the the Grill—the campus snack bar—and had a hamburger, or a milk shake, or a couple of frosted cinnamon rolls and exchanged a few words with the cook there, a stocky, fake-gruff man named Bucky, who was one of my favorite people at the Academy. And most nights after dinner, a few of us from Amen Hall would make the pilgrimage to Ferlita's for sub sandwiches, or have pizzas delivered. When Uncle Peter visited, he took to bringing up loaves of soft white bread from Brandano's bakery on Broadway, and Joey and I would make peanut-butter-and-jelly sandwiches and share a quart of milk before going to sleep.

Everything about my external situation at Exeter was fine and pleasant. I was rushing toward adulthood with a kind of half-childish abandon that felt like the end of mourning to me. Eating, rowing, learning, dreaming about girls, waiting to hear from colleges. . . . But, underneath all that, something else was breaking open.

One day during a particularly tough crew workout, that invisible something made itself known to me in an unexpected way. It was near the end of the practice. We were three-quarters of the way through a twenty-minute piece, full power. Our legs were burning, and the breath was moving in and out of us in great heaves. My whole torso seemed to have been dipped into a boiling pot of pain, and my mind was trying every imaginable strategy to get me to ease off a bit, to move away from the pain instead of into it, to do something sane with my afternoons instead of driving an eight-oared boat along the cold surface of the Exeter River with blistered hands and screaming muscles. For some reason, though, instead of easing off, I pushed on into the pain and the fear, and after twenty or thirty more strokes and another hundred breaths, my mind just seemed to give up, to stop, to go quiet. I rowed on, unwavering, the pain held at arm's length, until the coxswain rattled the wooden knockers and called out, "Paddle! Paddle now! Easy now. Long and slow, zero power. Breathe easy."

Afterward, everything was almost the way it had always been. I rowed along lightly, caught my breath. We turned toward the boathouse with the afternoon shadows on the river's steely surface, the oarlocks squeaking, the motor on Mr. Swift's launch puttering behind us. We climbed out, lifted the boat over our heads, and carried it into the boathouse on our shoulders. The gunwales dripped, the dock creaked and rocked under our bare feet, the smell of the river clung to our shirtfronts and faces.

Joey and I sat on the dock, laced up our running shoes, and, as we always did, jogged back to Amen Hall along Main Street, through a thin parade of women doing errands and town kids killing time after school. We showered and changed. He headed off to Advanced Calculus, and I went out for my walk in the woods. Everything was the same, except that my mind felt like a cottage on the shore that had just had its windows thrown open after a long, musty winter. I sailed along past the tennis courts and onto the fields, filled with a quiet jubilation that was nothing like any happiness I had felt before. It lasted for the better part of an hour.

A week passed. On Wednesday, a night when I wasn't required to wait on tables, I stayed out in the woods until the sun set and the first wooly shadows were gathering in the tops of the trees, and then I walked past the clearing again and saw Mrs. Coughlin there on her stone. I squatted on the path and watched her. It was a strange thing to see an adult that way, not moving at all; and stranger still to be spying on her. I watched until she opened her eyes, stretched her arms and legs, and then I made a little scuffing noise in the pine needles of the path so as not to startle her.

She was wearing hiking boots, blue jeans, and a red down vest, and from the pocket of the vest she took a pair of eyeglasses, hooked them over her ears, and calmly looked at me. "Hello again," she said.

"Hi."

She stood up and came toward me. She was a small, trim woman, with a round face that was attractive without being pretty, and light brown hair pulled up tightly in the back. She held out her hand. "I'm Lydia Coughlin."

"I know. I met you before . . . at the wake."

She asked if I was walking back toward campus, and I said that I was, and we went together along the path by the river. She asked what grade I was in at school, what I was studying, which sports I played, where I was from—all the usual questions. I wasn't the type of student who felt at ease in the company of my teachers, and so I associated her, at first, with the other middle-aged adults at the school, people from whom I was separated by twenty or thirty or forty years and a waist-high fence of formality and deference.

But when we crossed the bridge and started along the fields, I began to relax. Those fields were, after all, my territory, the place I felt most myself; and I began to see that she was speaking to me in a way fundamentally different from the way my teachers spoke. There was no armor of politeness, no subtle false suit of smugness about being older. "So, are you happy here?" she asked when we were climbing the small rise to the dirt road that ran past the gym.

"Three out of every four days," I said. It was a line I'd borrowed from my grandmother, who believed that the secret to happiness was to expect some disappointment, sorrow, and pain, not to resist it too strenuously, to think of it as the Fourth Day.

"Is today a good one or a bad?"

"Bad," I said. "Salisbury steak for supper. 'Cooked puck,' we call it."

She laughed—a quiet, lilting laugh. We walked past the tennis courts and stopped at the road, waiting to cross. In front of Amen Hall she stuck out her hand again, her arm straight and held up high from the shoulder. It was dark, there was no one else there. I don't know what came over me, but instead of just saying good-bye, I said, "I was really sorry at the wake. I said I was sorry, but really I was. My mother and father died when I was young . . . suddenly, like that . . . and I . . . "

"Thank you," she said, but it sounded to me as if she wished I hadn't brought the subject up, which made me feel young again, and foolish. "I'll see you," she said. "I'll have you over for dinner some night when they're serving cooked puck."

I laughed too loudly. I walked off toward my awful meal, feeling angry at myself for not having behaved properly. She had been so plain and at ease, and I had flipped from one persona to the next—the respectful schoolboy, the hockey player, the Revere guy, the respectful schoolboy there again at the end. All through the meal I fidgeted and worried about it. We filled ourselves up with milk and pudding, sliced off disk-shaped pieces of the inedible meat and slapped them back and forth on the tabletop with our knives. When we tired of that and brought our trays up to the conveyor belt, Higgenbotham turned to Joey and me and said, with his slight lisp and in the aristocratic tone we had come to love, "The sub shop, gentlemen?"

We walked across campus again in the sweet fall darkness, cut through one end of town, and consumed a second dinner under Ferlita's fluorescent lights with the jukebox playing Derek and the Dominos' "Layla" at top volume. Clapton and his friends were scooting happily down the drug-addled alleys of the early seventies when they recorded that tune. Even now, you can hear the crazed joy of those times in it, the manic, chemical jubilation. The Vietnam War hovered always in the background then, and death was on the news every night, real as the weather. War, riots, assassinations—it wasn't the happiest of times in America. But if you really listen to that song, you can hear in it a sort of rock-and-roll insistence that death always takes second seat to one god greater.

Fifteen

TWO WEEKS PASSED. I saw Mrs. Coughlin again in the woods, and we talked a little more. She did not have to work, she told me in that second conversation; she had "family money"—a term I'd never heard before coming to Exeter—and her husband's insurance benefits, but she put in five or six hours a day making stone sculptures, and she volunteered four mornings a week at a school for the blind in the next town east. Her grandparents had been émigrés from south of Moscow—her maiden name had been Svetlovskaya—and when she heard I was studying Russian, she spoke the expressions she remembered from her childhood: *"shto khochesh"*; *"tebya liubliu,"* and so on.

We bumped into each other again a few days after that, on the last Tuesday before hockey season began, my last free afternoon until the April vacation. The dining hall was serving Salisbury steak again, and I mentioned it to her as we came back across the river toward campus.

"Do you like Indian food?" she said.

"Never tried it."

"I made a rice-and-lentil dish yesterday. All I'd have to do is heat it up."

It took me a few seconds to realize that she was inviting me to her house for dinner. I almost said no, almost made some excuse about schoolwork or friends, and headed back to the safety of the dormitory and the dining hall, my ordered little world. Newfound maturity notwithstanding, I was still a seventeen-year-old boy, bashful and self-involved; it could not possibly have occurred to me that a grown-up woman might just want some company on a weekday night.

Her house was seven blocks from campus, on a quiet street of well-spaced Victorians with front porches painted in pastels. We turned off the sidewalk and walked down a gravel path. The light was on over her back steps, and I could see a built-in swimming pool covered with blue plastic and spotted with fallen leaves. Her back steps led up to a glassed-in porch, and then through a glass door into her kitchen. The kitchen did not feel like it belonged in such a sedate neighborhood: new white and green tiles on the counter and partway up the walls, new white cabinets without handles, a table made of pale wood that shone as if it had been polished for hours, and a single thick candle for a centerpiece. No saints on the walls; nothing on the walls, in fact. It was as spare and tidy as a hospital waiting room, but warmer and more elegant, a place so free of clutter and plastic surfaces that the table and stove and the glasses in the strainer seemed to pulse with their own quiet life.

After so many weeks of dormitory living, of looking at furniture that was identical to the furniture in every other room and belonged to no one, it was always a shock to walk into a real home again. You felt as though you shouldn't touch anything. Beyond that, there was still a way in which any house other than the ones I'd grown up around seemed alien. There were no garlic and tomato smells in Mrs. Coughlin's kitchen, none of the trappings of the Italian-American aesthetic—plastic table-cloths and garish mirror frames, crucifixes wherever you looked. And it was an odd thing to do, skipping dinner with friends to spend time with a woman so much older. It was something I never would have done a few months earlier, and in those first minutes, especially, I was self-conscious and anxious.

I had called her Mrs. Coughlin once or twice during the walk. When we were inside the house, she asked me to call her by her first name, Lydia, a name she admitted she had never really liked. She poured me a glass of grape juice and told me to wander around while she heated up the food. The other rooms on the first floor—a dining room, a parlor, a guest bed-room with the door open, a very small room with a foot-high stone Bud-dha on a platform and cushions on the floor instead of chairs—had the same unpretentious, orderly feel as the kitchen. I remember stopping in front of an end table next to the living-room sofa and looking into the faces in the picture frames there. A man I recognized as Mr. Coughlin was standing on a sailboat, one of his hands holding a rope that angled across the picture, and the other curling around the shoulders of a boy who resembled Mrs. Coughlin—Lydia—so perfectly that he looked to be a younger, male version of her.

In a moment, she called me into the dining room, told me to sit at the polished table there. She brought from the kitchen two steaming plates of rice and lentils and a loaf of French bread, sliced along its length, with butter melting into it, and she poured herself a glass of wine and sat down across from me.

When we'd been eating for a few minutes, she said, "Did you skip lunch today?"

"Sorry."

"It's alright, but there's plenty where that came from, you know, and no time limit."

"Sorry."

"I'd offer you some wine, but there's a rule at the school about drinking alcohol, isn't there?"

"I drink it all the time at home. Since I was five. I miss it."

But I had never tasted white wine. It seemed sweet and feeble to me, a diluted dessert. I remember finishing the first dish of rice and accepting her offer of a second, and eating two-thirds of the loaf of bread, then telling her, when she asked, that I drank coffee at home, too, and watching her pour the coffee and grate fresh coconut over three scoops of chocolate ice cream in a glass bowl.

Little by little, the plainness and straightforwardness of her manner wore away at my self-consciousness. I began to be slightly less polite, slightly less young. In a certain way, she was the polar opposite of Uncle Peter—still and straight-faced, where he would have been moving and joking—but I began to hear myself speaking to her as I spoke to him, in a voice that sounded like my own voice, unadorned.

I was so happy to be doing that, so at ease, that I talked too much that night. Way too much, as we used to say on Jupiter Street. I felt somehow compelled to tell her everything about life in Revere, everything from the layout of the planetary streets and the slow disintegration of the Boulevard amusements to the names of my aunts and uncles and the details of the menu at our Sunday gatherings. When the ice cream was finished, and the coffee was finished, and another cup of coffee was finished, and I knew I shouldn't stay much longer, I felt as if I had painted the floor of the room with my flood of words and had looked up to find myself standing alone in a corner, far away from her. "What do you do there in the woods?" I said, because it was the first thing that came to mind.

"I sit."

"And think?"

"No. I sit and not-think."

"How can you not-think?" I asked her, but the moment I spoke those words, it was as if a light clicked on in my mind's little seaside cottage. For a few seconds I was out on the river again, and jogging back through a downtown that was brighter and clearer than it should have been, a hundred times more precious. *Not-think*. I was sitting with my grandmother in Jerry the Zazz's and she was holding up a napkin in front of her as if a yellow piece of cloth held within it the key to life. Not-think. Not-think. The idea of it was so radical and impossible, and yet so completely familiar to me, as if people had been preparing me to understand it for years but I had simply never turned my mind in that direction. I wondered if all the adults in my life already knew about this but had just never found a way to convey it. I told myself then that I would make a career of not-thinking. I'd put it in the Exeter yearbook under "Professional Aspirations." Anthony Benedetto: Not-Thinker.

"We'll sit together sometime, I'll show you."

Why? I almost said. I remember catching the word in my mouth as it was on its way past my teeth. Not: Why sit and not-think?—I had some idea about that already. But: Why me? Why did you invite me here?

Why are you so nice to someone you don't know? Why are you different? What is it that makes you seem so different?

I don't remember leaving her house. I must have thanked her half a dozen times for the good food, and shaken her hand, and probably called her Mrs. Coughlin again. But I do remember walking back to Amen Hall that night, slowly, in the crisp autumn air, past the Exeter Inn and the Catholic church, and past the quiet, white-clapboarded homes on Main Street. I remember it, in part, because the town fire alarm was sounding, a series of air-horn blasts summoning volunteer firefighters from the far-flung corners of the county. Just as I reached the edge of campus, Joey Barnard was crossing the street. "You skipped hockey puck, you hockey puck," he said. "Want to go see if we can find the fire?"

"Is it close?"

He sniffed the air in answer, and we followed the smell toward the center of town. At the end of Main Street, the housefronts were washed by red and blue strobes, the road blocked by a police cruiser parked sideways and an officer standing next to it, waving traffic into a detour. Fire hoses lay like huge twisted shoelaces across the middle of the street, and as we passed the policeman and followed the curve of the sidewalk, we could see aluminum ladders angling up from the engines, and long stiff sprays of water.

Waterman's Cobbler Shop was burning. Waterman's Cobbler Shop and the two floors of wood-frame apartments above it. Firemen came and went in their helmets and rubber coats, training the spray from their hoses on scarlet tongues that curled through the top-floor windows, and on the two buildings to either side. A barricade of sawhorses had been set up on the opposite sidewalk, and Joey and I stood there in a small crowd. More fire engines arrived, two ambulances. Great clouds of smoke bubbled out the back of the building, and word spread among the onlookers that there had been two adults and two children in one of the upstairs apartments. So far, someone said, only one of the children was accounted for, a boy, badly burned but expected to live.

We stayed there three-quarters of an hour. Voices squawked from radios in the cabs of the closest engines, and shallow ribbons of water twirled along the middle of the street, making the pavement rippled and red-streaked. From the faces of the firemen and the silence of the little crowd, you had the sense that the second child and its parents were sprawled about the rooms above Waterman's shop, choked and charred, crossed over already into some other chamber of the spirit-maze. "Goddamn," Joey kept saying under his breath. "Goddamn it."

After a little while, there was more smoke and less flame, then no flames at all. Through a confusion of machinery and men we watched a stretcher being carried along in front of the store windows and into the back of one of the ambulances. The ambulance drew away without hurrying, and I saw a fireman, his face soot-streaked and shining with sweat, leaning straight-armed against the back of one of the trucks and wiping his eyes.

"Rough for the kid who lived," I heard someone behind us say, then Joey nudged me and pointed at his watch, and we turned away from the sad spectacle of it and headed home.

On the way back, I remembered an ordinary moment with my mother. We had gone swimming at Revere Beach. She was waist-deep in the sea, moving her arms back and forth across the surface in gentle strokes and encouraging me to come in deeper. I remembered her clearly then, perfectly, as one remembers a person in a dream—her voice, her shoulders, the way her wet hair fell along one side of her neck. I turned my face away from Joey and tried to hold the feeling of that vision. But it would not be held.

We said nothing on the walk back, and nothing at all as we pissed, and brushed our teeth, in the bathroom across the hall.

When we were settled in our beds and the lights were out, he said, through the darkness between us, "You have to wonder about God on nights like this."

"Yeah."

"You have to wonder if there's anything there at all."

"There's something," I said.

"Yeah. What, though? That's the question."

"That's the last little secret."

"Not little, Anth. Not to me."

In a few minutes his breathing changed. He turned over in the bed and moaned once, then was still. For a long time I listened to the night sounds: a breeze against the screen, cars passing on Court Street, the hum of engines and tires rising and falling away, and the empty spaces between them.

Sixteen

AFTER ANOTHER COUPLE OF chance encounters in the woods, Mrs. Coughlin and I began spending time together in a more or less regular fashion. It was an association of two lonelinesses, that's all.

On Sunday afternoons I would call her from the pay phone in Amen Hall, then walk the seven blocks to her house. She drove a new red Volvo station wagon. She would be standing outside near the car when I arrived—in her red down vest and the fleece-lined gloves that made her hands look comically enormous—and we would drive half an hour or so in one direction or another and find a place to walk. Sometimes we would go to the seacoast, to Rye, and walk along the ocean in the raw winter wind. Sometimes we would travel south and west, out into what was then New Hampshire farm country and is now Boston's outer suburbs, and walk along dirt roads past poor-looking clapboard-sided homes with barns tacked on out back, and stone walls running at the edges of cold pastures. Pickups rattled down the road. Men we did not know would raise a hand to us in greeting as they passed.

There was no more plan to those excursions than there had been to my solitary Revere walks. She drove as the mood suited her, stopped when we saw a place that looked empty and wild and good for walking. She was not very big on conversation, and I think she felt, at first, that there was something strange, almost wrong, about our friendship.

Partly because of that, a persistent awkwardness haunted the edges of those first afternoons. We were, after all, an odd couple, not relatives, or lovers, not teacher and student. I was a little more than half her age.

Over the course of that winter, though, a cold, icy winter with very little snow, we designed another arrangement, a free-form architecture of companionship that combined the emotions of all of the above. Since she did not spend a lot of time giving me advice, since she was always straightforward and unarmored, it was easy for me to let go of the cushion of deference and modesty with which I softened my relations with older people. She did not like sports, she said, and never came to my hockey games. So it was impossible for me to cling to my on-ice persona around her. Beyond what I told her, she did not know anything about Revere and the traditions and values of Italian Americans. She was unashamedly rich, unashamedly quiet; yielding in conversation yet without any of the lacy, false trappings of femininity I was used to seeing in the Greater Boston girls I spent time with during the summer months: the coquettish looks and laughter, the preening and teasing. She listened to classical music on the car radio and curled loose strands of hair back around her ear with her second finger. She drove with both hands on the wheel and flinched when trucks passed going the other way. When she locked the keys in the car once in Hurleysville, she said, "Oh, well, dammit then," and sat on the hood while I walked to the nearest farmhouse and called Triple-A. She listened attentively to her radio when there was news about the Vietnam War; she cooked Indian food and Moroccan food and wouldn't let me see her sculptures; she had a secret addiction to Mounds candy bars and allowed herself only one a day; she wrote checks to Amnesty International and the local animal shelter. Sitting with her in the car or in a restaurant was like sitting alone with your better self— and there was something tremendously pleasing in that. What connected us, I think, was the forced humility of people who have been roughly touched by death. An appreciation for the magnitude of absence. The absence of a person you loved, the absence of a Creator's mercy.

I was still playing hockey, still going out with Uncle Peter after the Saturday games. My grandparents would be there some days, too, if Grandpa Dom was feeling up to it. We'd always take Joey along, and go to the steakhouse we liked on the outskirts of town, and sit in a round booth there, talking about hockey or school or the wonderful future everyone assured us we would soon see. Sometimes my grandfather and I would have our wordless language going again. He'd sit beside me in his pressed pants and put his thin arm around my shoulders, and I would feel—as I sometimes felt with Lydia Coughlin—that words had been invented because the weight of a genuine intimacy between two souls, a real spiritual connection, was too much to bear for very long in silence. Too sweet. Too intense. You had to rise up out of it after a while and start breaking creation into nameable pieces again.

Grandpa Dom and I would sit that way for a little while, the meal over, half-full coffee cups in front of us, and it would seem to me, as it had seemed to me as a boy, that we were two parts of the same alert creature. There was the sense that we were waiting for something unnameable, but that we could afford to be patient about it. Conversation floated around us, the waitress came and refilled our cups, we sat there, connected, looking out at the world.

On the day after the game with Choate and a meal like that with the people I cared most about in the world, I went to Lydia's house just after noon and we drove up toward the foothills of the White Mountains. There was a lot of snow in the high terrain, and we rented snowshoes at a cross-country ski lodge and climbed up into the woods. It was a cold afternoon, but the sun was shining above the western hills, and the air was charged and sharp. She was a good snowshoer, and I had never done it before. Struggling and tripping, I followed her up the trail and across a high pasture of swirling white gusts, where the only sound was the *sluff*, *sluff* of the shoes, our breathing, the wind, and the occasional crack of ice in the frozen limb of a tree.

We made a large loop back to the ski lodge. We took off our snowshoes there, brushed the frozen coating from the cuffs of our pants, and sat drinking mulled cider next to a fireplace while the skin of our faces thawed. There was a small trouble in her eyes that day. I wanted to find a subject that would clear it away, so I said, "You promised you'd teach me this not-thinking trick. You said you'd show me how to meditate."

She held the cider mug in both hands with her fingers spread. She smiled sadly, a gold crown flashing on one of her back teeth. "I've been showing it to you the whole time."

"It's pretty subtle then?"

I'd meant it as a joke, but she looked steadily at me, her lips barely turning up. "It's ordinary," she said. "It's what's left over if you take all the fuss away. I spent a month at a retreat in a monastery in Nova Scotia once, and over the front gate they had a sign, 'No Fuss.'"

"Sounds boring."

"Boring is like a door you go through."

"To get to what?"

"To get to this peculiar kind of generosity and happiness that's different from any other happiness, that can't be taken away from you, no matter what."

I thought about that, I watched her. I said, "Sometimes, happy is the last thing a person would see on your face."

She brushed at the cuffs of her jeans. "It hasn't been the greatest year for me."

The sun was just going down behind the hills when we stepped outside again and into her cold car. On the highway, as if paying me back for my bluntness in front of the fire, she asked if I had a girlfriend. It was a subject we had never gone anywhere near.

"No."

"Why not?"

"There are nine hundred and ninety-six boys at the Academy, and eighteen girls. The ones I think are pretty all have steady boyfriends."

"What about in Revere?"

"There are a couple of girls I'm friends with. We don't go out, we're just friends. We go to the beach together with other friends, to movies sometimes when I'm home, that's all."

"Have you ever really dated anyone?"

I rolled the window down half an inch and let the cold air whistle in.

"Too personal?" she said.

I shook my head. "I'm just embarrassed, that's all. . . . Hockey player. Student Council rep. Never had a girlfriend."

"Don't you have mixers with girls' schools sometimes?"

"Sure."

"Do you go?"

"Sure I go. I dance a little. Sometimes I find a girl I like, and we hold hands and sit someplace and talk for a while. Sometimes I call her up the next week, or for the next few weeks. I just don't . . . I'm not good at it. I don't know what to say. I get shy. I've never even really kissed anyone, and I'm a goddamned senior in high school."

She laughed. I felt as if I'd shaved eight years off my age in the space of four minutes. Through the side window I looked out at the passing scenery, the hills, and the small towns tucked into cold valleys: white church spires and slate-roof houses. It was my great shame, this lack of a romantic life. My uncles and aunts joked with me about it, tenderly, affectionately, but it had gotten so that the edges of my brain went raw at the mention of the subject.

"What about you?" I said, because I felt she had pushed me tight into the corner of the seat.

"I guess I came at things from a different direction. I kissed my first boy when I was thirteen. My parents had a summer home in Delaware, and he and I took sailing lessons together, and we used to sneak down to the beach at night and kiss for a half hour at a time. I made love first when I was a freshmen in college, which was early for a woman in those days. It was my birthday, I'd gone out and had beer and pizza. I was underage, and I was a little bit drunk, and there was a boy who had a reputation for sleeping with a lot of girls. All I had to do was bump against him as we were getting up from the table, and that was that. He drove me back to the dormitory in his daddy's car, took a detour to the playing fields, and climbed on top of me in the front seat. Very romantic."

"What about getting pregnant?"

"A good Catholic question," she said. And then, after a moment, "It's a good question; I shouldn't have said that. I didn't get pregnant that first time. Purely by luck. After that I went to a doctor and got a diaphragm."

I did not know what a diaphragm was. We drove another few miles before I could bring myself to look over at the side of her face. She had a small, straight nose and gray eyes, and the top of her ski hat was pressed down against her forehead.

"I meant, what about boyfriends now?"

"My husband's been dead less than a year. He was having an affair when he died. I didn't know it. The woman came and told me herself, a week after the funeral."

"Who was she?"

"I shouldn't say." She looked across the seat at me. "You might run into her sometime in town, and then you'd have that in your mind, talking to her. I'd rather not say."

"Alright. I saw someone having an affair with my aunt once, when I was a kid."

"In the act?"

"What?"

"How did you see them? What were they doing?"

"They were in my cousin's bedroom, and my aunt was lying back. She had her clothes on. And he was kneeling down—he had one hand on her knee. I knew from the way she said my name that there was something wrong about it."

"Did your uncle find out?"

"I told him."

"Really?"

"A long time afterward. They were already divorced by then. Separated anyway. The man was dead."

"Is this the uncle who comes up to the hockey games?"

"Uncle Peter. You'd like him. I'll fix you two up if you want."

She took her eyes off the road and gave me an amused look, the first sparkle of happiness on her face that day.

We stopped about an hour from campus at a Chinese restaurant with exotic fish in large glass tanks along the walls. I remember the colors of the fish—impossible blues and golds—and I remember thinking that the conversation had changed the nice, easy feeling between us in a way I did not understand. It was late by the time we pulled into her driveway. She invited me in for coffee, but for some reason I said no, and took the long route back to Amen Hall.

Seventeen

THE MAIN QUADRANGLE AT EXETER is the heart of campus. Crossed diagonally by concrete paths, it sits in a shallow bowl of earth surrounded by four-story brick buildings: the Thompson Science Building; Phillips Hall, the Language Building; the Academy Building—which houses classrooms and the chapel and sits up on a rise so that it appears to be even larger than it is; and the Jeremiah Smith Administration Building, where the deans and the principal work and where there is a post office on the ground floor. All 1,014 of us had mailboxes there, with brass doors the size of cigarette packs, and individual combination wheels.

On that Friday, five days after my snowshoeing trip with Lydia, I worked the combination, opened my box, and saw three letters. Ordinarily I would have taken them to the Grill and read them in the company of friends, but after I glanced at the return address on one of the envelopes, I decided I wanted to be alone to open it.

I carried them outside, along one edge of the quadrangle, and down a path to Main Street. Not far along Main Street, you come to a sort of boulevard called Swasey Parkway, which angles off to the left between the widest part of the river and a patch of woods. Academy students did not walk there much. It had a reputation as townie territory, a place where Exeter High kids went to drink beer and make out, though I don't know if that was actually true.

I sat on a park bench there, by the river, placed my books on the green slats to my left, and held the letters in my lap for a few minutes before opening them. Compared to the weather we'd been having, the day was warm, a day when it was possible to believe winter would actually give way to a kinder season. Birds were darting here and there in the trees behind me. The sunlit bench was warm, but the air was cut by a sharp cold breath from the river.

I unzipped my hockey jacket and looked at the surface of the water, the boathouse flag stirring in the sun, the Milliken factory across the way with its rows of glinting windows and chimneys pumping smoke. I had a strange fascination with that building, and used to sit staring at it for minutes at a time before crew practice started. For some reason, I connected it with the men and women who worked in the dining halls, a sort of white-uniformed servant class that went about its duties quietly and unobtrusively, but with what always seemed to me a righteous bitterness, cooking for and cleaning up after boys like me, in our sport coats and ties and ridiculous naïveté. It seemed to me vaguely wrong that there should be human lives so different from each other, that I should be there, in that cold, hardscrabble state with its backwoods poverty and mill towns, studying Russian grammar in elegant classrooms and making loud jokes with my friends at the Grill while people not that much older prepared my food and washed my plates, or worked in factories and passed their days dreaming about the weekend. My father had worked in a factory. I knew he would have been proud that I was at Exeter, but my being there also slid a thin steel plate between his memory and me. I sensed that with my uncles, aunts, and cousins, too, as if I had gone off and joined the oppressor—which is what I felt like, sometimes, at the Academy.

Late at night, when we were finished studying, Joey and I would often walk down the three flights of stairs to what everyone called "the buttroom," a twelve-foot-by-thirty-foot stone den in the basement of Amen Hall. There was a vending machine, a place to play Ping-Pong, and a round, badly scarred wooden table where those students who had permission from their parents could smoke cigarettes and offer them to those students who did not. The buttroom was only a few steps from the outside door. One night a little boy from town walked through that door. Reggie, he said his name was. He was nine years old but had the face of an adult, a triangular, worn face sitting on top of a body with arms and

legs that were as thin and hard as sticks. He asked Madhur for a cigarette, lit it, took a puff, looked us over with a jailbird's eye, and said,
"What the hell are you queers doing down here?"

Reggie came back three or four times during the course of the winter
and early spring, amusing us with his swearing and smoking. But there
was something horrible about it all. One night, Joey had an argument
with Madhur about giving him smokes. "It's like he comes up from
underground, man," Joey said to me afterward, as upset as I'd ever seen
him. "Did you see the rings of dirt on his neck? Did you see his finger-
nails?"

Reggie was a like a figure in a dream for me, stepping out of the Exeter, the New Hampshire, the America that never showed themselves on
the Academy's neat lawns. Years later, I did, in fact, see him in a dream.
He was darting through traffic on a snowy street, scooting between the
bumpers of cars, away from me, and trotting down an alleyway like an
abandoned dog, runt of the litter, looking for a warm place to sleep.

I had the three letters sitting on my lap; I was looking across the river at
the factory. I was standing at the border of what seemed to me another nation. I took the thickest of the letters, put it on the bottom, and opened a
smaller, thinner envelope that had my name written on it in the spidery
glyphs of my grandmother's arthritic hand. I have that letter to this day.
"Carissimo, carissimo Antonio," it begins. *"Come ci manchi qui . . ."*

My dearest, dearest Anthony, how we miss you here, how terribly
we miss you. Your grandfather wanted me to write this letter to
you today because he is not feeling strong enough himself to
write it. He says he will probably not be well enough to come see
you play the hockey next week, but that Uncle Peter will come
and will tell him everything that happens. Here, with us, everything is fine, though Domenico suffers now from pain and is taking the medicine every few hours that the doctor gives him. I am
very well. I pray for you every morning and every night, that
God will give you all the happiness in life that Grandpa and I
have had, that Jesus will send his blessings down on you, and on

the souls of your mother and father in heaven. Soon you will be home with us again. *Non vedo l'ora. Con grande affetto*, Your grandmother who loves you. Nana Lia.

Non vedo l'ora is the Italian way of saying "I can't wait," though its literal meaning is "I do not see the hour."

There was a crisp five-dollar bill enclosed, as always. I put the bill in my pocket and the letter back in its envelope and set the envelope between the pages of my chemistry book. The next letter was even smaller, with unfamiliar handwriting, no return address. I opened it and found a card with a woodcut of a seated Buddha dressed in red-and-gray robes. Around the Buddha's head was a circle of red, edged in gold, which reminded me of the haloes around the stained-glass figures at Saint Anthony's Church. I've kept this card, too, all these years. It says, "Anthony, I have to go to Colorado to care for my sister, who is ill with breast cancer. I don't know when I will be back. Before you graduate, I hope. Go sit on my rock when you can and meditate, as I showed you. Your friend, Lydia."

I turned my eyes to the river and followed its silver surface north, toward the marshes, toward Portsmouth and Rye. A shrill whistle shrieked on the far bank. I looked up at the Milliken building and saw one of the windows on the top floor being opened, the sill being raised, a man's face pushing out into the air. I watched him leaning there on his forearms for half a minute. He looked over the whole landscape in front of him—the river and the town and the Academy buildings in the distance. He saw me and waved, and I waved back. Then he pulled his head in and slid the window closed.

The third piece of mail was from Brown University, something I had been waiting for all winter. The envelope was thick, and thick envelopes were supposed to mean good news, but I was afraid to open it. After hesitating a long while, I ran my finger beneath the flap and pulled out the forms and a page printed on fine stationery. It was addressed to "Mr. Anthony Benedetto," and the first line began, "We are pleased to inform you . . ."

Eighteen

THAT NIGHT, JOEY AND I skipped dinner at the cafeteria and went
to a place called Clarke's at the western edge of downtown, where the
tables were covered with linen cloths and the waiters addressed you
as "sir."

"This is allowance money for the next two months," Joey said when
we opened the menus and saw the prices. But we ordered steak, baked
potatoes, and coffee, and sat like princes at a corner table, eating very,
very slowly.

"Doesn't seem real, Anth, does it?" he said.

"Put a little more salt on and it will."

He shut his eyes and tilted his head back as he always did when he
laughed, a piece of baked potato the size of a sesame seed clinging to his
lower lip, and his new eyeglasses twinkling in the lights. His laughter
was quiet, almost apologetic—both of us half-expected to be put out on
the street.

"I mean, Brown. MIT. The world out there is *large*, man, and we're
going right into it."

"We're ready."

"Sure we are. But don't you feel it coming at you some days? It's like
a locomotive for me sometimes. It's like finals are tomorrow, and graduation is the day after tomorrow, and the days have only about five hours in
them. Do you ever feel that?"

"Sometimes. Other times I can't wait to be out where somebody
doesn't check to see if you're in your bed at night."

"You're more grown-up than me. You're more ready for the big world."

"Like hell."

"Sure you are."

The waiter, probably five years older than we were, came and stood beside the table and asked if he could take our plates, asked if we wanted dessert, said, "Yes, sir," to each of our orders for chocolate cake.

"You're already hanging out with older women, and I'm a virgin still," Joey said when the waiter had walked away.

"What older women?"

"I saw you in Mrs. Coughlin's car, man. Come on. Everybody knows about it. Maddy saw you walking on the playing fields with her. Jensen saw you coming out of her house. You're a legend in your own time."

"She's just a friend. We went snowshoeing once. We go for walks."

"Come on, man. This is your roommate you're talking to. The whole school knows, you're going to keep it from me?"

"I'm Catholic, remember?"

"So what? Shaughnessey's Catholic, and he's been balling what's-her-name from Concord Academy—"

"Kate."

"He's been balling Kate since they were in eighth grade."

"I'm not balling anybody. I'm a virgin. And she's gone away anyhow."

"Mrs. Coughlin?"

"Lydia."

"See? First-name basis. And you had a little thing in your voice, there, when you just said it. What did I tell you? You're all ready for the big world, man."

I shrugged; the waiter brought our desserts and refilled our cups from a long-spouted silver pitcher.

"This is the life, no?"

"Yeah. Until the bill comes."

"Speaking of graduation. You taking Lydia to the fancy lunch afterward?"

"Lay off."

"Reason I ask is that my sister wants to come up with my friend from home, Gloria. You've seen her picture, right? What about it?"

"Gloria?"

He reached out and touched the two knuckles of his fist against my forehead. "I guess it was because of the hockey stuff that they let you into Brown, huh? You think I'm taking my own sister to the Principal's Luncheon? I'd be in mad disgrace, man."

"Course you would."

"I'm trying to fix you up with my sister, Puck. She's looking for a white boy who's Catholic and not too smart and not going out with anybody and still a virgin and you're number three on my list. The other two already said no, for reasons of racial prejudice."

"Oh."

"She's pretty, don't you think?"

"Sure she's pretty. But didn't you tell me she had a boyfriend?"

"They just broke up. Another jock, like us. Football player."

"Worse than us."

"Tell me about it. He kept trying to get her to . . . you know, and she finally told him no, she meant it, no, and he never called her back. She's looking for somebody with a little brains this time. I've been telling her about Higgenbottham, you know."

"You have?"

"Course, course. But she saw his picture and that was the end of that. And the name turns her off. If it was Higgen*top*, she said, then maybe, but never no got-damned Higgen*bottoms*. What about your roommate? she asked me. She's seen your picture, you know, and the name Benedetto has a nice sound to it, she said."

"It means 'blessed' in Italian."

"There you go. You never told me. And you're a virgin to boot, a good Catholic boy, so I don't have to worry about you, am I correct?"

"You couldn't be more correct," I said.

Nineteen

WE FINISHED THE SEASON 14–2 and played in the New England Schoolboy Championships at Boston Garden, where we lost to St. Paul's 1–0, then beat Andover again, 2–1, in the consolation match. Several of my aunts and uncles came, and a contingent of cousins, but I barely had time to hug and kiss them all and ask about my grandfather before we were hustled onto the bus and shipped back to New Hampshire.

We'd each had bronze medals draped around our necks for finishing as the third-best prep-school team in New England. I wore mine to bed that night. I lay awake for a while, going over the final two games we'd played in front of the Boston Garden crowd, and then thinking back across the six years since my grandfather had first taught me to skate. I could remember some of the goals I'd scored, even as long ago as Bantam hockey. I could remember some of the injuries and defeats, riding home on a silent school bus once with my Revere High teammates after a particularly embarrassing loss to North Quincy, no one saying a word, Coach Zizza grinding his teeth in the front seat. Bruises and falls, beautiful cross-ice passes in practice, hours and hours of wrist shots and slap shots aimed at the corners of the backyard net Vito Imbesalacqua had made. My grandfather had been right, *era proprio l'idea per me.* Hockey had replaced a broken beam inside me, given me a way to live with myself—a kid from Revere, nephew of Pete Benedetto, who did not like to fight.

The next day I emptied my locker, put my skates and pads into a laundry bag, carried them back to Amen Hall, and stashed them underneath my bed.

I called Revere every Tuesday and Friday night from the basement pay phone. Uncle Peter would make a point of being downstairs at the appointed hour, and he gave me, sometimes in a quiet voice, the latest health reports. Grandma was fine, but Grandpa spent most of his days sitting in his favorite armchair, not saying much. He no longer had enough strength to work in the garden, or to make suits and blouses for his sons and granddaughters. Except for doctors' appointments and the funerals of his friends, he did not leave the house and yard. He could get himself out of bed, dress and feed himself, and use the bathroom on his own. Vittorio Imbesalacqua brought him *Il Mattino* every day at lunchtime, but he read it without really seeming interested, as if, now that he could no longer participate in it, the world beyond his immediate grasp had lost all attraction for him.

Spring break fell the week after Easter that year, and instead of going to the Canadian home of one of my hockey friends, I went back to Revere and spent most of the vacation sitting with my grandfather at the kitchen table, in the den, or out on the front porch. On some days he'd want me to tell him a story from school—he especially liked hockey stories—and I told him, more than once, how Higgenbotham had won the consolation game at Boston Garden: winding up for a slap shot from the point and completely missing the puck, then looking down, seeing it there, and just winding up a second time and blasting it into the corner of the net. "Everyone thought it was the greatest fake of all time," I said. "But he just missed it. He was so tired, Grandpa, he could barely stand up. He pulled the stick back and whiffed on it, almost fell over. But the defenseman had gone down to block the shot and slid right on by, so he just wound up all over again and hit it just right the second time."

My grandfather would nod, smile, close his eyes for five or six seconds as if picturing the scene. Grandma would set a glass of prune juice and a napkin in front of him, with the deliberateness of a priest performing a sacramental rite. And he would thank her, put his fingers around the glass, then rest his arm there for a time, gathering the strength to lift it. Uncle Peter came downstairs before work and stopped by again at lunch, and then came home, showered, changed into clean clothes, and spent the whole evening with him, holding his arm when he walked to the bathroom, playing checkers and games of cards, massaging the withered muscles at the tops of his shoulders. After his father went to bed, Uncle Peter would step out onto the back porch and smoke a cigar, or sometimes take a few puffs from a cigarette. He was working construction again, and it seemed he was taking on all the muscle his father was losing. I would stand beside him, almost as tall as he was by then, forty or fifty pounds lighter.

"This is going to be the end of the family now, Tonio," he said one night as we stood looking over the vacant lot at the streetlights on Park Avenue.

"No it isn't. You're not here during the day. You don't know how many people come by—Aunt Marie, Aunt Eveline, Uncle Francis, Uncle Aldo, all the cousins. Everybody comes."

"Sure. I'm not sayin that. I'm sayin it will never be the way it was. People will come to see Grandma, and you, and me, but the whole family's gonna change when Grandpa passes, you'll see. People will go their separate ways. That beautiful thing we used to have, that's gonna break apart." He shot his cigar out into the night, and I watched the red ash arc and sputter at the edge of the garden. "Your father was the only one who could have held everybody togetha."

"What about you?" I said. "You could hold us together."

"Me? With my track record? I couldn't hold togetha the two sides of my pants if the zippa broke."

I had a vision then of my grandfather as a skinny fifteen-year-old, booking passage back to Italy in order to fetch his parents and sisters, to piece his family together again in the New World. I imagined him sitting in the hold of a shuddering ship with strangers coughing and retching and pissing in pots around him. It did not seem possible that we could face any obstacle greater than what he had faced, that any of the forces of modern life could tear a fabric as tightly woven as ours. Which shows, I suppose, who was the wiser of the two people standing there on that night.

On Saturday, the night before I left to go back to school, Grandpa

Dom and I stayed up late to watch the boxing matches on the TV in the den, something we had not done more than four or five times since my parents were alive. He would drop off to sleep and wake up, drop off and wake up, and I spent as much time looking at him as at the action on the screen. My grandmother was praying in the back bedroom, as she always did before sleep; Uncle Peter was upstairs in bed, Rosalie out on the town. Grandpa Dom sat on the sofa in a bathrobe that looked two sizes too big for him, his hands pressing down on the pillows as if he were pushing with all his remaining strength against the gravitational tug of the grave.

When the last event ended, I turned the set off, and the small noise woke him. He patted the cushion of the divan, and I sat there, close enough to smell old age on him—old clothes, old skin, old breath. I looked through the lenses of his glasses at the watery whites of his eyes.

"What are you going to do now, Tonio, with your life?" he asked me in Italian, each word like a heavy stone he'd had to carry up through his chest and push out into the air. *Che farai adesso, Antonio, con la tua vita?*

"College, Grandpa."

He nodded. I could see the thin blue blood vessels on the sides of his high forehead, crooked little threads through which the last of his life was running. "After the college, I mean."

"I don't know. Something with Russian, maybe."

He closed his eyes and opened them. "Not a priest," he said.

I shook my head.

"A doctor?"

"No."

"A professor then maybe, in the university."

"Il professore," I said, puffing myself up and dragging out the word. It was an old joke of ours, a term we used, sarcastically, when we saw someone on TV who acted like he knew everything—a reporter, the governor, a political pundit. On certain summer afternoons, our neighbor Jim Shelston used to come by and watch us work in the garden, and offer a small encyclopedia of advice: "You should mulch those peppers more,

Dom." "You should pick those eggplants now, when they're small, they have more taste that way." "You shouldn't let your grandkids play ball here—look, some of your lettuce is broken." Grandpa would nod, thank him, and go on about his work. And when Mr. Shelston finally wandered back to his own home and his own garden, my grandfather would look at me, raise his eyebrows once, and say, *"Il professore."*

He lifted his eyebrows again now when I said it, pulled his lips back in a version of the old smile, then sank slowly into a tired silence, looking down through his glasses at his loosely folded hands. I would have taken him by the arm and led him to the bedroom, but I had the sense then that he was trying to gather the energy to say something. I looked out into the kitchen, where my grandmother had left the night-light on; the clock above the table was ticking loudly enough for us to hear.

"Ask me now," he said at last. *Fammi una domanda adesso.* "Ask me now, Tonio, if there's anything you want to know."

I looked at him, and then out into the kitchen. Through the window I heard angry voices, then a car door slam, then Rosalie's footsteps on the porch and on the stairs leading up to the apartment above us. I was suddenly assaulted by questions, overrun by a battalion of questions. What is important, your own work and success or trying to take care of the pain of the people around you? Can you manage both? Where should I live, in Revere or not in Revere? What did you do wrong that you don't want me to do wrong? Why did what happened to my parents happen? How could something like that happen to us? Why?

He watched me with some patience, though he must have been exhausted by then. Why did God set it up like this? I wanted to ask him. What is the point of it, of living, of suffering, of people you love leaving you, one after the next, of having to sit and watch all your dreams get picked up and twisted around and set down in a different shape?

He watched me, and I would have given anything then to have been able to find the question for me, and to have him offer an answer. I would give a great deal now to have been able to summon my Exeter eloquence on that night, some manly expression of gratitude. You saved me, I wished I had said, at least. All the time you spent reading through the catalogues of those schools, all the hours on the ice at the Public Gardens, your stories, your example about going where you were afraid to go, being a quiet, dignified, gentle man instead of something meaner. You saved me from the person I might have been. I know that now, I can feel it, I can see it. How can I thank you? How can I live so as to thank you?

But nothing came. Nothing, not one word, not a sound. My throat tightened up like a knot being closed in a rope. I knew he was telling me I would never see him alive again; and even with all the practice I'd had, all the warning, I could not bear the thought of that. After a few moments, I felt a tickling in my throat, and the sides of my eyes blurring. I looked away and then back, straight at him. He lifted his frail hand and rested it against the side of my face as he had not done in many years, and he rocked it up and down there once so that the skin and muscle moved back and forth over the bone, and a tear was shaken loose from my left eye, and ran down his finger and wrist and up under the cuff of his sleeve.

"Help me up now," he said at last. I stood and pulled him carefully to his feet. He seemed to weigh nothing. We squeezed side by side through the arched kitchen doorway and went as far as the threshold of his bedroom. He held me lightly at the back of the elbow. "Your cousin has her own life," he said, speaking quietly and hoarsely, almost whispering. *La sua propria vita.* "A separate life from you." He squeezed my arm once, and then stepped into his room, and I went down the short hallway and across the corner of the parlor, into mine.

Twenty

THERE IS NO FEELING on earth like the feeling of waiting for the death of someone you love. You cannot reach out your hands to help: he is too far away to touch. And, though you desperately want to, you cannot slow down, but must continue to lift your healthy thighs, and pump your healthy arms, and hurry on toward a future you can't see, and don't want to see, and want to.

Guilt, fear, helplessness, rage, impossible hope—every new day carries a new emotion, another bit of weight, as if you are trying to slow yourself down, trying to swing back into step with him. But he staggers on, falling farther and farther behind. Long past the moment when it seems he must surely collapse, he still moves forward on his feet, another breath, another minute, another day. The distance between you increases. You must look in front of you finally because you can't keep your head turned back at such an angle. You must look away, though you know what will happen when you look away. You know what you will not see, and want to, and don't want to.

I had to leave Revere and return to Exeter. I had to hold my grandfather's frail body against me on the front porch, and then finally let it go. I could not look into his face in that last minute, when he was standing so close to me. I turned away quickly and, through a gray, watery storm of tears, went down the steps and climbed into the backseat of Uncle Aldo's Oldsmobile. Uncle Aldo and Aunt Laura were in the front seat, ready to go; my young twin cousins Eliza and Alissa sat beside me, staring at me, perplexed, almost afraid, because of the scope of my grief.

My window was down. As the car moved away from the curb, I turned to look. He had come out of the porch and was standing on the top step, one hand resting on the railing. My grandmother was behind him, in the open doorway, and Uncle Peter was standing to his left, supporting him under the elbow. I knew he was trying to wave. I could see that he was trying to lift his hand from the railing and wave good-bye to me, I could see just the fingers move. He turned his head as we started off, following us, and I pushed my face out the window and managed some kind of grotesque smile, stretched, trembling, tears streaming down across it. I saw him open his mouth and lean forward an inch, as if saying one last word, in Italian, that I could not hear.

❯

DURING THE FIRST LONG DAY back at school, I expected, every minute, to receive the news that he had died. I made the walk from Amen Hall to my classes, watching for the assistant dean to step out of one of the buildings and signal to me, the way I had seen him signal to Johnny Grater when Grater's brother was killed in Vietnam. In calculus class, in Russian class, in the dining hall, half of me paid attention to what was being said and the other half held a constant vigil. I did not want to be surprised by the news. I did not want it to catch me unawares, the way a boxer is sometimes caught, the opponent's left hand coming out of darkness while you are watching the right, thundering against the bone to the side of your eye, and smashing you down on your back, on the gritty, sweaty canvas. That had happened to me, twice, and I thought I could avoid part of the pain of it if I saw it coming at me a third time.

I called home after dinner that night. "He's the same," Uncle Peter said over the line, "maybe a half a little bit bettah."

"Can he come to the phone?"

"He had a hard day, Tonio. He's beat."

"I thought you said he was a little bit better."

"Half a little bit, I said. He sat at the kitchen table, and Grandma fed him three spoonfuls of soup and a bite of bread. Vito came with the paper, like always, and Grandpa put the paper on his knees and he turned one page. That's how much bettah we're talkin about."

"You'll tell me if he gets worse?"

"Sure I'll tell you. Whaddaya think, I wouldn't tell you?"

"I'll call tomorrow night."

"Call every night this same time. He hears the phone ring, and he knows it's you, and it makes him happy. If he's feelin good enough, he'll get up and talk, okay?"

My grandfather lived through the next day, and the day after that, and the following week. For a short time it even seemed he might be growing stronger. Once or twice he was awake when I called, and feeling well enough to speak a few sentences into the phone. Those conversations were brief and affectionate scenes in a play. The script called for us to act like old friends chatting over a last peacetime lunch in the park, knowing all the while that an invading army was rolling in to the far side of the city, burning, looting, smashing through the streets and cafés and museums we loved. We talked about my classes, the weather, plans for the garden, expressed our love for each other in a word or two, and said good-bye.

On other nights my grandmother would come to the phone and say, "He's about the same, darlin. He sends his love, he's sleepin now, he loves you."

Lydia did not write again. I checked the mailbox three or four times every day—letters from the hockey coach at Brown, from an aunt or uncle or cousin, a card from Uncle Peter with a twenty-dollar bill inside, a note from my friend Leo Markin, saying he was thinking of enlisting in the marines after graduation, and was I interested. But nothing from Lydia. I called her, five different nights. The phone rang and rang in an empty house.

During the last days of April and the first days of May, I had more time to myself than I'd ever had at Exeter. I spent a lot of it walking. The fields and woods had burst into color after the long dreary winter, and in the afternoons I'd go along the path on the far side of the river, praying for my grandfather, fingering a whole rosary of strung-together memories; beginning—tentatively, guiltily—to imagine a life for myself without him. In those days I had the sense that the nonphysical part of me had grown into a larger size, and was waiting for a suit of clothes that was still being cut and sewn for it, that was not quite ready. I was in the last stretch of my last year, one of the oldest boys at Exeter now, gaining weight and muscle, the hockey season behind me, most of my academic challenges behind me. It seemed to me that one or two more stitches had to be sewn in and tied off, a sleeve finished, a cuff hemmed; another month or two, a few more lessons, and I would shake off completely the tight skin of childhood. There was a lining of impatience to every hour.

I avoided Lydia's flat stone, but not for any reason other than the fact that it stood close to the path, and I didn't want my friends to see me there, sitting with my eyes closed and hands folded.

In spite of that, though, I began to try to meditate as she'd instructed me, sitting quietly, a neutral observer over a parade of hopes. It was difficult. I found a log by the river, protected from view by a thick growth of underbrush, and I'd sit there for ten or twenty minutes at a stretch, trying to recapture the feeling I'd had during crew practice that one afternoon. It helped me believe I was maintaining some connection with her. It helped me forget, for a few seconds or a few minutes at a time, what was happening on Jupiter Street. On Wednesdays and Saturdays I would go out for a run and always take a route that led past her house. I'd slow down there, look up at the windows, peek into the yard as I passed, checking the door and the driveway and the lawn for signs that she'd returned.

After one of those runs I came back to Amen Hall via a roundabout route that brought me past the new library and through the door next to the smoking room. I climbed the iron-tipped concrete stairs, pushed through the brown fire doors into the third-floor hall, and saw my friend Chris Jensen there. He was waiting for Higgenbotham outside his room, twirling a squash racquet on its rounded end as if it were a top.

"Eliasis wants to see you, man," he said. "Right away."

So, in shorts and sweatshirt, I went back through the fire doors, up another flight, and knocked on the door of the faculty apartment. Mr.

Eliasis ushered me into his rooms—a real living space, carpeted and full of color. "Please sit down, Anthony," he said in an oddly formal voice, but by then I had made myself ready. I sat on his sofa. He sat on the edge of a soft chair, hands folded in front of him, forearms balanced across the tops of his thighs. For a second or two he squirmed and fidgeted, almost making eye contact, then he looked at me and said, "Your uncle called half an hour ago with some very sad news."

Twenty-one

I DON'T REMEMBER WHAT Uncle Peter and I said to each other on the ride home from New Hampshire that day, if we said anything at all. What I remember is that instead of going straight to Jupiter Street, he took a different exit off Route 1 and drove to Revere Beach. There would be people waiting for us at the house, we knew that, cousins, friends, neighbors, my grandmother, Uncle Peter's brothers and sisters. But it seemed the right thing to do to go and spend an hour near the beach before we saw them.

"Food up theah still lousy?" he asked when we were driving along the Boulevard.

I nodded, and he pulled into a parking space opposite Bianchi's Pizza. He bought four slices and two sodas, and we carried the food across the street to the hurricane wall and sat there eating and looking out over the sand. Revere Beach was not at its best that day: the tide low, the shoreline strewn with seaweed, litter, broken shells, and smelling of decay and salt.

"Why do people do that?" my uncle asked, sticking out his jaw to indicate a drift of plastic cups and pizza boxes against the foot of the wall. There was a trash barrel not ten feet behind us. I said I didn't know.

It was one of those days when the landing patterns of the big jets took them right over our sparkling little bay. From where we sat, if you looked to your left and out over the water, you could just see them beyond the Nahant Peninsula. A wavering gray smudge against pale blue sky, at first. Then, as they came in over the houses on Nahant, they grew larger—you could see wings, then the landing gear—but they still seemed not to be moving, or to be moving only at the speed a child might walk. And then they were suddenly enormous, right there, roaring so low across the water with the fuselage and windows glinting in the sun, and the wings dipping and lifting, and the tires looking as fragile and soft as the sugar-wheel pastries my grandfather used to buy me at Sully's store. It seemed absolutely impossible that something so huge and made of metal could hold itself up in the air like that, drop so quickly beyond the homes on Beachmont Hill, touch lightly down on the runway at Logan Airport, and bring its cargo of souls safely to the terminal. But all afternoon you could sit there and see jets strung out over the ocean in a long line, coming back to earth one after another, miracle upon miracle.

"He was lyin in bed," Uncle Peter said after the roar from one of the larger planes had subsided. "Hurtin pretty bad. We told him the ambulance was comin, and he said he had to get his pants on. I said, 'No, Pa, don't worry about it. You can go in your pajamas.' But he had to get his good pants on first; it meant everything to him to go to the hospital in his good pants. It was strange, Tonio. He sat up like he was as strong as he used to be, and he said, 'San Rocco,' just like that, and then he went. I stahted slappin the bottoms of his feet, hahd; I thought I could bring him back. Aunt Laura had to grab my ahms, imagine?" Uncle Peter threw the last crust of pizza into the box and closed the cover. "She said Saint Rocco's was the name of the church in the place in Italy where he grew up."

"It's where his sister was buried from," I said.

"What sista?" Another jet came roaring past. Uncle Peter didn't look at it, didn't seem to expect an answer from me.

"You know what I keep thinkin about?" he said. "I can't stop it, all the way up to get you I was thinkin about this, that one time he lent me money when I was really down and out and I never paid him back. I used to try to. I swear to God I tried as hahd as I could. The car, the house, money for Rosie—when theah was anythin left ovah I used to try to give it to him, ten bucks, twenty bucks. He'd take it and look at me . . . he used to look at me like, When are you gonna learn? I'd go out of my house on a Friday night at the end of a week of work, three hundred bills in my pocket, and I'd be plannin in my mind to go see him. But then I'd have to go to Broadway for gas for the car, then I'd remember he wanted some cold cuts from Rigione's, so I'd go to Rigione's. Then I was only five minutes from the dog track, so I'd go to the dog track. Three hundred, I used to think, what the hell good is three hundred when I owe him three thousand? I'll win the three thousand down Wonderland and I'll wrap the bills in a little piece of paper and stick them in there with the cold cuts, and then I'll sit down and say, 'Ma, what about a sangwich for Pa and me,' and she'd find it, and say, 'Pietro, what's this? My God, Pietro!' I'd imagine it just like that, you know, real as could be. And by the time I finally got to Jupiter Street that night, I'd have a dollar and forty-five cents in my pocket."

"He loved you," I said.

"Shuah, natchrally, he loved me. But I was the screwup who couldn't pay him back. When are you gonna learn? his eyes used to say to me. When?"

"He loved you more than anybody."

"What, *more*? What are you talkin about?"

"You were his favorite."

"How? What? What, favorite? Favorite screwup is what I was. Favorite moron. Big shot with the Cadillac and the new shoes."

Twenty-two

MY GRANDFATHER WAS WAKED at Alessio's, in the same room where my parents' caskets had once stood. Thick red carpet on the floor, ushers with somber faces and dark suits, rows of folding chairs, the smell of dozens of floral arrangements that were propped up near the long shining box in which he would be buried. My grandfather had led a quiet life—with the exception of his transatlantic voyages—but over the course of those two days, something like a thousand people came to pay their respects. Priests, tailors, retired presidents from the garment union, neighbors of my aunts and uncles, tough guys and gamblers and the friends who worked construction with Uncle Peter, old-guard Italian Americans—the men with big ears, coarse hands, and white shirts open at the neck, and the women with their hair colored various shades of brown and blue and patent-leather purses in their hands. My grandmother stood just to one side of the casket with a handkerchief and rosary beads in her fingers, and kissed the cheek or shook the hand of most of those visitors. I watched her, studied her. It seemed to me that two out of every three people said something that made her start crying all over again, but that even beneath the steady stream of sadness, there was something stable and confident about her. I wanted that for myself.

Once, when the river of visitors got dammed up near Aunt Marie, I watched my grandmother reach back, put a hand on her husband's arm, and squeeze it twice. His body was hard as a stone beneath the nice suit—I know, I touched it, too—but she squeezed it as if it were alive and warm, as if she were setting loose sixty years of companionship to do battle against the cold sureness of death.

Vito Imbesalacqua was there, of course, with his wife, Lucy, and their children, Peter and Joanie. My other close friends, Leo Markin and Ambrose Romano, shook my hand and squeezed my shoulder and sat with me for a while. Lois Londoner walked through the receiving line on Uncle Peter's arm. Johnny Blink leaned against the back wall of the room with his hands crossed in front of him. In the middle of the session, Angelo Pestudo showed up with two bull-necked bodyguards. Pestudo was a short, solidly built man with eyes that seemed to be always one-third closed, and a beautiful head of white hair. He was dressed in a silvery silk suit, a white shirt with no tie, and shoes that shone as if they were lightly coated in some precious metal. Though most people pretended not to, everyone watched him. As he stepped through the door, you could feel a quiet ripple of attention go across the room; and then you could feel people try as hard as they could not to stare, not to show that they knew what he was and what he did.

He did not take a place at the end of the long line, but walked right up to the casket and pretended to say a prayer there—making a foreshortened sign of the cross and bringing his fist to his lips. Then, with a movement that was as slick and forceful and natural as an Olympic figure skater's turn, he cut in front of someone who was talking to my grandmother and hugged my uncle hard around the neck. There was something elegant about the way he cut in line. His timing was perfect, effortless: he seemed to have been trained from birth to do things like that, to break a rule in public and dare people to stop him. Someone was holding my grandmother by both hands and talking to her, which created a small opening, and into that opening he stepped, canting his wide torso sideways a few degrees so that the movement gave you the feeling he was apologizing, but knew he did not need to. He was a head shorter than Uncle Peter, and when he reached up to hook an arm around my uncle's neck, the back of his suit jacket lifted up. I looked for a gun there, but there was no gun, no wallet, just the perfect cut of the silk trousers, a surface of fine cloth, without stain. He hugged my uncle and held him for a long time so that Peter had to lean over awkwardly, patting him on the back.

"Ma," I heard him say, turning to my grandmother when Pestudo finally released him. "Ma, this heah is Angie Pestudo. He's in a big rush, but he came by to say he was sorry." Pestudo leaned in to my grandmother and took one of her hands in both of his, the guards shifting their bullish bodies to either side and glancing quickly right and left as if assassins lurked among the cousins. I could not hear what he said to her, but from where I sat in the front row I could see her face clearly. She knew who he was; everyone in Revere knew who he was. He reached up and cupped the side of her face and her jaw in his hand, and that was the only flaw in his program, the only deduction as far as the judges were concerned. It was too familiar a gesture, and there was something aggressive in it, proprietary, as if, for the benefit of the audience, he was making a point about the relative worth of a heavyset old housewife and the king of the streets. My grandmother did not flinch. Gently, she reached up and took the hand away from her face, brought it back down to the level of her belt and held it there, all the while keeping her eyes fixed on his eyes. She was trumping the king. Without judgment, she was asserting what was right and proper in this room and what wasn't. Pestudo seemed to know it, too. He cut his act short, bowed to her in a false way, then patted my uncle once on the arm, turned his back on the casket, and paraded with his entourage past the rows of folding chairs, past the ordinary people, the type of people who waited in line, and out into the night.

Italian wakes, Irish wakes—there's something of the festival to them. The cousins kissed and talked and took turns standing in the receiving line, the men from the Holy Name Society came and said a rosary out loud; late in the session someone laughed once in the back of the room, and the noise knocked strangely against my ears. I wanted to observe everything—the pastiness of my grandfather's embalmed skin; the trembling and sobbing of my aunt Marie, who could not be consoled; the perplexed eyes of the youngest cousins; the rugged face of Vito Imbesalacqua, who sat in the front row a few seats from me, staring at the body of his older friend with an expression that was almost proud, as if Dom had been assigned some difficult tailoring job and completed it well. I wanted to remember everything, hold everything in my mind.

I wanted, especially, to talk to Rosalie. But she and Caesar huddled side by side in the receiving line and sat together in the folding chairs and stepped out the door for a smoke, exactly like a married couple.

On the second night, Rosie wore a short dress the color of the mussel shells at Revere Beach—a deep, shimmering purple, with white stitching at the hem—more appropriate for a fancy dinner date than her grand-father's wake. Halfway through the visiting hours, she came over and sat next to me. Her face was set in the beautiful half-smirk she wore when-ever she saw me, and there was tobacco smoke on her breath.

"It makes me think about your mother and father," she said.

I said it made me think about them, too.

"I don't know what to do with it, Tonio. It makes me just . . . it makes everything not make sense."

"I know."

"You don't seem like you know. It makes you sad, but it doesn't seem like it wrecks you inside the way it wrecks me."

I'm learning from Grandma, I almost said.

I had been looking at the banks of floral arrangements, at my uncles and aunts lined up there in their suits and dresses. Rosie had been talk-ing near my right ear, and I turned to face her and saw her eyes and mouth formed into an expression I had not seen there since we were very young. It was as if she were standing in front of me with no clothes on, Rosie without her act. In that one instant I understood her completely—her masks and toughness, her funny stand-up routines that always kept you at arm's length. I had an urge to say to her, But you'll die, too, Rosie. You can't stop it, you can't change it. Which would have been a terrible thing to say.

So instead I told her: "Everybody loves you. Your father loves you more than you can begin to imagine," and I put my arm around her shoulders and pulled her against me, so that our chests were a few inches apart and our heads side by side. She erupted in tears then, soaking the shoulder of my suit jacket, squeezing me and squeezing me and sobbing so loudly that eventually Caesar came by with some water for her in a paper cup. I took the water with my left hand and held it a little ways out from my body so it wouldn't spill on us. Rosalie went on weeping, not acknowledging him in the smallest way. He stood there a minute, awkwardly tugging together the sides of his sport coat, then retreated to his place along the wall and watched us.

Uncle Peter was watching us, too.

I held the cup of water out and pulled her close with my other arm, and I tried to concentrate on the fear in myself, a fear I'd been cultivating in some dark garden since I was eleven years old. Now, though, some new light was shining on it, illuminating Rosalie's life, Uncle Peter's life, my grandfather's dignity, Lydia Coughlin's plainness, my grandmother's constant prayers. For a moment it seemed obvious to me that the fear of dying was the whole driving force behind Angelo Pestudo. He had to master it; he had to wrestle it and pin it to the floor and convince himself and everyone around him that he was not worried about it, not afraid, when, in fact, he was more afraid than anyone. The prestige, pleasure, and power of his life meant everything to him: how could he even think about losing them? Being special, invincible, superior—his entire identity was tied up in those things: how would he ever be able to let them go and die like an ordinary man?

For that small moment I saw everyone I knew in the light of the fear of death: everyone faced the same music and made up a different response. But what it always came down to was a choice between running and standing still, between distracting yourself in one of a million different ways, and looking straight at the end of the world as you knew it and walking on, in spite of what you saw there. I made a little vow to myself then, as to how I would try to live. Seventeen, just stepping out into the world, not knowing half what I thought I knew. I made myself a little promise.

Eventually, Rosie leaned back and kissed me, then went off to wash her face and fix her makeup, and drive around the city until the early-morning hours with Caesar Baskine, trying to cobble together some kind of future for herself that did not include this room.

The wake ended; the aunts, uncles, and most of the cousins returned to Jupiter Street to eat and talk. Very late that night, when all the relatives and friends had left the house, I was knocked awake in my little room by a sound I could make no sense of. A faint, regular creaking. Some peculiar bird outside the window, I thought. Or my grandfather's ghost. I lay still beneath the sheets and listened, then got out of bed, pulled on a shirt and a pair of pants, and went into the kitchen. The sound was louder there, I recognized it. I went to the back door and saw my grandmother on the landing outside, wearing only her bathrobe and pajamas against the cool night. She had a basket of laundry at her bare feet, filled with her husband's clothes, and she was reaching down and pulling out wet undershirts and socks, one after another, shaking them, draping them over the clothesline, pinning them in place. The pulley squealed, a drawn-out shrieking in the Revere night. She bent down for a pair of his socks, pinned them up, tugged once on the hems, lightly, to stretch them into shape, pushed the rope out with one hand.

"Grandma," I said quietly through the screen, "it's late." But she didn't turn around.

Because I couldn't think of anything else to do, I went back into the kitchen, buttered two slices of Italian bread, and set them in the toaster oven until the butter in the center of each piece melted so that it almost looked as if an egg yolk had been broken there. When she finished her chore and came inside, she seemed surprised to see me, surprised that it was so dark out and there she was, in her bathrobe, barefoot, hanging clothes. I sat her at the table with the plate of toast in front of her, and she looked at it, then up at me.

"Eat a few bites," I said, as she had said to me so many times, "you'll feel better."

Book Four

One

I MADE THE TRIP back to Exeter, as always, with scraps of the fabric of Revere sewn into the lining of my coat: my grandmother on the porch in her bare feet; Rosalie's beautiful, unguarded face a few inches from mine; Uncle Peter scooping armfuls of flowers from the cemetery lawn and throwing them down into the open grave; relatives crowded into the kitchen at 20 Jupiter Street, picking at plates of food and letting themselves laugh, tell a story, or bubble over with tears, now that the funeral was over and the body in the ground.

Like Joey, I began to feel that the end of the school year was speeding toward me then, that the days were fractions of days, chips of sunlight that were being washed out of our hands and down a sluiceway into the past. There was less than a month left of school, and a languorous air blew in through the open windows of our classrooms. Our teachers pressed and cajoled and pushed us on toward graduation like drivers whipping teams of thirsty horses past a cold stream. We rented canoes, paddled up the Exeter River, roasted hot dogs there and sipped from an illegal beer or two; the seniors in Amen Hall took to staying up until two o'clock in the morning playing a double-elimination Ping-Pong tournament and printing the results on a piece of white cardboard on the wall. I called my grandmother every third night, felt my grandfather's absence tugging at me, at us, but I could not pretend I wasn't happy then.

On the next to the last Friday night in May, I was sitting in the butt-room playing bridge with Higgenbottham and Joey and Joey's good friend Sterner, when we heard the phone ring in the corridor. Sterner was sitting nearest the door and got up to answer it. "Suspend play for six minutes, gentlemen," Higgenbotham called out. A moment later Sterner was back. "Benedetto, some babe for you."

Lydia's voice was like a happy song in my ear. "The Coughlin pool is open," she said when I answered. "Can you come over on Sunday?"

I told her that I could, that I wanted to. When she asked how I'd been, I told her about my grandfather, and she said how sorry she was, that she knew how important he had been in my life, and I thanked her and went back to the table and finished the hand in a state of perfect distraction.

Two

ON SUNDAY AFTERNOON, Amen Hall was quiet as a library, my friends out on the fields or tennis courts, or finishing up a final science project in the lab. Joey had been invited to an end-of-the-season barbecue at the home of the track coach.

I sat on the side of my bed, unable to open a book, turning my eyes to the clock every two minutes. At 4:05 I put my bathing suit on under my jeans, took a towel from the rack in the closet, and went down the stairs and out into the hot day. Because of what Joey had said about people seeing me and Lydia together, I decided to take a roundabout route to her house, choosing back streets and circling around behind the Exeter Inn like a spy.

She was sitting by the pool. She stood up, said, "I'm so sorry, Anthony, really," and wrapped her arms around me, her head turned sideways and pressing in against the top of my chest. We had never been physical in that way before—it was always handshakes and nods and a safe distance between our bodies—and I had never seen her in a bathing suit, her middle bare, her round breasts pushing out against the yellow fabric. I turned my back to her quickly—in my confusion I may have been rude—dove in and swam several laps. It probably would have been better for me at that moment if the water had been cold, but the pool was heated. I swam a few more laps, letting my blood quiet, then turned onto my back and floated, watching the clouds in a blue spring sky as they broke apart and knit together again in new shapes. I tried not to think about the feeling of her body against me. I tried to relax again into the sense of being in a place where I did not have to keep any part of myself secret, but I was unsure about that now. Something had changed. I was afraid of it.

Lydia sat in a lawn chair, reading the *New York Times* and sipping from a glass of grapefruit juice, but I could feel her watching me. I could feel a strange sort of tightness in the air. "You coming in, Mrs. C?" I said in what I hoped was a casual tone.

When she put her eyeglasses on top of the paper, stood up, and walked to the diving board, I noticed, as if it were the first time I'd seen her, how small she was built. There was a scar running from the hem of her bathing suit bottom up to her navel, and I looked at it, then away. She dove and swam underwater the length of the pool. We made a couple of laps together a few feet apart, floated, hung to the rough cement edge at the deep end, keeping all but our heads and the tops of our shoulders in the warm water. She ran a hand up from her forehead, pushing the hair back, and glanced at the one other house we could see.

"Nice to have you on the same level as me for once," I said, but she glanced up again, over the lilac bushes that bordered her yard, then fixed me with a look that cut through any possibility of humor. She stared at me that way for what seemed like half a minute but was probably five seconds, then she took a breath and dropped down into the water.

I felt her hands on the bones of my hips, and my bathing suit being tugged down, over my knees, past my ankles, and off into the pool. She surfaced very close to me. Her eyes searched my face as if she was waiting for me to stop her, but the last thing I would ever have done then was stop her. We were each holding on to the lip of the pool with one hand. She took my free hand and brought it to her bathing suit bottom, and I tugged down, and then went under the water as she had done and pulled it over her legs and let it go. I could see the scar on her belly, the hair between her legs—darkened by the water—the muscles of her thighs. She was making a very small kicking motion. I rose up through the water against her and she took hold of my shoulder and pulled herself up and onto me so that I felt as if my whole body had been enveloped by her, that she was a second, warmer flesh pulled down tight over the thumping blood in my legs and hands. She held on to the muscles of my upper arms and leaned back so that she was looking into my face. I was breathing very hard and shaking violently; I could barely keep my eyes on her eyes. "Let go," she said. I thought she meant let go of the lip of the pool and I did, and we immediately sank and separated and found each other on the surface again. She was spluttering, then laughing quietly.

"Not let go of the pool," she said, coughing, treading water a few feet from me, the happiness in her face blending over into something else, something unprotected. I reached out—timid still, afraid she would stop me—curled my arm around the middle of her back and pulled her up and onto me again. She lifted her legs up over my hips and moved a few times against me, and I made a noise that echoed in the fenced backyard, and then she was squeezing me very tight with her arms and legs and sobbing into the side of my neck, pouring out all the pain I had not been able to see in her before that day.

"I hurt you," I said.

She was sobbing as if death itself were visible over my shoulder. My arm grew tired from holding on to the lip of the pool, but I didn't move. There were strands of her wet hair across the side of my face, and her ribs were against my other hand, moving back and forth in time with her quick breaths. I could see, beyond her shoulder, the yellow bottom of her bathing suit floating on the pale blue water.

"Tell me if I hurt you."

But she was shaking her head and pressing it hard against the side of my throat, and could not speak. We stayed that way a long time. At last, she said, near my ear, "Come inside the house now."

I dove for my bathing suit. I could see the maroon square of cloth lying against the drain, and I felt, for the time it took me to retrieve it, that perfect clearness of mind I remembered from the river, as if all my life I had been wrapped in a tight suit of thoughts, wrapped in a false belief about who I was, and what God wanted from me, and what was wrong, and what wasn't, and now I had burst through all that and was diving down into a bright, open adulthood that had no limits. When I surfaced, she was already in the house. I pulled my trunks on, climbed out and quickly dried myself with the white, dormitory-issue towel, and saw that the bottom of her bathing suit had been tossed carelessly over the back of a lawn chair. She was standing on the kitchen tiles, naked, young-seeming, with the top of the bathing suit in one hand. Her breasts were formed like the rest of her, small and muscular and yet somehow fragile-looking, with tiny nipples like a boy's and a spray of freckles across them. In a certain way it was like coming upon her that first afternoon in the woods: she seemed not to have a particle of embarrassment about her, not to have the capacity for shame. More than anyone I have ever known, she treated sex as if it were a wonderful, almost holy event, and it made everything easy and natural for me, in spite of the frenzy of my body. My first instinct was toward guilt and regret, toward apology; she broke that apart for me without speaking.

She took me by the wrist and led me to the small guest bedroom. She pulled the covers back and we slid under them, wet in places from the pool, our hair damp against the pillows. The shade was drawn in the room. The light was dim. Her skin was cool against my skin at first, and she shivered slightly. We lay there silently for a little while, and then she kissed me very tenderly and lovingly, and I took my cue from her and kissed her back the same way, as if I had done it a thousand times before. And when she turned and pulled me on top of her, I remembered my grandfather's fingers against the wineglass, and I tried to hold her that way, my hands against the sides of her breasts, and she did nothing to make me feel awkward or clumsy. When we had made love, I lay on top of her for a long while. I remember her running a hand slowly up and down my shoulder blade, and I remember feeling surprised that it had all seemed so natural, as if being intimate with a woman was something I had done countless times before and somehow forgotten about. A moment later I drifted down into a sleep so deep and warm, it was like being covered from forehead to feet in the fur-covered bodies of small animals.

When I awoke, it was dark in the room and I was alone in the bed. I turned onto my back and looked up at the ceiling. I could smell the clean cotton smell of the pillowcase. I rested both hands across my stomach with the tips of my fingers touching, and concentrated on the breath moving in and out of me. It was very quiet in the house. My life at Amen Hall was thousands of miles away. For a long time I did not seem to think anything at all, but coasted along in a single feeling, the deepest calm, as if I believed I would never have to strive again, or accomplish anything again, or prove anything to anyone ever again, as if there could not be any sadness again ever in my life.

After a time the door opened. "Are you sleeping?" I heard her say. She stepped into the room, and I could see her head and shoulders, half-lit by the light from the hall, a faint line of reflection along the frames of her glasses. She sat on the bed and put one hand on my chest. "You're awake?"

"Drifting."

"It's quarter to nine. What time do you have to be back?"

"Ten."

She put her hand on the middle of my chest. "Get dressed, and we can eat something, alright? Are you hungry?"

"Make me eleven sandwiches," I said.

She made me two. Grilled cheese on rye bread with thin slices of tomato. And she poured me a glass of white wine without asking. Instead of sitting at the table, we carried the plates and glasses onto her sun porch, and sat in the white wicker chairs with the food on our laps and only the light from the street on our faces.

"I'm sorry I lied to you," she said.

"About what?"

"I told you I went away because my sister was ill. She is, and I did go to see her. But I went away because I wasn't sure what would happen to you if we did this, what would happen to your last two months at school."

I studied her, studied the leaves of the plants on the table between us. "Where did you go?"

"I went to see Anastasia, and then I went up to where we have a cabin in the Allegheny Mountains, near where I grew up, and made a kind of solitary retreat."

"Why did you cry there in the pool?"

She did not answer for so long I thought she was angry at me for asking. I could see a shadowy figure passing along the sidewalk at the front edge of the yard, a woman walking her dog. "That's right," the woman was saying very loudly. "That's right now, that's my boy, that's my little sweetheart."

"My neighbor Helen," Lydia said, nodding in the woman's direction. "She's a little bit deaf and half blind. Good thing for us."

"Why did you cry, Lydia?"

Helen went on spewing endearments into the night. Two cars hummed down the quiet street, one after the other. Lydia didn't answer.

After a long while I asked, "Can I come back?"

She was staring at me now, staring right through the adolescent wrapping, as if to measure the amount of affection I was capable of accepting from her, or giving in return. There was only one thing I was afraid of then, one word.

"I want you to come back," she said at last. "I just don't want you to be thinking about coming back. Do you see?"

"Almost. I think if I come back a few more times I will."

She laughed her lilting laugh then, sunlight in the room. I looked at her, smiled, felt that nothing stood between us—not our ages or histories or personalities, nothing superficial like that.

She took my plate to the sink, gave me a mint to cover the wine on my breath, and kissed me once lightly on the mouth before I left.

Three

IT WAS IMPOSSIBLE NOT to think about her. I thought about her in my classes, in my bed at night with the rough wool blanket against the skin of my forearms and hands, and the sound of Joey stirring and muttering in his sleep on the other side of the room. I'd sketch her face in the margins of my textbooks. I'd leave my friends at our table in the dining hall and go up for a second helping of chicken à la king or a third brownie, or a fourth glass of milk, and my inner eye would be filled with visions of her: lying beneath me in the guest-room bed, looking at me in a way I had never been looked at, making soft humming sounds during the lovemaking—the language of another life; sitting in the wicker chair with the plate balanced on her thighs and held lightly in the fingers of both hands and telling me, "I don't care what other people think, Anthony; I just don't care about things like that anymore," in a voice that sounded so certain and calm, it seemed she had never been afraid, that she could never be hurt.

Everything in her world—from the jars of flour and cornmeal on her kitchen counter to the strands of her hair, wheat-colored with a few threads of gray, held back in the teeth of her barrette—seemed clean and ordered, immune to ordinary complications.

It wasn't true, of course. Her life was, in fact, ordered and calm, more so than most lives I knew before or have known since. Sitting quietly in meditation for two hours every day, as she did, is almost a guarantee of an ordered, calm life. But there were also deep layers of trouble and grief in that life. Her sister's illness. The lingering, nagging sorrow—too small a word—caused by the death of her husband and, especially, of her son, Robert, who had celebrated his fifteenth birthday a week before the accident; the haunting memory that she had stayed home that day, instead of going with them, because she had wanted to finish one of her sculptures. There was, too, a particular brand of middle-aged loneliness that I could sense at certain moments, dimly, but would not, for another twenty-five years, even begin to understand.

We made love nine times in all, and always afterward she wept. It was a quiet, restrained weeping that lasted only fifteen or twenty seconds, a kind of orgasm in reverse. She would pull my face down against her neck and turn away, and I could feel the pulse of sadness running up through her chest and throat. I would hold her and let the sorrow run its course, and then lie next to her on my back, feeling the warmth of her leg against my leg, and resting my left arm across my belly so that the ends of my fingers touched the scar that ran up toward her navel. That scar fascinated me. I know now what event it marked, what profound joy, but I did not know it then, and I ran my fingertips across it as if it were the mysterious key to her, which it was.

Over the last two weeks of the term, I went to her house on Wednesday afternoons and Sunday evenings—the times I could get away from my friends and from the dormitory without attracting attention. On Sundays, we had more time together, and after the lovemaking, she would talk more than she had ever talked since I'd known her. I understood that she had made the decision to allow me into the secret room where she kept her old trophies of happiness, and I tried to be the perfect guest there, the perfect listener.

Lying beneath the single sheet in the darkness with the sound of the drawn shade knocking against the window frame, I would listen especially carefully to her voice, as if the essence of her could be distilled from its sure, quiet notes. She liked to tell me stories about her travels: the canals and gilded onion domes in Leningrad, old kerchiefed women on the corners selling strawberries from cones of newspaper, their hands as gnarled and worn as if they'd been scratching out a living in the dirt for centuries; a plain poor village in the mountains near the Yugoslavian coast, where a man had been killed on the train tracks outside, while she drank beer and ate chocolate with friends in the depot bar; a road that led from a city called Domodossola in Italy, south and west into France, winding down out of the Alps past soft-looking cliffs with old French men fishing in the river that curled around the base of them. As a single woman, and later, with her husband and son, she had traveled widely— to Africa, to Argentina, to a Norwegian city called Narvik, a hundred miles north of the Arctic Circle, where she and her husband had lived for two weeks in a cabin at the mouth of a fjord, and where they'd returned ten years later with Robert.

"Traveling is the purest joy for me," she said. "No house, no car, no things. It's like the feeling you have sometimes when you're running. You have no weight. And everything has a richness to it, a newness. When you're finished with college, you should take off for a year or two and just see what there is to see."

"We could travel together," I said. "I speak Italian. We could go to Italy, to the villages where my grandparents were born."

There were eighteen days until graduation, until I was supposed to leave Exeter. There were two weeks. I consoled myself by creating elaborate scenarios like that in my mind's eye: we would travel to Europe together; we would find a house on the beach at Cape Cod, where I would get a job as a carpenter and she'd have all day to work on her sculptures; we would book passage on a freighter and sail to Hong Kong. Or, if I was in a less expansive mood, I would imagine borrowing my uncle's car on Wednesday afternoons in the summer and driving up to Exeter to be with her—to make love, meditate, walk in the woods, drive to the seacoast for a cold swim.

From time to time, in that shadowy warm room, one of those dreams would rise and break the surface, and she would let it make its fabulous splash there in the darkness, and then let it fall back and sink again, without comment. Instead of taking up the thread of my fantasies, she'd put my fingers on the pulse in her wrist, or she'd say, "Look at the way that band of light falls across the walls and the ceiling." Anything to tow me back into the actual present.

"That's not light, that's less-darkness," I would say, or something like that, some seventeen-year-old's clever quip, because her wordless resistance to my fantastical plans felt like rejection to me.

Once, she brought me down into her cellar workshop and showed me a sculpture she was almost finished with. There were tools lying in one corner of the room—chisel, mallet, goggles, a power sander—and next to them, on a wooden pedestal, a piece of white marble about the size of a basketball, that she said she had gotten from a quarry in northern Vermont and carried in from the car herself on a dolly. She'd carved faces into the four sides of the globe, elongated faces with noses, cheeks, and foreheads as smooth and speckled as a grapefruit skin. A woman weeping, a woman smiling, a woman who appeared to be in pain, a woman who might have been asleep, or in a state of deep relaxation, or in a state of bliss. "No one in particular," she said when I asked who it was. "I've been working on it for two and a half years. There are some other versions out in the shed and up in my bedroom. I'll show you sometime." She led me back up the stairs and kissed me good-bye there, patiently, playfully, and slapped her hand lightly against the seat of my jeans when I turned to go out the door, so that I made the walk back to Amen Hall singing to myself.

Twice she had me sit with her in the small "shrine room," as she called it, and meditate cross-legged before her Buddhas and her beads. My meditations would be full of images of her body, or echoes of things we had said or done in the bedroom, nothing like the little empty stretches of peace I had sometimes experienced in the woods. When I confessed that to her, she told me, "Think of it as a thousand-year project."

In the other hours of the week, I went through the motions of my former life, crossing the campus with textbooks under one arm, sitting in the Grill and talking with friends about summer plans, going out onto the playing fields on the last Saturday afternoon of the sports season and watching Joey Barnard fly around the gravel track in his maroon shorts and maroon EXETER shirt and set the school record for the mile—four minutes, twelve and two-tenths seconds, a record that stands to this day. I would talk to my grandmother and Uncle Peter from the basement telephone, and wander alone in the woods before dinner, practicing not-thinking. One night, I had such a vivid dream about Rosalie that I sat bolt upright in bed and shouted her name, waking Joey out of a solid sleep. In the dream, she had borrowed Caesar's car and driven up to Exeter in the middle of the night, and had been tossing pebbles against the screen of my room and calling my name, but by the time the sound woke me, and by the time I went to the window, she had somehow rigged up a rope to the windowsill and looped it around her neck and was dangling from it. Her feet were twitching, she was reaching up one hand to the rope, to me, but her body was too heavy to reel in, and there was such a space between us that I could not reach down and save her.

Classes ended, exams ended, the underclassmen packed their trunks and suitcases and headed off in their parents' cars or in airport limousines. The seniors stayed on. We had three empty days in which to pack our belongings, collect our yearbooks, and tie up any loose ends in the bursar's office, at the bookstore, at the Grill. I had Uncle Leo's Instamatic, and I remember using half a roll of film taking pictures of the ten-foot-high wrought-iron gate that led into the main quadrangle, something I'd passed by four times a day for two years without giving more than a glance. We were nostalgic like that, excited, nervous, a bit tired from the strain of examinations. I was caught up in those feelings like everyone else, but beyond that, there was a constant note running through every hour of every day for me. Lydia, Lydia, Lydia.

Graduation was scheduled for the first Saturday in June. On that Friday, after lunch, I met her in a side street behind the fire station, two blocks from Amen Hall, and we headed west in her car. She was wearing a short-sleeved black jersey and a loose summer skirt the color of cornmeal. The skirt rode a little ways up her legs as she worked the pedals and clutch. The day was humid and warm, and we could hear thunder grumbling in the western distance. There was a tangle of traffic on Main Street, some intermittent drops against the windshield. When we had worked free of the town and were heading into the countryside at last, we saw a spectacular display of lightning in front of us, and then a hard rain began to fall. "Do you have a lot of people coming up for graduation?" she asked above the sound of it.

"Two cars' worth. My grandmother, uncles, aunts, cousins."

The wipers squeaked and slapped; she leaned forward and peered at the road.

"You'll be there, too, won't you?"

"I don't think so, Anthony."

"I thought you said you didn't care who knew."

She didn't answer. We were traveling west on Route 101, the highway where her husband and son had been killed. Trucks sped past in the opposite direction, throwing clouds of dirty spray against the windshield. The heaviest rain had ended, but we could hear thunder behind us, and see the occasional bright flash in the mirrors.

"The ceremony is going to be outdoors if the weather's good," I said, trying to sound nonchalant and grown-up, though something about the conversation, something about her posture and tone of voice and the way she would not look at me, made it seem that the wet ground was moving sideways under the wheels. "There will be a couple thousand people there. . . . You could just hang out on the fringe and give me a little wave or something, couldn't you?"

She didn't smile or speak and seemed to me to be concentrating on the driving more than she really needed to. I did not like to think about the graduation ceremonies, partly because it meant leaving her in Exeter, and partly because I had promised Joey to take his sister, Regina, to the Principal's Luncheon after the diplomas were awarded. Ever since I had slept with Lydia for the first time, it had been gnawing at me. I knew Regina wasn't coming all the way from Sacramento just to meet me. On the other hand, I knew Joey had been building me up to her, that the Principal's Luncheon was no ordinary date (there was a tradition at Exeter having to do with the number of boys who had eventually married the girl they took to the luncheon), that Regina would be coming east to visit an aunt in Bridgeport, Connecticut, for two weeks in late July, that I was supposed to be a virgin, and unattached, that I hoped to stay friends with Joey for the rest of my life. I couldn't tell him about Lydia yet—it was still too private for me, too precious—but I did not like the feeling that I was living a lie.

We turned off the highway and away from the darkest part of the storm. In a gusty rain we went north along a smaller road, two tar lanes that snaked past houses with rusty bicycles on their porches, peeling shingles, wheel-less pickup trucks on concrete blocks in muddy front yards. It was the domain of the poor of rural New England, another secret life. We came upon a sagging, dripping little town, and as we passed through the pitiful commercial strip, she said, "My sister's gotten worse, she's going to have to be hospitalized. I'm going out there to help care for her kids."

Her voice broke slightly on the last word. It made me happy to hear that break, to think that she would miss me, and then, arcing over that mean little happiness came a spark of understanding of what she was saying to me, and an explosion of self-pity. "It's the truth this time?"

She looked across the seat. "Not a very nice way to ask. Yes, it's the truth."

"When are you going?"

"Tomorrow."

"When are you coming back?"

"I don't know. I don't know if I will. . . . After she dies. After everything is settled there, maybe."

We were in the country again, hills covered with fir trees, everything green and black and wet. We passed through another hard shower and a hard stretch of silence.

"You're just going to go then and not come back. That's it?"

"You make it sound like . . . like it's as simple for me as—"

"Isn't it?"

She didn't answer, and I bit down hard on the inside of my cheek to keep the rest of the words in. One more step in that direction, one more ugly sentence, and I felt we would be instantly transformed into enemies. I felt the possibility of that, the sweet, miserable power of it. Hurt for hurt. But I had never had much taste for purposely hurting people, and I thought there might still be some hope, something I had not understood correctly. So I swallowed once and took a breath and said, "I'm sorry. I'm sorry about your sister."

She drove on for a minute without speaking. I turned to look at her. "We're very close," she said at last. "I told her about Phillip and his girlfriend. I told her about you."

"I didn't tell anyone. No one would understand it the right way. They wouldn't believe it or they'd think I was bragging or they'd think it was about something else. My friends would think that, my family. Everybody."

She nodded twice as I said this, two small dips of her head that felt like love to me. We had never used that word, not during the hours when we were together in bed, not sitting on her sun porch, or saying good night at the door. There was real warmth in those times, friendship, physical joy, vulnerability, but now something new was set in place around them, the thin membrane of trust that always surrounds real love, and can be broken open with a single selfish action. She kept her eyes forward, but I could sense another wave of relaxation in her, the quick approach of tears. There is no feeling in the world like the feeling of losing someone you love to an early death. It is an immense experience, excruciating and absolute. It presses your face against a cold stone wall and holds you there like the hand of a torturer, giving you every opportunity to cry out that you believe in nothing, no kindness, no spirit world, nothing but the reality of your own pain and loss. Everyone cries out then. Everyone curses goodness into nonexistence.

And then time passes; some people step back from the sharpest part of the pain and are able to look around and see that they are not unique, that they have not been singled out after all, that there is yet one more dimension to things, a dimension they had not seen or imagined. That kind of pain, and that movement into something beyond it, had marked my life, the way it had marked Lydia's.

For a moment then, I was able to step out of my dark closet of concern about myself and imagine what the breathing days were like for her, what that drive was like on the other side of the front seat. The wound of the death of her son had been reopened for her on that day—driving through the same countryside, with a young man she was trying to say good-bye to. Somehow I understood that, and somehow I was able to let go of the last of my hope then. It was as if, after months of probing and trying, we had at last stumbled upon the line of intimate contact between us, the deepest surface where we were joined, and that was enough.

"Anastasia understands," she said. "She's in a great deal of pain now. You can hear the pain in her voice when you talk to her on the phone. Her body is breaking down in a dozen different ways. She can no longer urinate. There's no longer enough moisture to lubricate the lids of her eyes. She says it feels as if her bones are being cut with electric saws. But she laughed for a second when I told her. She said I was crazy, that I had always been the crazy sister. I could tell by her voice that she understood it the way I wanted her to, and didn't judge me."

"Because she's dying," I blurted out. Lydia looked at me with two strokes of surprise at the corners of her mouth and one tear trembling at the side of her eye. She turned forward again, brushed at the eye, and after another minute, said, "Someday there will be someone special in your life, and you'll want to tell her."

"I don't think so."

"Wait till I die, and then tell anyone you want."

I looked away from her, out the side window at the black tree trunks. I had hoped to make one of my little jokes, but I could not get the words to come out. We went a mile in a miserable silence, and then I took a breath and said, "I'll wait then, alright? That's what I'll do." And that's what I have done.

We drove the back roads of eastern New Hampshire in the rain, listening to one of her tapes of Bach, a music I did not like then. We went all the way as far as the southern tip of Lake Winnipesaukee. In place of my elaborate fantasies of a future with her, I was left with a drizzling present moment—the silvery drops, the wipers knocking, the sight of the veins beneath the skin of the backs of her hands—and something fine and rare slipping away from me.

We stopped for sandwiches and coffee in a place called Alton Bay. I remember a jukebox in the restaurant, and posters of Red Sox baseball players on knotty-pine walls. I remember trying to punish her with my stubborn silence, and then seeing how foolish it was to do that, how childish, how wrong.

I insisted on paying for the sandwiches. By the time we finished eating, the rain had stopped, and we left her car in the unpaved lot and walked along the western shore of the big lake, the wind kicking up bits of grit against the sides of our faces, licking at the hem of her skirt. I had then, with her, a feeling I've known only rarely in my adult life. Walking along beside the lake, with the sun trying to break through the western edge of the rain clouds, I had the very clear sense that we were two pieces of the same living self. There were differences, of course—we were male and female, young and middle-aged, taller and shorter; we had different names and different histories and different ideas about things—but those were the equivalent of slight irregularities in the two halves of a peach that has just been sliced open. I turned, and our eyes met for a second as we walked, and it was as if we were each other's reflected essence. I believe she felt it, too. She smiled. She reached out and put four fingers in the back left pocket of my jeans for thirty or forty steps, the way a grown woman might touch a grown man, and we walked as far as an old wooden bandstand in a park, then turned around and headed back along the shore.

Epilogue

IT SO HAPPENED THAT my cousin Augustine—named after my father—had come home alive and unhurt from Vietnam that same week, and so the party held at Jupiter Street on the day of my Exeter graduation was really for both of us. Rosalie and Caesar never made an appearance (though I thought I heard the *ah-ooh-gah* horn once on Park Avenue). Other than that, and my grandfather's absence, and the way my little success seemed to highlight, all over again, the fact that my parents weren't alive, it was not so different from the spontaneous gathering that had formed when our number came in, six summers before, almost to the day. Cousin Mike stood at the grill with an apron on, turning over sausages and hot dogs with a pair of tongs. The uncles smoked cigars and sipped from cans of beer, the aunts commandeered the picnic table and sent gales of laughter out over the yard. My grandparents' old friends sat on lawn chairs in the shade, and the younger cousins raced back and forth at the edges of the crowd, screeching and shouting, building a little happy history for themselves.

My grandmother sat on one of the metal lawn chairs under the grapevine, and I sat beside her there for the last part of the afternoon, getting up from time to time to refill her glass of orange soda or to bring her something sweet from the dessert table. The uncles, aunts, and older cousins gave me envelopes with cards and money in them; that was the tradition. My grandmother kept the cards in her lap, and it was nice to have that money, and nice to receive the compliments and congratulations, but, really, I was embarrassed by the fuss, especially with Augustine there.

My mother's friend Lois Londoner came, my cousin Angelo walking beside her holding a large, wrapped box. I took off the ribbon and the paper and found, inside, probably a hundred dollars' worth of new drawing pencils, sketchpads, pastel chalks, brushes, and books on how to sketch and paint.

"I just had a hunch," she said, holding one of her shaking hands on my knee and leaning toward me for a kiss. "Probably you would have rather gotten money, but I remembered your mother saying you liked to draw and paint when you were a little boy. I just had this feeling."

The hot afternoon light changed and slowly faded. My grandmother kept the stack of envelopes on her lap, as if for comfort. From time to time she would reach out and lay a hand on my wrist. Once, she said, "Did you find somebody for yourself, Ahndonyo? The girl you like?"

I said yes, I thought I had, the sister of a good friend, but it was too early to be sure, and she smiled, patted my arm, and looked at me for so long and with such love that it made me uncomfortable, and I turned my eyes away. I said, "I miss Grandpa."

"He has a gift for you."

"He does? He did? He left something?"

"He told Uncle Peter to give it to you."

"What is it?"

"You'll see—Uncle Peter said he'll give it later. After it gets dark."

There is a beautiful quality to summer evenings in Revere, a certain light, a certain softness to the air that has to do, I think, with its proximity to the ocean on the one hand, and its proximity to the smoke and steel of the city on the other. The salt and grit and moisture in the atmosphere seem to catch up the edges of sounds and spin them off into the shadows. The shouts of children, the slap of a screen door, even the rumble and mutter of the bus engines on Park Avenue—they reach your ear as something frail and sweet, accordion keys touched lightly beyond a gauzy curtain.

Night fell, some of the neighbors left. Just when it seemed the party was finally ending, we heard someone cough loudly on the raised square patch of yard that was bounded on the south by the grapevine, on the east by the back of the house, and on the north and west by neighbors' fences. It was full dark by then. I turned to look over my shoulder but, in the light from my grandmother's back porch, I could make out only the bottom part of a pair of gray trousers, a sharp crease, expensive shoes. There was another cough, sort of a drawn-out throat-clearing, and everyone stopped talking and turned to try and see what was going on. "Your present, Ahndonyo," my grandmother said.

An empty moment, a hesitation, and then a beautiful voice striking and holding a long first note. It took me a few seconds to realize the sound was coming from my uncle's mouth, because it had nothing in common with the voice he used for speaking, but was much higher and sweeter, as clear as a crystal bowl being tapped with the tip of a spoon. By the second note I already recognized the song he was singing. "Lenta Va La Luna, Lenta La Luna Va," it is called ("Slowly Goes the Moon, Slowly the Moon Goes,") a tremendously sad Neapolitan ballad about a grown man's gratitude for the women in his life—his mother, his daughters, his wife. It is an appreciation of the purity and power of genuine emotion, and the territory—profound, mysterious, utterly vulnerable—onto which emotion opens the soul.

His voice went around and around through the notes, twisting like sweet smoke above the yard.

> *Tendo un braccio*
> *Tendo una mano*
> *Cercando il proprio cuore*

It was a high, elegant voice, something he would never have offered us on that night if Caesar Baskine or Johnny Blink or Angelo Pestudo had been anywhere within ten blocks of the house. He would never have shown himself to them in that way because he had come of age in a country of competition and money, in a subculture shadowed by terrified and violent men who believed their only hope of salvation was to terrify others, to close them up, to shake them free of the warm inheritance of their heart.

Not a person in the yard moved or spoke; even the smallest children were fairly quiet for the two or three minutes the song lasted.

I have to admit that when my grandmother told me about the gift, I'd pictured something like the inheritances of my Exeter friends—ten thousand dollars in my bank account, the deed to the house, or at least to the upstairs apartment, a car of my own, the horse Uncle Peter had once promised Rosie and me—something grandiose and expensive, some shiny symbol of my grandfather's abiding love. Instead, all he had left me was this: a boxer, a former tough guy, singing in a high, beautiful voice on a summer night in Revere. I hugged Uncle Peter when he finished, and thanked him, and thanked my grandmother, but it was years and years before I really understood what had been given to me on that night.

CONWAY, MASSACHUSETTS
August 2000–June 2002